The Ones We *Hate*

Katie Golightly

Copyright © 2024 Katie Golightly

All rights reserved

The characters and events portrayed in this book are fictitious. Any similarity to real persons, living or dead, is coincidental and not intended by the author.

No part of this book may be reproduced, or stored in a retrieval system, or transmitted in any form or by any means, electronic, mechanical, photocopying, recording, or otherwise, without express written permission of the publisher.

ISBN Print: 979-8-89372-866-8

ASIN Ebook: B0CWGT5DY8

Cover Design by: Sam Palencia at Ink&Laurel

Editor: Maryarita Kobotis

Sensitivity Reader/Spanish Edits: Allie Garza

Layout: Kristen Hamilton at Kristen's Red Pen

To the good girls who hide behind a smile and the people who see right through them.

Playlist

I Won't Back Down by Tom Petty
Walking On Sunshine by Katrina & The Waves
She Brings Me The Music by RPA, United Nations of Sound
You're An Ocean by Fastball
Sugar, We're Goin Down by Fall Out Boy
My Body by Young the Giant
We Can Work It Out by Cast of Zoey's Extraordinary Playlist,
David St. Louis, Alex Newell
Heaven In Hiding by Halsey
Dangerous Woman by Ariana Grande
Animal by Neon Trees
Favorite Poison by Fuller
She's so Mean by Matchbox Twenty
Smooth (feat. Rob Thomas) by Santana, Rob Thomas
I Wanna Dance with Somebody by Whitney Houston
Crush by David Archuleta
Electric Love by BØRNS
Here It Goes Again by OK Go
Teeth by 5 Seconds of Summer
Good Girls (from the "Ghostbusters" Original Motion Picture
Soundtrack) by Elle King

Dirty Little Secret by The All-American Rejects
Lose Control by Teddy Swims
Iris by The Goo Goo Dolls
Come Over by Noah Kahan
Suddenly I See by KT Tunstall
You Should Probably Leave by Chris Stapleton
So Alright, Cool, Whatever by The Happy Fits
Lean on Me by Bill Withers
Make You Feel My Love by Adele
Breathless by The Corrs
Wouldn't Change a Thing - From "Camp Rock 2: The Final Jam" by Demi Lovato, Joe Jonas
Tiny Riot by Sam Ryder
Steal the Show by Lauv
Dress by Taylor Swift
Green Green Dress - bonus track by Andrew Garfield, Alexandra Shipp
Mine by Bazzi
The Way I Loved You (Taylor's Version) by Taylor Swift
Parachute by Song House, Kyndal Inskeep
The Great War by Taylor Swift
Simply the Best by Billianne

Author's Note

Content/Trigger Warnings: Off-page death of family members (drunk driving, cancer), off-page sexual assault/harassment, brief mentions of an off-page character's pregnancy complications, on-page panic attack, manipulation, discussions of alcohol abuse, explicit language, and sexual content.

In my first novel, I wrote myself into the characters, and while that is still true with this book, I relate the most heavily to a side character you will meet. When I sat down to start this novel, having already mapped out the entire plot, this character did not exist. In true me fashion, the undercurrent of the novel changed and warped into yet another healing journey for me. I thought this book would be about grief, and it is, but the most prevalent theme, after pouring even more of myself into it, is friendship.

    Piper and Leo are simply the friends I wish I would have had —the friends I deserved—when I experienced betrayal and heartbreak. They are the embodiment of my true friends on the other side of the country, who were and are equal parts angry and compassionate on my behalf. The ones who dusted me off, who said that I was allowed to feel and that I wasn't burdening them by sharing—the ones who told me that I deserved better.

So, if you are that person who feels alone, like you don't have friends who would burn the world down on your behalf, this one's for you. If you've ever gone through something and begged for your friends to listen, only to find out that they weren't your friends at all, this one's for you. If you're a family member of mine, this is *not* for you, and you should definitely put this book down. The likelihood that the sexual content will mortify you is high. If you frequently run into end tables, trip over uneven ground, or hit doorframes on your way into a room, for once, you're in luck, this one's for you.

If you love flawed characters and emotional battlegrounds, you guessed it: this one's for you.

Prologue

15 years ago - Age 6

PIPER

Every once in a while, there was a rare moment when Piper got to be on her own. No brothers to poke and prod her or show her gross bugs from the backyard. No friends or teachers at school expecting anything from her. It had been a while since the last time, so when her mother came to wake her up for school that morning, Piper miraculously came down with a nasty cold. She thought she had gotten pretty good at pretend sneezing by that point, but only one of her parents fell for it. Her father, Cole, seemed to notice immediately that it was all an act, and Piper had no idea why he didn't tell on her. Instead, he looked right at her, tapped his nose, and winked before declaring that he, too, would skip going to the office. After that, because her parents owned a business together, it was only a matter of time until he roped Piper's mom, Paisley, into staying home with them after they had dropped Piper's brothers off at their respective schools.

That was how Piper ended up in the kitchen, legs swinging under her chair as she fiddled with a sunflower head, forever suspended in the small glass dome her mom had gifted her earlier that day. Markers were strewn atop the table, and her fingers were stained at the tips from the sky she'd colored in on her house drawing. The pop song playing through the surround sound had been on the radio so much lately that Piper knew the lyrics vaguely well enough to sing along while her parents chopped carrots and boiled noodles behind her. She wasn't fabricating an illness anymore, but her dad had insisted on the chicken noodle soup anyway, claiming it could cure even a restless heart's ailments.

"I think it needs salt," Piper's mother announced, reaching for the saltshaker.

"Now, hold on just a second, Pay." Cole rounded the island and caught Paisley by the waist. "We have our very own, super special taste-tester sitting right over there. And she's only home for one day."

A smile spread across Paisley's face, and Piper mimicked it with her own, knowing exactly who her dad was talking about. Piper's mom lifted her hand and placed it on her forehead as if she were trying to peer through a crowd. "Who? I don't see any super special taste-testers."

"Me, me!" Piper giggled and kicked her legs harder.

"Oh my goodness," Paisley gasped and clutched at her heart. "*You* are a super special taste-tester? I had no idea! I thought you were a singer."

"I'm both," Piper decided on the spot. "And a house designer like you!"

"Ah, a multi-talented girl." Her mom beamed.

"She's been taste-testing for me for years!" Cole puffed out his chest with pride, and Piper grinned up at her father, her nose scrunching and eyes squinting. "I think we should put her to the test. What do you think, honey?"

"Absolutely!" Paisley agreed and brought over a silver spoon teeming with soup, blowing on it before she held it up to Piper's mouth. The warm liquid coated Piper's tongue, and she screwed up her face in thought as her parents stared down with wide, expectant eyes. Despite her parents' faith in her, Piper had no idea what the soup needed, if anything, and opted to copy what her mother had said earlier.

"It needs salt," Piper said. Both her parents seemed to take this well.

"Genius!" Cole declared, turning to Paisley. "Didn't I tell you she's a genius?"

"You did." Paisley nodded and walked over to the large pot on the stove to add salt. Cole moved in beside her, pulled the wooden spoon from the pot for a taste, and hummed his approval. "Since you're so smart," Piper's mom called out. "What color do you think I should paint the cabinets?"

Piper looked down at her markers and contemplated them before eyeing the color she had accidentally smeared across her hands. "Blue!"

"Blue." Cole nodded. "I like it."

Paisley stepped back from the stove to get a wider look at the white-primed cabinets as if she were already painting them in her mind. Piper watched a spark of excitement pass through her mom's features. "Blue is perfect. We can do dark blue and maybe a gray stone for the backsplash?"

"Love it," Cole said.

The song that had been playing finally faded out, and a new one started in its place. It sounded old, slow, and boring, not at all the fun, upbeat music that Piper liked to listen to. She was just about to voice her complaint when her dad yanked her mom into his arms and whispered something into her ear.

Paisley threw her head back with a laugh. "You'll step on my feet again, Mr. Hartrick. You're a bull in a china shop when it comes to coordination."

"Excuse you. I am a *fantastic* dancer," Cole argued. Piper giggled because just as her father had somehow known she had been lying earlier, she knew *he* was lying, too. Her dad looked weird when he danced. His hips always jerked back and forth like the robot in her favorite TV show. "Dance with me, Pay. You know you want to."

"Okay, okay." Paisley gave in and wrapped her arms around Cole's neck, where his apron emblazoned with the words "Grill Master" hung. Piper watched in rapt attention as her dad pulled her mom in and started to sway. The song continued and built to a chorus as Piper's father twirled her mother under his arm, his eyes soft and never leaving Paisley until it was finally over, ending with a slow press of lips.

"Ugh, gross." Piper gagged.

Part One
I hate you

One

Present - Age 21

PIPER

It was happening again. Piper looked up at the tree branches crisscrossing the patio area of the coffee shop and rubbed her thumbs into the pressure points on the back of her hands in anticipation of a headache. She simply refused to witness whatever arrogant facial expression her now ex-boyfriend was wearing. If her emotions were as unforgiving as her lack of spatial awareness, they would compound and spill out in the form of rage. Unfortunately, her pent-up anger would probably just fizzle out while she ate ice cream later, and she would never think about Todd White again. If she could just blow up once, maybe word would get around campus and shitty guys would stop lining up to declare their feelings for her just to snatch them back a few months later. But she couldn't fucking do it. It was blatantly clear that she was doomed to forever be the pleasant girl whom everyone could rely on for a smile. If she didn't, it would only take someone two seconds flat to tell her she looked prettier when she did.

"Are you even listening to me, P?" Todd interrupted Piper's

train of thought with the nickname she had always hated. It had initially been a joke, like *ha, ha, the first letter of your name is also a word for urine*, but Todd continued to use it relentlessly, always laughing and acting as though it were a term of endearment or some inside joke between the two of them. As usual, she went along with it. Why rock the boat?

"I'm listening." Piper offered Todd a tight smile.

"Good." The undertone of his response said there should have been a "girl" at the end of his praise. If Todd was expecting her to stick out her tongue and wag her tail for a compliment, he would be a bit disappointed. *Sorry, I didn't bring my leash today,* Piper thought.

Being a pushover didn't mean Piper enjoyed degradation. It just meant she frequently let her opinions fall by the wayside and carefully chose which battles she fought, most of which just happened to be on behalf of other people, not herself.

"So, you understand why we have to go our separate ways. You're a smart girl, so I'm sure you knew this wasn't going to last forever." Todd got up from his seat and shrugged down at her.

The way her exes always acted like Piper had somehow misinterpreted the relationship was beyond frustrating. There wasn't much to misinterpret when Todd had said, verbatim, "I want to spend all my time with you" and "best sex of my life." That was why when the guys Piper dated dumped her like used trash, claiming to have never felt a thing, she always swore up and down that she would be the dumper the next time. Yet, here she was, sitting in a public place, staring up at an ex who was just like the others after she'd wasted the entire summer with him. The words "it was fun, but I don't see much of a connection anymore" were still ringing in her ears. And, really, she couldn't blame him. It wasn't like she was in love with Todd. She had tolerated him at best. That was what she had liked about him: he was a human person who made her not so completely alone. A warm body she would never be at risk of falling in love with.

The "we need to talk" conversation always materialized after one of Piper's "mental breakdowns," as a previous ex-boyfriend had termed them. When guys realized they only liked her when she was happy, they'd leave. The root of Piper's emotional turmoil could always be sourced back to one thing: her parents. She was decent at holding back her emotions, but occasionally something would trigger her memories and she'd find herself sobbing—not alone, like she preferred, but with someone who could never fathom or care about the devastation of losing both her parents. But who was she to expect understanding when she had never chosen her boyfriends for their listening capabilities?

The perfect guy would be someone with whom Piper could have a mutual agreement. A transactional relationship was the only kind that wouldn't end up breaking her. Neither one of them would be in love, but they could warm the bed, get each other off, and go to the occasional party together. He would never ask why she sometimes froze up behind the wheel of a car or why she refused drinks at parties, and even when he inevitably found out through the grapevine about the drunk driver who had killed her parents, he'd never mention it. He would just leave her be. He could be that person who realized when she went missing and reported it to the authorities in a timely manner. No one had to be left dead and unattended in their apartment until someone noticed the smell. Unfortunately, any guy who wasn't a walking red flag seemed to require love. And the red flag guys loved to proclaim what Piper already knew: no one liked her unless she was dolled up and smiling. *Good girl, Piper. Good fucking girl.*

"Yep. Totally understand." Piper ground her teeth together. Anger wasn't going to get her anywhere with Todd. If she lost her cool, he'd just end up telling the entire student body of Fletcher University that she was a crazy bitch. Finally having a blowout fight with one of her exes wasn't worth having the word "crazy" always tacked on to her name. She had carefully curated her image to avoid the emotional turmoil that came with remembering anything painful. She redirected her thoughts when they were going somewhere unhealthy and replaced them with ambition and niceties. She did it now, too, just to cover her bases.

"I knew you would understand." Todd grinned, his obnoxiously white teeth now looking like a wolf's. Then, hovering over her with a sly smile wrapping his fangs, he nailed her with the kicker. "But you can feel free to hit me up anytime you want to take a roll in my sheets. We were always really good at that."

Piper wouldn't be hitting him up for any booty calls, late at night or otherwise. While Todd had proclaimed her to be his best sexual partner, she hadn't orgasmed one singular time in his company. The urge to throw that in his face was a powerful one, but not powerful enough to follow through. Telling everyone that Todd White was bad in bed would probably get her on some sort of campus-wide blacklist. She wondered if there was a secret club out there somewhere made up of all the women Todd had slept with, like a support group for scorned and orgasmless women. She workshopped support group names while Todd continued spelling out exactly what he wanted from her.

The Perpetually Edged. Nope, that one didn't work. Piper hadn't even gotten close to edging. *Never-O-land.* They could be the lost boys of terrible sex. Scratch that—no one was flying anywhere with Peter Pan over the edge of anything. *The Sisterhood of the Lackluster Man.*

Todd smirked as he finished off his list of good deeds he wanted Piper to accomplish. Yet again, he was the only one who ever got to finish. "Remember that one night at that house party? We could do *that* again."

"I think I'll pass. I should focus on studying." Why Piper felt the need to have a legitimate excuse not to sleep with him, she had no idea. Her internal voice, which was now just a mere whisper, was telling him to go fuck himself. The more passive part of her was already listing off a whole study guide for an upcoming exam in her business class.

"Always focusing on school." Todd rolled his eyes and began

to walk away, only looking back to offer some unwanted advice. "You should try being fun sometime. See ya around."

In her last year of college, Piper was too close to the finish line to release the reins on her schoolwork, but Todd's last barb before he left cut like a knife. She couldn't win. She was either too perfect or too imperfect. What the hell did people want from her? That was it. Swearing off men, for real this time, was her only recourse. Piper got out her planner from her backpack and slammed it down on the table. The force rocked the break-up coffee that Todd had made her pay for on the rickety metal table, and the cup toppled over, directly onto the binding of her planner. The cheap plastic lid easily popped off and slid to the side, allowing the coffee to dump freely onto the table.

"Ugh!" Piper exclaimed and launched out of her seat. Her purple sundress was already a lost cause, a brownish stain soaking into the spot around her crotch. *Lovely.* The liquid dripped over the edge of the table until a hand swooped in from behind Piper and slapped a wad of napkins onto the puddle.

"Thank y—" Piper turned and came face to face with the one person who could possibly make this day worse and snapped her mouth shut to glare. Leonardo Diaz. He had his backpack casually slung over one shoulder as if he had just happened to pass by at the exact time she'd spilled her coffee everywhere, which was par for the course given how her day was going. The latte river had made its way around the haphazardly tossed napkins and was dripping over the edge of the table again. Leo's white sneakers, the only bright thing about his outfit, carefully sidestepped the stream of coffee as he frowned at it like it had disobeyed a direct command to stay on the table. Everything else—his Henley, his pants, and his backpack—was as black as his soul, solidifying his perpetual storm cloud persona. The scowl he always wore sealed the deal.

After Piper learned that Leo would be attending Fletcher University alongside her, three years of hell ensued. The problem hinged on Fletcher's renown for having the best arts programs in the entire state of Oregon. Piper was double-majoring in interior design and business because as soon as she graduated, she would eagerly be taking on the role of owner and CEO of Hartrick Designs, which her parents had grown from a family business to a flourishing hundred-employee company. She should have guessed that Leo would be working on his own Bachelor of Arts for something revolving around theatre or film given that he was self-important enough to pursue a career in the entertainment business. Any job that involved bossing people around and having a superiority complex would be the perfect fit. Plus, if it wasn't perfect, Leo would just smash his foot into the shoe à la Cinderella's evil stepsisters. The shoe, incidentally, did fit, and Leo became the talk of Piper's hometown when he won a big, fancy nationwide scholarship from some famous director. All that bravado and confidence was probably where Leo's secondary business major came into play and how he and Piper ended up in at least one class together every single year. To put it bluntly, she fucking *hated* him and was pissed that after already dealing with him enough for two lifetimes in high school, the universe was hell-bent on torturing her more.

They had originally met in Spanish class their junior year, where Piper got stuck with Leo's condescension and snickering all year long. She had been so used to school coming easy that her difficulties in Spanish threw her for a loop. The entire school year her parents had died was a blur, but she would never forget Leo tossing around ridicule like his life's purpose was to critique everything she did. His haughty attitude was the stuff of nightmares, not to mention that his personality seemed to be the exact antithesis of hers. Piper always cared what people thought. Leo, on the other hand, didn't give a single fuck what anyone thought and steamrolled over every person he encountered. Piper meticulously ironed her clothes. Leo made little effort in his appearance, and yet every hot-blooded woman in the vicinity seemed to gawk over his tanned skin, smoky eyes, and sharp tongue. His hair was a wild mop of dark curls he never tried to tame, and it didn't seem to matter that he didn't tower over anyone. What Leo lacked in height, he made up for in sheer will. Spanish constantly slipped from his mouth—usually in a grumbling undertone when directed at her—and, for some stupid reason, that made even Piper's best friend, Thea, go weak in the knees. Piper had already dealt with enough assholes who hid their misogyny to deal with one who openly hated her from the start.

"You gonna finish your sentence, princesita?" Leo asked. The nickname he always used for Piper came out right on cue like he was trying to win a prize for irritating her.

"Sure. Thank you so much for appearing like a surprise zit before school photos. You want a gold star?" Piper shot back.

"Careful, someone might notice you're a little ungrateful." Leo cocked his head and continued with an evil lilt, "I know you just got dumped, but it'll really ruin the whole *My Little Pony-*glitter-rainbow vibe you try to give off if you don't hand over all of your gold stars immediately." The asshole actually held out his hand, palm up, like he was ready to receive something.

Piper's face turned beet red. She hadn't realized anyone, let alone Leo, had overheard her conversation with Todd. Snatching her planner from the table, she shoved it into her backpack, no longer caring about the moisture clinging to the cover. It was a mess she would have to deal with when she got home. She quickly swiped at the coffee with the wad of napkins and collected her empty cup.

"Can I help you with something, or are you just pretending to be a knight in shining armor with napkins I could have easily gotten myself?" Piper ground out.

"Fine. I guess gold stars are only for douchey frat boys." Leo's hand fell away, and he smirked. "The gold stars you give are fool's gold, anyways." It was the running insult with him. He'd call her fake, and then she'd point out the obvious: he was a dick.

"Have a nice day, Leo." Piper turned up her nose at him and stormed toward the nearest stone staircase, disposing of her trash on the way. The entire campus was built into the side of a hill, so there was no lack of stairs anywhere. Turn a corner? Staircase. Walk two feet? Staircase. Piper's naturally muscular legs had gotten even sturdier since attending Fletcher. There seemed to be a lack of the stereotypical "Freshman 15" on campus as well, what with all the cardio everyone had to do just to get to class.

"Go F-U," Piper muttered as her thigh and calf muscles worked to get to the first landing. With a jolt, she reared back, suddenly yanked by an unknown force. She stumbled a bit before her ribcage met the metal railing on her left, and she winced as she grabbed on to stay upright. If balance and spatial awareness were college courses, she'd fail every time.

Upon investigating the source of her almost-tumble down the stairs, Piper found her bag was hooked on a bush. Typical. Several hard pulls later, the greedy plant still wouldn't let up. She genuinely thought she might have to give in and let the bush have this one.

"Bush versus Piper, who will win?" Leo's voice called as if he were an announcer at an MMA fight. Piper looked over her shoulder to watch him walk up the staircase wearing an amused expression. It always irritated her how graceful he looked doing mundane tasks. He was like a cat: fluid and arrogant.

"Following me around like a pesky fly now?" Piper asked, still trying to free her bag and getting more frustrated by the minute.

"*Buzz*," Leo deadpanned before reaching out and unhooking her bag with one deft flick of his wrist. "Maybe you should work on learning how to walk instead of dating every guy who thinks he's God's gift to humanity."

"Says the guy who has a massive god complex."

"My partially Catholic mother would be none too thrilled with that assessment. Just out of curiosity, do you have some weird kink where you enjoy getting slapped around by both man-children and inanimate objects?" Leo gestured to the bush.

"I don't have eyes in the back of my head, and if I wanted to date a man-child, I would just date you." Piper gave him her best villainous smile, but she hadn't perfected the art of being rude like Leo had, so she probably just looked constipated.

"Mmm." Leo tilted his head from side to side like he was weighing the options. "I'll pass. My standards are a little higher than that. I'm forever curious as to when you're going to grow a spine and get some standards of your own, though." He held up one finger for each name he listed off: "Harden, Christopher, Parker, Tre, Dante, Tristan, Conrad, and finally, Todd. I almost ran out of fingers, Piper. Each one of them was a walking red flag, and you fell for it every time."

"Okay, one, you pay way too close attention to my dating history, and two, we're in the twenty-first century. Slut shaming is in poor taste. Plus, if I recall, you're not doing so hot on the dating front, either. I haven't seen you flaunting a new girl around campus lately." Piper folded her arms over her chest, eyebrows raised.

"Slut shaming wasn't what I was going for. Sex is fun. I don't knock anyone for it. And if by 'flaunt' you mean holding hands because that's what couples do, then sure. You don't have to be jealous just because whatever douchebro you're dating at the time doesn't act like a real boyfriend."

"Fuck you." Piper scrunched her nose, trying to search within herself to come up with anything better. But Leo was right. Todd, for example, had claimed that he wasn't into PDA until any given house party, where his concerns magically evaporated and he'd make out with her against a wall in front of everyone. Todd was horrendous at that, too. His mouth was always uncomfortably wet, and his tongue usually tasted like stale beer. She had only ever felt like a conquest when it came to guys, but admitting that didn't make Leo's words hurt any less.

"You know I'm right, don't you?" Leo lifted his chin with pride. "You only date them because they're meatheads with surfer hair and money. You'd be able to see right through them if you could get past their appearance and status."

"I don't date them for their looks or money!" Piper shouted.

A group of baby-faced freshmen sitting on the lawn a short distance away looked up from their books, and Piper cringed, lowering her voice. "I don't."

"Whatever you say, princesita." Without another word, Leo looked her up and down with distaste and jogged back down the stairs, most likely slinking off to the underworld so he could go back to being Satan's personal bitch.

Piper stared after him, seething. It wasn't her fault that the only men who ever showed interest in her were jerks. They always pretended to be nice in the beginning. Granted, there had been plenty of red flags waving for each one of her ex-boyfriends, but red seemed to be her favorite color, and oddly enough, those guys were the safest option to cut ties with. It was impossible to have a broken heart when she had no real stake in the game to begin with. No one could hurt her if she didn't allow them that power. Love was for people who could handle heartbreak or for bitter people like Leo who could move on easily because they never had a heart to begin with.

Two

LEO

All broke college students scraping by on a hefty scholarship and sheer will were bound to have a lemon of a vehicle that couldn't be counted on for shit. Leo's bucket of rusty bolts required a bit of finagling to get running, and it was perpetually in need of a new part he couldn't afford. That was how he ended up jogging two miles to get to class and how he had witnessed Piper Hartrick getting dumped for the hundredth time by some shit-for-brains guy with a flat-brimmed hat. Frankly, it was none of his business how many entitled assholes Piper wanted to date, but her "I'm perfect" act had always pissed him off.

Every encounter with Piper always had Leo running home to his boxing gloves and punching bag that was a little worse for wear with its multiple duct-taped patches. He'd been feeling tired earlier that morning, but Piper had turned him electric and energized with one bickering conversation. Talking to her always felt like a live wire current was running through his veins. He could have arguments with other people and not get so easily ramped up, but Piper was different. Her words always pricked his skin and drew blood, burrowed into his muscles and sank into his bones.

He had told himself a thousand times that he didn't care what fake, spoiled brats believed about him, and yet, he was currently drenched in sweat and probably going to piss off his neighbors with how hard he was going to town with his boxing drills. At least he'd purposely gotten a ground-floor apartment for that specific reason. He wasn't completely inconsiderate, despite what Piper thought.

Hatred fueled Leo's punches as every *psh-psh* of his mitts had him huffing and puffing. Boxing was always the best way to run him ragged. That, or sex, and the latter hadn't happened with anything other than his hand in a while. Unfortunately, his cock tended to have a mind of its own when it came to Piper, too. Anatomy didn't care that her personality was the epitome of I Can't Believe It's Not Butter, and *his* had decided that it didn't mind the verbal abuse. If he wasn't so dominant in the bedroom, he would have thought he might be a masochist or something.

Growing up as the son of a part-time boxing instructor had its perks, one of which was knowing how to school his anger and his sex drive. When Leo was a kid, he and all his siblings had practically lived at their father's second job in the evenings thanks to their free admission to the gym. Mateo made sure his kids could defend themselves. For a long time, before both Leo's parents got jobs at Lydia's Grocery and moved them the hell out of California, they had lived in the bad part of a town where gang activity was heavy and witnessing drug deals was scarily frequent. Everyone learned to keep their nose out of everyone else's business, but they could also hold their own if they needed to. Hell, because of their father's instruction, Leo's sister would probably never need him to defend her. Mariana could easily bury a body herself. But if she ever did need help, Leo and his three brothers would happily wipe the floor with anyone who bothered to mess with their little sister or their mother. The Diazes could either be your best accomplice or your worst nightmare.

The door swung inward, and Leo momentarily paused his drill to look toward the doorway, where his best friend and roommate, Sam, was standing. "It sounds like someone's getting it on in here."

"If you thought that, why did you just barge into my room?" Leo scoffed.

"Good point." Sam tapped his temple and then called out over his shoulder. "He's still not getting any!"

"Thanks for the play-by-play," a voice called back.

"Wes is here?" Leo asked, peering over Sam's bony shoulder.

"Yeah, we're doing flashcards for his next organic chemistry exam, so if you could keep it down with your non-sexual activity, we would appreciate it." The twang in Sam's voice had a scolding tone to it, but it lacked any real heat. Sam jabbed a thumb over his shoulder then combed his fingers through his straight blond hair. "Wes is a stress case right now."

"You know I can hear you, right?" Wes yelled from the living room. Sam's boyfriend was pre-med and frequently had a mound of things he needed to study for. His expertise came in handy any time Leo was sick or injured. Despite the fact that Wes wasn't an actual doctor yet, both his rich parents were, and when he didn't know the answers, he didn't mind making his parents pro bono for Leo and Sam since neither of them had a pot to piss in—a phrase Leo had picked up from Sam's Kentucky vernacular.

"While I'm here," Sam blazed ahead, ignoring Wes, "any update on the Sarah Brown situation?"

"Don't remind me." Leo frowned and pulled his boxing gloves off, tossing them onto his dark green comforter before starting to peel off his hand wraps with clammy fingers.

"Pressure's on." Sam nodded. "I get it."

The Sarah Brown situation was constantly looming in the back of Leo's mind. If Sarah were a real person and not a fictional character in the musical they were putting on, he would hate her. Both the headliner and understudy had conveniently dropped out of their production of *Guys and Dolls* after casting. The vocal ranges were so wildly different between Sarah and Adelaide, the other female lead in the play, that Leo couldn't in good conscience snag the understudy for Adelaide to fill the role. He had called some people from the original audition, but anyone who was remotely decent had already found a use for their extracurricular time and was unavailable.

"Sorry," Leo groaned. "I'm exhausting all my options here."

"I am but a frog without a princess to kiss." Sam shrugged, trying to play it off as a minor deal, but Leo knew it wasn't, despite Sam's acting skills.

Like Leo, the only reason Sam was attending Fletcher University was to study under Alejandro Moreno. Their professor, a renowned director, had once been called a "trailblazing pioneer in his field" and dubbed sixteenth place in an edition of *People* magazine's "Sexiest Man Alive." Sam was headlining Fletcher's winter production of *Guys and Dolls* as Sky Masterson, a high roller gambler and the romantic counterpart to Sarah Brown. Without a Sarah, Sam had no one to practice lines or scenes with. Wes couldn't even be a stand-in because he was busy practicing his own lines as Nathan Detroit. The three of them were itching to be part of a show with Moreno's name on it again, and Leo especially. This would be his first time claiming the role of assistant director after three years under Moreno's tutelage. That is, if they could find a Sarah Brown.

"I'm just spitballing here, but what if—"

"If you're going to suggest the karaoke bar again, I might use myself as a punching bag," Leo harrumphed.

"Come on!" Sam looked at him with pouty puppy dog eyes.

"No. This isn't one of your romance novels. We aren't going to find the perfect Sarah Brown just waiting to be discovered at a bar where everyone scream-sings and slurs their words because they're sloshed."

"What if we just go for fun? The new bartender at the Hot Mic is, well, hot. You could let off a little steam?" Sam gave Leo a suggestive pump of his eyebrows.

"Stop trying to set me up with every person that breathes. And you don't even like women!"

"I can objectively see when a woman is hot and your type. Dark hair? Tattoos?" Sam's mouth quirked because he knew he was right. That was exactly Leo's type.

"Fine." Leo gave in but raised a finger. "But it's not because of the bartender. This is strictly a work outing that will fail miserably."

Three

PIPER

Piper's planner was a lost cause. The pages had dried and stuck together by the end of the school day, but, like her mother before her, she was never without a backup planner. And so she sat at her dining room table in the small bungalow she rented close to campus with a tub of Umpqua ice cream and a set of custom highlighters and calligraphy pens, ready to rewrite all of her events and assignments in a tasteful and colorful display of organization. There was something so relaxing about seeing her entire life laid out on paper. Everything could be broken down into a check box and a completed task. If only her personal problems were that easy.

With the first spoonful of her coffee-flavored ice cream suspended in front of her mouth, Piper's stomach growled in anticipation. She made it about an inch away from her lips when the glob of ice cream made a break for it and slid off the spoon directly into her lap, joining the other stain from earlier that morning. "Oh, fuck me!"

"I'm sorry, but I am just not interested in you that way." Piper's roommate, Thea Galanis, said dryly as she plopped down beside Piper with her own heaping bowl of ice cream, her springy, dark curls bouncing with the movement.

"No one is," Piper groaned.

"Oh, come on, now! That's not true. Todd's just a little bitch. Didn't I warn you about him?"

Thea was the type of friend who told it like it was. If you were dating a scumbag, she would tell you right to your face to make better choices.

"You did, but he was nice to me." Piper looked down at her hands with a sheepish expression. "Kind of."

"Why is being occasionally nice the only qualifier for men now? Did he give you mind-blowing orgasms? No. Did he ever buy you flowers or carry your bag? No. He made you pay for all your dates, Piper. I'm down for splitting a bill, but you know he's here on his daddy's money and could afford to pay for your food occasionally. You deserve better."

"Right now, what I need is for my dress not to look and smell like cream, sugar, and mistakes. I think I'm going to call it and change into sweatpants."

"I know exactly what to do!" Thea slapped her hand down on the table, and Piper flinched.

Thea was a fixer, and it was both exhausting and wonderful. She would be a fantastic therapist someday. Piper did her best to school her facial expression into something remotely grateful, but all she wanted to do was crawl into a hole for a bit and not come out until the next day. Thea wasn't the wallowing type. As a matter of fact, their friendship meet-cute had taken place when Piper's first college boyfriend dumped her at a bar during their second semester of freshman year. Thea, who was sitting on a stool at the counter behind him at the time, had heard every word. She promptly dumped her drink into his lap with an "oops, it looks to me like someone had a little accident" and proceeded to pull Piper out onto the dance floor.

Since then, they had been inseparable. Through every breakup and late-night study session, Thea was a constant. Even after she met Yuri, her boyfriend, Thea made plenty of time for Piper. Piper was still Thea's emergency contact despite Yuri knowing Thea's body way more than Piper ever would. (The walls were thin, and they weren't quiet.) The only thing Piper didn't talk about with Thea was her parents. After several attempts to get Piper to open up, Thea backed off the subject. What Piper lacked in vulnerability with her friends, she made up for with acts of service. It was the least she could do.

"All right, let's hear it." Piper waved Thea on, knowing that she would have no choice but to comply with whatever the plan was.

"Drumroll please," Thea said dramatically. Piper sat back in her antique chair, waiting while Thea put on a show, using her fingers as drumsticks and rolling her tongue to make a popping drum sound. Thea finally finished when Piper let out an exasperated sigh after waiting entirely too long for her theatrics to end. "We're going to that karaoke bar I told you about last week!"

"Nope." Piper popped the P and flipped open the cover of her planner to drown herself in more work. She would have said yes if the reason they were going was for Thea alone, but she knew that was not at all why Thea had suggested it.

"Oh, come on!" Thea begged. "You gotta get out and have some fun! You sound like a goddess in the shower when you're singing."

"I think my brothers would beg to differ." Piper laughed.

"Your brothers!" Thea exclaimed. Piper narrowed her gaze, not liking the excitement behind Thea's eyes. "Do they happen to have any attractive friends you could date?"

"You're not actually suggesting I date one of my brothers' friends."

"Colin's cute. He has to have cute scientist friends, right? And what about Carter? He's just plain sexy. He probably has some friends here that are hot. His roommate, maybe?"

"I'm pretty sure Carter would be annoyed if I was dating his roommate considering they live together and I'd be invading his privacy. And you're not allowed to think my brothers are attractive." Piper got up from the table, snatched up the tub of ice cream, and wandered into the kitchen to put it away.

"I can't help it if your brothers are hot. If I didn't have Yuri, I would definitely ignore the girl code for Colin or Carter."

"Here." Piper grabbed a pan from the decorative hanging rack she installed when they first moved in. "Hit me over the head with this, will you?"

"In all honesty, your uncle is—"

"Fucking hell, will you shut up?" Piper interrupted. "I already have to hear gross things about my uncle from my aunt. I don't need you talking about it, too."

"Oh? Well, don't be close-lipped about it. What did Talia say? I bet Walker's a real freak in the sheets. All those tattoos scream *sexual deviant*." Thea bounced on the balls of her feet, always extremely into any discussion revolving around sex.

"You could just ask her yourself," a voice said from the living room. Piper jerked her head to the open olive-green front door, and she and Thea broke into grins as they sprinted to envelop Piper's aunt in a tight hug.

"You didn't tell me she was coming!" Thea complained to Piper. "I could have made scones."

"She didn't know I was coming," Talia explained. "She told me about Todd this morning. Amala's covering the store, and I told my 'freak in the sheets' that I had to take a little trip to cheer Piper up."

Back in Piper's hometown, Talia and her best friend, Amala, ran a grocery store that had finally been renovated completely from its original look. The modern color-pop design Piper had helped create was one of her favorite designs to date. It was weird that she missed grocery shopping, of all things, but she did. One more year of school, and she'd get to finally return home for good.

"So, he *is* super kinky, then?" Thea asked, with no self-consciousness whatsoever.

"Whatever Walker is, I'm much, *much* worse." Talia winked, and Thea high fived her.

"Ew, ew, ew, ew, ew!" Piper slapped her hands over her ears, and Talia barked out a laugh.

"Okay, so, what's the plan? Are we eating ice cream out of the container, dyeing your hair a different color, watching a sappy rom-com, blasting grunge music—my personal favorite—or slashing Todd's tires?" Talia set her hands on her hips.

"We're going to a karaoke bar!" Thea announced.

"I already said no." Piper sighed.

"We have to. Piper, if I had your voice, I'd be forcing it on people all day long," Talia said.

"You still *do* sing all day long," Piper pointed out. "I'm surprised that Walker hasn't completely lost his hearing by now. And, speaking of, you didn't tell him, did you?"

After taking guardianship of Piper and her siblings when their parents died, Walker had become a bit pissy and protective when it came to Piper's dating life. The last time she had gotten dumped, she had to beg him not to drive down and threaten her ex. It was a four-hour drive to campus from Archwood, and Walker had already gotten one hour in when Piper—or Talia, rather—convinced him to turn around.

"I told him you got a B on an essay. What he doesn't know won't hurt him. Ah, speak of the devil..." Talia pulled her vibrating phone out of her pocket and held it up for show. A picture of Piper's uncle on their wedding day was displayed on the screen with a video chat request. Talia swiped to answer. "Hey, hun. I made it!" She turned the camera to include Piper and Thea in the shot, both girls waving at Walker.

"Good." Walker smiled on screen and waved back. "Piper, let me know if you need any help with your B that I know is really a boy problem." Talia's mouth dropped open, and she offered an apologetic glance in Piper's direction.

"Nope! Don't need any help, thank you," Piper said quickly.

"Okay, but—"

"We're just about to leave to go karaoke," Talia cut off her husband.

Walker grimaced and asked carefully, "You're gonna... sing?"

"Okay, no need to be rude." Talia feigned offense. "No, I'm not singing. I'm aware that I sound like a garbage disposal."

"A *cute* garbage disposal." Walker laughed. "Piper, you're singing, though, right?"

Every eye turned toward Piper to get her response. Ultimately, it wasn't her family or her best friend who made her decision: it was Todd's annoying voice, still stuck in her head.

You should try being fun sometime.

She *was* fun. She was exciting. She lived life on the edge—well, just a few feet back from the edge. She could do this: one night of singing and fun. Fuck Todd.

Rocking back on her heels, Piper closed her eyes and nodded. "Yeah, I'll sing."

Cheers erupted in the room and over the phone. At least, if nothing else, she could lose herself in a song and in the company of people who didn't think she was a stick in the mud.

Four

LEO

The Hot Mic was packed and too loud for Leo's liking, in no small part thanks to the absolute train wreck on stage. Two drunk girls were singing "Elastic Heart" with enough vigor to curdle milk. Making eye contact with the barkeep, Leo gave her a slight smile to entice her his way. Sam wasn't wrong about her being his type—this woman dripped sex appeal, and Leo wasn't mad at it. If she was interested, maybe the night wouldn't be a total bust. Leo was typically a long-term relationship guy, but it was a bit hard to find something that lasted more than one night when the women he was attracted to were all so confident in themselves that they didn't want or need a relationship.

"What can I get you?" the bartender asked with a flirty lilt.

"I'll take a shot of tequila. Cheapest shit you have." Leo ordered the singular drink he would allow himself to pay for that evening. "And a lime if you're planning on watching me take it, cariño."

"You wanna lick salt off something, too?" The sexy bartender passed Leo a lime wedge as he cocked his head to the side and dragged his eyes over her slender, tattooed arms.

"There are many, *many* things I'd like to lick salt off of." He leaned farther over the bar, hitting her with his bedroom eyes as she set a shot glass in front of him.

"Like *you* need to be saltier."

The snide voice didn't come from the bartender. Heat spread through Leo's body, and his muscles went rigid as he turned to face Piper *fucking* Hartrick.

"Whatever this girl orders," Leo said, directing the comment to the bartender as he scowled at Piper, "you don't need to add any ice to it. If she stares too long, it'll freeze over no problem. She's got the ice queen thing down pat."

The outfit Piper was wearing added no value to Leo's statement. Her black sundress printed with bright yellow sunflowers hugged her breasts so well that the tasteful amount of cleavage peeking out the top begged him to look. The fabric—cotton, maybe, given how soft it looked—jutted out from her hips in flowy pleats that fell partway up her thighs. Cork wedge heels accentuated her legs, with straps encircling her delicate ankles that tied in neat bows at the top. Leo's mouth went treacherously dry. It was the kind of outfit that had his brain scrambling to fight off a desire to flip up the hem of her dress and fold her over the bartop. Good girls, Piper especially, were not his type, but sundresses—well, those were his kryptonite.

"I'm a goddamn ray of sunshine, and that's ice *princess*, to you," Piper corrected. All sundress fantasies were lost to the wind when Leo was reminded a second later why he hated her so much. Like someone had flipped a switch, Piper's face transformed from irritated disdain into a pleasant smile as she lit up for the bartender. "I'll take a Shirley Temple with an extra cherry, please." If he looked up "two-faced" in a dictionary, odds were he'd find a picture of a blonde with newly dyed lavender tips.

"Sure thing." The bartender nodded and barely gave Leo a second glance before making Piper's juice and running off to place more orders, no longer interested in him.

"Thanks for that." Leo sighed and threw back his shot, slamming it down on the wooden bartop. He cringed as the bite of the inexpensive alcohol hit the back of his throat. Then, taking the lime wedge between his lips, he made direct eye contact with Piper and bit down into its flesh, sucking hard. Piper's eyes flicked briefly to his mouth and then back up to his eyes.

"I saved her a lot of trouble." She shrugged, her expression falling back into identity numero uno. Piper took her own turn at whatever game they were playing. Bendy straw perched between her lips, she took a long pull from her kiddie drink all while staring at him with an unblinking glare.

"Yes, you're a true hero. I can see the headlines now." He mimed an invisible banner with his hand. "Piper Hartrick, saving women everywhere from multiple orgasms."

Piper jerked her hand up to create her own banner. "Breaking news, men still have yet to figure out that women know how to fake orgasms."

"Aw, princesita, you probably think you're really good at faking it, huh?" Leo crooned. "I'd be able to see right through you."

"Doubt it." She rolled her eyes.

"See, the trick is, I keep going, even when they say they've finished. Because if I've really done my job," he dropped his voice into a low rasp and leaned forward so only she could hear, "everything will be so sensitive that they'll *beg* me to stop touching them." Piper stood, completely speechless, as he leaned back on his elbows, relaxing against the bartop. *Point Leo.* The blush staining her cheeks should have just been amusing, but instead, Leo found he had to quickly cut the tension with another biting remark before his thoughts went down a rabbit hole of sundress-related daydreams. He pointed to the drink in her hand. "You got a hot date with a crayon box and glitter glue soon?"

"I don't drink, and Shirley Temples are delicious. Plus..." Piper fished a cherry out of her glass, plopping it onto her tongue and wrapping her lips around it to pull it from the stem. Leo swallowed as he watched, his tongue dipping out of his mouth to involuntarily swipe over his bottom lip. "I can tie a knot in a cherry stem with just my mouth."

"You know what that means, right?" He played along.

"That I'm a good kisser," Piper stated with a definitive lift of her chin.

Leo smirked. "I was going to say it means you spend too much time doing useless shit." Now that she'd mentioned it, he couldn't for the life of him stop staring at Piper's lips as she stuck the cherry stem in her mouth. The bright red lipstick she was wearing accentuated her cupid's bow, and the fluorescent bar lights illuminated her blue eyes like electricity was flickering behind them. For his libido's sake, he wished Piper looked like an evil witch with a pointy nose instead of a freckled Margot Robbie.

Piper pulled the stem from her mouth with her thumb and forefinger to reveal a tight knot in the center. "A useless trick it may be, but I think your bartender is now more interested in me than in you." She pointed across the bar, and he found she wasn't wrong. The bartender had the same flirtatious smile from earlier on her face, but she was no longer looking at him. *Point Piper.*

Leo took one last stab at Piper. "Maybe you'd choose better women since you aren't very good at choosing men."

"I seriously wish I swung that way. Too bad you're missing out, too." Piper took a long sip from her drink and turned to leave, running right into two other women. She stumbled back into Leo, and his hands shot to her hips to steady them both.

"Woah." Leo dug his fingers in and pushed Piper into a standing position.

"Get your hands off me!" Piper batted his hands away from her hips like he hadn't just saved her ass.

"Gladly!" he shouted back. "Learn how to walk, and I won't have to protect myself and everyone else from you spilling more drinks!"

"Funny." She rolled her eyes and turned to face the two

women she ran into. "Can we please leave now?" It was then that Leo realized he recognized the other two. He had been in a few prerequisite classes with Thea Galanis his freshman year, but he couldn't quite place the slightly older woman, who looked to be in her thirties.

"No! You haven't sung yet," Thea protested.

Piper singing was the exact last thing Leo needed. She was probably one of those types who thought they could sing because no one in her rich-kid family had ever told her that she was terrible. Everyone was always happy to pass out participation trophies to those types.

"I signed you up already, so we can't leave," the older woman said, cheerfully pointing toward the signup table.

"Talia, I appreciate you trying, I just don't know that I'm in the mood to sing right now." Piper sighed.

Talia. The name sparked a memory, and a split-second later, Leo remembered who the older woman was. "Talia Cohen, right?" he asked, weaving around Piper, who he could see glaring at him in his peripherals.

"It's Talia Hartrick now."

"Oh, right." Leo tapped his temple. "I forgot. My parents went to your wedding." He neglected to mention that he had also met Talia's husband once.

At the time, Leo had been in high school, trying to pay for an online directing class and save up for film school—efforts that eventually proved pointless when he got the rejection letter in the mail and had to reroute his plans. Tutoring Spanish was a quick way to make money, and Harden, Piper's boyfriend at the time, had rich parents who were willing to pay up the ass for Leo's expertise. After Harden blew him off one too many times, Leo had invited himself out to lunch with the jock crew to try to cram some knowledge down his tutee's throat before his parents could notice he was still flunking. Instead, Leo had run smack dab into the most entertaining altercation he had ever been part of. Walker, Piper's uncle, had accosted Harden for being a good-for-nothing creep by literally hopping into the driver's seat of Harden's showboat of a car. It was insane behavior, so, naturally, Leo had eagerly taken a front-row seat to watch while Walker explained that under no certain circumstances would Harden be allowed to contact Piper again. And then, as one does when fed up with entitled jerks who were wasting one's tutoring time, Leo offered to tell the whole school that Harden had a micropenis.

Talia gave him a kind smile, and Leo stood a little straighter, trying to make a good impression. His parents would have his head if he wasn't the epitome of respect in front of their employer. Plus, from the way his parents had spoken of Talia and her business partner Amala, they *deserved* respect.

"You know him?" Thea asked Talia.

"His dad is the head butcher at Lydia's, and we just promoted his mom to the manager position this morning before I left," Talia explained.

Piper leaned conspiratorially in Thea's direction. "His parents are both super nice. No idea where Leo came from."

Leo ignored the jab, focusing on the news he hadn't yet heard. "I didn't know she got the job. That's great! I'll have to call her and send her some flowers or something." Leo pulled out his phone and made a note to himself to call his mother. This was a big deal. She had been so nervous about the interview process. The fact that she'd gotten the job filled him with his usual familial pride, and he practically beamed down at his phone as he made the note.

"You're going to send your mom flowers?" Thea squeaked, darting her eyes to Piper.

"Yeah, I think I can swing it," Leo said. The endless calculations to determine what exactly he could afford jump-started in his head. It would have to be the cheapest bouquet he could find. If nothing else, he could call up his siblings, and they could all chip in on something. College was expensive. Adulthood was expensive. He didn't often fork out money for extra things, but he would spend a little extra on his mom. She deserved it.

"Let me take care of it." Talia tossed her hand in the air, and Leo pulled his eyebrows together in confusion. "Just let me know which flowers she likes, and I'll leave them on her desk with a note from you."

"Okay, just let me go to an ATM, and I'll—"

"No, no! I got it, don't worry about it." Talia smiled. "We *love* your mom at the store. I'll make sure she knows they're from you."

"Um... are you sure?" Leo's eyes shifted to Piper and then back to Talia. "I wouldn't want to impose."

"No problem. Just text Piper and let her know what you'd like to say on the card and which flowers, and I'll make sure to get it to her." Talia yanked on Piper's arm so she was forced to stand beside her.

At the same time Piper said "he doesn't have my number," Leo found himself yelling "I don't have it!" like a nervous head case. It was her freaking dress. That was what had his head so far up his ass. He just could not stop staring at Piper. Never before had she looked so... enticing. Okay, technically, that was a lie, but most of the time he could just use that as fuel to hate her more.

"Here." Thea yanked Piper's phone from her grasp and passed it to him. "Put your number in."

"Oh." Leo took the phone and looked at Piper as she stood stock-still.

Flipping her phone around, Leo held the camera up to Piper's face. It recognized her and unlocked, and he felt a small power trip from it, like he was holding her whole life in his hands. Piper must have sensed it, too, because her body went even more rigid than her normal stick-up-the-assery. He typed in his number and hit dial so he'd have hers, too, and let the phone ring as they locked in a staredown. Finally, when he ended the call, Piper reached for her phone. He held it out to her, then pulled it back at the last second.

"Not so fast." Leo gave her a sly smile and turned the camera on himself, snapping a picture and saving it as his contact photo before labeling himself as "Leo" with a purple smiling devil emoji.

Then, unable to help himself, he held up his own phone and pointed it at her. "Smile, princesita. I need a contact picture. I know a lot of Pipers."

It was a flat-out lie. She was the only Piper, and there wasn't a single person in his phone that had a picture with their contact. He was never that thorough with phone numbers. He actually had someone labeled in his phone with just the letter K, and he had zero clue who it was. Instead of smiling, because she never smiled for him, Piper held up her middle finger. He took the picture at an angle that showed the most of her dress, because he was a self-indulging asshole, and labeled her as "Piper" with a sunflower emoji next to her name.

"You could just put my last name in if the number of Pipers is throwing you for a loop." Piper held her hand out again, palm up, waiting for her phone. Still feeling the need to tease her, he held it high above her head.

"What song are you singing?" Leo asked. "Who am I kidding, it's probably something that sounds like the artist took uppers beforehand. 'Barbie Girl,' maybe? 'Here Comes the Sun'? Or... 'Walking on Sunshine'?" Piper's eyes went wide, and he smirked. "It *is* 'Walking on Sunshine,' isn't it?"

"It's not my fault that you hate joy, Leo." Piper ripped her phone from his hand.

"You're singing a love song when you just got dumped?" He couldn't help how intrigued he was. There was no way Piper was constantly this happy. The only time she seemed to show any other emotion was in his presence. Anger was her favorite flavor when it came to him. And she equally irritated him enough for several lifetimes. "Seems a little fake, if you ask me."

Piper rolled her eyes. "It's a good thing that no one asked you, then. It's a song, not a declaration. I don't know if you know this, but it is possible for a girl to be okay after getting dumped. Just ask all of your ex-girlfriends."

"All I'm hearing is that I have experience doing the dumping, and you have a lot of experience *getting* dumped." Leo shrugged.

"Damn." Thea gawked beside Piper. Leo blinked, suddenly realizing that Thea was still there, and so was Talia. It was probably in poor taste to be insulting the niece of his parents' employer.

He shot a nervous glance at Talia and decided a quick exit was in everyone's best interest before he and Piper could get into a more heated argument. "Anyway, I have friends waiting for me. Good luck with sunshine walking."

Leo departed like a bat out of hell, forcefully slowing his steps so he wasn't jogging through the bar to Sam and Wes's table. When he sat down next to his best friend, Sam was looking at him like he was privy to some tantalizing information. Wes had his hand pressed over his mouth like he, too, was attempting to hold something in.

"What?" Leo asked dryly, already waiting for the punchline.

"I just figured you'd get the bartender's number, not the girl you constantly complain about." Sam broke into a grin. "But I think you now hold the world record for the amount of times you can check someone out."

"Oh, fuck off. I did not check her out," Leo grumbled. He definitely had, but a world record seemed extreme for the way he had very casually noticed Piper's figure.

"The tension is tensioning," Wes singsonged.

"You two are clearly bored," Leo said. "I can't stand her."

"Thou doth protest too much," Sam said in his Shakespearian accent.

"That's your worst accent to date," Leo critiqued.

"I apologize, Mr. Director Man." Sam saluted him. "Don't think I didn't notice that segue into a different conversation, though."

"I'm not entertaining a conversation that is so off-base it's not worth my time." Leo rolled his eyes. "This entire night is a waste of my time. There hasn't been a single person I'd cast for even the smallest role in our show."

Just then, the emcee for the evening practically ripped the

microphone out of a guy's hand on stage after a very loud and pathetic performance of "All By Myself" to announce the next act. Leo mentally prepared his ears to take a hit.

"Next up, we have Piper Hartrick singing 'Walking on Sunshine' by Katrina and the Waves!"

Five

LEO

The beat started the second Piper grabbed the mic off the stand in the middle of the stage, and Leo waited on bated breath for her either to cut and run or botch the song. Piper looked like she wanted to throw up, her face a little green as she peered out over the loud bar. He almost felt a little bad about making fun of her until her voice wafted through the speakers.

Leo's eyes widened as his self-righteous smirk fell away from his face. "Shit," he hissed.

She was good. *Too* good. So good that it instantly filled him with dread.

Leo snuck a glance in Sam's direction and knew instantly he was in for a world of hurt. Sam was entranced.ABes was entranced. They were both hunched toward each other, discussing something in hushed whispers. Leo didn't have to guess to know exactly what they were thinking.

When their heads popped up to peek in Leo's direction, Leo gave one indignant and firm shake of his head.

Absolutely not.

Sam's eyes blazed with a passionate plea, and Leo shook his

head again, mouthing "no" as he jerked his head back to the stage to watch Piper grow even more confident in her voice. It was unruffled and pure. The sweet kind that made you feel like you were floating on a cloud. A good-girl voice, like Mandy Moore's in *A Walk to Remember*.

Leo let out a long sigh, looking over at his friends again. Wes's eyebrows rose, and he cocked his head to the side as Sam whispered something in his ear. Leo groaned to himself, massaging his temples. They were never going to shut up about this. Not when they thought they had found the perfect Sarah Brown. It was even in the name of the musical, *Guys and Dolls*. Piper looked like a literal doll up on stage, swaying with the music and singing in a happy and energetic voice. And she was smiling the entire fucking time like the sun was shining and everything was right in the world. Sam and Wes were not allowed to find their Sarah Brown in Piper. Leo didn't think he could stand having to see her almost every day, let alone having to work with her on a project that could make or break his resume for after college.

Piper sang out and swung her hips back and forth, her dress seductively drifting across her thighs. Leo's eyes dropped without his permission to watch her body, then quickly darted back up to her face just in time for her to point and direct the chorus at him. Her blue eyes met his, and she did a little kick step and turn. She was obviously trying to prove a point that she was capable of walking on sunshine despite her shitty morning, and unfortunately, it was working on everyone but him. Sam chuckled next to him, and Leo shoved his shoulder.

"She's good," Sam whispered.

"I already said no," Leo replied with a chop of his hand.

"It's not about you," Sam retorted. "Take one for the team."

"She'll say no, too. Did you see the look on her face when she got up there? She has stage fright. No way she'll be able to pull it off."

"Seems like she's pulling it off to me," Wes interjected, keeping his voice down.

"She's..." Leo searched for the right word. The one he finally landed on fell flat. "Aggravating."

"To *you*. She's in one of my classes, and *I* think she's a delight," Sam said.

"She will be an absolute diva to work with," Leo argued. "She's a faker. She's not actually sunshine and roses like everyone thinks she is. No one is that happy all the time."

"Well, we work with *you*, and you're not as hard-headed and grumpy as you think you are." Wes chuckled.

Leo muttered, "I need a drink," as he threw back his chair and started toward the bar.

When he reached it, he slapped his hands on the bartop, like the sound of his confidence alone would rein in the out-of-control feeling that was taking hold of his body. The same tattooed bartender from before walked over to him.

"What can I get you?"

"Are you doing something when you're off your shift?" He spewed the question so quickly that he could tell it took her a second to understand what he had even asked.

"No. Are you offering to change that?" She leaned over the counter toward him, flirtation easily sliding back onto her face.

"I would very much like to change that." He held out his hand. "Leo. Nice to meet you."

"Sasha." She shook his hand slowly, locking eyes with him.

Sasha was exactly what he needed. The wild look about her was on par with every other girl Leo had ever dated. But with Piper's voice filling his ears, every muscle in his body wanted to revolt against the idea of doing anything but going home to look at the contact picture in his phone and stew over Piper's annoying talent. The spark with Sasha had been there until Piper had ruined it. He needed it back, and he was determined to force it back if he had to.

"What about your ex?" Sasha asked.

"My ex?" Leo knit his eyebrows together in confusion.

"The hot girl on stage." Sasha pointed.

"She's not my ex. She doesn't date men that don't treat her like shit."

"And you'd treat her better?"

"What? Why does everyone—? No. I'd never date her to begin with." Leo shifted on his feet. "She's not my type. *You* are."

"That was not the impression that *I* got." Sasha gave him a sly smile.

"Do you want to go out with me or not?" Leo huffed.

"Do *you* want to go out with *me*?" Sasha took a rag and wiped at some spilled mystery liquid on the bartop.

"I..." He snapped his eyes shut in defeat. She was right. He just wanted to high-tail it out of the bar before something terrible happened. He could feel that something looming in the air, as if Piper's voice were going to set the entire room aflame. "I'm just gonna go home. Have a nice night, Sasha."

The song finally ended as Leo made his way back to his table to grab his hoodie. He snuck a glance at the stage, where Piper was walking toward the narrow staircase in her death trap shoes. Leo's hand twitched as he watched her get to the first step. He scanned the bar, hoping someone would do the respectable thing and assist her, but not a soul got up from their seat. Sam and Wes were in a very spirited argument about heaven knows what and brushed him off when he tried to get their attention.

"Fuck," Leo cursed under his breath as he stomped closer to the stage.

Piper looked like a glass breakable teetering on the edge of the highest step. The nagging voice in the back of Leo's head—which usually sounded like one of his parents—said chivalry wasn't limited to only the people you liked. And yet, Leo found himself stalking toward the side of the stairs and holding his hand up to Piper with a scowl.

"I can do it myself," Piper bit off.

"You're going to break an ankle. Or an arm. Or your neck." Leo sliced his pointer finger over his neck and made a gagging sound for effect.

"You'd like that, wouldn't you?" She gripped the railing harder and carefully made her way onto the first landing, which wasn't enough of a ledge to hold an entire foot.

"I mean, death seems a bit drastic, but if you accidentally broke a couple of fingers right now because you're too stubborn to accept help, it would be amusing."

"I'm fine." Piper took another few steps without grabbing his outstretched hand, smiling when she only had one step left. "See?" Stepping forward one last time with misplaced confidence, Piper slipped off the last step and stumbled forward, trying to regain her balance, arms flying about at her sides. Leo took one step in her direction and caught her under her elbows to stabilize her.

"The last step is always covered in alcohol and whatever else people are drinking." Leo smirked. "They'll probably be sued at some point for not putting up a Slippery When Wet sign."

"You could have mentioned that," Piper snapped.

"Mmm, but where's the fun in that?" He dropped his hands away from her body and stepped back to look at her. "You think you can make it to your table without falling on your face, or do you need me to fireman carry you over my shoulder, princesita?"

At first, the thought of Piper's body bent over his shoulder with her dress hiked up around her hips sent a pang of need through Leo's chest that he didn't want to examine. It wasn't like it was the first time he had ever imagined Piper bent over something, except he was usually standing behind her in those daydreams as they spewed curse words at each other in a fervent round of hate sex. Luckily, the realization that her whole ass would also be on display to half the bar if he did toss her around like a sack of potatoes was a bucket of ice water dumped over his head.

"I'll keep my dignity intact, thank you." Piper snorted.

A snide breath of laughter left Leo's lips. "Oh, I think you lost *that* a long time ago."

"You're a real dick." She trudged past him and paused just in time to lift her foot to stomp on his toes. It was a bold move, but a fruitless one. She wound up too much for him not to know exactly what she was about to do. Boxing had trained him enough to know when he was going to take a hit. He sidestepped her easily.

"If you break my toes, who's going to help you walk upright?" Leo asked.

"I hate you," Piper snarled.

"And I hate you," he snapped back. "*So* glad we can finally agree on something."

"Your ego is the size of Texas."

"My *ego* is what got me to where I am." Leo angrily folded his arms over his chest. "Try having to work for anything, Piper. All you need is a fake smile and the world hands you whatever the fuck you want."

Piper's face was as red as a tomato, and she looked away for a moment before meeting his eyes with a newfound fire. "At least I don't treat people like shit just to make myself feel better." And with that parting blow, she turned and walked to her table.

The deep, choppy breath of air Leo inhaled didn't help him regain his center. It took several before he felt at equilibrium again. Piper was on the wrong side of this argument. He was sure of it. He had snide remarks, he could admit that, but since high school, she had been nothing but nasty to him. They had been in opposition from the moment they met. A large assumption on Piper's part had snowballed so far out of control that every second after, they had been in constant battle. Back then, Leo had refused to explain himself on principle, but now, he wondered if everything would have been different if he had just said something. There was no way to backtrack and course-correct when they had so many years of arguments and clashing opinions under their belts. The best thing he could think to do was to avoid Piper at all costs. And that was going to be rather difficult with the way Sam and Wes were looking at him from across the bar with hope in their eyes.

Six

PIPER

All you need is a fake smile, and the world hands you whatever the fuck you want.

Leo's latest dig at Piper's character rang in her ears like the aftermath of an explosive. She wanted to march back over to him, offer him her most dazzling smile, and petulantly say, "There. Now, since that's supposed to give me whatever the fuck I want, I'd like my parents back, thank you."

She wasn't completely out of touch with reality. It was easier to get what she wanted because her family had the means to do it. The major difference between herself and Leo was that Piper would never step on people to get to the top. She wouldn't walk into a room, claim superiority, and demand to be treated with respect. Her respect was earned.

"They're talking about you," Talia interrupted Piper's seething with a nod over to where Leo, a guy named Sam from one of Piper's classes, and another guy she didn't recognize seemed to be in some sort of an argument.

"Ooo, they *are*." Thea wiggled excitedly in her seat.

"No, they aren't." No sooner did the declaration leave Piper's lips than all three men started off toward their table. Talia let out a knowing hum, and Piper furrowed her brow, wondering what the hell any of them would have to say to her.

"Piper Hartrick!" Sam beamed once the guys were standing directly in front of her, as if the two of them had been best friends for years. Leo, with his arms crossed over his chest, looked even grumpier than normal, which was saying a lot considering he seemed to have a permanent resting bitch face.

"Sam—uh, I don't know your last name," Piper replied awkwardly, trying to figure out where the hell this conversation was going.

"Gosling. Like Ryan Gosling, but less hot." Sam grinned. It was interesting that Leo was friends with this guy because from what Piper knew about him, Sam was pretty much the epitome of a golden boy Southern beau.

The other guy beside Sam waved. "And I'm Wes, Sam's boyfriend. I don't have a cool last name. It's just Williams." Wes matched his boyfriend's wide smile.

"Like Robin Williams," Sam suggested.

"Good point," Wes agreed.

Leo didn't budge or offer up any commentary, so Piper decided to snatch up the reins on the bizarre introduction.

"And he's Oscar the Grouch," she said, pointing at Leo.

Sam barked out a laugh. "That he is!"

"For the record, I'm opposed to this entire thing," Leo practically growled.

"No one cares what you think." Sam shot Leo a look that Piper couldn't read before he turned his full attention to her. "Piper, have you ever performed?"

"Performed... what, exactly?" She was not even kind of tracking this conversation. One glance at Talia and Thea said that they, too, were trying and failing to suss out where the line of questioning was headed.

"Well, he doesn't mean sex acts," Leo huffed and then shifted an apologetic glance in Talia's direction. Talia just lifted her hand in surrender and leaned back in her chair, amusement playing across her face. The tattletale inside Piper was secretly hoping that Talia would run back to Archwood and tell Leo's parents that their son was a belligerent asshole.

"He means theatre. Acting. Everything in between," Wes offered up.

"Uh, no?" Piper responded warily.

"See, like I said—no experience. I guess we have our answer," Leo exclaimed and turned to walk away just for Sam to grab his shoulder and jerk him back into position.

"But you can sing," Sam stated. His soft blue eyes were staring expectantly at Piper, and it made her feel a bit exposed.

"I mean, kinda." Piper shrugged. She had a feeling this was leading somewhere bad.

"We want you to star in our play," Wes jumped in. Piper blinked up at them in shock for several long seconds, trying to find the punchline of the joke.

"Just to be clear," Leo raised his hand, "*I* do *not* want that, but apparently my opinion doesn't matter even though this is *my* job."

"Correct, your opinion does not matter." Sam nodded and then tipped his head to Piper again. "So, what do you think?"

"I'm very confused," Piper managed to get out.

Leo let out an elongated sigh, and both his companions glared at him before he shook his head and pointed at Piper. "They want you to play Sarah Brown in our production of *Guys and Dolls*. It's a musical, hence the singing aspect. Sam is playing Sky Masterson, and Wes is playing Nathan Detroit. We have an Adelaide, but we're missing a Sarah Brown because our leading lady ran off with her literal understudy, and now we have to replace both of them. These two idiots seem to think you're perfect for the role."

"Me?" Piper gawked.

"Exactly my thoughts." Leo jerked his head toward Sam. "See, I told you she wouldn't be interested."

"Oh, but you would be amazing, Piper!" Thea joined the conversation, bouncing in her seat.

"I've seen that musical before," Talia chimed in. "You'd be perfect."

"Exactly! You have a sweet-sounding voice that's *very* Sarah Brown," Sam agreed.

"She doesn't even know who Sarah Brown is." Leo frowned.

"Yes, I do," Piper said. It was a lie. She had never seen the show before and was hoping Leo wouldn't call her bluff. Either way, it didn't matter. There was no way in hell she was ever going to agree to this. "But, for once, Captain Hook and I are on the same page. I don't think I could pull that off."

"Sure you could!" Sam took a seat across from her and folded his hands on the table. "You practically *are* Sarah Brown."

Piper trod carefully, still trying not to get caught in a lie. "We do have a lot of the same characteristics, sure, but I'm not an actor."

"So you're admitting to being a good girl who gets easily swindled?" Leo smirked.

Fuck. Before Piper could respond, Wes shoved Leo's shoulder and sat down next to Sam, leaving Leo looking out of place as the only one standing. Leo wore it well, though. If Piper had to bet, he would continue to stand for the entire discussion just to drive home the point that he was uncomfortable *nowhere*.

"What Leo *means* to say is that you're kindhearted and see the best in people," Sam said.

"And you might have a bit of a wild streak underneath it all," Wes tag-teamed.

"No, that's not at all what I meant." Leo laughed, but it wasn't the kind of laugh that transformed his face into a smile. Instead, it was cold and unamused. Piper gave him her best death glare. She didn't have a strong one, considering her brothers and Leo were the only people in the world who ever got on her nerves enough that the look was necessary, but there needed to be something that conveyed the sheer amount of hatred vibrating in her veins.

"Sorry about him," Sam offered. "I think he had the hots for the last Sarah Brown."

Leo rolled his eyes. "Now we're making things up? Cool."

"Shh, I'm trying to sell it." Sam held a hand out and pushed Leo's face away playfully. Leo looked like he wanted to rip Sam's head off, but instead, he shoved his hands into his pockets with an even deeper scowl.

"Yeah, unfortunately, Leo liking the last girl is definitely not going to sell it for me, but I'm so happy that the last Sarah Brown managed to dodge that bullet." Piper quirked up the side of her mouth and met Leo's eyes. "And what's your role in this play? To sleep with the leading ladies and stomp around proclaiming superiority?"

"If I say yes, you'll just *really* want the role." Leo shot her a cocky wink, and Piper feigned gagging.

"If you say yes, it'll guarantee that I say no."

"Perfect. Then *yes*." Leo turned up his nose.

Piper cocked her head to the side and shrugged, folding her arms over her chest. "*No*."

"He's the assistant director!" Sam shouted. Piper swiveled her head to Sam at the same time Leo did.

"Ha!" Piper's outburst had Sam, Wes, Talia, and Thea all staring at her with wide eyes. Leo just looked furious.

"Don't think I can do it?" Leo challenged.

"No, I think you'd love bossing people around. I'm laughing because there is no way you could convince me to do this. Especially if you're directing."

Leo scoffed. "I'm not the one trying to convince you of anything. *They* are. I thought I made that very clear."

"Oh, and here I was thinking you were trying to convince me that you're an asshole. It worked, by the way. Ten out of ten performance. Take candy from a baby next, and I'll be even more convinced."

Leo grinned like the conniving little shit he was, and he bent forward, dipped his fingers into Piper's glass of mostly ice, and pulled out the last remaining cherry, twirling it between two fingers. She fumed as he stared directly into her eyes and plopped the cherry onto his tongue. Leo chewed at an arrogantly slow pace before she watched his Adam's apple dip on a swallow. "There. I took candy from a baby. Happy, princesita?"

"Not quite." Piper stood up from her seat abruptly, no longer in control of her emotions as her hand whipped out to grab her glass. And then, with the heat of anger licking up her spine, she tipped it over Leo's head. She'd never done something so impulsive before in her life, but the look of utter shock on Leo's face was worth it. The look of horror on Talia's, on the other hand, was not. Thea had slapped a hand over her mouth to cover a very loud gasp, and Sam and Wes both had their jaws hanging open, so it was sufficient to say that Piper's response might have been overkill.

The entire bar was staring at them, and Piper could feel her face heat in mortification as Leo stood with hunks of ice on his shoulders and in his hair, glaring at her. She hadn't really realized that they had been practically shouting at each other until the bar quieted, only the karaoke music still playing through the speakers. Even the current vocalist on stage had stopped their performance to watch the altercation.

The fury behind Leo's dark eyes and the rigidity of his posture as he finally shook off the ice, his face dripping from whatever had melted in the bottom of Piper's glass, said that their battle wasn't even close to over.

Leo glared. "You are the most—"

"Hey!" Piper's eyes widened as the tattooed bartender Leo had been hitting on earlier stomped her way over to them. "You two. Leave."

"Me?" Leo argued. "Sasha, I didn't do anything!"

"Didn't do anything, my ass!" Piper barked.

"I don't care." The bartender—Sasha, apparently—pointed at

the door. "You made a giant mess, and I want you both out of my bar." Piper had come down from her Hulk-level anger enough to realize that dumping ice all over Leo's head, though satisfying, had just created yet another mess that someone who was underpaid would have to clean up.

"Uh, do you have a broom?" Piper started frantically kicking the ice on the floor with her feet to sweep it into a pile. Leo jumped into action simultaneously, swiping napkins off the table and dropping them on the ground to soak up the water. "Leo, that's not going to help, you're just blocking me from getting all the ice."

"There's sugar water everywhere, too, thanks to you. It's going to be sticky, and you're just spreading the liquid around more." He stepped on the stack of napkins with his foot and shifted his stance to block her from getting to a few more pieces that had flown under the table. Even when cleaning up a mess, Leo found new ways to aggravate her.

"Stop it! I'm trying to—"

"Get. Out." Sasha cut Piper off with an indignant clap of her hands. "Both of you. *Now*. Before you manage to tip a fucking table over."

"We'll go!" Talia was clutching Piper's arm, practically shoving her out the door as Thea grabbed hold of her other arm.

"No problem at all. We'll get him out of here." Sam yanked at one of Leo's arms as Wes took the other.

Before Piper knew it, all six of them were standing outside the karaoke bar, and she was staring at the door as if that would magically make everything from the last half hour of her life replay in a way that didn't get her kicked out of a bar for the first time in her entire life.

"Thanks," Leo said under his breath when he finally shrugged off his friends.

"You ate my fucking cherry!" Piper snapped. The statement sounded incredibly sexual, and she realized it entirely too late after it had already shotgunned out of her mouth. Thea let out a small cackle from beside Piper as Talia tactfully looked away. From the look on his face, Leo hadn't missed the double entendre, either. Piper's cheeks flamed, and she quickly spun around to avoid whatever cocky retort Leo was about to respond with.

"I think I'm gonna head home," Talia said, raising an eyebrow at Piper. "Think you can stay out of trouble?"

Piper bit her lip. "I think I can manage. *Please* don't tell Walker about this." Even though she was a twenty-one-year-old woman, she still had the urge to hide any missteps from her uncle, the man who had dropped his entire life to pick up the pieces after her parents died.

When Leo saddled up beside Piper, she thought he was going to make a quippy comment about how she was acting like a child by trying to appease her uncle, but instead, he just looked nervous and ran a flustered hand through his hair. "Are you going to tell *my* parents about this?"

Talia curled her lips over her teeth like she was trying to bite back a smile before she said, "There are certain people in life that make us lose control. I've had my fair share of battles with someone who got on my nerves, so I'm gonna let you two deal with this on your own."

Leo let out a deep exhale and nodded before walking back over to Sam and Wes, who were waiting in the wings. Curiosity piqued, Piper asked "Who?"

"Who what?" Talia furrowed her brow.

"Who makes you so insane that you'd dump ice over their head?" Thea asked for her.

The grin that Talia gave Piper said who the culprit was before she gave her answer, and Piper immediately regretted asking.

"My husband," Talia replied, the implication heavy in her voice.

"Sexual tension is not the same thing as hatred." Piper rolled her eyes. She was ready to fight her aunt on this until her dying breath. Talia and Walker's love story had been obvious from the start. It might have taken them entirely too long to figure it out, but the comparison was borderline insulting.

"There's a reason they say all's fair in love and war," Thea mused.

"I'll take the war," Piper said and rubbed her hands over her arms, steeling herself against the chill of the night. She could hear Leo arguing with Sam and Wes off to the side and could vaguely tell that Sam was *still* being relentless in his pursuit to make her the next Sarah Brown. She had to hand it to him, he was persistent, but it was *not* going to happen.

A somewhat sad look crossed over Talia's face. "I just want you to be happy."

Piper stepped forward and squeezed her aunt's arm. "I *am* happy, I promise." She finished off her statement with a smile. "This was just a momentary lapse in judgment. Leo and I should just stay away from each other, and this won't be a problem."

"You'll call me if you need me?" Talia asked, digging her keys out of her purse.

"Of course." Piper nodded. It wasn't altogether untruthful. She *would* call if she needed her aunt, but there were just some things that Piper didn't quite feel Talia or Walker needed to know. There were parts of herself she locked away on purpose. There was no use burdening other people with her problems when those problems could never be fixed.

By the time Talia had said her goodbyes, Piper had regained control over her emotions enough to face Sam and Wes again. Regardless, Leo was forever going to receive the cold shoulder from her.

"I'm going to have to say no to the Sarah Brown role," Piper said curtly. She could practically hear Thea's disappointment beside her. "I don't think I'm your girl. I also think being in the same room with your friend seems to always end in disaster, and the idea of him directing me makes my skin crawl."

"I'm right here, you know." Leo threw up his hands. "I can hear you!"

"I'm pretty sure she knows." Sam cringed.

"You know I'm right." Piper turned on Leo. "I *never* get in trouble. The only times I've ever been reprimanded by a teacher or tossed out of a bar, you were there. You make me *livid*."

"The feeling is mutual," Leo grumbled back with a resigned shake of his head. "Let's just steer clear of each other so we don't end up burning down the entire campus. I'll sit as far away from you as possible in Hornbill's class."

"Sounds good to me." Piper shivered as a gust of wind blew over her arms and was surprised when Leo, out of everyone, yanked off his hoodie and handed it to her. "I don't need that."

"Uh, Piper..." Thea's wary voice said.

"You're cold," Leo stated. And then, his eyes briefly dropped lower, and she followed his gaze down to her chest, where her nipples were standing on end, poking through the fabric of her dress. Any misconstrued notion that Leo was being nice for once was thrown out the window. She ripped the hoodie out of his hands and threw it on over her head as even more humiliation seeped into her veins.

"Jerk," Piper muttered under her breath as she turned on her heel to leave, shoving a giggling Thea along with her.

"You can give that back to me in class on Monday," Leo called after her. It took every ounce of self-control in Piper's body not to hit him with a scalding remark, but she managed to keep her head forward by focusing on one thought:

He can rot in hell before I ever give this hoodie back.

Seven

LEO

Somehow, Leo managed to refrain from telling Sam "I told you so" a thousand times on the way back to their apartment. He was still sticky from the small amount of liquid in the bottom of Piper's drink, and he smelled like he had bathed in a child's fruit cup. His hair was matted and clumped together in a disgusting medley of mocktail and regret. He probably shouldn't have stolen her cherry, but Piper's reaction was exactly why she would never be the right choice for Sarah Brown. A good girl she might be, but she had a temper up her sleeve that, when unleashed, would make most people cower in fear. For some reason, it just egged him on.

Once Leo slammed the door shut, Sam rolled his eyes and flopped onto their shitty couch in the middle of the living room. The foam cushions audibly compressed and let out air on impact. Every piece of furniture in the living room had a chipping surface, and their TV had to be smacked around occasionally to get a good visual, but the couch, even with its ugly burnt orange color, was more comfortable than either of their beds. All the pieces they had acquired over the last three years were functional. There was no need for aesthetics when the end table they had picked up for free on a street corner was holding up just fine.

"If you've got something to say, say it," Leo said. He made his way to the fridge and opened it to find a hell of a lot of nothing before closing it and leaning one hip against the counter.

"She would have been perfect. You ruined it." Sam shoved his face into the knitted throw pillow Leo's grandmother had made and groaned theatrically. "Now we're back at square one."

"Did you miss the part where she dumped her drink on my head? I have to take a shower, and I already took one this morning."

"You poor, pathetic thing." Sam sat up from his sulking. "Between checking her out, purposely antagonizing her, and taking what wasn't yours, you did a bang-up job. She's practically a walking, talking, singing Sarah Brown!"

"I was *not* checking her out!" Leo rebutted. "She was going to poke my eye out with her nipples if I didn't give her my hoodie."

Sam raised a finger. "My eyes seem to be fine, and I didn't stare at her ass when she walked away."

"You're gay!" Leo snapped. At the smirk on Sam's face, he realized his error immediately. "No, no, don't be weird. This is not a thing. Fine, I checked her out. She's objectively hot. I still despise her."

"You have been bitching about Piper for years. And don't think I didn't see you help her down the stairs."

"I'd help little old ladies down the stairs, too, and you don't try to set me up with them," Leo pointed out.

"Are you into older women?"

"¿Qué?" Leo cringed. "No."

"Then my point stands."

"That makes literally no sense. You don't get it," Leo ran a hand through his hair. "She's—there's something about her that drives me up a wall."

"That's called sexual tension, my friend." Sam grinned.

"No, it's because she's a fraud. I can notice when someone is attractive and also hate every single thing about their personality. She acts all sweet with other people, but she treats me like I'm scum on the bottom of her shoe. She dates every asshole she can get her hands on. She lets people walk all over her in the name of perfection."

"Hmm, seems like you think she's putting on a show. *Acting*, even." Sam looked entirely too pleased with his deductive reasoning.

"No." Leo raised a finger in warning but had no better argument. "Just no."

"You think she'd be bad at it?"

"I..." Leo trailed off with a grimace. He didn't think Piper would be bad at it at all. She had the entire audience at the bar eating out of her hand when she was on stage. "It doesn't matter because we can't get along."

Sam stretched his legs out with an air of condescension Leo was none too thrilled with. "You're telling me you can't be professional and let bygones be bygones? You? King of telling everyone to *leave it off the stage*?"

"I'm aware that I've worked with people in my career that I don't like, but it doesn't mean I have to hire them when I know how difficult they'll be to work with."

"So, you think she's the one who can't be professional?" Sam pried.

Unlikely. Piper was always organized and punctual. Most people enjoyed her presence and got along with her fine. She barely showed emotion apart from false pleasantries, so everyone who didn't notice that her entire personality was a front found her delightful. But Leo *did* notice, and he could barely control himself when it came to her. Given the fiasco that very night, who was to say that she would be able to control herself, either?

"I don't know," Leo admitted.

"Well, I think you know where I stand." Sam stood up from the couch and yawned. "We need someone, and working off the list of people who originally tried out for the role has been fruitless. You're down to our fifth pick now that everyone else has other obligations, and quite frankly, Millicent Underwood has the acting chops of a toddler."

"I'm aware. Why do you think Moreno and I haven't picked her yet?" Leo wrung his hands.

The pressure had been on for two weeks. One of the most influential Latino directors of his time was breathing down Leo's neck to find a replacement, and the lack of options was making Leo want to pull out his hair. If he didn't figure this out promptly, the letter of recommendation he was hoping to get from Alejandro Moreno for his film school application—which would all but guarantee his acceptance this time—could burn in a fiery pit along with all his hopes and dreams.

"You and I both know Piper could do it. Just think about it." Sam left the room on that note, not even giving Leo a chance to deflect.

"Fine. I'll think about it," Leo huffed to the empty living room.

After wearing a path into the floor pacing the length of his tiny living room, Leo took a shower and headed to bed. The phone he had left charging on top of the particle board desk in his room glowed in the darkness like a silent taunt. Somehow, having Piper's number felt like an invasion of privacy. Like she could peer through his phone into his soul and suck the life out of him.

"Ridiculous," Leo muttered before getting up and snatching his phone off the desk. He burrowed back under his sheets and decided that getting the text out of the way immediately would be in his best interest. He was fairly certain that his mom liked lilies, but after perusing the internet for a bit, he ultimately decided on something a little more cheerful and typed out a quick message to the most annoying person in the world.

LEO 11:52 PM

Sunflowers.

The three little dots indicating that Piper was typing popped up a second later.

PIPER <SUNFLOWER EMOJI> 11:52 PM
Fine.

Leo chuckled at her response before tapping her contact, homing in on the sunflower he had added to her name. He squinted at it in irritation when it dawned on him that his flower choice and emoji choice were aligned, and he considered typing out a new message to switch the sunflowers to lilies out of spite. But, in the end, that would require him to send Piper another text, which he should be avoiding at all costs. Deleting her number and any trace of her from his phone should have been his next move, but after his thumb hovered over the delete button for too long, he tapped her contact picture instead. His body shifted under the sheets as he stared at Piper callously flipping him off on his screen, and then down her body at the sunflower dress she had been wearing.

You didn't choose that flower because of her dress, he tried to convince himself.

Leo groaned and rolled from his side onto his back, his phone hovering over his face as his cock twitched between his legs. His fingers itched to get himself off just so he could sleep, and he would have obliged if he wasn't so frustrated that the picture of Piper was what seemed to be starting him off.

"Chingada madre," Leo cursed under his breath and threw his phone on the floor before snapping his eyes closed.

Sleep. He could just go to sleep.

It was easier said than done when the backs of his eyelids unhelpfully played back the memory of Piper shivering outside the bar, the swell of her breasts covered in goose flesh, her hardened nipples stabbing through her bodice. It would have been so easy to flick at the buttons near the top of her dress, holding everything together. Just as easy as pulling up the bottom hem around her hips or sucking her middle fingers into his mouth.

His chest rose and fell in rapid, ragged breaths, his cock now standing at attention and aching between his legs. It was so wrong the way his body liked the abuse while his morals screamed at him from the sidelines. So, he pretended he *wasn't* thinking about Piper when he finally gave in, fisting his cock and tugging to relieve the pressure. He imagined someone who looked like her, with the same blond and lavender hair, with the same dress, and with the same piercing blue eyes, but with a personality that didn't make him want to chew gravel.

The pumping of his fist quickened until the sheets were kicked off his legs and his hand was a blur of self-indulgence below him, his mind taking the shaky moral loophole and running with it until all he was left with was shame and a mess to clean up.

EIGHT

LEO

The stage was Leo's happy place. The orchestra pit was where he could contemplate and take a step back from anything weighing on him. The seats in the theatre were where he came alive, especially while watching something marvelous happen on stage. He felt the same when he was behind a camera. Unfortunately, all he felt sitting in the front row of the theatre now was the urge to plug his ears. Millicent Underwood was truly botching his favorite song from *Guys and Dolls*, "I've Never Been in Love Before." On top of that, Alejandro Moreno was sitting at his right, stiff-backed and searing a hole into the side of Leo's head as if to say "*What the actual fuck is this?*"

Before Millicent could get to another high note that Leo was sure would either blow out his eardrums or send him into a deep depression, he stood up from his seat, raised a hand to stop the pianist in the corner from continuing, and cleared his throat. "Uh, thank you for... that. We'll let you know if you got the part by the end of the week."

Millicent gave a bright smile and walked confidently off the stage, probably thinking that she had nailed it, but Leo would rather gouge his own eyes out than listen to her sing on repeat. Someone should really let the poor girl know that she couldn't even sing "Old McDonald Had a Farm," let alone a Tony Award-winning song. Despite what Piper thought, however, he wasn't cruel. It wasn't his job to tell Millie that she sucked. It *was* his job to find the people who didn't suck. He waited until he knew Millicent was out of earshot before turning to Moreno, now standing and looking irritated.

"I'll find someone else," Leo sighed.

"We're out of time, Diaz. Do I need to step in? Ninety percent of directing is casting. You know that. I don't have to tell you that if you can't find someone, the assistant director's position will be off the table," Moreno warned. Alejandro was strict, but he wasn't an asshole—Leo knew that. "I'm trusting you on this."

"Yes, sir." Leo bobbed his head. Moreno was right: if Leo couldn't find someone to be the next Sarah Brown soon, he didn't deserve to direct at all.

"What's your plan?" Moreno's eyebrows lifted in expectation. The only plan Leo could think of was one he knew wouldn't go over well. Not with Moreno, of course—he usually agreed with Leo's choices—but with the talent herself.

"I have someone. She's perfect for the part." Leo blinked slowly, trying to come to terms with it. Sam was going to have a field day.

"Well, why the hell isn't she here, then?" Moreno motioned to the stage. "If you have the perfect solution, why do my ears feel violated right now?"

"Because," Leo pounded his palm against his forehead. "She despises me, sir. Like nuclear-level hatred."

"What'd you do? Sleep with her?" Moreno asked. "And, for the love of God, stop calling me 'sir.' I am *not* that old."

"I didn't sleep with her!" Leo practically shouted. "And why do you assume I'm the one that did something? We're just fundamentally different. She fights me on everything."

Moreno's mouth parted in surprise before the corner of his mouth tipped up. "Ah, okay. So you *want* to sleep with her, then."

"I—what? No." Leo tried to school his expression away from what he assumed was the very guilty-looking one on his face.

"Listen, I don't give a single fuck what you do in your spare time. I used to say that sleeping with the actors or staff is a terrible idea, and I still think it's a terrible idea, but I'm self-aware enough to know that I'm a hypocrite. If you can keep everything professional, then I don't care."

The torrid love affair between Moreno and his wife had been big celebrity news back in the day. They were still, to this day, one of Hollywood's favorite It couples, even two kids and eight years later. They had met on the set of Moreno's Regency era box-office hit *The Promenade*. Leo really couldn't blame Moreno for sleeping with or falling in love with the lead actress, Quinn German. He had seen the movie... and her tits. The famous nude scene where the duke and the daughter of his father's enemy, played by German, had sex in the library was probably the only reason that most of the guys from Leo's high school and Fletcher had seen it. Maybe, at some point, Leo would grow a pair and ask the question he had been dying to know since he started shadowing Moreno: what was it like to direct a scene like that? Was it better or worse when you already knew someone's body well? But today was not that day as he stared back at Moreno, whose eyes were narrowed at him like he could tell Leo was thinking about his wife's tits.

"I don't want to sleep with Piper." The statement soured in Leo's mouth like the lie it was. Saying he didn't want to see Piper naked was like saying he didn't repeatedly watch the sex scene from *The Promenade* for... research purposes.

"If you're going to direct actors, you should probably get better at acting." Moreno scoffed. "I assume you can both get over your vendettas enough to be professional?" Leo nodded. "Perfect, then figure it out. Get her to take the role. Beg. I don't care."

"Yes, sir."

"I thought working with college kids would make me young and hip again, but you all still call me 'sir' like I'm your grandpa," Moreno grumbled as he turned to walk down the aisle, looking over his shoulder. "And Leo?"

"Yeah?" Leo called back as he sat down in one of the cloth director's chairs facing the stage.

"Stop thinking about my wife's breasts."

It was a good thing Leo wasn't a blusher. His face was hot with embarrassment as he fumbled out a response. "No, I-I wasn't—"

"I'm just fucking with you," Moreno called back in a singsong voice, pushing the crash bar and leaving Leo to sit alone with his mortification.

"Dios mío," Leo groaned and massaged his temples. Quinn German's rack aside, he had a serious problem on his hands.

Piper was never going to agree to this, but he would have to get her to. If she wanted his left arm, he'd have to chop it off for her. Giving up the opportunity to assistant-direct alongside Alejandro Moreno was not an option.

Nine

LEO

It was never hard to find Piper in class. All one really had to do was clock the nearest straight man, follow his line of sight, and *bingo*. If that failed, she could always be found sitting at the very front of the classroom, meticulously rearranging her notepad, pens, and highlighters like the eager good girl she was. The space next to her was usually open because no one wanted to be a target for Professor Hornbill, and today was no different. Piper was bent over a notebook, writing a header at the top in neat calligraphic script. Leo would never understand the type of person that made their notes an entire art project. His notes were shoved into a binder that was falling apart at the seams. Not as pretty, but it got the job done and didn't require tens of thousands of dollars in fancy pens he couldn't afford.

After waving to Emma Planter, the other female headliner of the musical, who was seated where he usually sat in the back of the class, Leo wandered to the front, hyping himself up for what would no doubt be the battle of his life.

"Where's your quill and ink?" Leo asked as he dropped into the seat next to Piper, who was still carefully scrawling out the date with perfect penmanship. Her head swiveled to him in a way that made him think it might just keep spinning, *The Exorcist*-style, all the way around her pretty little neck. She glared at him for only a second before turning back to her art project.

"That seat's taken," Piper said.

"By whom?"

"Anyone else," she grumbled. "We said we would stay away from each other."

"That seems a little extreme to me." Leo shifted in the seat to get comfortable.

Piper's stormy eyes stared him down, cold and unwavering. "It was your idea. Seeing as it's the only good one you've ever had, it makes sense that you've decided to abandon it. Go sit somewhere else."

This is going so well, Leo thought as he slid out his notes, ignoring her stab. Piper glanced at the frayed edges of the notebook he had pulled from his bag, little bits of paper still caught in the spiral from where he had torn pages out of it. Her shoulders stiffened as if his lack of organizational skills were a personal attack. While she was busy judging his study habits, Leo scoured every corner of his brain for the right thing to say that would somehow end with Piper cast as Sarah Brown. He decided a compliment was the best way to go.

"The purple is nice." Leo practically spat the words. The way Piper's face screwed up in confusion said that she had no idea what he was talking about, so he rambled on. "In your hair. It's like lavender or lilac or some other L word that has to do with purple." Jesus, he was botching this. The problem didn't even lie with finding something to compliment her on—his brain was clearly capable of indecent thoughts on just *how* compliment-worthy her body was—but stating his dirty thoughts didn't seem like the right way to get her to agree to the role, and he had no idea what *was* the right way

"Thanks?" Piper reached a self-conscious hand up to touch her hair.

"What do the colors mean? You change it a lot. Is it like a mood ring for your hair?" Leo said. *That* turned out to be the wrong thing to say, because her face returned to its scowl.

"Yep," she said. "That's exactly it. I'm always emotional, and I need people to know it. Purple means 'stop talking to me.' Why don't you try it?"

"You know," he forged ahead, "we have like thirty different wig colors in the theatre department. If you ever wanted to test out a new color, you could come try them out."

"Oh, so now you want me to change my hair?" Piper scoffed.

"What? No, I just..." Leo sucked in a breath of air, hoping to come up with something to convince her in the time it took him to exhale. "Esto no está funcionando." He came up with nothing. Nada. Zilch. "I'll just come out with it. The Sarah Brown role is open if you want it."

Piper cackled loudly, and he flinched. "No need to save it for me. I don't want it. I'm not sure when you got the impression that I did."

"You don't want a chance to prove yourself?" Leo goaded. "To show that you're capable of leading?" He knew he was framing it in a way that made it sound like Piper wanted the role and not that he was desperate for her to take it, but his pride was getting the better of him. She was still glaring at him, so he pulled out the small bit of reconnaissance he'd done on her earlier that day. "I mean, my mom said you're taking over Hartrick Designs when you get out of college, so this could prove you know what you're doing."

Piper cocked her head. Whatever Leo's expression was, it gave him away, because she immediately broke into a sinister smile. "Oh, I get it. I'm your last option, aren't I? You're screwed, and you're trying to twist this in a way that seems like you're doing me a favor, is that it?"

Leo's hands were starting to sweat profusely. He really should have consulted Sam, Wes, or literally anyone else on how to go about this beforehand. But he hadn't, so he did the only thing he could think to do: he told the truth.

"You aren't my last option." Leo sighed. "I think you'd be just as good as who we originally cast for the role, though. My last option would be a list of people who are well-intentioned but would botch the role so thoroughly that it would tank my future career. If I don't find someone to play the role, my assistant director position is off the table. Casting is a major, if not the most important, part of directing, so I need to get this right."

"I'm surprised you don't think you could just cast anyone and force them into whatever box you want them to fit into." Piper didn't say it as a slight so much as an observation, like she truly believed directing meant Leo just bossed people around all day. But being strict didn't mean forcing people into submission.

"Alfred Hitchcock said that actors should be treated like cattle," Leo paraphrased. "But if it wasn't obvious from that quote alone, Alfred Hitchcock was a complete and utter asshole. In *The Birds*, he had people throw live birds at the lead, Tippi Hedren, because she wasn't reciprocating his sexual advances."

"Jesus." Piper's mouth dropped open.

"So, no. I don't subscribe to the forcing-people-into-a-box mentality. I like to think I'm collaborative, if a bit of a hardass."

"You were just trying to sell it to me like it was my idea," Piper pointed out.

"I do think it's a good opportunity for you. Yes, I get something out of it, but so do you," Leo insisted.

"What? Your extremely pleasant company?"

"You had stage fright at the karaoke bar before you committed and won over the crowd," he explained. "You'll have stage fright when it comes to running your own company."

"So, what, exposure therapy?" Piper asked. He was losing her, but he didn't have any other idea how to get her to agree. "I think I could work on confidence without getting up in front of a hundred people to embarrass myself, let alone having *you* of all people order me around for months leading up to that. You'll get some sick pleasure out of telling me what to do."

"The Olson Theatre seats seven hundred and fifty people. And I'll make you look good. You won't embarrass yourself," Leo pleaded. He wasn't going to negate the fact that he would be giving her orders and suggestions; it was his job to do so. He also wouldn't deny that he loved the idea of Piper complying with those suggestions. He wouldn't misuse that power, but it was still exciting.

It was as if Piper could see the thrilled glint in his eye with how fast she shot him down. "The answer is no."

Shit. Shit. Shit.

His heart freefell from his chest, his hopes and dreams sailing into hell with it. Leo frantically reached out to touch her arm, and when she stiffened against his fingertips, he ripped his hand back. "Isn't there something I could give you in return?"

"Now you're prostituting yourself out to me? You're going to do wonders in the entertainment business," Piper said scornfully.

Leo let the smirk spread across his lips. He couldn't help it. "I meant like a favor, princesita, but it's very interesting that your mind immediately went to sex. Do you think of me naked often?"

"I don't think of you *at all*," she hissed.

Leo had to admit the jab stung a little considering the sheer amount of mental space Piper seemed to occupy in his head. Even he wasn't delusional enough to continue pretending that it wasn't her he had been imagining when he'd gotten carried away the other night. It annoyed him to no end how she was always there in the back of his mind. He constantly replayed her comments on a loop like a never-ending movie. The number of times he had pictured her plump, pink lips parted...

Leo groaned. "Piper, I'm serious. What do I need to do to get you to agree to this?" He was practically taking Moreno's suggestion to beg at this point, and he didn't even care. Desperate times called for desperate measures.

"There's nothing you can do," Piper bit off. "Go find someone else to torment."

Before Leo could offer up his actual body (as a blood sacrifice rather than a sexual sacrifice, since Piper was clearly repulsed by the latter), Professor Hornbill strode his way over to the center of the room and leaned back against the whiteboard, arms folded over his chest as he surveyed the classroom. Leo liked the majority of his professors, but Hornbill was the emphatic exception to that rule. The guy was classically handsome, with a chiseled jawline, sandy hair, and stormy gray eyes, so most of his classmates had dubbed him 'Professor Horny,' which, while not the most original of nicknames, got the point across. General physique aside, there was something off about Hornbill, something that set off every alarm bell in Leo's head. If his father had taught Leo anything, it was to always trust his gut, and his spidey senses tingled every time Hornbill was around.

"In the front row today?" Hornbill made eye contact with Leo, sending a sideways glance at Piper. If there was any implication behind Hornbill's observation, it wasn't obvious, but Leo couldn't help but think it had nothing to do with him and everything to do with the pretty blonde beside him.

"I'm just very excited about ethics," Leo said smoothly.

"Please." Hornbill smiled humorlessly. "No one is excited about ethics. Not even me." The class laughed at this, but Leo kept his mouth in a flat line. A glance over at Piper confirmed that she, too, wasn't laughing. Leo offhandedly wondered if Piper got the same vibe from Hornbill that he did.

As the class proceeded and Hornbill started to discuss the material for their next exam, Leo pulled a pen from his bag, ripped a sheet from his notebook, and scrawled one word on it before sliding it over to Piper.

Please?

Ten

PIPER

Please?

    The word ran through Piper's mind like an earworm song all day. She could almost hear it in Leo's voice, soft and pleading, even though she had never heard him speak it aloud. It invigorated her to see such an overconfident guy reduced to someone who had to beg to get what he wanted. The power she felt from that single word made her wonder what else he would beg for. It was a ridiculous thought, but she had lied when she said she never thought about Leo, naked or otherwise. Most of the time, when her brain conjured up anything Leo, it was because he'd pissed her off, but there was still the rare occasion when her thoughts ran away with illicit images of Leo underneath her—solely to teach him a lesson, of course.

    Leo's chicken scratch handwriting seared a hole in the back pocket of Piper's jeans as she made her way to the campus library. Her fingers itched to take out the note and look at it again, but the compulsion was getting a little out of hand. The fact that she had even brought the stupid slip of paper with her was pure insanity. Even with the note living rent-free in her head, there was no way she would step foot on stage as Leo's pet. The only person gaining anything from the agreement would be him. She couldn't think of anything Leo could give her in return that would even out the playing field. If he wanted her to play nice, then he should have thought about that long before he continually used the word "nice" in association with her name as an insult.

"Hey, Piper!"

Piper smiled as she approached the brunette girl wearing heavy eyeliner, fishnets, and ripped black jeans who was sitting casually atop a table with a *Best Business Practices* textbook perched in her hand. Emma Planter was *way* cooler than Piper would ever be, which was why Piper had never really interacted with her. Once, in high school, Piper had tried out the whole goth vibe, even dyeing the tips of her hair black. In the end, she had only been doing it to appease her boyfriend at the time and quickly reverted back to her colorful dresses and sweaters. Emma radiated confidence and bad bitch energy, so Piper was shocked when Emma approached her after class to request a study session for their ethics exam.

"Hey, Emma." Piper slid into a seat at the table.

"Thanks for meeting me." Emma clicked her pen. "My grade in this class is fighting to climb out of a pit right now. I've been meeting with Professor Hornbill once a week, but he said that you and Leo have the highest grades in the class, so I figured I could weasel my way into studying with you."

Piper fought the urge to cringe, and surprisingly enough, it wasn't on Leo's behalf. Professor Hornbill gave her the creeps. No one else seemed to have that impression of him, though, and she had no real reason to dislike him other than the occasional glance at her that lingered a little too long. The man was married and had children, so Piper had told herself about a billion times that there was no way he was anything other than a man with an occasional wandering eye.

"Thanks for saving me from having to talk to Leo at the end of class, by the way." Piper pulled her ethics textbook and notebook out of her backpack and set them on the table. When she reached back into the bag for her highlighters, her fingertips brushed over a small wooden box with a metal clasp on the front that was tucked safely away at the bottom. After a silent deliberation, she set the box in her lap.

To anyone else, the contents of the box Piper carried with her everywhere would look like nothing but a random assortment of objects, but to her, they felt like pieces of her soul, catalysts to her dreams. Each piece represented something. When her anxiety got the best of her, she'd pull something from the box and use it as a talisman for strength. The small apatite stone she pulled out now was one of her favorites, the vibrant blue of its smooth surface soothing her senses. Also inside the box were a collection of peachy paint swatches in warm and inviting colors, a tiny sunflower encased in glass, and a piece of square-cut, gray cashmere fabric that represented Piper's soft side. Her mother used to say the color felt like storm clouds, too, a testament to the wicked temper Piper had when she was little. Her thumb brushed over the cool surface of the blue apatite stone several times before she put it back, reclasped the box, and gently set it on the table.

"So, I take it you don't like him?" Emma asked.

"Can't stand him," Piper affirmed and flipped to a clean page of her notebook.

"I am so sorry for this." Emma scrunched her eyes shut like she was in pain, and Piper looked up from uncapping her pen.

"Why?"

"What's all this?" Leo's voice asked abruptly.

Piper jumped out of her skin, smacking her elbow on the table. She winced and turned to face the culprit. "Ow! Why the fuck are you here? Are you seriously stalking me now?"

"Don't flatter yourself. Emma said she needed help studying." Leo sat down beside her.

"You two know each other?" Piper asked Emma, pointing between the two of them. Emma certainly seemed like the type of girl Leo would be into.

"Emma's playing Adelaide, another headlining role in the musical." Leo's mouth quirked up, and Piper suddenly felt like a caged animal, a mouse caught in a trap. A mouse with Leo's handwritten note burning a hole in her back pocket.

"Does Emma speak for herself, or are you planning on talking over her the whole time?" Piper bit off.

"Holy *shiiiit*," Emma cackled. "Did you two use to date or something?"

"I would never touch him with a ten-foot pole," Piper spat.

"You wound me." Leo rolled his eyes. "And to answer your question, Emma, the SparkNotes version is that we went to the same high school. Piper decided that taking my advice in Spanish class was beneath her even though I'm literally fluent, and now, here we are."

"You forgot the part where you purposely ripped apart everything I did in that class. You didn't give your so-called 'advice' to anyone but me. It was your mission to make me look stupid in front of everyone the same year my parents died." Piper scrunched her nose at the memory of each humiliating encounter with Leo back then. She'd meant to keep the last part in her head, but it had come out regardless.

Leo dared to look aghast at this. "That's not what happened, Piper."

"Whatever." Piper swallowed and looked away before thoughts of her parents could overwhelm her senses. "Hopefully you're better at helping people study now because we have a lot of stuff to cover. Emma, I don't know if he's tried to rope you into asking me about the play, but I'd rather not discuss it."

"It's a musical," Leo corrected.

"He only told me that he was trying to get you to do it." Emma lifted her hands in a show of innocence. "I'm just here to study. I wasn't lying about my grades. Hornbill said you two were my best shot—other than him, of course." Piper watched Leo's face momentarily scrunch in what looked like disgust before relaxing.

"We should get to work, then." Piper nodded.

"First things first, I need to know what this is." Leo pointed to the open wooden box Piper had slid off to the side earlier. Emma glared at Leo, and he shrugged. "What? It looks like a little treasure chest. You can't possibly tell me you don't want to know, too. My entire existence revolves around storytelling, so a mysterious box in the middle of the table? Yeah, I'm gonna ask."

Emma chuckled. "Okay, fine. I was curious, but it just looked personal." She turned to Piper with a small shake of her head. "If there was a button that said 'don't press me' on the table, I bet he'd immediately press it."

"That's not even in question." Leo scoffed. "Obviously, I'm going to hit the button. What's in the box, princesita? Mementos from boyfriends past?"

It was just a box. Logically, Piper knew that, but her body still locked up with the thought of having to explain. Leo would no doubt find it silly to hold onto things so seemingly meaningless. When she didn't respond, Leo pulled the box toward himself and peered into it. Piper wanted to throw up. Everyone was going to find out how pathetic she was. That she could never get over something that had happened over five years ago.

To Piper's utter shock, Leo pulled out the apatite stone first and held it up, squinting at it. "This matches your eyes."

"Yeah," Piper finally spoke, and the corner of her mouth tugged upward. "That's kinda the point. The whole box represents me."

"You just carry around a bunch of things that remind you of yourself?" Leo's normal asshole behavior was back, and Piper was grateful for an excuse to fight.

"What a power move. I like it," Emma chimed in.

"No," Piper laughed. "My mom called them inspiration boxes. She'd make one for each client during the designing process of their house. They had pieces of wood, rocks, paint swatches, fabrics, that kinda thing."

"She made you this one?" Leo asked, seeming genuinely

intrigued as he pulled out a plaid square. "What does this signify?"

"I like everything in organized boxes, just like she did." Piper forced a smile in the Pavlovian way she always did when either of her parents came up. She had trained herself well.

"Hm. I'm more of a creative chaos person myself." Leo tipped his head to the side. "I think mine would look like one of those paintings where up close it looks like just a bunch of dots, but if you back up it makes a picture."

"Pointillism," Emma said.

"They have a bunch of paintings in that style hanging up in Roaster's Republic back home." Piper nodded. "My uncle bought one from them a while back for my aunt. It's an open book, but the whole thing is made up of tiny little dots."

"Huh. I'll have to go in and look sometime when I'm back in Archwood. I've never actually gone inside, even though my sister-in-law's the manager." Leo carefully pulled another item out of the box.

"What? Really?" Piper gawked.

"Yep, my brother practically stalked her in that coffee shop for half a year before asking her out. Now they're married, so I guess it worked out."

Piper shook her head. "No, I meant really, you've never been inside?"

"Half of my meals are Top Ramen-based. You expect me to drop six bucks on coffee?" The question came out teasingly enough, but it still gave her a prick of shame. Leo held up the glass sunflower dome from her inspiration box. "Is this for your sunny disposition?"

"Yeah. It's supposed to represent my smile." Piper blushed. It was a bit uncomfortable to talk about herself so casually. She was just repeating back her mom's words, but explaining the reason behind each piece in the box felt conceited. Every time Leo pulled out a piece and inspected it, it felt like he was inspecting *her*. Seeing her right down to her core without even looking at her.

"Makes sense." Emma gave a considerate bob of her head.

"Your real smile, maybe," Leo said flatly before placing the sunflower back in the box. It always unnerved Piper how he constantly called her out on the smile she had practiced a billion times. She had convinced herself that he couldn't actually tell when it wasn't real, that he just enjoyed calling her fake any chance he could. There was a difference between being fake and protecting people from your emotions.

"Okay, enough about the box." Piper waved them off and ran a flustered hand over her supplies, picking up a yellow highlighter. "It's time to study."

It was late by the time they finished going over their notes and, at Emma's request, set another study date. Emma had finally declared that her brain was eating itself with the influx of information and she needed to eat real food before cramming to memorize her lines for the musical. To Piper's surprise, Leo didn't use that as a segue into recruitment and only informed Emma of the pages they'd be running tomorrow before she scurried off. But Piper could almost see it in his eyes—the *please*—and she wondered what she would do if her dream hinged on Leo doing something for her.

"Do you think Professor Hornbill will test us on the marketing strategies he introduced last class, too, or just the ethics lessons we've been doing for the last month?" Leo dragged his finger down a page in his textbook as they packed away their supplies.

"The syllabus says ethics, but I wouldn't put it past him to include the marketing stuff. That last test he gave us was a doozy."

Leo shrugged. "I aced it."

"So did I," Piper ground out. Why he always felt the need to one-up her, she would never know. Even just trying to connect with him on a basic human level was hard.

"Well, I have the ethics lessons basically memorized at this point. I'll have to work on the marketing strategies."

"Really? I feel like you could use an ethics lesson," Piper quipped.

"Funny." Leo flipped several pages forward in the textbook. "We should focus our studies on marketing next time considering you're already a walking, talking ethics textbook."

"There's nothing wrong with following the rules," Piper insisted. Everything coming out of her mouth was clipped and irritated. It was late, she was tired, and Leo was doing what he did best: pushing her buttons. They were still in a library, though, so she needed to control herself before they ended up in a screaming match.

"And yet," Leo snapped his textbook closed, "the people that make history are the ones who break the mold."

"This isn't politics," Piper scoffed. "It's about treating employees with respect and improving workplace dynamics. I'm not planning on running my company by breaking HR rules. My parents never had to do that to succeed." Her parents had run their business so well that even after they died, Hartrick Designs still ran like a well-oiled machine. Cole and Paisley had rewarded their employees when they delivered on their assignments. They had granted leeway when someone was having a rough time. They were the kind of bosses that people dreamed of working with, and Piper had every intention of taking on the role with the same level of care.

"Who's running the company right now?" Leo's eyebrows rose, his interest clearly piqued.

"My uncle designated the business to be run by the manager and assistant manager. He has to sign off on things occasionally, but he's mostly hands-off since he knows nothing about interior design or running a business. Talia makes up for the business side of things, but she doesn't have much time for it with the grocery store. My parents have," Piper cleared her throat, "*had* one hundred and thirteen employees, so shutting down the business when they died would have meant that everyone would lose their job. Plus, Walker knew that my dream was always to work with my parents. So, basically, when I graduate, Hartrick Designs is mine. If my siblings want in on it, I'll share, but currently, the only one who seems mildly interested is my sister, Pearl, and she's a sixteen-year-old who romanticizes the idea of everything. The job is mine."

"Don't you think current management is going to have a problem with the nepotism and you stepping in to take over after they've been running it on their own for several years?" Leo challenged.

"I..." Piper swallowed, trying to formulate her thoughts before she spoke again. Leo had just voiced every insecurity she had about taking over her parents' business. What if everyone thought she was untalented and unworthy? The nagging voice in the back of her head agreed that she was incapable despite how much she loved the company. While the rest of her siblings had no desire to be involved in the business, Piper always had. Her parents used to bring her along to the office, and she had years of knowledge stowed away just from watching them work. Watching her mother talk to customers and agonize over design plans. Watching her father negotiate deals and harp over numbers. "I'm not planning on snatching up the responsibility all at once. And yes, they might think that when I first start, but I'm going to prove myself. I'm not doing this because I'm a beneficiary of the business. I'm doing it because it was my dream to work with these people and do this job. It was my dream to work with my parents, and if I can't have that, I'm going to build their business into something even greater, and I'm going to do it *with* the people my parents entrusted their life's work to. I don't have to take things away from them in order to lead. I'll keep everything above board."

"Hm." Leo gave a perfunctory nod of his head.

"What?" Piper sighed. "You have some opinions you want to share with the class?"

"It doesn't matter what I think."

"Your face seems to tell a different story. You think I'm not good enough."

"I think, as a boss, it's not your job to prove you know what you're doing. Obviously, you have to know things, that's a given, but to lead you have to be confident, and you're too nice. You care too much about people's feelings. If people argue with your capabilities, despite your qualifications and skill set, you'll give in instead of doing what you think is right."

"And, let me guess," Piper drummed her fingers on the table in irritation, "you don't care about other people's opinions. You think your way is the right way, always."

"I want to be a director. So, sure, there's an element of creativity I'll take input on, but in the end, what I say goes. I'm not going to constantly ask people if they think I'm doing okay at my job. It'll make them think that I don't know what I'm doing." Leo shrugged. "I'm their boss, not their friend."

"I think I can be someone's boss and their friend."

"Where's the line? At some point, you'll get taken advantage of because they'll think of you more as a friend than as someone who could fire them."

"I'd rather be nice than overbearing." Piper shook her head. "I'm not in it for a power trip like you are."

"Power trip?" Leo laughed. "I want to create something. So, I might be a hardass, but it's what needs to happen to get the work done. You have all these pens and highlighters telling you to stay on track. I don't need that because I'm already on track. I'm not here to make friends. With what I want to do, I won't get anywhere by palling around. I can elevate people by showcasing their talent. I don't need to be their best friend, I need to be their boss. No one will listen to me if I'm not sure of myself."

"Isn't Sam your best friend?" Piper pointed out. "He seemed to have no problem telling you what he thought the other night."

"Sam knows the second we're in work mode, I'm not there for fun and games. That's why our friendship works. It's about respect. And, sure, the other night, he gave me his opinion on you, but ultimately, what I say goes. If I decided that we weren't going to entertain the conversation, he wouldn't have even spoken to you about the role at all. I told him he could try."

"You sound like a pompous ass," Piper scoffed.

"And you sound like someone without a backbone," Leo shot back.

"Guess we'll find out which one of us is more successful later," Piper taunted him.

"Ah, yes, and we'll judge this success off of what, exactly? The fact that your parents left you a Fortune 500 company, and I have to build my way up from the ground?"

"Well, you seem to think I'll run my parents' business into the ground, so if that happens, you win."

"I don't think that. I just think you'll make it further if you stop caring so much about what everyone thinks of you."

"That's bold coming from the guy who constantly judges me." Piper pointed at Leo's chest. "You want me to stop caring about what people think? Fine. I don't care what *you* think."

Leo hummed introspectively. "See, I think you *do* care what I think. And I think it bugs you that you care."

"And I think you get off on making people feel small, and that's disgusting," Piper snapped.

"You make *yourself* feel small," Leo enunciated, his black-rimmed eyes staring directly into hers. "I just point out the obvious. You won't stand up for yourself, and eventually, other people will eat you alive."

"I stand up to you just fine." Piper lifted her chin. He might have been right about her when it came to other people, but for some reason, she never had a hard time going on the attack with Leo.

He massaged his knuckles like he was contemplating something and then shook his head. "That, we can agree on. It's probably why I can't get you to agree to the show. I'm usually pretty persuasive." The *please* note in Piper's back pocket suddenly felt like a dead weight. "Any chance your answer has changed?"

If there was one thing Leo was good at, it was having the balls to ask for something, even after he'd just torn apart her managerial tactics. "It's still a no," Piper said. He practically deflated in front of her, so much so that she wanted to take it back before she reminded herself that he was a dick, and a singular moment of humanity didn't change that.

"Can you just think about it a little more?" He took the apatite rock from her inspiration box, still on the table, and sighed deeply as he ran his thumb over it. He must have watched her do the same thing before he'd sat down at the table for their study session, or the action would have felt strangely personal. A little color returned to his face when he looked from the rock to Piper. "You're good at acting. I can still tell when it's not real, but I'm an expert at telling the difference between fiction and reality." She gave him one of those smiles that children did when their parents told them to smile for a photo: exaggerated and toothier than necessary. Leo chuckled, set the rock back in the box, and picked up the sunflower. He tapped it on the table as if he were testing its durability, then put it back in the box before he folded his hands on the table, business-like. "What do I have to do to get you to agree to the show, Piper? Beg?"

"Yeah, definitely," Piper snickered. "I'd love to see that."

Before she could even grasp what was happening, Leo had pulled his chair out and risen right behind her seat. She turned her chair just in time to watch him drop to his knees.

"This work for you?" Leo assumed a begging position, lacing his hands and holding them up in prayer. Her eyes blew wide as she gaped at him. "*Please*, Piper. I need this opportunity. I'm desperate. I will do literally anything you ask me to."

Piper's cheeks were flaming as she jerked her head back and forth to scan the library. People were staring. Not only staring, but pointing and whispering. Leo didn't take his dark eyes off her, his chin held sturdy like he couldn't give two shits that he was degrading himself in front of her. By the time someone wolf-whistled in their direction, her entire body felt like it was on fire. But her body's reaction wasn't entirely due to embarrassment, either. How could it be when an objectively attractive guy was practically bowing at her feet?

"Isn't this embarrassing to you?" Piper asked, keeping her voice low.

"Only if you say no." Leo cocked his head and grinned. "Say yes, Piper. You know you want to." Those words did something even worse to her body, and she swallowed hard, shifting her eyes anywhere but Leo's face. Her gaze landed on her inspiration box. And that was when the idea hit her like a slap to the face.

"I want to design the set."

Leo's smirk faltered. "What?"

"If I can design the set, I'll be in the show."

"We already have a set designer." He got up from the floor and shook his head as he dusted off his knees.

"You don't have *anything* without me," Piper rebutted. "I'll use my own supplies, I'll pay for it, and I'll collaborate with whoever's in charge now. I want this in my portfolio."

Leo brushed off his knees and tipped his head from shoulder to shoulder. Without saying a word, he walked over to the black backpack he had thrown on the table when he arrived and pulled out a thick white packet of papers bound together with a binder clip.

"Rehearsal is at six tomorrow." He tossed the packet on top of Piper's textbook. "I checked your schedule with Thea. You're free. Memorize pages twenty-two through forty. I already highlighted all your lines. We aren't practicing your musical numbers tomorrow, but you'll need to download those and study them as well. I know you aren't familiar with it, but *Guys and Dolls* is a widely popular musical, so you can find the soundtrack on any major platform where you stream music. The sheet music is in the packet as well. Feel free to purchase the movie, too. Since you're springing for the set design, I'm sure you can afford it. After rehearsal, you can meet Elliot, the lead on set design." Without the briefest of glances her way, Leo zipped up his backpack, slung it over his shoulder, and turned on his heel to walk away, leaving Piper staring after him dazedly. When he reached the end of the row, he looked over his shoulder with a sinister smile. "Happy studying, princesita!"

Piper watched Leo disappear behind a shelf and stared into the empty space there for an inordinate amount of time before picking up the packet and smacking it against her forehead repeatedly as punishment.

She had just gotten fucking played.

Eleven

PIPER

"I'm mad at you."

Thea broke free from her liplock with Yuri on the couch when Piper stormed into the house. "Is this because of Leo?" Thea asked.

"Why would you tell him my schedule, Thea? *Why*?" Piper came to stand in front of her best friend, hands on her hips, eyebrows raised. "Do you want to give a serial killer or a Mormon my address while you're at it?"

Yuri shifted on the couch. "This seems like a conversation for—"

"I'm fucked, Thea! Fucked!" Piper bulldozed over Yuri's attempt to escape and slid her bag off her shoulder, ripping out the massive packet that Leo had bestowed upon her. She threw it, a little forcefully, at Thea's torso but missed and hit her smack-dab in the middle of her forehead instead.

Thea winced, then picked up the packet. "Um, *ow*! How many times have we talked about you throwing things? You have terrible aim. It's a wonder how you ever played soccer."

"I wasn't very good." Piper shrugged.

"And what am I looking at?" Thea thumbed the packet.

"*Guys and Dolls*?" Yuri asked, peeking over Thea's shoulder. "I love that musical!"

"I'm now a freaking headliner." Piper gritted her teeth.

"I thought he was going to ask you out on a date. I didn't know," Thea deflected.

Piper ran a frustrated hand through her hair. Her fingers caught in a tangled knot at the bottom, and she had to fight to pull them free. "I can't believe you. I don't want to date Leo! You were there when I dumped my drink on his head."

"I *was* there, and it was all very hot. The ice felt like a metaphor for cooling off, if you know what I mean. Plus, Leo is fine with a capital F." Thea grinned, then turned to Yuri. "Sorry, honey."

"Oh, no worries, I've seen the guy. Your assessment is accurate. Plus, I'm very secure in all of this." Yuri gestured from his head, where his crew-cut brown hair matched his sharp jawline, all the way down to his crotch, and then gave an extra jerk of his hand toward his junk for emphasis.

"Ew! Now is not the time to talk about your Russian Beast," Piper groaned.

"If I'm being honest, I love that my dick has a reputation." Yuri grinned.

"The *reputation* album is actually about your dick," Thea tacked on.

Piper wrinkled her nose in disgust. "I hate you both." She didn't, not in the slightest, but they both knew that. While Piper didn't allow herself to love many people, Thea was one she had to fight against loving too much so it wouldn't be as painful when they inevitably went their separate ways after college. And Yuri treated Thea in a way that reminded Piper of her parents. She couldn't have it for herself, but she was happy that her friends had that kind of love.

"Okay, why didn't you just say no to doing the role?" Thea

asked. Piper bit her lip and looked away, mumbling sheepishly under her breath. "You caved, didn't you?"

"Well, not exactly. I kind of negotiated?" Piper's voice cracked at the end of her sentence.

"I love negotiations! What did you get? You should have asked me. I probably could have gotten you a better deal." Yuri, a pre-law student, frequently acted as if he were Piper's lawyer. His advice was usually helpful—or it would be, if Piper ever found the courage to barter with her teachers.

"I, uh, get to do the set design." Again, Piper had murmured it, as if making the words feel smaller would make the problem go away.

"So, let me get this straight, you're mad at me because you agreed to the part *and* volunteered yourself for the set design?" Thea folded her arms over her chest. "We both know Leo would have just convinced you to do the musical with or without your availability. You don't know how to say no to people."

Piper searched for a response, but came up empty-handed. She took a deep breath and let it out slowly as she turned and fell back beside Thea on the couch. "I've been swindled."

"There's no way to get out of it?" Yuri asked

"I don't think so." Piper shook her head. "I'm sure Leo's told half the school by now that I agreed to the role. If I back out now, he'll have more fuel to torment me. Plus, I do kind of want to do the set design. I researched *Guys and Dolls* while I was at the library, and I think I could do something really cool with it."

"Aren't you a bit overbooked with classes, the musical, and the set? That seems like a lot." Thea gave her a look of concern that said everything Piper hadn't voiced yet.

"You know me. It'll be a little stressful, but I'll figure it out." It was the understatement of the century, but Piper was experienced in the art of never being able to say no and always offering more of herself than humanly possible. Taking on too much was a mere fact of life for her now, and as long as she had her mental breakdowns alone, no one would be the wiser. Thea lived with her and usually noticed when things were spiraling, but Piper had gotten pretty good at hiding the plight of her personality. She was and would always be a helper, regardless of the toll it took.

"Are all the highlighted lines yours?" Thea sifted through the script, her eyes widening as they took in Leo's sloppy highlight work. Piper wished he would have left the script alone so she could meticulously highlight her lines with the pen set her brother Carter had gotten her for her twenty-first birthday. They didn't bleed through and had tips that made it easy to guide the marker in a straight line. Leo's lines were all over the place and distracting.

"Mm-hmm." Piper took the script from Thea's hand and thumbed through it. "I have to memorize a bunch of lines before tomorrow, so I should probably get to it."

"Can we play the other characters?" Yuri's eyes practically sparkled with excitement, and Piper tried not to let her shoulders sag with relief.

The plan when Piper had walked into the apartment had been to guilt trip Thea into helping her, but as it turned out, Piper was terrible at manipulation and also terrible at asking for help—both things Leo Diaz seemed to excel at. She took a page from his playbook. "*Please*? I swear I'll do your laundry for a week if you help me."

"I don't need you to do my laundry, Piper," Thea scoffed. "I don't need to be bribed to help you. What scenes are we working on?"

Twelve

PIPER

The Olson Theatre was on the opposite side of campus from the majority of her classes, so in her time at Fletcher, Piper had only been inside once. Her boyfriend during her sophomore year was a concert violinist, and an extremely pompous one at that. She had sat alone for his entire performance to cheer him on despite hating classical music, only for him to dump her right after, high off the attention he was getting from the other musicians.

The air was frigid when Piper finally entered the theatre through a heavy black door. A chilly gust of air blew back her hair, and she shivered, vaguely wondering if Leo had control over the thermostat. She wouldn't put it past him to purposely make everyone mildly uncomfortable while they rehearsed. Lucky for her, she was sporting the hoodie Leo had lent her the other night, which she was planning on never returning. She had worn it as a sort of fuck-you to flaunt in his face.

"It's colder than a witch's tit in here!" a voice shouted from below.

When Piper made it to the ledge on the first flight of stairs, she swallowed and looked down toward the stage. She once again regretted her decision to attend a university that was built into the side of a hill. The elevator in the lobby or the wheelchair ramp to the bottom of the hill would have been the better option than the main entrance, but it was too late now. People onstage were starting to slowly notice her presence as she descended. Her footing was careful, but the cascading rows of folding maroon cloth chairs were still an ominous threat to her poor balance. "We're not doing a musical about Antarctica, so why is it negative two degrees in here? Even if we were playing Santa's elves, I am not a method actor," the voice continued, and Piper finally tracked it to Leo's friend and her male counterpart in the play, Sam.

"No, but you *are* dramatic as fuck," Emma replied. "You're in the Pac Northwest now, honey. It's cold here."

"All right, all right. I know it's not ideal, but maintenance is coming by tomorrow to fix the heating," an older Latino man with perfectly styled dark hair said as Piper got to the halfway point of her descent.

Sam spotted her and waved ecstatically. "Piper!"

Despite being fifteen minutes early, Piper wished she had shown up even earlier so she didn't have to make the trek to the front of the theatre with an audience. Leo stood next to the older man with a victorious smirk aimed in her direction, and she wanted to slap it right off his face. She was suddenly the center of attention, and the nervous energy she had when stage fright set in started to bounce off the walls of her body.

"Ah, you must be our newcomer," the older man said with a warm smile.

"Uh, I guess so," Piper called back as she made her way down another step.

And that was when everything went wrong.

The ground slipped out from under her zero-traction flats, and Piper was freefalling. Shouts from the stage were followed by her arms waving about frantically like she was trying to stay upright on roller skates. There was nothing to hold on to on the way down the two steps she hadn't completed yet. By the time she felt the searing pain of her kneecaps smacking down on the hard surface of the black floors, she was almost grateful the wait was over. Then the embarrassment set in, turning her face red. If her legs weren't screaming in pain, she would have bolted, changed her name, and moved to a small island off the coast of nowhere.

"Demonios, princesita." Leo was now directly in front of her, squatting down to her level. Piper winced as she moved to sit back on her butt. "Are you okay?"

"Fine," Piper croaked. She nervously scanned the rest of the theatre only to find exactly what she thought she would: everyone looking at her with a mix of shock and pity.

"Mira, I know I said I wanted you to headline, but there was no need to make a grand entrance." Leo chuckled.

Piper's eyes pricked with tears as the panic set in. "I don't know why I'm here at all. I can't do this." She started to adamantly shake her head as Leo's eyes widened.

"Piper, look at me," he urged. When all she could do was continue to shake her head, his hand reached up, cupping her cheek. Warm fingers curled under her chin and stopped the motion of her head. With a steadying pressure, he tipped her chin to look at him. It should have been repulsive, but it was oddly comforting. "Yes, you can," Leo said softly. The fear of her backing out was written into the creases of his face. "That was a bad joke. Sorry. I should have told you there's a back entrance to the theatre."

Piper swallowed and sniffed back any remaining emotion. "Was that your first time apologizing for something?"

Leo let out a breath and relaxed his shoulders with a grin. "Was that your first time walking?"

She shoved his hand away from her cheek and rolled her eyes. "Help me up, asshole."

Leo obliged, gripping her hand and hauling her to her feet with so much force that she had to stop herself from toppling forward by planting her hand against the center of his chest. He caught her by the waist with his free hand, and that was when her body decided that breathing wasn't something she was capable of doing.

"Piper?" Leo's voice was all gravel.

"Yeah?" Piper squeaked.

"You're bleeding."

"Oh, shit!" Sure enough, when she looked down, blood was dripping down her shins, leaving a trail of red behind.

"We've got a first aid kit in the back." The older man was suddenly at her side, with Sam's boyfriend, Wes, in tow.

Leo took a large step back from Piper, dropping his hand away from her waist. With an unreadable expression on his face, he whipped his hand out from his side and shoved Wes forward. "He's pre-med, and both his parents are doctors. He can fix you up." Then Leo left, leaving her bleeding and staring after him, wondering what had suddenly gotten him spooked.

Thirteen

LEO

"No." Leo held up his hand in a stop position when Sam barreled toward him across the stage.

"You don't even know what I'm going to say," Sam whined.

"I know you, and I know exactly what you're going to say," Leo said. He'd bet a hundred bucks he didn't have that Sam was going to say something about all the touching, and Piper was quite literally the last thing he wanted to talk about. The hand at Leo's side flexed and unflexed, trying to rid the feeling of her cheek against his palm. He opted for curling it into a proper fist, one he wished he could take out on his punching bag back at his apartment.

"You flipped out when she fell." Sam gave him a wry smile.

"Cool, so we're ignoring my consent to have this conversation," Leo muttered. "I would have done that for anybody. I don't need a reason to help someone who fell down the stairs. Now, if you'll excuse me." Leo shooed Sam away and made his way over to Moreno, who was scanning his clipboard. Piper's fall felt like it reflected more on Leo than it did on her, and he was a bit worried his mentor would judge his casting capabilities solely off one accident. Moreno looked up when Leo cleared his throat. "So, I know that was a rough start, but I'm sure she's just a bit nervous, and—"

"Do you know how many times I've tripped on theatre steps?" Moreno asked. The question seemed rhetorical, so Leo waited. "A lot. No one tells you how many steps you'll have to climb up and down on the way to success. You're bound to trip up occasionally."

"That sounds like a metaphor." Leo tipped his head to the side.

"Does it?" Moreno waggled his eyebrows in a way that said he was trying to sound like a fortune cookie on purpose.

Leo grinned back. "I promise you'll love her. She doesn't know it yet, but she's perfect for the role."

"I'm sure I will." Moreno took a glance at his notes and then, with eyebrows raised, held the clipboard out to Leo. Confused, Leo peered down at the script, searching for anything that could give him a hint of what Moreno wanted. "I'd like you to take the reins today with rehearsal."

"The entire time?" Leo's eyes practically bugged out of his head.

"Yep. I'm going to observe." Moreno wiggled the clipboard in the air a bit, goading him.

Leo grabbed the clipboard and pulled it to his chest for safekeeping. "Thank you, sir."

"Show me what you're capable of, and we'll discuss what the rest of the rehearsals will look like." Moreno clapped Leo on the back with a firm hand as Leo warred with his face to appear calm, collected, and professional. The corners of his mouth tugged up anyway as the excitement roiled in his chest. He had directed his fair share of smaller productions, but never something this large or beside someone as prominent and respected as Moreno. This was his shot, and he'd put every morsel of his talent into it.

"We're all bandaged up!" Wes announced from the wing as he and Piper stepped into view.

The cast erupted with applause and whoops of joy. Theatre kids cheered for anything remotely exciting, and finally getting a leading lady was emphatically one of those things. Leo balanced the clipboard in the crook of his arm and clapped along with everyone. A blush dusted Piper's cheeks with an adorable shade of pink that made him want to brush his thumb over her skin and see if it felt as warm as it had earlier, even after being exposed to the chill of the room. The thought vanished just as quickly as it had arrived when he saw Piper's false smile. A glance around the room confirmed that no one else noticed the lie written on her face. Even Moreno, with his trained eyes, couldn't tell that Piper's enthusiasm was fake. She was already acting.

"Okay!" Leo clapped his hands together and shouted over the dying commotion. When the room fell silent and all eyes were on him, he set his shoulders back and lifted his chin. "Professor Moreno is giving me the opportunity to lead today's rehearsal. For our first order of business…" Leo locked eyes with Sam and cleared his throat, hoping Sam would take to his idea quickly. Leo pointed over to the audience area. "Raise your hand if you've ever tripped on those steps."

Sam's hand shot into the air, and Leo grinned as every other cast and crew member, including Moreno, raised their hand. Leo shifted to lock his gaze with Piper's as he slowly raised his clipboard into the air. The dust that seemed to constantly coat the black theatre steps was a travesty to the wrong kind of footwear, and even Leo wasn't exempt from his fair share of mishaps. A real smile tipped up the corner of Piper's full lips as she raised her own hand. Eliciting a true smile from Piper felt oddly powerful. Leo slid his eyes over to the rest of the cast.

"Great! Good to know that this musical is being put on by the most accident-prone people in the world." The cast all laughed at his joke, and Leo could feel the camaraderie in the room solidify as Emma stepped into Piper's side and squeezed her arm in excitement. "Sam, Piper, let's start from the top of Act One, Scene Eight."

"I don't get it," Piper sighed. She plopped down onto a chair they had set up as a temporary placeholder for the real set. "Sarah Brown goes from buttoned-up to punching a dancer in a bar brawl in the span of a day?"

"She's drunk." Sam shrugged from his spot beside his dancing partner, an ensemble member named Miranda.

"And extremely jealous," Leo added. They had been practicing the sequence of events that led up to an all-out brawl in a Cuban bar and had finally reached Leo's favorite part of the entire musical. Sky Masterson got whisked away by a dancer while on his date with Sarah Brown, and Sarah, after a few dulce de leches, got fired up enough to wage a dancing war. The script summed up the whole encounter in a short paragraph and said to take liberties with the brawl, and Leo was planning on doing just that. There would be breakaway props, a choreographed fight, chairs flying, and enough chaos to make the audience feel as if they were smack dab in the middle of the bar. "Haven't you ever met someone who makes you go insane enough that you want to punch someone?"

"Yes." Piper fixed Leo with a hard stare that said she was mentally replaying the moment she had dumped ice all over him at the karaoke bar.

Leo refrained from rolling his eyes. "I meant because of love, Piper. She's having this incredible night with this man where she gets to be free for once in her life. She's finally let loose a little on her good-girl behavior, and this random woman is trying to threaten that."

Piper got up from her seat with a new look of determination. "Okay."

"Okay." Leo bobbed his head. He had thought there might be more resistance on her end, but he had been right to assume that Piper was a professional. Despite their issues, they could get through this without an actual brawl. "So you and Ian," Leo gestured to Piper's dancing partner, "are going to salsa back to here." He pointed to a taped X on the ground that marked the spot. "This is when you'll be close enough to reach Miranda, and you'll take a drunken swing at her. Sam, come demonstrate with me. Piper, go stand a little behind Sam so you can see what I'm talking about."

They both complied, and Leo reached an arm out to test the distance between his fist and Sam's face. "You'll want to keep an entire arm's length between you and Miranda when you swing. And when you do so, you'll have your arm bent the whole time until the follow-through. Sam will clap a cupped fist to his chest when he reacts. Ready?"

Sam nodded, and Leo swung at the air between them. Dramatic as ever, Sam made the hollow clap noise against his chest and dropped to the ground, writhing around like an idiot as he clutched his face.

"He hit me!" Sam cried out in fake agony. Leo could hear Moreno quietly chuckling from his seat as he observed in the audience.

Piper launched forward and dropped to her knees in a panic at Sam's side. "Oh my God! What the fuck, Leo?"

"Honestly, I think that was a bit overplayed," Leo drawled. "The knap was solid, but you look like a professional soccer player trying to get a penalty kick."

Sam dropped his pretense of agony. "Damn, really? I thought it was pretty good. She fell for it, at least." He gestured to Piper, whose mouth dropped open. Her eyes shifted between Leo and Sam as Sam hopped back to his feet, dusting off his legs.

"He didn't hit you?" Piper asked.

Sam dusted himself off and flicked an invisible speck of lint off his shoulder. "Nah, I'm just really good at knapping."

"What does sleep have to do with anything?"

"K-n-a-p, princesita." Leo slapped a hand against his chest, making a quieter version of the sound that had Piper convinced Sam was injured earlier. "It means he hit himself out of sight of the audience and timed the noise with my missed punch. If I had hit him, Sam would be knocked out, not wiggling around on the floor."

"I would argue, but I've seen him actually knock someone out," Sam said.

"Hit people often?" Piper asked Leo.

A roguish smirk took over his face. He didn't know why he liked Sam informing Piper that he could win a fight, but he did. "I box," Leo explained and stepped toward her. "Can I touch you?" he asked.

"W-what?" Piper's eyes blew wide, and he held back a laugh.

"To show you how to execute the punch," Leo said quickly. "You can say no."

"Oh." She nodded and glanced down at his hand. He wondered if she, too, was stuck on the strange intimacy they had accidentally stepped into when he touched her after she fell. "Yeah, of course you can."

"Perfect. Miranda, come stand where Sam was originally." Any tension Leo was feeling dissipated as he flipped back into his directing role and watched as Miranda immediately followed his instruction. He reached down to Piper's side and held her arm out straight in front of her to measure the distance between her and Miranda. "This is just right. Now, when you swing, bend this elbow." He suspended her arm, gently bent it to the right angle, and moved it in front of her so she could see how her arm would swing during the real thing. "It'll be right... here," he stopped her arm on a swing, "when you straighten out to make it look like you connected with her jaw."

"Are you going to teach me proper boxing form?" Piper's face was so close to his when she asked the question, his hands still on her arm, that he could smell the mixture of sugar and lemons in her shampoo—because even her hair had to radiate sunshine.

He cleared his throat. "No, Sarah Brown isn't a boxer. She doesn't know what she's doing, and she's also tipsy. It's okay if you make the swing a bit sloppy as long as you're the right distance away from Miranda and you don't actually hit her."

"Okay." Piper nodded.

"Great." Leo dropped his hands away and paced behind Miranda to both put space between himself and Piper and get the right angle to watch. "Miranda, when you take the hit, time it with a knap and a reaction like Sam did, but, for the love of God, stay upright, and don't roll around on the floor like he did. Just reel back like you would if you'd been punched and stumble a bit." Miranda gave him a nod and practiced the motion once before Leo continued. "After you recover from the hit, you'll step toward Piper. Sam will come around this side," Leo pointed over Miranda's right shoulder, "and he'll block you, shielding Sarah while also squaring off with Sarah's dance partner. Ian, you'll take one hit from Sam, the same way I showed Miranda, and go for a chair."

Sam and Ian moved in sequence with Leo's directions, and they continued to block the fight scene, practicing it several times in slow motion before Leo felt comfortable enough to move on. Piper took to her role quickly. By the time they'd finished the first chunk of choreography, her motions looked more realistic and less forced. While Leo thought she could fine-tune the drunken behavior a bit, her acting had only solidified his decision to cast her.

"Sam, you'll then throw Piper over your right shoulder so the crowd can see her, and Sky and Sarah will escape stage left. And Piper," Leo turned to face her directly. "When he has you over his shoulder, I want you to squirm a little, flail your limbs around like you still want to be there and you're vaguely annoyed that he's taking you out of the fight."

"So, throw a tantrum like a petulant child?" Piper said.

"Exactly." Leo grinned and moved on to Sky's part. "Sam, Sky is panicking. He brought her here, and she's no longer safe. The only goal is to get out before something terrible happens, like the love of his life getting injured. So, when you throw her over your shoulder, put some pep in your step to jog off the stage."

"You got it, boss." Sam saluted him.

"Okay. Let's do this, from the top of the salsa dancing." Leo clapped his hands together, and everyone took their positions. He was all too aware of Moreno silently observing from the front row, but for the time being, Leo tuned him out. There was no use in overanalyzing his approach to appease Moreno. The execution of this particular scene would prove his talent and his ability to lead, and he would run it into the ground until it was perfect.

Fourteen

PIPER

Fake fighting was a workout, and more a mental one than anything else, but the one arm Piper had used to repeatedly mimic punching Miranda felt like a limp noodle. It was probably why Leo's arms looked so strong in comparison. She got a long, hard look at the way his black shirt stretched over his chest every five seconds as he pointed and shuffled all the actors around the stage.

In fact, when Piper and Sam discovered that it wasn't the easiest thing to toss someone over a shoulder, she had gotten an entire show. After several failed tosses and subsequent fits of laughter between her and Sam, Leo gave them better instructions by tossing all six feet and two inches of Sam over his shoulder like he weighed nothing. At first, Piper thought Leo was going to test it out on her, but when he stepped in her direction, he scanned her from head to foot and then sidestepped her to get to Sam. Because he was very committed to the role, Sam thrashed around on Leo's shoulder as if he were Sarah Brown herself, which only made Piper fall further into hysterics. Leo gave a short laugh of his own, letting them have their moment of fun before clapping his hands loudly to call order to the chaos.

The older man Piper now knew as Alejandro Moreno had been sitting quietly in the front row of the theatre the entire rehearsal. Originally, it had unnerved her, but she relaxed as rehearsal continued, and focused more on Leo's direction rather than waiting for any commentary from the elusive director. Even so, she kept trying to remember the name of the one movie she knew that he'd directed. It was set in the Regency era, and she distinctly remembered watching it when she was younger. At fourteen, Piper hadn't particularly loved watching a graphic sex scene while sitting beside her parents on the couch. Her dad had tried to cover her face with a pillow to block out the nudity, while her mom had laughed about his "sudden modesty," making some flirty joke that had her dad turning a deep shade of red. At the time, Piper was an embarrassed teenager, mortified that her parents had anything to do with sex. Now, she'd give anything to see her mom make her dad blush and to hear her dad call her mom 'sweetheart' or 'Pay' again. Her father would probably be just as uncomfortable as, if not more uncomfortable than, her Uncle Walker was about the idea of Piper fooling around with anyone. People always assumed she had gotten her propensity to blush from her mother along with most of her looks, but the blushing had come directly from Cole Hartrick, along with his clumsy balance.

When Leo finally called it quits on rehearsal, they had the fight scene mostly blocked out. Piper had to remember to focus on cheating out several times since she wasn't used to angling her body for an audience to see, but she hoped at some point that it would become second nature. Then again, walking was supposed to be second nature, and she had already failed miserably at that today.

"All right, and now, a few words from our sponsor," Leo said, diplomatically passing the torch to Moreno.

"Ha." Moreno shook his head with a chuckle and waved Leo off when he attempted to hand him the clipboard. "Great work today." He turned to Piper, and she swallowed in anticipation.

"And Piper, it's a pleasure to have you on board. I think Leo chose well."

"Thank you," Piper mumbled, folding her arms over her chest. Compliments always made her uncomfortable. They directed the attention where she didn't want it: onto her. That was why playing a character felt so freeing. Everything was about what Sarah Brown would do, not what Piper would. Sarah Brown could drink and not be subjected to generational alcoholism. Sarah Brown could fall in love and come out on top.

"And Diaz," Moreno turned to Leo, who stood straighter. He was the picture of calm, but Piper could sense something else underneath it all: the same fear that had made him so desperate for her to join the show in the first place. "Fantastic work today."

Leo's mouth twitched, and his shoulders relaxed a bit before he gave a short nod. "Thank you, sir."

Moreno then turned his body and projected his voice to the rest of the cast. "As some of you know, my wife, Quinn—" Some of the cast members cheered, and Moreno's face transformed into a grin. Piper looked around in confusion as Moreno continued to speak.

"His wife is Quinn German." Sam leaned over to whisper in her ear.

"You probably know her. She's wicked talented and a major A-lister," Wes chimed in from behind her.

"They met on the set of *The Promenade*," Emma added from her right. The movie name Piper couldn't remember earlier filled in the gaps of her memory.

"The one with the...?" Piper whispered, trailing off.

"Extremely hot sex scene that made me question everything I know about myself?" Emma asked. "Yep, that's the one."

"Emma," Moreno called out in an authoritative teacher voice, and Emma turned back to the front. "So glad you could all fill Piper in on how wonderful intimacy coordinators are, but if you could pay attention for two seconds, you're going to want to listen to the rest of my speech."

Emma, Sam, and Wes all adopted identical guilty facial expressions, and Emma muttered "sorry" under her breath.

"Perfect." Moreno clapped his hands together, the same way Leo had when he was pivoting a scene earlier, Piper noticed. "I'll start by saying this is top secret information, and if you leak this to the tabloids, there will be hell to pay." Moreno paused for effect, then gave a curt nod when he saw everyone bobbing their heads back at him. "Quinn and I are having another baby."

The stage erupted in cheers for what felt like the hundredth time that day, and Piper clapped with them, smiling at the group's earnest enthusiasm. They celebrated anything and everything worth celebrating. They laughed together. They collectively got annoyed when they weren't nailing something. She could see how easy it was to get sucked into the culture.

"Thank you, thank you." Moreno lifted his hands and motioned for them to calm down. "Three years ago, I took this job to teach, but I also took it to be closer to my family while my kids are still young. This will be our third child, and I have my wife's permission to tell you all that when she's pregnant, she gets very ill. She has gestational diabetes and is at extreme risk for preeclampsia since she had it with our son." The room went completely still. "On that front, we are fortunate to have the best medical professionals working with her to keep her healthy, but when it comes to our family, my wife and I agreed that I would need to be around more often to help take care of our kids and her during the pregnancy, which is why I will be taking a step back from this show."

A collective gasp rang out on the stage, and Piper had no idea why, but her instant reaction was to look at Leo, who wore a worried expression. "I will still be here, and I'll still be teaching, but I'll be here a lot less. I'm demoting myself to assistant director," Moreno said.

"Then who's going to direct?" Sam asked.

"Ah, good question, Sam." Moreno's face split into a wide smile. "Today was a test run, and I'm happy to announce that your new director is as devoted, if not more devoted to the role than I am." He turned to Leo, whose mouth gaped as he blinked up at the professor. "From here on out, Mr. Diaz will be taking up the position."

Piper knew where Moreno's speech was headed partway through and thought when he eventually got to the kicker, it would fill her with impending doom. But it didn't. It might have been partially attributed to the fact that the entire cast was shouting and jumping around in excitement, but it was also because she had been there for the last several hours and had witnessed how deserving Leo was of the job. She wasn't petty enough to say he wasn't good at directing, because he was. Leo, on the other hand, looked as though someone had hit him over the head with a frying pan.

"Congratulations, Diaz. The floor is yours." Moreno gestured for Leo to take over, and Piper watched him hike up the sleeves of his shirt to his elbows before he cleared his throat.

"This is... wow." Leo pressed his hand over his heart.

"Speech!" Sam shouted.

"Thanks, Sam." Leo sighed. "I—uh—I want to assure you all that I'm extremely grateful for this opportunity, and I won't take it or any of you for granted." He made direct eye contact with Piper, and she had the urge to hide from his piercing stare. "I may be a bit hard on you, but just know it's because I think this is important. We're all going to have our names permanently attached to a show with Alejandro Moreno." He gave Moreno a nod and continued. "I don't take it lightly that he's entrusting a piece of his reputation to us. We're going to work hard, and I'll be expecting a lot from each of you."

Piper found herself bobbing her head along with his speech, swept away by the camaraderie and energy of the room.

"In the end, we'll do this show justice."

Fifteen

LEO

Leo was going to either throw up or perform a touchdown dance. Both seemed unlikely due to his stomach of steel and his lack of desire to ever play American football or dance, but so had getting the head director position. His name was going to be printed on a program with Alejandro Moreno as a fucking director. Not even with him, but *above* him. The weight of that was terrifying. It was also something Leo could finally point to and say that all of his hard work hadn't been for nothing. It didn't matter that he hadn't gotten into film school—all those producing, filmography, and directing courses he had saved up for by painstakingly tutoring rich people's kids in high school had landed him a full-ride scholarship to Fletcher. A theatre major was a roundabout way to get where he wanted to go, but he'd had to make sacrifices, and Moreno had lobbied for him during the entire scholarship process after his first video interview. Leo had kept his grades up. He had worked his ass off, and now it was finally paying off, both figuratively and literally. The director position paid more than assistant directing, and while it wasn't a lot, it was still something.

After a brief stint in the bathroom, where Leo determined that he was in fact not going to empty the contents of his stomach, he made his way back to the stage, passing cast members along the way. He shook hands and took the congratulations with a smile. Compliments, when they were sincere, made him feel like he was doing something right. Something worthwhile. Especially when they were from his family, who were all blowing up the family group chat.

VARO 8:32 PM

Yooooooo. Get that dinero!

MAMÁ 8:32 PM

We are so proud, mijo. Abuelita dice buen trabajo.

PAPÁ 8:33 PM

Buen trabajo mijo.

MARI 8:33 PM

Leo's going to be famous!

MARCOS 8:34 PM

¡Felicidades! Harper and I are expecting to see your ugly face in the tabloids soon.

ANTONIO 8:35 PM

¡Con la novia!

ANTONIO 8:35 PM

Oh, right. Pero no tiene.

ANTONIO 8:35 PM

And Saanvi and I say congrats!

As usual, the group chat had turned into a roasting session, and Leo quickly shot back something snarky in response.

> **LEO 8:36 PM**
> I don't need a girlfriend to be wildly successful.

> **VARO 8:36 PM**
> There's that humble guy we all know and love.

> **MARI 8:36 PM**
> Varo, go look in a mirror.

> **MARCOS 8:37 PM**
> La reina del fútbol can go look in a mirror, too.

Leo let out a puff of laughter through his nose and shook his head.

"What's so funny?" Piper's voice asked.

Leo's breath caught in his lungs. She was sitting on the edge of the stage while Emma and the pianist rehearsed one of Adelaide's songs in the corner. He'd forgotten that Piper had shown up wearing his hoodie, no doubt as some sort of statement. But when everyone was getting sweaty during the brawl scene, despite the near-freezing temperature in the theatre, she'd taken it off. Now she was wearing it again, and the idea of her nipples standing at attention underneath made his mouth water.

"My family is blowing me up after the news," Leo explained. "Elliot should be here shortly, and then we can discuss the set and—"

"Here!" Just then, the set designer himself jogged out onto the stage, pushing up his glasses while simultaneously swiping his dark hair out of his face. He paused for just a moment to give a timid wave of his hand at Emma before crossing the distance over to Leo.

"Thanks for joining us," Leo said as Piper got to her feet. "Moreno had to run, so I figured I'd make the introduction." He watched in real time as Elliot's eyes drifted to Piper and widened before dropping to his feet. Leo cleared his throat and shoved down the strangely venomous feeling creeping up his chest. Elliot was probably one of the sweetest guys Leo had ever met. The guy was just as tall as Sam, but nerdy and meek in the way he carried himself. Between that and his soft-spoken voice, Elliot's personality probably lined up with Piper's perfectly.

"Hi." Piper smiled and stuck out her hand. "I'm Piper. I hear that we're going to be working together?"

"Uh—yeah." Elliot bobbed his head and wiped what Leo was sure was an incredibly clammy hand on his pants before sticking it out to shake hers. "Elliot. Nice to meet you."

Piper jumped right in. "So, I don't know what you have already, but I brought a bunch of color swatches and some notes I researched last night."

"Great!" Elliot's voice was a little too cheerful. "I have some architectural blueprint drawings, but nothing that can't be altered."

"We could work on it at my place if you're free?" Piper suggested. Leo's stomach felt like a lead brick. *My place.* Once again, everyone got her warm and inviting persona but him.

"That sounds great. Let me grab my bag and—" Elliot's sentiments were cut off by the sound of a piano in the corner and Emma fixing her stance on stage to open up her diaphragm. The sound that came out of her mouth was masterful. Emma's voice was old-timey, like at any moment a nonexistent saxophone could start playing in the background as her cool and raspy tone lingered in the air.

"Holy shit." Piper gasped at Leo's side.

"Yep," Leo agreed. "She's our secret weapon."

"Sam's voice is a killer, too, but Emma?" Elliot trailed off wistfully.

"Why am I even here?" Piper asked. It was stated as a joke, but when Leo turned to look at her, he could tell she was dead serious.

"Because I chose you," Leo said.

He couldn't tell whether the surprised look she returned was because she didn't expect to be chosen by him or because she wasn't used to anyone choosing her *at all*.

Sixteen

LEO

"We're doing the third kissing scene on Tuesday."

They were standing between two bookshelves in the campus library when Leo decided to spring the information on Piper. It was just after one of their study sessions with Emma, and Piper seemed exhausted. She always brought a peppy energy to the stage, and seeing her a little worn out made him wonder if she was losing steam from all the demands he had been making of her lately. He thought telling her they were going to do the kissing scene might rile her up, but she just glanced over her shoulder with a bored expression and put one of the marketing books they had been looking at back on the shelf. Her blasé response to the scene he was most looking forward to torturing her with made him want to poke the bear until the claws came out.

Eleven rehearsals after Piper's introduction, Leo felt like they were finally getting somewhere with the production. They'd blocked out several major scenes, and everyone was starting to lean into their roles more. So, after their last rehearsal, Leo had altered the schedule a bit to include the third kissing scene between Sarah and Sky, feeling comfortable enough with basics to dig into something a little more substantial. It was the most heated and romantic kiss in the whole musical, taking place after a duet about how neither of the characters had ever been in love before. In his opinion, it was the most pivotal moment of the play.

"Think you can pull it off?" Leo prodded.

"I don't know." Piper shrugged. "I did fine with the first one, and it was kinda fun to slap Sam across the face, even if it was fake."

"This kiss is completely different. You have a very limited amount of time to make the audience believe that Sarah and Sky are falling in love right before their eyes." Leo snapped his fingers for effect.

"I know that," Piper ground out. "I told all of you I wasn't right for the part, and you kept fucking pushing, so now we're about to find out if someone who's never been in love can convince everyone that she's in love." The words were a jackhammer to Leo's brain, and he gaped at Piper as she moved to leave.

"Wait." Leo latched onto Piper's arm with a grip firm enough to stop her, but not so much that she couldn't leave if she was determined to. "You've never been in love?"

"I don't feel like being made fun of today, okay?" Piper's eyes were pleading for him to stop, but he couldn't. Not because he wanted to make fun of her, but because he wanted to know how it was possible that she had dated so many people and never fallen for any one of them. The curiosity launched its way out of his throat before he could take it back. Even if it wasn't true love, he could see her thinking in a naive way that she'd been in love with some of the assholes she had dated in the past, so how had she never felt it? Then again, he knew how it was possible.

"No one should make fun of you for not falling in love, Piper." It came out as sincere as he could make it. He dropped his hand away from her arm when he noticed he was still holding on. "I haven't been in love, either."

"You haven't?" She seemed genuinely shocked by the statement, which gave Leo a modicum of solace that he wasn't completely unlovable, even to Piper Hartrick.

"No, but it's easy to make people believe that you're in love. It's the same way you're good at faking it when you smile."

Piper let out an indignant sigh. "There's the insult."

"I'm serious. You have a tell when you're smiling for real. Your nose crinkles at the bridge, and your eyes get all squinty, like you can barely hold them open because you're so happy." Leo cleared his throat. "And when it's not real, well, then it's not nearly as defined, and it's missing that sparkle people get in their eyes when they're truly feeling it."

Piper just stared, blinking for several agonizing seconds before she finally spoke. "So, then, how do I pretend to be in love?"

"You do what I do. You study other people. It's the same thing psychopaths with no emotional bandwidth do to blend in." Leo laughed.

"Ah, so you're finally admitting to being a psychopath?"

"I'm admitting that I know what love looks like on other people."

"And what does it look like?" Piper relaxed, her body language no longer looking like she was gunning for a quick exit.

"It's a bunch of little things." Leo considered what he could say to get his point across. "It's the way my mom comes home after a long day at work and wants to tell my dad every single thing that happened to her even though they work at the same grocery store and have for years. It's Wes snatching Sam's grandfather's watch to take it to get it fixed as a surprise just because he knew it would be important to him. It's—"

"My uncle smiling every time my aunt scream-sings to emo music in the kitchen while she cooks," Piper added.

"My brother cleaning his wife's windshield every time they go to a gas station and drawing a heart on the window with the filthy squeegee water."

"Thea kissing Yuri on the cheek when whatever awful dad

joke he told didn't land. It's..." Her face fell, and she shook her head, looking up at the ceiling for a second. Whatever she was about to say completely snapped her out of their conversation. "It's the little things."

Leo almost asked. Almost begged to know what she was about to say. Whatever it was, it had Piper looking like she was on the edge of tears. That was the kind of emotion they needed in the show. The kind that took over and consumed you the way his emotions seemed to skyrocket every time Piper was around. Usually, the emotion was anger, but lately, it was starting to feel more like desire.

Instead, Leo offered a word. "Exactly."

"So, then, I'll just study other people who are in love." Piper wouldn't meet Leo's eyes any longer, and that made him feel desperate to keep the conversation going.

"And maybe, for Sam's sake, go watch *The Promenade* so you know how to kiss," Leo teased. "I don't think cherry stems are an accurate test for that."

"I don't need lessons." Chin lifted, Piper flicked her lavender-tipped hair dramatically over one shoulder, her mood lightening and vibrant color returning to her face.

"Practicing with Elliot?" Leo quirked a brow. He had no right to even ask, but his mouth ran off without permission. After each of their rehearsals, he had watched Piper and Elliot leave together, always laughing and bouncing ideas off each other the way friends and lovers do.

"Elliot?" Piper's face screwed up in confusion, and she shook her head. "If you seriously think we have time for anything but set design when we're together, you're insane."

"Elliot's a cool guy," Leo said. And why he felt the need to push it, he had no idea.

"*You* kiss him, then. I don't have that kind of time. Maybe he could teach you a thing or two. You probably need help in that department."

Leo barked out a laugh. "No, I really don't."

"I bet you're all wet and sloppy." Piper lifted a pointed finger and waved it in a taunt in front of his mouth.

"Get your finger out of my face, princesita." He snatched her wrist and pulled it down to her side but didn't release his grip.

"I bet you're selfish," she continued.

"You know *nothing*." Leo glared furiously at her and stepped in her direction.

Piper took a step back into the bookshelf on the back wall. Never one to back down, she reached out her other hand and jabbed her pointer finger into his chest. "You probably barely draw out the tension before you're trying to get into a girl's pants." His eyes dropped to where her finger was wrinkling his black Henley before he stepped toward her again, caging her with his body against the shelves. "I think you." Poke. "Should take lessons from *me*." Poke. "Mr. Director." *Poke*.

Leo had become so pissed off and fed up with her assessment that he snatched up her wrists and pinned them against the shelf above her head. One of his hands was big enough to wrap around both her wrists, and where he didn't have a good enough grip, the shelf and the textbooks gave him leverage. His entire body was pressed into Piper. Each hot breath that mingled in the air between them had her breasts pressing into him, and his cock surged in his pants at the feeling of it. Piper didn't struggle to break free, just hit him with her searing ocean eyes, the pure hatred behind them somehow making it harder to conceal the growing problem in his pants. They didn't say anything for what felt like forever, just panted in a furious stalemate before Leo finally broke the silence.

"I can show you if you're so desperate to know for yourself, Piper." Leo's voice came out hoarse as his eyes flicked across her face, cataloging every feature to memory.

"You wouldn't dare," she seethed, but she was stubborn enough to press her chest into him another inch.

"Don't test me. If you tell me to show you, I will." He

dropped his gaze to her lips and back up to her eyes to make his point perfectly clear.

"I think you'd chicken out." Piper's hot breath danced just below his mouth, and he could feel her quickened pulse in her wrists.

"Try me," Leo urged. He was so sure she was going to say no. She had to because her lips were a fraction of an inch away from his, and he had imagined how they would taste one too many times for this staredown to end anywhere good.

"Do it." It came out as a whisper, but he heard it perfectly. *Fuck.*

"Fine." His self-control splintered. One arm still pinning her wrists above her, Leo jerked forward and met Piper's lips with his mouth, breathing her lemon cake scent in through his nose. With one hard, demanding kiss, there was no mistaking exactly where his thoughts went when it came to the curve of her ass or what he wanted to do when her nipples were pointing at him in the cold outside the karaoke bar. He couldn't pretend he wasn't attracted to her anymore. The proof that he could easily lay her down right there on the floor and ruin her if she wanted him to was in the kiss. The desire that coursed through his veins rivaled his anger.

There was no reaction from Piper for a second, and Leo was just about to pull back in horror—because what the actual fuck was he thinking?—when she moved. It wasn't slow like how she had implied she would want it earlier. She pressed into him and warred with his mouth, her tongue slipping past the seam of his lips and dragging in a rough swipe along his bottom lip.

Leo was gone. There was no return from this. And it seemed whatever invisible cord there was between them had finally snapped—no, burned—for her, too. The hand he wasn't restraining her wrists with found her waist, his fingertips digging into her with an all-consuming want. A soft noise of pleasure left Piper's throat and vibrated against his mouth before her teeth bit into the pillow of his lip. His cock hardened against his zipper, straining to press into her. It would go down in infamy as the worst decision he ever made, but his body refused to stop. Despite how reckless and stupid it was, it felt like everything was aflame and would burn him alive if he didn't get more. Everything inside him would be satiated as soon as he got *more*.

At some point, Leo relaxed his grip on her wrists. One of Piper's hands gripped the fabric of his shirt to pull him closer, and his now freed-up fingers found the back of her head, lacing into her hair and pressing into her scalp to slant harder over her lips. Nothing was enough. He licked into her mouth, and her tongue met his with fervor. The hand gripping her waist slid up her side and found her breast, cupping her through the fabric of her dress. It was exactly how he thought it would be, firm, warm, and *everything*. He could only stop devouring her lips long enough to trail wet, sucking kisses up the column of her throat. Piper bucked her hips into his groin and hitched her leg over his hip.

Leo groaned. "Me vuelves loco."

Their lips slowed.

Speaking at all was the wrong move, or the right one, depending on how Leo was looking at it. Declaring how crazy turned on he was was too much. They could have pretended before that this was inevitable, but the second the words left his hungry mouth, it brought them crashing back to reality enough to jerk apart with mutual alarm.

Piper's eyes were wide and alert as she pressed her palm over her mouth with the hand she just had fisted in his shirt. Leo took a giant step back, his mouth hanging open. Whatever the hell that was, the sobering reality of his surroundings was a hard slap to his face. Anyone could have walked in on them grinding against each other like two people who didn't claim to despise one another. Maybe someone *had* seen them. It wasn't as if hiding in a row of bookshelves were very discreet.

Unable to meet Piper's stare for longer than it took to see the sheer shock on her face, Leo backed up, tripping over his shoes. He quickly escaped to the end of the bookshelves but stopped just before he was out of sight to look back over his shoulder. Piper was a statue and looked like she would stay there forever unless he said something, so he let his self-indulgent side have the floor again for one statement. "I guess now you know."

In the time it took him to get to the exit, Leo's self-beratement ranged from a simple "chingada madre" to "What the hell is wrong with you? Pinche pendejo." Beyond all the insults he could hurl at himself, there was still a devil on his shoulder who wondered what it would feel like to have Piper naked and moaning his name if just kissing her felt that good. The small gasping sounds she had made against his mouth played on a loop in his head like his own personal *Groundhog Day* hell, a broken record that felt equally destructive and like a perfect harmony. A symphony in the orchestra pit nailing the crescendo of a song while a perfect voice on stage hit every note of the performance with ease and grace. Piper's voice.

Seventeen

PIPER

Obnoxious crunching noises echoed in Piper's living room as her brother Carter sat on her couch eating what was left of a bag of barbecue chips while smiling ridiculously at his phone. Piper was both thrilled that her brother was so sickeningly happy and annoyed by the same thing. This was the first time she had seen him in two months even though they went to the same college. Despite wanting her brother to find love, she didn't want him to disappear on her completely because of it. There was always some excuse as to why he couldn't come over to her place or travel back to Archwood with her. The only difference today was that his girlfriend had canceled on him in favor of other plans. Piper was always second fiddle when it came to Stella, but she didn't care. She would take what she could get.

"I see how it is. You came over just to eat everything in my pantry?" Piper scolded.

"I didn't eat the kale chips." Carter grinned.

"Wow, thank you so much for being so considerate."

"And I'll try to be around more! I just—"

"Yeah, yeah. I get it." She waved him off and plopped down on the couch next to him, shoving one of his broad shoulders.

"And how are *your* romantic prospects? Anyone remotely good enough for our Perfect Piper?" Carter's eyebrows rose.

Piper groaned. "God, you know I hate it when you call me that." She sidestepped his question entirely considering her only romantic entanglement of late was with Leo Diaz, of all people, in a library, where she had practically dry-humped him against a bookshelf. One more minute alone with him, and who knew what egregious mistakes she would have made? Even in the aftermath, she could not stop thinking about the kiss. The way it felt like Leo had fucked her with all her clothes on.

"That's why I do it. It's my job to annoy you." Carter cut through Piper's sexual fantasies, effectively dousing her in ice water. And then, because little brothers were disgusting, he started to lick the barbecue residue off his fingers.

"You're very good at it," Piper said.

"One of my many talents." Carter sat back and stretched out his long, muscular legs, clad in the basketball shorts he wore even during winter, and propped his feet on the coffee table, all while setting the chip bag in his lap like he was the king of the world. Piper snatched the bag up, the foil crunching under her fingertips.

"You're so gross. Get your athlete's foot off my table." She shooed his feet, and he made a dramatic show of setting them back on the floor. "And is your other talent being a human garbage disposal?"

"Ask Stella what my talents include." Carter smirked.

"Ugh!" Piper stuck out her tongue.

If there was one thing her brother was good for, it was making a sexual joke out of anything. It might be funny if she hadn't grown up with him and didn't know that he always chewed way too loudly and that his basketball shoes smelled like death incarnate. Growing up with three brothers meant Piper was accustomed to gross smells. Growing up with a younger sister meant being accustomed to loud screeching when Pearl came across said smells.

Cooper, though his shoes smelled a bit better than Carter's, had an investigative streak that was equally as annoying as Carter's pervy jokes. Cooper was the reason Piper got caught sneaking out of the house a few times during her senior year of high school. He had also drawn attention to her messy hair after an evening out with one of her asshole ex-boyfriends enough times to make her want to wring his neck. At one point, Piper was certain that Walker had begged Cooper to stop noticing things so he wouldn't have to guess what she'd been up to. It always led to a discussion with Talia about how Piper should be more careful, or at least better at hiding her sexual activity.

"So, you're really doing the whole play thing?" Carter asked, barely looking up from his phone as it vibrated in his hand with yet another text from his girlfriend.

"Yes, I'm really doing it. They practically begged me to." Remembering the way Leo had looked on his knees, pleading with her to take the role, somehow made Piper's brain jump right back to when his mouth was on hers, not just kissing her but unraveling her.

"I've never seen *Guys and Dolls*, but I assume that you're the doll in this scenario." Carter chortled.

"You're hilarious," Piper said with as much enthusiasm as Emma during their business class study sessions. "Sarah Brown. That's my role. She's a sergeant of the local mission." She looked down at her hands, knowing exactly what Carter's smug face would look like.

"Should I start calling you Saint Piper?" He laughed.

"She's not always that good! She falls in love with a prolific gambler and gets into a fistfight at one point."

"Ooh, saucy."

"You're such an ass."

"Am I going to have to watch you make out with some dude on stage?" Carter grimaced, and Piper had to laugh at how weirded out he was given the number of times she'd seen him slobber all over his girlfriend's face.

Unfortunately, the thing her brain wanted to focus on—even worse than Carter sucking face with Stella—was Leo, pinning her to the shelf in the library and kissing her senseless. They hadn't seen each other since the incident, but that was going to change at rehearsal tomorrow, when she and Sam were supposed to act out the very scene that had gotten her into this mess in the first place. Sam would be easier to kiss. Her body wouldn't take over like it had with Leo, but, either way, Leo's eyes would be drilling into her while she practiced the scene, and that made her want to crawl out of her skin.

"Sam is very gay, so you don't have to pull the protective brother act."

"If it comes down to it, I can just pretend you aren't my sister. That's the beauty of being adopted." Carter lifted his umber fingers and wiggled them for effect.

"God, I hate it when you make up stories about how we know each other," Piper grumbled.

"Oh, come on, you're no fun. I need new material." Carter flashed her a toothy grin before he dropped his gaze to his vibrating phone again.

Thea was really the only person Piper had gotten to talk to about the musical apart from the cast and the occasional conversation with Talia and Pearl, so she was excited to explain it to someone new. But again, her brother's phone seemed to be the biggest distraction of the century. "Will you put that thing away for two seconds?"

"It's Walker." Carter flipped his screen around as proof of the video call request before answering it. "Hey! I'm with Pipes." Piper squeezed in next to Carter so that Walker—and, apparently, Talia—could see them both in frame.

"Good, you're both here!" Talia chirped. "We were going to call you next, Piper."

"Are we in trouble?" Carter teased.

"We're just calling to see what's up with Thanksgiving and to figure out what time you two are coming down." Walker's mouth lagged for a second on screen before the image caught up to his words.

"Oh..." Carter didn't make eye contact with the phone, his eyes also darting away from Piper.

"Carter?" Walker asked, catching on to his hesitation.

"You're not coming home with me, are you?" Piper guessed. Clearly, Carter had Thanksgiving plans that had nothing to do with his family this year. The bitterness came out in her question, and she fixed it by offering Carter a sad excuse for a smile. Since their parents died, spending time with family felt more sacred and important to Piper than ever before. She knew Carter felt the same, but his time had to be split between the different people he loved. Stella was nice. Stella made him happy. There was no evidence to conclude that Stella was anything but perfect to Carter, but Piper's gut feeling about her wasn't a good one.

"Stella invited me to her house for Thanksgiving. It's a whole thing." Carter blanched, then quickly added, "But maybe I'll bring her home for Christmas?"

"That'd be great!" Talia smiled on screen as Piper watched Walker's face fall a little before he regained his composure.

"Yeah, totally cool." Walker bobbed his head. The next question was directed toward Piper. "What about you?"

"I'm coming!" Piper plastered her signature smile on her face to reassure him and watched Walker's mood lighten a little.

"Okay, then, I want you to know I had absolutely nothing to do with the next thing we have to tell you, and I'm actually very opposed to it now that Carter isn't coming home." The image on the screen jerked to the side as Talia shoved Walker's shoulder, mumbling something Piper couldn't quite hear. Piper furrowed her brow and looked over at her brother, who just shrugged, as unaware as she was.

"I may have volunteered you for something," Talia started carefully, clearly trying to lace her voice with innocence. "Well,

Amala and I really were just trying to do something nice for someone, and—"

"Spit it out, already. I'm on the edge of my seat!" Carter interrupted. Piper was thankful for her brother's interjection because she could already feel her stomach dropping with whatever news she was about to get hit with.

"Okay, fine," Talia grumbled. "We told Leo's mom that you had plenty of room in your car to drive him home to Archwood for Thanksgiving."

Piper's mouth dropped open, and her next words came out in a garbled, stuttering mess. "W-what? No. Leo? But I... I can't. We don't—that's not even—"

"Woah," Carter chuckled. "Take a deep breath, will you?"

"I can't be trapped in a car with Leo for that long." Piper shook her head frantically.

"Why?" Talia asked at the same time as Carter. Walker muttered something under his breath and got a scalding look from his wife in response.

Because he kissed me, and I can't stop thinking about it. "You saw how we were at that bar. We'll murder each other!" Piper said.

"But you're in his show. How is that any different?" Talia argued.

"Hold on, *his* show?" Carter turned to Piper with a devious smile. "You neglected to mention that it's Leo's show. I thought you said you were just kissing the gay guy."

"I *am* just kissing the gay guy!" Piper yelled. It came out too loud and flustered. Too much of a tell for her entire family. All eyes stalled on her for a moment before someone finally spoke.

"Leo's directing," Talia explained, the corner of her mouth pulling up as she looked over at Walker, who just ran his hand through his hair—one of his stress tells. "If you can deal with each other five days a week at rehearsal, I'm sure you can handle being in a car together for six hours."

"But I have to leave *after* rehearsal, so it's going to be late. We'll be driving in the dark." Somehow this statement was supposed to help her cause, but all it did was make her brother incredibly suspicious.

"Afraid of the dark?" Carter's tone had an undercurrent of accusation.

"I just mean it's not safe," Piper replied quickly.

"Yep!" Walker nodded on screen. "Totally agree. It's not safe at all. You should come on your own."

"Walker," Talia hissed. "If anything, driving with Leo will be safer. Having another person to keep you company at night is a good plan."

"Yeah, I don't want you driving alone," Carter agreed and tossed Piper a knowing smirk. Her brother was way too good at reading her, but even his smirk fell away a second later as he touched her shoulder. "Really, though. I don't want you to go alone. I didn't know you were going at night."

Out of anyone, Carter knew how much Piper hated driving, especially long distances. Driving at night made it that much worse. Drunk drivers were out at night more than any other time of day, and her family would always be hyperaware of that fact. Carter was much more confident in his driving than Piper was, so he usually drove when they made trips back to Archwood. She could see the guilt on her brother's face clear as day: he hadn't quite thought it through when he'd decided to go home with Stella for Thanksgiving.

"It's okay," Piper gave in, not wanting to burden him or make him feel bad for wanting to spend Thanksgiving with someone he loved. "I'll go with Leo."

"Great!" Talia grinned. "I'll let his mom know he's good to go. He wasn't planning on going home at all because his car is broken and he can't afford the gas. Lucia tried to give him the money, but he's too stubborn to take it. I figured if we worked it out so he could get home for free, then both parties would be happy."

"So... he doesn't know he's going with me yet?" Piper bit her lip. "I don't have to tell him that, right?" The thought of having to offer Leo anything at all was painful. He already thought she was a spoiled rich girl, and she didn't feel like telling him that she knew he couldn't afford a trip back home, let alone swooping in with the solution.

"Lucia will tell him herself as a surprise," Talia supplied.

"I'm sure he'll be elated," Walker added with a sarcastic scoff.

"What is your problem?" Talia chastised, turning to glare at her husband.

"Piper driving in the middle of the night with Leo Diaz. That's my problem. You know what I think about this, and you won't listen to me."

"She's an adult!" Talia argued. "And you said you liked Leo."

"He's still a twenty-something man with a high sex drive and—"

"Um, hi, I'm still here," Piper interjected with a jerky wave of her hand. Her aunt and uncle snapped their heads up to look through the camera again as if they had forgotten they were still on the phone. Carter was silently wheezing next to her, his body shaking as he covered his mouth with his palm to try to hold back his laughter.

"Sorry, Piper. Your uncle will refrain from being an overprotective asshole now," Talia stated.

"Hey!" Walker shouted.

"Nothing is going to happen with Leo. *Nothing*. I can guarantee that." Piper crossed her arms over her chest in defiance then raised one finger in warning. "Not that if I wanted to you would have any say in it. And Walker, since when do you even have an opinion on Leo at all?"

"Since I—uh, I don't know, really. Talia told me some stuff." Walker looked away from the screen, coming off extremely suspicious, but Piper was too annoyed by the conversation to dig into it further. "Anyway, we'll see you late Tuesday night, then? We'll probably both be up no matter how late it is because I'll have anxiety and Ponytail here will be reading smut." Walker tugged on the high pony on Talia's head.

"He's not wrong." Talia grinned.

"Yeah, I'll see you then," Piper agreed. The prospect of seeing her family again made her relax a little. Even if she had to endure six hours with Leo on the road, there would be a bright light at the end of the tunnel.

"Grab a bag of sunflower seeds like your dad used to eat," Walker suggested. A pang of grief zapped through Piper's chest at the mention of her father. It was accompanied by a memory of her sitting shotgun beside him in the car that was ultimately totaled in the accident that took his life. Cole was eating sunflower seeds and explaining, yet again, how they kept you alert and focused while driving.

"I will." Piper nodded.

They said their goodbyes, which ended mostly with Walker and Talia describing all of the food that Talia and Amala were going to make for Thanksgiving dinner. Piper was assured that Walker would not be doing anything remotely involved with cooking and would be strictly chopping things or cleaning up. In the five years since her uncle had been married, despite Talia's multiple attempts to teach him, he still managed to burn the majority of the things he cooked.

Once Carter hung up, he immediately rounded on Piper with a wide grin. "Okay, what the fuck is up with you and Diaz?"

"What? Nothing is up." Piper hopped up from the couch to avoid her brother, but Carter called her on it a second later.

"You liar! Spill. And I don't mean tell me all the nasty details." Carter cringed, squeezing his eyes shut as if the mere thought of her ever getting laid were the most disgusting thing ever.

"Nothing really happened," Piper said, then quickly backtracked. "I mean, we kissed—er, he kissed me. But it was just the one time, and it was a mistake."

"Why are you freaking out so much, then? Did you kiss him back?" Carter narrowed his eyes and leaned forward.

"No! I—okay, I did, but it was an accident!" Piper chopped the air with her hand. "I hate him." Carter started laughing, collapsing back into the couch like it was the most hilarious thing he'd heard all year. "I'm serious!"

"Dude," Carter wiped under his eyes, "I'm pretty sure you don't make out with people you hate."

"I didn't say we made out." Piper pointed at him. Carter just curled his lips over his teeth, trying to keep from laughing further. "Fine! It was only a little making out. Like thirty seconds. A minute, tops!" Carter completely unfurled, doubling over and clutching at his middle. "It's not fucking funny, Carter."

"Colin, Pearl, and Coop are going to love this." Carter heaved air into his lungs. "You've been complaining about this guy for *years.*"

"He's an asshole!"

"An asshole you apparently like to suck face with," Carter said. "Did you know I hated Stella before we started dating?"

"Really?" Piper's expression softened.

"No," Carter laughed. "But you should see your face."

"Oh, fuck you! You'd probably like him. You're both assholes."

"You're right, I probably should get to know my future brother-in-law."

"I hate you," Piper hissed.

"You seem to overuse the word 'hate.' Your words mean nothing now." Carter reached for the bag of chips on the coffee table, and Piper leaned forward to slap at his hand, snatching up the bag before he could grab it.

"Only brothers who are supportive of my vendettas get chips."

Carter raised his hand with his thumb bent over his palm as if he were taking an oath. "I hereby solemnly swear that I support your vendetta regardless of the fact that you like to swap spit with Diaz on the side. Happy?" He ripped the bag out of Piper's hand with a cocky smile as her face went bright red.

Choosing to say nothing at all for fear of giving away just how much her body had liked the kiss—how much she still craved the spark that had ignited between her and Leo when his lips raked over hers—she slumped into the seat next to Carter and dipped her hand into the bag of chips. With a grumpy hand motion, she shoved a large chip into her mouth and bit down hard. The chip was somehow supposed to keep her mouth occupied from thinking about Leo's tongue entwined with hers, but it accomplished nothing.

The new action movie that Carter talked Piper into watching for their movie night didn't distract her, either. There were enough shootouts and dead bodies to break anyone out of a trance, and yet she continued to fixate on Leo's mouth, the idea of driving across the state with him, and how horrible it would be tomorrow when she had to practice kissing Sam—not because it would be uncomfortable to kiss him, but because pretending like she could ever recreate a kiss of the same magnitude as Leo's was a joke. No one would believe that Sarah Brown was in love with Sky Masterson, because the best kiss of Piper's life was with someone she hated, not someone she loved. And just how fucked up did she have to be in order to want to do it again?

Eighteen

LEO

In the aftermath of Leo recklessly smashing his face into Piper's like an unhinged child against the glass in an aquarium, he had successfully avoided her at all costs. It actually wasn't that hard since she had no idea where he lived. He had hidden in the apartment for the entirety of their two-day break from rehearsal, emerging only to attend the classes Piper wasn't enrolled in. He had even avoided the library, which was a problem because he now had two days of studying to catch up on. The discomfort from the shitty chair at his desk and the thin walls separating his apartment from the noise of the other apartments had his head so scattered, he'd barely gotten anything done. Thanksgiving break was coming up, though, so he figured he could catch up then since there would be nothing else to do. It would be a good distraction from thinking about how this would be the first time he couldn't make his budget work enough to spend the holiday with his family. Between skyrocketing gas prices and the part his car needed to even make it two feet, he couldn't pull it off. His mom had tried to hide the sadness in her voice when he told her— she would never guilt-trip him about not being able to afford something—but Leo could still tell how disappointed she was. His dad was always far more practical.

"La honra y el dinero se ganan despacio y se pierden ligero, mijo." Honor and money are earned slowly and lost quickly. It was his father's favorite catchphrase. Leo wondered where his honor was in the grand scheme of things. Kissing Piper might have tipped the scale into the "lost quickly" category.

The disappearing act Leo was pulling with Piper was about to come to a close, so he would find out soon enough if his honor was gone forever. He pulled open the back door of the theatre and shuffled along the glazed concrete to the office space that had been Moreno's alone before he permitted Leo to use it. Nothing was ever organized in the office. There were papers everywhere. Scripts were stacked and shoved into every available space, with colorful tabs and sticky notes hanging off of pages covered with chaotic scribblings. Anyone else coming into the room would have assumed that its occupant was a madman, but Leo knew better. Alejandro Moreno was a genius. The mere fact that Leo got to come anywhere near a space where Moreno's thoughts were sprawled across every surface felt like a dream, let alone that he got to sit in Moreno's chair and come up with his own ideas.

Over on the desk, Leo's clipboard had a coffee stain on it, and his handwriting crammed into the margins was so illegible that he should have been a doctor. His methods were just as scattered as Moreno's, and his brain was even more scrambled with the knowledge of what scenes they were practicing later. "Adelaide's Lament" about continually sneezing due to psychosomatic symptoms would be easy enough; Emma could sing practically anything thrown at her. The bar fight scene in Havana, Cuba, had been rehearsed more than any other scene because of the choreography that went into it, so it would be more of a refresher. No problem. The scene that had him so wound up and nervous was Sky and Sarah singing "I've Never Been in Love Before," punctuated by a passionate kiss. Act I, Scene 10 was going to be hell. When he had made the schedule last week, there was no way he could have known that just a few days prior to rehearsal he would make the terrible mistake of locking lips with one of the leads. It was so wildly unprofessional and uncomfortable for him to be directing Piper on how to kiss now. He had thought about postponing the scene entirely, but if he did that, she would know why, and he would look like a coward. He had spent enough time cowering in his room, hiding from her. Time to bite the bullet.

Every muscle in Leo's body seemed to lock up as he made his way to the stage. He could hear Sam's voice warming up his vocal cords and a smattering of other voices from the cast, but his ears ignored all of it to home in on one voice alone.

"Ready to make out, hotshot?"

Leo froze behind the curtain on the side stage just out of sight when he heard Piper speak.

"It's going to be the best kiss you've ever had, sunshine," Sam crooned back teasingly.

"Ah, yes. The best kiss I've ever had being with a gay guy does make sense for how my love life typically goes." Piper sighed.

Despite never wanting to speak of the library incident again, Leo's pride still hoped that he was Piper's best kiss because, unfortunately, she was definitely his. He really wished he could stop thinking about it, but the way Piper's mouth had moved against his was nothing short of mind-fuckery. Her lips had somehow been both soft and aggressive. Before, he had really thought that the taste of a woman's mouth should only be described in Sam's romance novels as "sweet," but he was wrong. What the hell was he supposed to do with the knowledge that Piper tasted like lemon cake? He could have gone his whole life without knowing that.

"You want me to make it really wet or something instead?" Sam's voice offered.

Leo held back a chuckle and shook his head, still hiding in the wings. Piper and Sam were getting way too close for his liking. They couldn't be friends because that would mean Leo would see way more of Piper, and that was a problem because he couldn't quite keep his hands to himself. Sam had asked several times over the last few days why Leo was in such a mood, but he had managed to dodge all the questions using his Thanksgiving situation. It was probably best he got out onstage before Piper let loose their secret and he'd have to deal with Sam's continuous pestering. But that also meant facing Piper, and that thought was equally unappealing. A double-edged sword.

"Ew, no! You keep your spit to yourself, Gosling," Piper laughed.

Leo couldn't quite hold back his laugh this time as he stepped out on the stage. His best friend and his arch nemesis-slash-one-time makeout buddy both looked in his direction, and he fought the urge to swallow nervously. Technically, the first thing on the schedule was the kissing scene, but Leo couldn't even make eye contact with Piper, so he spontaneously decided that it would have to be last so he could get his bearings.

"You two practice your lines," Leo called out, speaking only to Sam and then turning to Emma, sitting in the corner. "We're starting with Adelaide's song first."

"The schedule says we're supposed to do 'I've Never Been in Love Before' first," Piper cut in before he could give further directions to Emma. He turned slowly toward Piper, meeting her eyes for the first time since their kiss.

"Figured you'd need more practice since you were so worried about the scene." His combative tendencies with her were coming right back to the surface after the short hiatus.

"I don't think I need more practice at all." Piper glared. "I think I've had too much practice, actually. *Way* too much. Some would say I'm even *over*prepared."

Leo glanced away and ground his teeth together. He knew exactly what this underlying conversation was. He paused for only a second to fume before he took his turn in the ring. "I don't think you're overprepared. I actually think that you could use a lesson or two. I get that you have a lot of hands-on experience, but that doesn't really translate to acting."

Piper's mouth fell open, and she crossed her arms over her chest. Leo was starting to really think that it was a tell for when she was self-conscious, and watching her do it after something he had said made his stomach drop. If he kept up this petty game, there was no telling whether Piper would continue to keep their kiss on the down-low. He should've been thanking her for not blurting it out in the first place instead of taking a stab at her. One look over at Moreno confirmed Leo's suspicion that he was being an utter ass. The man was giving him a stern look that a parent would give a child who was misbehaving. Leo cringed and reeled it back, finding his professionalism before responding.

"But I'm sure that's not what you meant by being prepared, and I'm sure you are capable of doing the scene," he backtracked. "I'm only suggesting that you haven't yet worked on the logistics with Sam, and Emma's scene is a solo, so it will be easier to start with her while you two go over everything."

"Right. Well, I guess we don't really want to be surprised and thrown off guard by a kissing scene, now, do we?" Piper finally responded. "Better to know exactly what we're getting into. I know I really hate it when things are just sprung on me."

Leo scoffed and decided to stop playing nice. Piper could pretend all she wanted that she hadn't been expecting the kiss, but she had blatantly told him to do it and then kissed him back. With enthusiasm. "I think you're a little more flexible than you're giving yourself credit for." He dropped his eyes to scan over her legs, specifically the one she had propped against his hip when she was grinding into him. She noticed and rolled her eyes. "I don't know," he continued. "I just have this really weird feeling that if someone were to spring something on you, you'd end up just really throwing yourself into the role."

"I guess you would know, as someone who's adept at springing things on people. On the stage." Piper's folded arms pressed up and in, accentuating her cleavage as she cocked her head.

Leo let out a breath through his nose as his fingers twitched in remembrance of the way he'd cupped her and felt her swollen breasts in the library. He opened his mouth to think of a quick comeback, but Sam cut him off.

"Why am I so confused by this entire conversation?" He looked back and forth between them with his eyes narrowed into slits. "I can't tell if you're insulting each other or complimenting each other right now."

"Complimenting," Leo said. "We're on the same page. Sometimes we do things that are unplanned, and people end up really enjoying it." He gave Piper his best lopsided smile to really piss her off. Sam's eyes continued to dart back and forth between Leo and Piper, and before he had time to figure out what was really happening under his nose, Leo turned back to Emma with a commanding confidence. "So, Adelaide's song, then."

Nineteen

PIPER

By Piper's standards, Emma's song barely needed any touch-up. She sang it flawlessly, so Piper attributed the fact that Leo had made Emma redo the song an unnecessary amount of times to his clear desire to avoid the kissing scene. The same thing happened when they moved on to the club brawl until Moreno declared that it was near-perfect. Next, Leo had her and Sam performing their duet only to cut them off just before the kiss an infuriating number of times. He practically jumped onto the stage, the ending note of the song not even complete before he'd yell, "Good. From the top!"

It was all under the guise of directing, and, sure, Leo gave them constant suggestions—Sam forgot one of his hand motions once, and Piper was sharp on one of her notes—but, for the most part, there didn't seem to be a valid reason to cut off the kiss each time. It felt deliberate. If Leo was trying to piss her off and make her nervous on purpose, it was working. During one of their practice rounds, she had fumbled over the name Obediah, the name coming out as "Obed-uh-what?" which sent Sam into an unhinged laughing fit. It took her a hot minute to get her bearings again, and when Leo again cut off the kiss and she was about to let him have it, Sam jumped in instead.

"Are we going to practice the kiss sometime today? Why do we keep restarting?"

"Just wanted to fine-tune some things," Leo mumbled.

"Okay, well, it feels like we're putting it off for some reason," Sam argued.

"Is there a reason we can't move on and finish the scene?" Moreno chimed in. Apparently, Piper wasn't the only one who noticed the delay.

"No reason other than I want to get it right." Leo flicked his eyes between Sam and Moreno with confidence, but Piper noticed his hand flex at his side.

"You want to show me how it's done?" Sam grinned and waved his hand toward Piper, who did her best to act like nothing at all would prevent her from practicing the kiss with Leo, with Sam, with a brick wall, but she could feel the heat creep up her neck anyway.

"No." Leo's voice came out calm and reserved, but his fingers quickly ran through his hair. "We'll do the kiss now since you're so eager." He turned his back to them and hopped off stage, crossing his arms and signaling for the pianist to start the song with a jerk of his hand.

The piano chords started, and Sam's deep vibrato rang out. He looked deep into Piper's eyes, and if she didn't know better, she'd almost believe that he was in love with her. Sam was good. So good that Piper would be shocked if he didn't end up an A-lister someday. Her own voice came out a bit shaky now that she knew the kiss was happening, but it solidified as she sang and blended her voice with Sam's. When they reached the end, she was clutching onto Sam's forearms the way they had blocked it out, and their voices meshed together with the final notes. Sam jerked forward and crushed his mouth to hers like he was dying to kiss her. Piper's body, on the other hand, went rigid as she attempted to press back. When they pulled away, Sam scrunched his eyes shut with a grimace.

Okay, so, that was bad, then. Her thoughts were confirmed a second later when Leo stood at the edge of the stage gawking at them.

"What the fuck was that, Piper?" Leo asked. Whatever hesitation he had exhibited earlier about the kiss was gone. "You looked like you were kissing a dead fish."

"Am I the dead fish in this scenario?" Sam raised his hand diplomatically.

"You're the dead fish," Leo confirmed, pacing over to Piper. Moreno had his hand pressed over his mouth like he was trying not to laugh at just how horrendous it was, which only made Piper wish they could go back to avoiding the scene entirely. "What happened?"

The blush Piper had mostly been able to hold back earlier sprouted across her cheeks. "I... uh, I don't know."

"You can do better than that. I know you can." Despite the fact that he was scolding her, Leo looked more amused than anything else. An ache of longing replaced the embarrassment in Piper's stomach. If he thought she could do better, then he must agree with her on some level that their kiss had felt like an oasis after nearly dying in a desolate place.

"How exactly do you know?" Sam asked, the implication heavy in his voice.

"Intuition," Leo stated. "We're going to try this again. Piper, tilt your head this time. Move like you need more, and you're desperately trying to get the right angle to achieve that."

"Okay." Piper nodded, but her nerves got the better of her when Sam stepped in front of her. It wasn't even Sam that was the problem, other than her obvious lack of attraction to him; she just couldn't handle Leo staring at her or the fact that what he had just directed her to do was exactly what she'd done when he had her pressed up against the bookshelves.

"Sam, put your hands on Piper's waist." Sam gave her a reassuring smile and followed Leo's direction. "Piper, when you kiss him, throw your arms around his neck, but make sure your right hand is low enough to not block your faces."

"You got it." Sam nodded. Piper clutched harder onto Sam's biceps and found he was surprisingly toned. Yet another thing that would get him further in the entertainment industry.

"We'll sing the last line to lead into it, and then I need you to really go for it. You're desperately in love. Piper, you're rethinking all your life choices and letting him pull you under his spell."

All Piper could do was nod. Leo's tips felt prophetic, and not in any way she wanted them to. It was like she had gotten carried away by a rip current when she had kissed him and was, for some inexplicable reason, still drowning.

The song started up, and Piper elongated the last note like they had practiced. She tossed her arms around Sam's neck as he crouched down to kiss her. She pressed harder against his lips this time and tilted her head, hoping that it looked somewhat okay. It was blatantly apparent that it did not when they broke their liplock.

"Is it me?" Sam asked, looking at her with pity. "Am I not bending down enough? Because you are stiff as a board, and I'd have more chemistry with the board."

"Ugh!" Piper covered her face with her hands. "I'm sorry. I'm really in my head."

"What do you think?" Moreno asked Leo.

"I think Sam's bending down enough to make up for the height difference, but Piper looks unnatural." Leo sighed. "I can practically see her thinking about the stage directions instead of the feeling behind it."

"Can you just... I don't know, show where I'm supposed to be putting my hands or how far I'm supposed to tip my head?" Piper groaned. "Maybe if I practice that part enough, it'll become second nature, so when I go to do it I'll relax more?"

"Here." Leo walked over to her, and Piper stiffened, her mouth propping open. "I'm not going to kiss you, so calm down." His voice was low, eyes staring directly into hers, their shared secret heavy in the air between them.

"Okay," she breathed.

"We're going to change the stage directions I gave you originally. Don't do anything I said earlier. Where would you put your hands if I didn't tell you to put them around his neck?"

"I'd..." Piper stepped forward, and she saw the muscles of Leo's body go taut. "Can I touch you?"

"Yes." His voice was shallow, like he was barely breathing, and she liked it entirely too much for her own good.

She brought her right hand up to the back of his bicep. "Probably this."

"Okay." Leo swallowed. "Can you use your other hand to do that on my—I mean Sam's—other arm?"

"Yeah, I think so." She switched hands, her left hand caressing Leo's shoulder blade instead.

"Good. That's going to be a little lower on Sam because he's a lot taller than me. So just make sure it's not on his ass." A raspy chuckle left Leo's mouth. He was still standing with both his hands at his sides, not touching her. The lack of contact made Piper feel touch-starved and desperate to egg him on. "And now we figure out what to do with your other hand."

Piper had an idea, but the second she did it, he would know where she was getting her inspiration from. She took a chance and did it anyway, reaching her right hand up and grabbing a handful of his shirt. Leo's breathing stopped entirely, the muscles in his back going hard under her palm.

"Ooh, that's good," Sam chirped from the sidelines. Piper immediately let go and stepped back, blinking back into the present, where she was still at rehearsal and not in a library with Leo's hot mouth against hers.

"Yeah, I think that's much better. It's fully visible from the audience, too, especially after the hand switch," Moreno said. "Good call, Leo."

Leo cleared his throat. "Sam will be wearing a suit jacket

during the show, so I think grabbing his lapel or his tie will work best."

"I can go grab one from storage," Moreno offered. "Keys?" Leo pulled them from his pocket and tossed them across the room into Moreno's waiting hands.

"While he's doing that, we'll practice the shirt grab." Leo backed off and swiveled his pointer finger in the air, indicating for them to run it again. "And Piper?"

"Yeah?" Her voice sounded too eager, and she hated it. Hated him for reducing her to this person waiting with bated breath ever since their kiss.

"If the problem is that you're not physically attracted to Sam, and you need that to make the kiss good, just imagine the last person you kissed," Leo said nonchalantly, as if he wasn't continuing in their unspoken mind game.

"I'll imagine the last *good* kiss I had," Piper said with a pointed look.

The playful spark behind Leo's eyes dimmed, and his frown deepened. "From the top!"

~

An hour later, Sam was being a giant baby about his chapped lips, but they had finally gotten the kiss to look sufficient. "Sufficient" was the exact incredibly underwhelming word Leo had dubbed it. Considering how hard Piper had worked and how many times she had pretended that Sam was Leo, his reaction felt a bit like a punch in the stomach.

Then there was the matter of the road trip. Piper had spent the last fifteen minutes slowly drinking water out of a plastic water bottle, trying to figure out a way to bring it up—or, at least, figure out if Leo knew about it yet. By the time she was supposed to go home, she still hadn't worked up the courage.

With Emma on her left and Leo and Sam trailing behind them out the back door of the theatre, Piper fiddled with her chipped nail polish, wondering when the other shoe was going to drop. Leo still hadn't said a word about their Thanksgiving plans. Unlike Piper's, Emma's chipped black nail polish still looked cool with a few missing chunks as she shoved her hands against the push bar to hold the door open for everyone.

"So, Professor Hornbill said he'll give me an extra credit assignment when I meet with him after Thanksgiving, and I think that will help pull my grade up," Emma said. Things were finally looking up for her, and Piper could tell, whether it was because of her instruction or Leo's, that Emma was finally getting it.

"That's great," Piper said and heard Leo murmur something under his breath behind her. She was starting to get the impression that he didn't like Hornbill because every time she or Emma brought him up, Leo got even grumpier, if that was possible. Piper would tell him to pull the stick out of his ass if she didn't secretly feel the same way.

The sound of Leo's phone ringing interrupted Piper's curiosity to know more about their shared disdain for Hornbill, and Piper froze.

In one fluid motion, Leo pulled his phone from his pocket, glanced at the caller ID, and swiped to answer it. "¿Ma, todo bien con Abuelita?"

Piper had lost most of her high school Spanish, but she could still recognize when someone was asking about the well-being of their grandma and determined that she was most likely safe from discussions of their upcoming road trip for now. That was until Leo's eyes slid over to her.

"No. No quiero—" Leo shook his head adamantly, his eyes wide with alarm, still staring at Piper. "Mamá. Ya sé, pero—" Piper shifted closer to him, and the closer she got, the more she could hear Leo's mother speaking in rapid-fire Spanish on the other line. This was clearly about the trip and not about his grandmother. "Yo también los extraño." Leo raked his fingers through his hair and down over his face before hitting Piper with a grimace and letting out a long breath through his nose. He groaned and muttered a reluctant "sí" into his phone. A happy-sounding squeal came from the other line, and a few more words were spoken between mother and son before Leo hung up and pocketed his phone. He turned to Piper with a jerk of his shoulders. "How long have you known about this?"

"My aunt told me yesterday. Trust me, I am just as thrilled as you are," Piper snapped.

"What's going on?" Emma asked.

Leo scowled and ignored her. "We're going to fucking kill each other. This is a terrible idea."

"Why exactly are you going to kill each other?" Sam's eyes flicked repeatedly between Piper and Leo, a wry smile playing across his face. "You seem friendly enough to me."

"My mom apparently can't take no for an answer and has set it up for me to hitch a ride back to Archwood with Piper for Thanksgiving," Leo ground out.

"You two, stuck in an enclosed space for a six-hour drive?" Emma chuckled.

"The sexual tension is going to be off the charts!" Sam exclaimed.

"That's called hatred, not sexual tension." Piper shoved Sam's shoulder.

"Sure, and I'm the King of England," Sam deadpanned.

"Would you rather be the king of the dead?" Leo muttered. "Because I can make that happen."

"Mark my words." Sam raised one finger and switched to a posh British accent. "Something is going to happen on this trip."

Part Two
You're my weakness

Twenty

PIPER

The silence in the car was deafening. Besides the brief argument they'd had when trying to play Tetris in the back of Piper's Mini Cooper with her five bags and Leo's singular duffel, he had barely spoken a word to her in over an hour, only breaking his silence to ask her a question about the musical or to reply with one-word answers to her questions. The tension felt so thick she was practically wading through mud just to maintain any conversation at all.

Leo seemed to have plenty of things to do during the drive, the most recent of which was poring over the *Guys and Dolls* script for what must have been the thousandth time given the unorganized tangle of notes on every square inch of margin space. Piper, on the other hand, could do nothing but stare forward at the miles of freeway stretched before them. When she'd finally had enough of the feeling of his eyes occasionally darting to her and away again, she reached for her bag of snacks in the console just for something to do.

"Sunflower seeds?" Leo asked, finally breaking the silence. "That's fitting." He had no way of knowing that sunflower seeds were a sore subject, so Piper attempted to keep her voice from dipping into anger or sorrow when she responded.

"Yeah, um, my dad used to always eat them while he was driving to stay awake." She fought the urge to mutter the obligatory morbid afterthought: *a lot of good that did him*. She had never seen it in the aftermath, but she imagined when the drunk driver had plowed into her parents' car, the impact had scattered sunflower seeds all over the dash. "Anyway, it's a trucker thing, but my brother, Colin—"

"The basketball star?"

"No, that's Carter. Colin is my older brother, and he's definitely not into sports."

"Too many C names."

"Yep. Colin, Carter, and Cooper because my dad's name is Cole. And Pearl and I are Ps because my mom's name is Paisley." It had been a long time since she'd explained the significance of their names, and she realized too late that she had mentioned her parents in the present tense, as if they were who she was going home to see for Thanksgiving. The thought made her stomach sour. "Anyway, Colin says that the nutrients in sunflower seeds help keep you awake better than an energy drink, and the process of opening the seed with your teeth and working to remove the seed with your tongue gives you something to work on that keeps you alert."

The blandness of the information helped reign in her emotions. Maybe that was why Colin spoke mostly in statistics. She would swear to anyone who would listen that growing up with Colin had taught her more than school did. She never could understand a damn thing he was talking about when it came to his job, though. Cancer research was reserved for people way smarter than she was, or, rather, tall blonds with wire-rimmed glasses and a propensity to grade their sexual partners with a literal chart they'd created in high school with their tutee-turned-fuck buddy. Carter had swiped a copy of one of the charts back in the day, and it was unsurprisingly thorough. Piper would forever wish she could burn the memory of it from her brain. No one needed to know that their brother enjoyed it when a woman used her tongue to... *fucking gross.*

What little conversation had passed between them died out when Leo nodded and went about his business, pulling out a textbook from the backpack at his feet. Piper always became violently ill when reading in the car, so it made sense to her somehow that Leo didn't seem to get carsick. Every fiber of their beings was different, which was further affirmed when she chose a radio station and could see Leo side-eyeing her music choices. Luckily, he stayed silent, or she was going to have to fight him to the death on Taylor Swift.

The music playing through the speakers wasn't enough to quell Piper's nerves as they drove on, and having Leo in such close proximity to her made every cell in her body alert, sunflower seeds or not. The fact that he had said nothing about their kiss felt like a declaration that he had either hated every second of it or thought it had been so boring that it wasn't even worth mentioning. Whatever electric chemistry she had thought they had—and gotten herself off to several times since—must have been fabricated in her head.

So, Piper did what she did best: she overthought. Each replay of the kiss in her head gave her no clues as to how she'd gotten it so wrong. All it did was make her core ache for release again until the question burst out of her like a popped balloon. "It was bad, right?" she blurted, cringing when Leo flinched beside her.

"The... sunflower seeds?" Leo knit his eyebrows.

"When you—we, you know, in the library?" Piper stammered.

"What the hell are you talking about, *princesita?*"

Piper was starting to genuinely think that her wires had gotten crossed. Had she dreamt up the whole thing? The press of his lips? The feeling of his tongue battling hers? No, she wasn't delusional enough to make that up. She set her shoulders back and hit Leo with a sidelong glance that said she wasn't playing games.

"You kissed me," she stated.

"I'm aware," Leo bit off. "I was there." He had the audacity to look irritated, which riled her up even more.

"Well, why the fuck did you do it?"

Leo straightened his back and hit her with narrowed eyes. "Why did you kiss me back?"

"I didn't—" She cut herself off when she saw Leo's eyebrows rise in disbelief in her periphery. "I don't know why I did, but I'm the one asking the questions here."

"You blatantly asked me to kiss you."

"Okay, well, you brought it up first."

"Mira, your guess is as good as mine. Maybe I just wanted to see if the cherry stem thing was true. Maybe you were annoying me, so I wanted to shut you up." He shrugged. "It won't happen again."

The last piece of Leo's speech came out in a disgruntled huff, and for some reason, Piper's stupid heart dropped into her stomach. She shouldn't want to do it again. She should wholeheartedly agree with him that it was a massive mistake, but her body said otherwise. He was minimizing the best kiss of her entire life, and her stomach sank at the thought of not being good enough yet again. It was her destiny to finally enjoy a kiss only to realize that she was alone in her enjoyment.

"Right." Piper nodded and looked back out the window, finding a tree in the distance to focus on. "Yep."

Leo massaged his temples earnestly before letting out an exasperated sigh and rifling through his bag for something. Piper kept her eyes on the road, but curiosity had her sneaking looks. When he found what he was looking for, he turned the small jar over in his hands a few times before ultimately holding it up for her to see.

"This was meant as a truce." A jar of maraschino cherries stared back at her. "It's also a statement of sorts."

"You think I need to practice tying knots in cherry stems because I'm a bad kisser," Piper guessed.

Leo groaned. "You're not making this easy on me." He fisted the cherries tighter in his palm and shook the jar a little. "I thought it was pretty fucking obvious that I liked the kiss, Piper. I think you're infuriating. I think you're fake. And—"

"Gee, thanks."

"I wasn't finished. Don't interrupt me," Leo warned before continuing. "I must have temporarily lost my sanity when I kissed you. But it was a fucking good kiss, Piper. I went home and got off immediately. That's why I bought these. You don't need practice at all. You were right about the cherry stems. I still despise you, and you still piss me off. But you're a good kisser."

There was no way to prevent the blood from creeping into her cheeks, so Piper stopped trying to hold her embarrassment. The way Leo blatantly talked about sex always made the heat surge between her legs, but knowing he had thought about her when getting himself off made the heat fester into a throbbing, unsatisfied ache. She fought the urge to ask more questions. Fought to keep the image at bay of Leo lying on a bed and imagining her as he stroked himself. If she had enough guts, she would have admitted to using her wand vibrator when she got home, too, but she wasn't that confident.

"All right." Piper let out a slow breath, thankful that she had to focus on driving so she didn't have to look at him. "Then... I guess I should say the same." She'd let him decide which pieces she was admitting to. "You're an asshole, you walk all over everyone to get what you want, and you perpetually have a storm cloud over your head. But you're a good kisser."

"Great. Are we done rehashing this now?" The words were as grumpy as ever, but one glance in his direction before her eyes locked on the road again confirmed the slight smirk tugging at the corner of his mouth. He probably couldn't help but feel a little self-righteous. She was feeling high on the praise herself, which was odd considering compliments usually made her feel uncomfortable. It was easier to accept her kissing abilities when she knew that Leo hated her. The fact that he had said it at all meant it had to be true. Even if the compliment had followed a bunch of insults to soften the blow to his ego, he had still said it.

"You didn't tell Sam, right?" The question sprang to the forefront of her mind in a panic. If Sam knew, it was only a matter of time until Thea found out and got livid that Piper hadn't told her.

Leo let out a bark of laughter and shook his head. "Fuck no. As much as I love the guy, he'd be absolutely relentless about it." She watched him stiffen next to her, his arm shooting out to touch her shoulder, equally panicked. "Did you tell Thea?"

"No." Piper shook her head. Leo relaxed back into the passenger seat, leaving her arm without the warmth of his palm. "I don't plan to, either, for the same reason you aren't telling Sam."

"Okay, we're on the same page for once. We never speak of this again."

"Fine by me." Piper removed one hand from her steering wheel and held it out, palm up. "Cherry me."

Twenty-One

LEO

Two and a half hours passed without another hitch and without Leo prattling on again about his masturbation sessions. Whatever had possessed him to tell Piper that little tidbit was firmly wrangled back into his mind and his pants. Since then, they had devoured an obscene amount of cherries and managed to not kill each other. He was counting it as a win.

Knotted cherry stems and sunflower seed shells filled a paper cup in one of the cup holders. It reminded Leo of his brother Marcos, who'd chewed tobacco for a hot minute in high school before he had gotten caught by their mother. Marcos had received a long lecture about hygiene and tooth decay while Leo and his other two older brothers snickered at their brother from the side. It was how all four of them had ended up scrubbing the bathrooms in Lydia's Grocery from floor to ceiling to "learn discipline." Really, all they had learned was that Antonio, the eldest of them, thought that the manager of the store at the time was hot. They gave him endless shit for it, especially when they found out that Amala Winston was over ten years his senior and also married. Leo's brother had always been into older women, so nobody in the family was surprised when Antonio married a sweet-as-pie receptionist at a car dealership who was three years his senior. Antonio had managed to knock Saanvi up less than two months after they got married. It was one of the many reasons Leo agreed to carpool with Piper in the first place. He had only gotten to see his baby niece three times since she was born, and it felt wrong. Then again, most of the things he missed out on felt wrong. Antonio and Marcos were both living the married family life. Alvaro, the wild child among all his siblings, was living out of a converted van like a Portland hipster. Mariana was at a state school on a soccer scholarship. She was only about two hours from Fletcher University, but Leo still didn't have the resources to see her as much as he wanted to.

It was only going to get worse when Leo moved to LA for film school. He had known that going in. His career choice, his passion, would lead him away from his family for a while, and it was going to be painful. Being away at college was like a four-year practice course on how to survive without the constant bickering of his siblings or his abuelita's cooking. Being Lucia and Mateo Diaz's son meant that you fought for what you wanted, but, in the end, family always came first. It felt like a betrayal to be so far away and detached from the commotion of his family for so long.

"What are you thinking about?" Piper interrupted Leo's inner monologue and then shook her head at herself. "Never mind. It's none of my business."

"It's not a big deal," Leo assured her. "I was just thinking about my family. I haven't seen them in a while."

"Hence why you were guilt-tripped into driving down with me."

"At least we're kind of getting along. It hasn't been that bad, right?"

As if to prove Leo wrong, the car lurched forward with a pop of sound, catapulting him toward the windshield. The seatbelt caught and held him back as another loud *thwack* slapped the undercarriage of the Mini Cooper, vibrating under his seat. His spine went ramrod straight as everything unnaturally tilted to one side—his side. Unbridled fear snapped him into action as he leaned toward Piper, who was white-knuckling the steering wheel.

Then they spun.

"Chingado," Leo cursed, clutching onto the side of Piper's seat. If he didn't lean harder, they were going to flip. Someone was screaming. He was vaguely aware that it was Piper, but the world outside was so disorienting and topsy-turvy that her screams felt like thoughts or a dream rather than reality.

The whole thing couldn't have lasted more than thirty seconds, but everything had moved in slow motion, almost as if Leo were a bystander to it all. A bystander who had no idea what the hell was going on until the car came to a stop on the shoulder of the freeway, mere inches from a guardrail. It was the middle of the night, so the majority of vehicles on the road were truckers, and they hadn't seen any for the last few minutes.

"A tire must have popped," Leo murmured, more to himself than to Piper, as if working out the logistics of that or saying it out loud would help him reconcile what had just happened. He was shocked that Piper had no response at all, though. His ears were still ringing from her blood-curdling screams. A quick examination revealed why she had said nothing.

Piper's hands were still latched onto the steering wheel. Her face was sheet white as silent tears trailed down her face, and her entire body shook. Leo had snapped out of the disorienting incident the second the car had stopped, but Piper looked like she was still there, stuck in the in-between, wondering if she was going to die today.

With a stiff-fingered jab, Leo unbuckled himself and leaned as far over the console as he could get, latching his hands around both her wrists and pulling them away from the wheel and to his chest.

"Hey," he whispered. "It's okay. We stopped."

"M-my..." Piper stammered. Leo had never heard her voice so

shaky before, so frightened. Her hands were ice cold, so he folded his hands over hers to warm them up.

A new fear ripped through him. "Are you hurt?"

Piper's head shook repeatedly. Over and over and over again as he searched her body for injury. "P-parents," she managed to get out.

"Parents?" Leo repeated. A second later, he realized just how bad it was. Eyes widening, he shook his own head. "No pasa nada. It's okay. It's going to be okay." He repeated it over and over again and took Piper's head in his hands, staring into her eyes, which were still brimming with new tears. This meant so much more to her than just a blown tire. Her breathing was erratic, so he leveled his own as best he could. "Breathe, princesa. In and out with me, okay?" Piper managed to nod once before he led her in several deep inhales and exhales.

Color returned to her face after five deep breaths, and the pulse point under his hand slowed by ten. Piper sniffed and let her eyes drift shut as Leo finally let her go and leaned back into the passenger seat.

"I'm sorry," Piper murmured when her eyes finally fluttered open.

Leo jerked to face her in his seat. "What the hell do you have to be sorry for?"

A morbid laugh left Piper's lips. "I freaked out."

"Do you often apologize for your feelings?" he asked. She just stared back at him, confusion cinching her eyebrows together. "The tire blew out. It's the middle of the goddamn night. You're with me, of all people. And you have a history with bad car accidents. That was terrifying, Piper. Don't apologize to me for being scared. That's ridiculous. You're allowed to feel things. You're not a robot."

"I could have handled it better," Piper argued.

"You didn't need to handle it better. I'm not judging you. The only time I feel like you're a genuine human is when you're bitching at me about something, so seeing you just feel was…" Leo swallowed, unsure of the right adjective. Enlightening? Scary? "Well, it felt like you were being real for once."

"So what?" Piper snapped. "You'll start enjoying my company if I have panic attacks more often?"

"That's not at all what I meant." Leo groaned. "Why are you always twisting everything I say? It's like you want me to be a bad guy."

"It's not hard to jump from one thought to another when you say I feel 'real' when I'm having a mental breakdown." Piper aggressively unbuckled her seatbelt and flung her door open. Leo ripped at the passenger-side handle and stepped out into the night to meet her eyes over the hood of the car. "I'm not a fucking science experiment for you to study. I'm not required to be vulnerable with you or with anyone, for that matter. I don't owe you my trauma. I'm not going to share my deep-seated feelings about my parents' car accident just because you think I'm a little more real when I'm miserable."

"I didn't ask you to!" Leo shouted back. "I'm just saying it's okay to be miserable sometimes. The world isn't all sunshine and roses."

"Your world *is*!" Piper's voice escalated even louder. "You're directing your own musical. You're going to get into film school. You'll do everything you want to do. You know what my dream was, Leo?" When he just stared back, she answered for him. "To design rooms right alongside my mom. To go over the business finances with my dad. Your parents are alive. They'll get to see you grow up. They'll get to watch you get married. Have kids. Mine are six feet underground, so I don't want to hear your self-righteous declarations about what I'm allowed to feel. If I want to put on a smile or fake it till I make it, that's what I'll do. That's what I have to do to survive. To stop thinking about everything I've lost. So, yes," Piper threw her hands in the air, and Leo flinched despite being nowhere near her flailing limbs, "I apologize for my feelings. It's easier to shove them down, and if I was going to share them with someone, it wouldn't be the person who's made it abundantly clear that even being near me is an inconvenience. You don't like this version of me? I can guarantee that you wouldn't like the messy one, either. No one does, and you're not special."

Leo rounded the car and folded his arms over his chest. "You don't get to diminish things I've struggled with because you've struggled, too. My life isn't all sunshine and rainbows. It has been ten times harder for me than it would be for someone in your position to get where I'm at. I fought tooth and nail to be who I am. I worked my ass off. So, yes, it fucking sucks that your parents aren't here, Piper. And yes, I'd take all of my struggles with money and status over being without my parents any day, but that doesn't mean that you get to tell me that my life is easy. The likelihood I'll end up with only a small portion of my dream is the reality that I live in. I do not apologize for who I am, and I don't hide from it. If people want you to cover yourself up with a smile just so they can feel better about themselves, then they aren't worth your time. Life isn't easy. If it was, we wouldn't be shouting at each other on the side of the road at two a.m."

"If I ditched everyone who thought my emotions were a burden, I'd have no one." Piper's voice cracked, and she looked off in the distance. Whether it was to search for cars or just to break eye contact with him, he didn't know.

Leo's heartstrings pulled taut. Piper was even more jaded than he had originally thought. "I don't believe that. I think that's what you tell yourself to make it hurt less when you don't want to feel."

"Please, feel free to grade my participation in life." Piper ground her teeth. "Would you like to grade my outfit, too?" She spun around with an exaggerated twirl. She was wearing a Johns Hopkins University hoodie and tight biker shorts that had caught his attention more than once on the drive over. "This okay for you? The sweater was a gift from my brother. Would you rather I dress in all black and line my eyes with thick eyeliner? You want me to play the part of the sad little broken girl?"

"If that's what you want to do, then yes." He didn't mention that if she did change her outfits to be more punk, he'd miss the sundresses. He'd miss the way she looked now: comfortable.

"What I want is none of your business."

"You're right. It isn't. Stop searching for validation in other people. That's my entire fucking point." Leo let out a long sigh as a truck driver passed, the first they'd seen in a while. The truck didn't slow down, so he gently shoved Piper a little farther away from the road. "We are never going to agree on this. I take what I want. I refuse to apologize for being... what was it that you called me earlier? A perpetual storm cloud? I will never soften myself just to appease people. I'd rather piss people off and learn their true colors. I'd rather my happiness mean something when it's real."

"My happiness, even when it's forced, means something. It means I'm kind. It means I'm empathetic. I choose to smile because the alternative is being cold and bitter like—" Piper closed her mouth, cutting herself off.

"Like me," Leo finished her sentence with a scoff. Piper just stared back at him, and the fact that she wasn't denying it made him even more annoyed. Being real didn't mean he was a stick in the mud. "You don't know me very well, then. Happiness doesn't have to look one way."

"Neither does grief."

A dry swallow did nothing to alleviate the tightness overtaking Leo's throat and chest. The sickening feeling that wrenched at his stomach told him that she was right. He had never disagreed with someone so vehemently on so many levels, and yet, maybe everything wasn't black and white. Faking joy wasn't necessarily wrong. Shoving your personality down people's throats wasn't necessarily right. Everything was gray, just like the storm cloud that apparently followed him around.

"Okay." Leo gave a slow nod of his head. "Nothing is cut and dry. There isn't one way to do anything. I would never do what you do. You would never do what I do." When Piper nodded back, seeming to come to the same conclusion, Leo took it as an opportunity to move on. "Let's call a tow truck. I can maybe get my dad or one of my brothers to come out to get us."

"I have to stay with my car here." Piper looked around. "Wherever the hell that is. I'll just get a hotel." She drew her phone from her pocket, and the screen lit up, illuminating her tear-stained cheeks.

"By yourself?" Leo blinked.

"Yes, well," Piper shrugged, "I can't very well leave my car here, even though I know my uncle or Colin would come to pick me up."

"Can't you have one of them come down to stay with you in the meantime?" He was sure he was practically begging her with his eyes, but they were in the middle of bumfuck nowhere. It felt like the only lodging she would find would resemble the Bates Motel. Hell, they were parked right next to a wooded area where he was sure the Blair Witch lived. Piper wasn't as naive as he originally had her pegged, but leaving her alone to fend for herself when they had gone on this road trip together felt wrong.

"I don't want to bug them. It's really late. I'll just stay the night and leave in the morning when my car is fixed." Her statement made his jaw tick. It would be so easy to offer to stay if he could afford to. The wheels turned in his head as he tried to figure out a way his bank account could magically acquire more zeros. The only way he could cut it was if he made a call to borrow the funds.

"I'll stay. I don't know if you noticed, but it feels like we're in the Twilight Zone." Leo gestured to their surroundings. Everything was washed in a dark, creepy hue—a filter he'd use if he ever directed a horror film. "I don't think it's safe for you to be here on your own."

"If you want to stay, I won't stop you," Piper said. It looked like she was trying to put on a brave face, and given that she had already confirmed that she often put up a front, he ignored the stubborn tilt of her chin. He couldn't leave her stranded.

"I want to. I don't want to burden my family to come to get

me, either." It was a lie, considering it would be much more of a burden to borrow money from someone in his family than to ask Antonio to come and get him, but what she didn't know wouldn't hurt her. Leo pulled out his phone and nervously ran his fingers through his hair, mulling over his options as he started to pace. The endless questions started up. Who was the most financially stable person in his family? Who would even be awake at this hour to answer him in time? Who would be the least disappointed in him that he had to borrow money? Who would be the easiest to pay back? His parents came to mind first because his dad was a night owl, and if he knew why Leo needed to stay, to make sure Piper wasn't alone, he wouldn't hesitate.

"What are you doing?" Piper asked.

Leo stopped kicking the gravel around as he silently panicked about having to call his dad for money—one of the many things he promised himself he'd never do when he went out on his own. "I—uh, I'm calculating my finances. I pretty much always have a running tally in my head."

"You're trying to figure out how to afford a hotel room?" she guessed correctly.

"Yeah." Leo nodded. "I think I'm gonna have to call someone. There's a reason I wasn't going to come down for Thanksgiving. My rent is due soon, and... shit, I don't know if—"

"Leo, stop." Piper cut him off. "You don't have to do that. I can pay for us both."

"I can't let you do that. That's so much money." He knew logically that in the grand scheme of things, a hotel room probably wasn't going to put a dent in her pockets, but he couldn't stomach the idea of feeling like he owed her something.

"Then just stay with me."

Leo blinked and looked at her. "With you? In your hotel room?"

"Yes. We can get a room with a pull-out couch or something. It usually doesn't cost more. Does that work for your moral compass?" The glow of Piper's phone illuminated her face, making her look like a supervillain as she tapped on the screen. She might as well have been one with the way the idea of sharing a hotel room with her was making all sorts of indecent thoughts swirl around in his head.

"That's—" He paused, trying to think of any other reason he could decline other than the glaringly obvious one: sleeping in the same room as the girl who starred in way too many of his carnal dreams was a terrible idea. And yet, he couldn't very well bring that up without sounding sex-crazed and presumptuous. "Yeah, I guess that will work."

Twenty-Two

LEO

The key tag smacked against the wooden door when Piper jammed the key into the lock. The loud noise, coupled with the jiggling as she practically wrestled with the doorknob, put Leo on high alert. His shoulders were hiked up around his ears as he anxiously waited for what was bound to be the longest night of his life. When she finally got the door open, his shoulders fell, and he stood speechless, staring into the room. Right beside the bed was the supposed pull-out couch that looked like his worst nightmare. The corners of the beige plaid fabric were peeled back, revealing the yellow foam underneath. He could almost feel the springs prodding against his back already. The bed beside it could only be described as dusty, with its brown, floral-printed covers and ornate wooden bedpost that looked about a hundred years old.

"Ew. You are not sleeping on that," Piper declared, pointing at the couch.

"I've slept on worse." Leo shrugged.

"Just let me buy you a room."

He gave her a cool and exacting shake of his head. "No."

"Fine." Piper looked around the room with a grimace before saying, "I'm gonna change the sheets on the bed."

"They gave you spare sheets?" Leo asked. He had watched her entire encounter with the leering concierge, and he didn't see extra sheets change hands. He did, however, get the moral confirmation he needed that staying in Piper's room was the right choice, given the concierge had stared at her chest for the entirety of the interaction.

"I have a brand-new set of sheets in my bag. My sister is trying to make her room look more 'adult,' so I got her some that I thought would complement her romantic spirit but are still mature. Point being that I have sheets, and I'll just wash them before I give them to Pearl. Help me make the bed?"

"Sure."

Everything felt like it was moving in slow motion, the car spinning out of control all over again. Piper unfolded the mauve sheets and held them out to Leo. His fingers accidentally skimmed over the back of her hand. They maneuvered the fitted sheet over the mattress, then lifted the flat sheet in unison so it parachuted above their heads, and he could see her underneath it like one of those romantic movie scenes where they put the camera under the fabric to catch the way it folded in around a couple.

Leo's body felt hot all over. It was brisk out, and they hadn't turned on the heater yet, so there should be no reason for him to feel that way, and yet a fire was stoking in his veins.

"The shower is pretty nice, actually," Piper noted after Leo flicked the light on in the bathroom to inspect it. The tile and grout looked fairly new, and the glass panes encasing the shower were more modern than the rest of the hotel room. An image of Piper naked in the shower with water slicking down her body unhelpfully popped into his head. The rest of the night was going to be torture, and he'd no doubt have to hide a raging hard-on in the morning. "It's like they renovated this bathroom but forgot about the pull-out couch and the wallpaper in the main room," she continued.

"Not a fan of merpeople and lumberjacks?" Leo chuckled.

"We aren't near the ocean, and even if we were, that wallpaper would be a travesty. The lumberjack aesthetic is a fine line between tacky and homey cabin-in-the-woods. That couch looks like it belongs on a street corner with a 'free' sign."

"You're the expert," he said. "Your sheets are probably the nicest thing in that room." When they had been remaking Piper's bed, he couldn't help but run his hands along the silky, soft fabric. Someday, he'd have enough money for high thread count bedding, but for now, the cheap sheets back in his apartment would have to do.

"I'm not an expert yet." The way she so easily brushed off the compliment annoyed him. He didn't pass out compliments unless they were earned.

"Elliot has been singing your praises. He says your set ideas have all been genius."

"Really?" Piper perked up, and Leo couldn't help but feel elated that he had been able to give her a sliver of real happiness after such a long day.

His pride fell away in a flash when he realized that it was technically Elliot who had made Piper smile, not him. It felt worse than getting punched in the jaw in a boxing match with one of his brothers and made him want to escape the claustrophobia of her presence. There was no room to breathe when he could feel the sexual tension radiating in the space between them.

"I'm gonna go check out the hot tub we saw when we pulled in. It's been a long night, and my back is going to hurt when I sleep on that couch," Leo announced and quickly turned on his heel for the door.

"But it's three in the morning. It's closed," Piper called after him.

"So?" He didn't give two shits if the pool area was closed. He needed to relax, and he needed to do it far away from Piper Hartrick.

"How are you going to get in?"

"You mean how am I possibly going to get over the really tiny fence? I was thinking I might go all out and ninja-roll over the top of it."

Piper gasped. "You can't just jump the fence!"

"Why not?"

"It's against the rules."

Leo sighed, mildly amused that the good girl inside her couldn't even break a rule as small as this one. "Let's play a game. What's the worst that could possibly happen?"

"You get arrested for trespassing." Piper was quick with her response. She probably thought of worst-case scenarios all the time, an unfortunate byproduct of losing loved ones so suddenly.

"That seems unlikely, princesita. Who's going to call the cops? The concierge who'd rather just watch porn at his desk?"

"Is that what he was doing when we walked in?" Piper balked.

"Yep." Leo nodded. "This hotel is surprisingly nice considering the staff they employ. You didn't hear the moaning coming from his phone?"

"I just... hoped it was a movie."

"It is technically a film of sorts. Not the field that I'd like to go into, though." He'd meant the joke to fend off any sex-related thoughts, but it had the opposite effect. His brain was scarily fast with how it jumped to the idea of filming Piper naked. It honestly sounded like the most pleasant career ever.

"You're just going to use the hot tub anyway?" Piper squeaked.

"Yep."

Piper snatched a pair of flip-flops out of her bag and walked toward the door. "Okay, fine. I'm coming." Now Leo was the one staring. She wasn't supposed to join. He had been banking on her not joining. She opened the door and looked back at him with raised brows. "You coming?"

Puta madre.

Twenty-Three

LEO

"This is ridiculous. Just hop over."

Leo shook his head as he watched Piper take a running start at the fence and stop, yet again, right before she should have easily lifted herself over it. If she didn't commit soon, he would have to toss her over himself before he lost his damn mind.

"I can do this," Piper psyched herself up.

"It's four feet off the ground. I'm pretty sure a toddler could do it." He gestured for her to get a move on. The street lamp right outside the pool area provided just enough light to see Piper's golden hair and concentrated features. "You look like you just escaped your tower and can't decide if you're a bad girl for disobeying Mother Gothel. Hurry up, Rapunzel, I'm getting bored."

She scoffed and rolled her eyes. "Does that make you Flynn Rider?"

"Fuck yes, it does," Leo retorted. Flynn Rider was the best Disney prince, and he challenged anyone to disagree with him. Flynn's character was a calculated one from directors who had encouraged a panel of thirty women on staff to tell them what physique and characteristics made a man attractive. While Leo didn't have the desire to become an animator and couldn't draw for shit like Emma could, he admired the tenacity and dedication of the job.

"I never pictured you as a Disney buff, but it makes sense that you like the morally gray prince. I assume Aladdin is your second favorite because he lied for half the movie?" Piper bounced on the balls of her feet and backed up to get a running start again. Leo huffed out a breath, both annoyed that she was correct in her assumption and that she still wasn't taking his suggestion to lift herself up on the fence instead of sprinting toward it with all the grace of a newborn deer. The only time she took his suggestions was on stage even though he'd wager he was right ninety-nine percent of the time they sparred.

"Don't talk shit about Aladdin unless you're willing to fight to the death," Leo warned. "And groundbreaking technology in the entertainment field has always interested me. Rapunzel's hair was seventy feet long in *Tangled*, and it took software engineers six years to tweak the 3D animation program enough to make it move like real hair." Piper cocked her head with curiosity. He shrugged. "Sam gets pissed off that I pause movies to explain pertinent information while we watch. So, basically, never watch *The Polar Express* with me unless you want a five-minute lecture on the first feature-length film made entirely from motion capture tech."

"So, what you're saying is that if software engineers can do that, I can jump over this fence and break the rules?" Piper said hopefully.

"I was just sharing movie facts, but, sure, whatever works for you. I'm about to get in the hot tub without you," Leo taunted. The threat of FOMO always worked.

"Fine." Piper ran at the fence with an adorable battle cry of "I can do this!" Her hands met the top metal rung, and she jumped to fling herself forward. Leo had positioned himself right on the other side, assuming something would go wrong, when one of her flip-flops caught in a column and she plummeted toward the concrete. He swooped in and clutched under her arms, propping her against his torso as he wordlessly untangled her shoe from the metal post. When her feet found the ground, their bodies were only inches apart. Her hands clutched his forearms, and her nails dug into his flesh. The idea of the same nails raking down his back popped into his head.

Leo shook off the thought. "I'm starting to think it was a bad idea to bring you." *Terrible idea.* He dropped her arms and took a step back when he was sure she was balanced enough on her own. "You're a klutz." Now that he was freely looking at her body, checking for injuries, he noticed her legs were banged up with old bruises and scrapes. The wounds from her fall on her first day of rehearsal were still healing. She was a hot—emphasis on the *hot* —mess.

"I run into a lot of end tables," Piper admitted, catching where his gaze had landed on a particularly nasty purple splotch on her thigh.

"Didn't you use to play soccer?" He knew for a fact she did. "That usually requires coordination."

"I did play, but I sucked," she said. "One time, I broke my ankle tripping over a clod of grass on the soccer field." Leo knew that, too. His sister, Mariana, was trying out for the varsity team at the time, and he had watched Piper's whole debacle play out live from his spot on the bleachers. Piper had just called him a dick in Spanish class earlier that day, and his younger self wasn't above muttering a "karma" under his breath when he watched it happen. "And I know what you're thinking. I didn't fall just now because of the running start. I would have fallen regardless."

Leo looked up at the black sky and pinched the bridge of his nose. There was no point in arguing, no matter how badly he wanted to or how infuriatingly wrong she was. "Fine. Whatever."

"Great. Now it's time to soak the new bruise on my ankle." Her tone was lighthearted, but when she stepped forward on the foot that had duked it out with the fence, her face pinched in pain.

"Chingado." Leo jogged the two steps to get to Piper and wrapped his fingers around her wrist. The memory of her hands pinned above her head against the bookcase sliced through his thoughts like a hot knife in butter. He watched her eyes widen as he moved into her side and carefully lifted her arm to drape it over him so he could shoulder most of her weight. "I'll help you get there, daredevil."

"Thank you."

A few steps, and they had finally made it to the edge of the hot tub. What would have taken Leo at most five minutes had turned into a fifteen-minute ordeal by the time he was peeling off his shirt.

"Jesus, fuck." Piper's curse took him off guard. He jerked around to face her again as he tossed his shirt onto a nearby pool chair.

"What? Your ankle?" He quickly crossed the distance between them.

"No, um, you just..." Her eyes roved over his chest, and he felt his heart rate pick up. "I wasn't expecting you to be so..." She gestured to his chest with a self-explanatory hand motion.

Leo looked down at himself, amusement pulling at the corner of his mouth as he rattled off some options for her to choose from. "Rugged? Hot? The most sexually appealing person you've ever met?"

"Whatever sex appeal you briefly had, it's now gone." Piper folded her arms over her chest. The corners of his mouth quirked up as he reached for the button on his pants. Piper's eyes widened. "What are you doing?"

"I'm not whipping my dick out, if that's what you're thinking, but I'm also not swimming in jeans." He probably should have changed into shorts before heading over, because now he was about to be stuck with Piper in a hot tub wearing only his black boxer briefs. The water would hopefully be obscuring enough to hide any growing problems down below, and he'd turn on the jets just to make sure of it. The fact that he decided to make direct eye contact with her while he dropped his pants and stepped out of the legs was yet another on the long list of things he should have reconsidered. To his surprise, Piper reached for the waist of her bike shorts. "Wait. What are you doing?"

"Same thing as you. I'm going to wear my underwear so I don't get these wet. I want to sleep in them." Piper gave him a shy smile, and he had to take a deep inhale to refocus after she used the words "wet" and "underwear" in the same sentence.

"This is a fucking strip tease," Leo mumbled under his breath as he sat down on the edge of the hot tub after turning on the jets. He did his best not to look up and utterly failed. Pink lace underwear peeked out from under the hem of Piper's long T-shirt once her bike shorts had pooled around her ankles and she'd removed her hoodie. He hadn't failed to notice her lack of a bra earlier in the car, either. The slow, shaky breath he let out as he slid into the hot, steaming water did nothing to quell his hunger for another taste of her. He had been right about the relaxing feeling of soaking his travel-worn limbs and entirely wrong about it relieving any sexual tension. "You coming?" he called back to her.

I want you to come, his brain aptly supplied.

"Mm-hmm." Piper slid into the water beside him, carefully babying her ankle.

"How bad is it?" Leo inquired, trying not to focus on her shirt in the places it floated around her breasts or clung to her figure.

"I'll be all right." She shrugged.

"I'll drive tomorrow, okay?"

"I was going to ask if you could." Piper looked away and bit her lip, her face falling into a somber expression. The way he'd known exactly what she was thinking before she even asked had his chest feeling tight.

"You're scared to drive again," he stated.

"I'll get over it like I do every time I get into a car, but..."

Leo bobbed his head in understanding. "You want to wait a bit. I get it. I'll drive. I'm glad I stayed."

"Me too."

"Can I see it?" He lifted his eyebrows and then added "your ankle" for some unnecessary clarification. Piper lifted her bare leg out of the water and stretched her foot toward him, leaning back against the hot tub wall with her hips tipped toward him in a painfully erotic motion that made his cock twitch. He gingerly grabbed her calf to steady her, desperately wanting to slide his hand up to part her legs with his fingers. "It's a little swollen, but ice and heat will help."

"I guess we're starting with heat," Piper murmured. He made eye contact with her as he slowly dropped her leg back into the water, and he really didn't mean to skim his fingers over her leg again, but he couldn't help but to touch her just a little longer. The puff of air Piper let out made him rip his hand back.

"S-sorry." Leo winced. He was really digging himself into a hole with every burning need for touch that he acted on. Reeling it in would be a much better option.

"Is it really so horrendous to touch me that you have to have that reaction every time?" Piper curled her lips over her teeth and scooted a few inches farther from him. "I realize we don't like each other, but if you keep jumping away from me when we so much as brush shoulders or practice a scene, I'm going to get a complex." She played it off as a joke, but he could tell she meant it, so he made the stupid mistake of shifting closer to her. Her breath hitched when his leg knocked against hers.

"You're sitting next to me," Leo licked his bottom lip, "wearing only your underwear and a T-shirt that does nothing to hide the fact that you aren't wearing a bra." It was too late to make better choices. He twisted his torso to face her more directly. "I want to do more than just touch you, Piper."

"What do you want to do?" Piper angled herself toward him and leaned forward a little, her eyelashes fluttering. The only thing that separated them was the steam billowing up between their wet bodies.

"I want to make you lose control." His chest rose and fell in quick breaths as he scanned her face, waiting.

She grinned maliciously. "I don't think you could."

"Don't tempt me with a good time." To test the waters even more, he let his fingers drag over one of her thighs. She squirmed a little in her seat.

"It's not as easy as you think it would be." Whatever confidence she had displayed a mere second ago vanished as she blushed prettily. He was desperate to know if she did that when she came, too. "No one's ever made me..."

"You can say 'come,' Piper," Leo teased and scooted even closer, his breaths getting shallower when he felt her leg press harder against his. Her chest tipped closer to him, like she couldn't help herself, and he dropped his eyes to admire her body with a smirk. "I think you're wound so tight that I could touch you through your underwear and get you off with just my fingers."

Piper stayed painstakingly silent for several long seconds, and then she turned toward him and whispered "fuck it" before her lips slammed down on his, and Leo was already grabbing at her waist to pull her closer. He groaned. It was just as good as the last time. Piper was like a drug, and his addiction was getting so far out of control that his hand was already wandering to find its spot between her legs. Their mouths worked in frenzied tandem until his fingers pressed on the outside of her underwear, right where her clit should be. He was rewarded with Piper bucking into his hand and tipping her head back, mewling for him. The sound shot straight to his cock, and he pressed harder.

"I can get you off, princesa," Leo promised, sweeping his fingers deftly over the thin fabric at the cleft of her thighs. Judging by the way she reacted—with a desperate press of her hips—she liked it when he walked her through how determined he was to do exactly what she wanted. "I think this pretty pink lace is going to be the death of me. You need it harder, don't you?"

"Yes," Piper cried out with a roll of her hips into his palm.

"If we weren't in a hot tub right now, I'd be able to feel just how wet you are. Were you wet before we got in here?" He increased the pressure of his fingers, and she gasped.

"Yes," she admitted, the sound coming out as more of a cry of pleasure.

"I was getting so hard just thinking about what's under this shirt, Piper." Leo dipped his head down to one of the perky nipples rippling the front of her wet tee and set his mouth over it, sucking at the warm fabric.

"Don't stop," Piper ordered. He'd never heard her demand anything she wanted with such vigor before, and the idea of her ordering him around just about made him lose it.

"So bossy," he growled against her chest and sucked through her shirt even harder.

Not only was Leo not going to stop, he'd do more. His hand worked between them, pressing and rubbing in slow, forceful sweeps from side to side. It almost felt like the small barriers were allowing him to claim innocence. He wasn't sucking on her breasts; her shirt was in the way. He wasn't fingering her within an inch of her life; her underwear was blocking him from touching flesh. On the other hand, the barriers made him go relentlessly harder over the top of her clothes. The arm he was working her over with was flexed from pressing so hard. His teeth bit gently against her pebbled nipple, eliciting a sound from Piper he wanted on vinyl.

"Tell me everything you want, princesa. Tell me where to touch you." The words left his mouth in a plea. He'd usually never be caught dead begging for anything, but this was now the second time she'd made him do it. *Please, join the show, Piper.* "Please. Tell me, Piper." The voice didn't feel like his own. He was usually commanding in bed, but this time, he sounded whiny. Oddly enough, he couldn't care less how pathetic he sounded as long as Piper opened her mouth to shout orders at him again. They were always fucking fighting. Maybe that was why he always felt the strain of sexual tension between them. He *liked* it when she was direct and mean about it. She bent over backward for everyone. And, God, if he didn't want her to yell at him to bend her backward...

"Go left with your fingers a little more, and—God, *yes.*" Piper reached for his hard length in his boxers and stroked him over his underwear like a reward for doing what she'd told him to do, and fuck if he didn't like that way too much. He needed all the gold stars.

"And?" Leo coaxed, wanting even more of her sweet demands. He let his eyes close on a groan when her thumb found his head and pressed the fabric of his boxer briefs against it.

"Go harder. Everything harder." She punctuated her direction with a firm jerk of her hand over his erection. He leaped forward, crushing his mouth against hers.

Piper's face was sopping wet. At some point during their tryst, the weather had done what Oregon weather did best and taken a turn for the worst. Leo hadn't even noticed it was raining until he found himself slipping his tongue into Piper's mouth, but he didn't mind it so much when it made her lips slide so easily with his. His hair soon matted to his head as her fingers dove into his thick, waterlogged curls. Rain pelted his face, but the cold did nothing to put out the inferno inside him. His body sought out the heat of Piper's tongue and the feeling of her hands against his chest and his cock. It shouldn't have felt nearly as good as it did to have Piper's mouth parted for him, and his brain had conjured up an image of what those same lips would look like wrapped around his cock.

A loud crack of thunder was what finally ripped them apart. Water and lightning didn't mix, the same way Leo had thought he and Piper didn't mix. As it turned out, they mixed rather well, but they were bound to have the same destructive properties as electricity in a hot tub.

Piper jerked out of the water and then freefell back into the hot tub, grabbing at her ankle and wincing. "Ow! Fuck."

"Christ! You okay?" Leo whipped across the water and pulled her into his chest to hold her up.

"I just forgot about my ankle." She let out a breathy laugh, and the whiskey and honey tone of it sent desire coursing through his core. He needed to get whatever this was under control before he did something truly terrible like have sex with her. "I think I should go back to the room. To sleep."

Message received—the entire thing had been a horrendous mistake.

Excuse after excuse spewed from Leo's mouth. "Right. It's late. We're tired. We survived a car accident and whatnot." Suddenly her shirt and her underwear didn't feel like good enough barriers at all. There was no denying that he had just finger-fucked Piper in a hot tub.

"Yeah. Exactly." Piper gave a fidgety nod of her head, but he didn't miss the way she squeezed her thighs together. "Long day."

"The longest." Now he was just parroting things back to her like an idiot. "So late, too."

You already said that, he reminded himself.

"It's probably four in the morning by now." Piper was rolling with his dumb statements, so at least he wasn't alone in his apprehension. "Bed—uh, I mean *sleeping*—is a great idea."

"On the scale of good ideas, it's the best one. Are you good with me carrying you? I think it'll be faster so we can sprint right to bed—sleep. Fuck, I meant sleep."

"To sleep!" Piper shouted the words into the night as if she were saying "Our chariot awaits, good sir!" Her arms were around his neck a moment later, and she held on as he lifted them from the site of their blunder.

Cradling Piper prevented her from seeing how hard he still was, which was probably for the best as Leo scrambled around for their discarded clothes. He made quick work of pushing through the self-latching gate and sprinting through the rain as Piper clutched their clothes to her wet chest.

His plan was simple. They would change out of their wet clothes, crawl into their respective real bed and pull-out couch bed, and forget any of it ever happened by morning. They'd go on like they had last time: ignoring it. They had never kissed in the library. They had never fondled each other in the hot tub. It didn't happen.

None of his plans held.

When Leo kicked the door shut behind them and went to gently set Piper on the ground, her pebbled nipples and her wet T-shirt that clung to her body like Saran Wrap pressed into his bare chest as she slid down him, inch by painfully slow inch to her feet. She grazed his still-hard cock on the way down. Both of them took sharp inhales. He only snuck one small glance at her face, and it was all it took for the entire plan to fall by the wayside. Out the window. He never even had a plan. It didn't exist.

Twenty-Four

PIPER

"Once?" Piper dropped their wadded-up clothes to the floor.

She had to be possessed by the ghost of a merperson or whatever seventies spirits lived in the room because there was no way she was seriously considering sleeping with Leo. But even as she scolded herself, heat licked up her spine at the sight of Leo's darkened eyes devouring her with a need so palpable that she pressed her chest into him even more. "We'll get whatever this is out of our systems, and then it'll be over."

"Once." Leo's head bobbed, and a dark curl swept over his forehead as his tongue wet his lower lip.

"I still hate you." She leaned forward and barely cared that it was a bad decision. This one could be labeled in her scrapbook of horrendous choices right under kissing Leo back in the library and letting him feel her up in the hot tub.

A short huff that sounded more like a growl of anticipation left Leo's throat. "Your personality still sucks."

"And you're an asshole." Her voice was so breathy that the insult carried no weight at all. She felt just as weightless, floating toward something inevitable and destructive. A balloon filled with helium tethered by one singular piece of ribbon in her grasp. All she had to do was let go, and she would be soaring.

"Hate sex, then?" Leo's mouth was almost touching hers, tipped up in a wry and irritating smile. Piper could feel the tiny, hot puffs of air dance across her lips as he spoke, and she drank in every word. *Hate.* Sip. *Sex.* Sip.

"Perfect," Piper whispered.

"Perfecto," he murmured back.

"I'm going to take what I want. I don't care about your feelings," she warned. Every wet article of clothing on her body was a vise, clinging to her where she wanted to be laid bare. The anticipation was torture.

"I'm fine with that. More than fine." His eyes were stripping her of her remaining clothes, too, dragging over her hard nipples and the shirt he had sucked them over earlier. The barrier separating his hot mouth from her skin in the hot tub had been agonizing. She should have known going back to the room wouldn't lead anywhere good. Leo couldn't just sleep on the pullout couch in the same room with her. That was never going to happen.

"You said you'd get me off," Piper reminded him. "The guys I've dated have never been able to, and I doubt you'll be any different." She had issued a challenge. They both knew it. Given how trigger-happy Piper's body had seemed in the hot tub, she had no doubt he could do it, but she wasn't going to let him know that. She was perfectly happy with pissing him off. Maybe that would make him sink into her harder.

"Pendejos," Leo scoffed and pressed his hand into the small of her back so her breasts smashed harder into his bare chest. "They were all idiots, Piper. I'm going to make it so that when you sleep with anyone else in the future, the only way you'll be able to come is by thinking about what I did to you."

"And how are you going to do that?" Piper had never brazenly rubbed against someone before, but there she was, wantonly pressing herself into Leo like an animal desperate for attention.

Leo's eyes scrunched shut with a groan when her body rolled against his erection. She could feel he was just as rigid as he'd been in the hot tub, ready to be played with. "I'm going to get you off by obeying every single one of your commands," he breathed. "And when you finally let go, we'll know which one of us is really in control, won't we?"

A battle of wills. That was what this was going to be, and Piper was desperate to win. She could be demanding tonight. She could be whoever she wanted because Leo would never be anything more than a one-night stand. Everyone had a breaking point, and she would find his. Getting him there, she decided, would be easy. All she had to do was deny him the power he usually had, and he'd call the whole thing off.

"Get on your knees." Piper pointed to her feet with smug satisfaction.

To her surprise, Leo promptly dropped to the floor in front of her with a thud. The insistent pang between her legs built. She backed up, keeping her eyes on him and most of the weight off of her swollen ankle as she carefully lowered herself onto the edge of the bed, beckoning him in a come hither motion. "Now *crawl*." She was so sure he wouldn't do it. She doubted anyone had ever treated Leo like this in his entire life, and yet...

Leo moved swiftly and crawled the distance between them, keeping his obsidian eyes trained on her. In no time at all, he was sitting back on his heels and kneeling between her legs. He didn't look even remotely embarrassed, and the sight of him peering up at her made her breath catch.

"Good boy," Piper praised, ruffling his hair like a dog and purposely degrading him. He leaned his head into her touch and let out a low, throaty chuckle.

"What's my reward for this?" Leo parted her legs with one hand and traced his fingers over her underwear. Piper's lashes fluttered, and she sucked in a sharp breath. The loss of that small amount of pressure made her eyes snap back open. Leo had removed his fingers from where she needed them and was gripping the edge of the bed on either side of her. "Say it, Piper. Tell me what you want me to do, and say it with confidence. Demand it."

The confidence Piper had was diminishing quickly, her face turning crimson, and she bit down into the pillow of her lower lip. She was so sure they wouldn't even get this far with her demands, and now that he'd already taken to each one with such ease, she wasn't sure how to proceed. She wasn't like this in bed. She wasn't like this *at all*. She didn't order people around or command any room she was in, let alone the bedroom.

"I'm not doing it until you tell me," Leo said.

"I want you to..." Piper knew what she wanted, and so did Leo, but saying it felt like crossing some line.

"You want me to what?" he pressed, each word punctuated with a period.

"Go down on me. No one has ever done that to me, so you better be good at it." The words came out slammed together, each one crammed into the sentence like if she didn't word-vomit the whole thing in one quick breath, she'd never say it.

"I am," Leo said. It was stated as fact in a deep rasp. The sky was blue. The mitochondria were the powerhouse of the cell. Leo was good at cunnilingus.

Then his fingers were ripping at her soaked underwear, peeling them down her legs as if he were desperate to complete his task. When Leo tossed her underwear on the bed beside her, Piper had little to no time to fret about how exposed she was before his strong hands gripped her behind her back and yanked her so far to the edge of the bed that she was close to falling off, the hard seam of the cheap mattress digging into her tailbone under the new sheets she'd no longer be giving her sister. Then his tongue blindsided her. It swept over her center in a ferocious swipe that made her see stars. She moaned, hips tipping toward his mouth to give him better access. The pressure he was using with his mouth and hands pinned her to the bed so she was grounded enough to not buck off the ledge, but she was still falling into something earth-shattering.

The tip of Leo's tongue found her clit and flicked at it from different directions until her legs jerked with one specific angled motion. A low hum rumbled from Leo's mouth, and she could see the corners of his lips pulled in a grin, a congratulations to himself for finding exactly what was going to get her off. Smug bastard. His tongue vibrated against her, causing fireworks to go off in her body and her back to arch in a stiff bow. She gripped the sheets hard for something to hold onto.

"Oh, fuck," Piper hissed, snapping her eyes closed for a moment to home in on the pleasure. He did it again, and her hips thrust into his mouth with no hesitation.

Leo came up for air and licked at two of his fingers before slowly pushing them inside her. "Enjoying yourself?"

"L—" Piper cut herself off before she did something truly embarrassing like yell out his name.

"I'm gonna hear my name on your lips tonight. And it won't be pissy this time. It'll be when you finish. Don't worry, I'll earn it." He drove his punishing fingers in farther, and her mouth dropped open with a whine.

"If your mouth isn't on my clit in the next two seconds, I'm going to finish this myself," Piper threatened. If he wanted her to be bossy, she'd give it to him.

"Yes, ma'am." Leo grinned and bent his head down to reach her again, doing one long swipe of his tongue before going in tandem with his fingers, pushing and pulling and stroking. "God, you're so fucking pretty like this," he murmured against her thigh before diving forward with another determined drag of his tongue.

"Shit. Oh, God, *yes*." Piper fell back onto the bed, writhing and sliding her hands over her peaked breasts. Her muscles tightened as he continued, her toes curling behind Leo's back where he had draped her legs over his shoulders. A wave of something cataclysmic pooled low in her stomach as his fingers and his mouth threatened to end her before he pulled back.

"My name, princesa. I want to hear it," he rasped. "You're never going to have anyone as good as me again."

"Fu—I need—" She thrust her hips into the air, and Leo chuckled.

"What do you need, Piper? Let me give it to you. I want to help."

"Tongue," she moaned. "I need your tongue."

Leo obeyed immediately, dipping his head forward. "You're going to finish for me right now because I've been so good, aren't you?" He shoved his fingers in deeper and stroked relentlessly. "Don't forget my name when you come. I need to hear it from those gorgeous, fuckable lips of yours."

"Fine. Do it now, for fuck's sake!" Piper yelled. Leo laughed, enjoying her torture too much before he finally licked up to her clit. The overwhelming sensation of it made her muscles twitch with a building tension again. "I'm gonna—*Leo.*"

The second his name left her lips, Leo increased the pressure, lapping at her with unhinged fervor. A starved man who had finally sat down for a feast. Before Piper even realized it, she was spiraling into the most extreme orgasm of her life. His mouth sucked at her clit, and she gasped, pulling her hips away from the sensitive pain. He yanked her closer, licking her anyway until she felt like she might keel over and die.

"Leo, I—stop," she shouted. He finally retreated, and her body went limp with relief. The heady swarm of stars plaguing her vision finally faded, and Piper found her body again. She had gone slack against the comforter, her soaked shirt dampening the fabric below her.

"Are you okay?" Leo's voice called from the end of the bed. He genuinely seemed concerned, which made her break into hysterical laughter. She clutched at her stomach as her eyes watered, her cackling bouncing off the mostly bare walls of ridiculous mermaid wallpaper.

"Piper, what the hell?" Leo jumped up from his knees and wiped at his glistening mouth as he sat down on the bed beside her, reaching down to yank her off the mattress by the shoulders to stare into her face.

"Holy shit," she wheezed. The panic in Leo's eyes dimmed, and a complacent smile replaced it.

"Can't say I've ever had this reaction before," he mused, which only made her laugh harder.

"That was," Piper held a shaky laugh back, trying to control herself, but couldn't quite form any words.

"Transcendent?" Leo offered. Piper finally stopped laughing enough to roll her eyes.

"Mm, maybe it was just a fluke," she said, falling back on her defiance.

"I can prove it wasn't." His eyebrows rose, and her eyes flicked down to his lips. She shouldn't want to kiss him again. If she told him she didn't want to go any further, he would obey, but the desire was already fizzing in her stomach like champagne bubbles.

"Prove it."

Twenty-Five

PIPER

Soft lips pressed into Piper's as if a giant question mark were looming over Leo's head. His tongue parted the seam of her lips, asking, "How far?", his teeth nipped her bottom lip to ask, "Is this okay?", and her body responded with a resounding "yes" at every turn. She slid one hand under the elastic of his boxers and palmed his hard cock to make it clear that they were going all the way, just like they had agreed on earlier. The moan Leo let out felt like vindication. She was reducing him to his most basic needs, and she'd be the only one to deliver them. The pressure between her thighs was already building again even though just a moment ago she thought she'd never have to be fulfilled that way ever again. Her body was insatiable when it came to Leo, and that was a massive problem. A problem for future Piper.

"Take my shirt off," Piper ordered, offering him a quick stroke of his length in return before she let go and set her arms at her sides.

"Gladly." Leo slid his hands down to the hem of her wet T-shirt and folded his fingers underneath, his warm knuckles pressing against her torso as they glided up her body. She lifted her arms as he pulled the shirt over her head, tossing it onto the floor. He swept his tongue over his lips, the same tongue that had just brought her so thoroughly to release a minute ago.

"Underwear." She snapped the gray band at the top of his boxer briefs. "Off."

"I don't even get a please?" He grinned, already sliding them down over his thighs and leaning back to drag them down to his ankles.

"It's not a request." When Leo finally relieved himself of his underwear and slingshotted them across the room, Piper gave his chest a firm shove so he fell onto his back.

Leo's only response was a muffled grunt as he reached to stroke himself.

"You aren't allowed to touch yourself yet," Piper snapped. Seeing him obey did something kink-altering to her brain. She watched with rapt attention as Leo forcefully pried his fingers away from his cock and fisted the comforter on either side of his naked body with each hand, his biceps flexing with self-restraint. His heated eyes fixed on her face as his eyebrows knit together in concentration.

"Please," Leo murmured. It was her undoing. Her self-control fractured as she snatched her underwear up from the foot of the bed and hauled herself over him, straddling his legs.

Piper's chest heaved as she held up the scrap of pink lace between them. "Give me your wrists." Again, he heeded her command and suspended both arms in the air, pinning his wrists together in front of her chest. "Now you won't be able to touch anything until I let you," she explained as she tied her underwear around his wrists, locking them together before she pushed them over his head.

"Fuck, I think this is the hottest thing that has ever happened to me," Leo groaned, glancing down at his erection bobbing in front of her thighs. He clearly wanted to touch, and the idea of not allowing him that made her even slicker with lust.

"Condom?" Piper asked. Having sex with Leo hadn't been on

her bingo card for that year, let alone for the trip, but she was always prepared. If he didn't have one, she would provide for them, but she didn't want to give away that she must have subconsciously thought she would need them.

"My bag. Side pocket. You should grab your vibrator while you're up," Leo suggested.

Piper stilled, her mouth ajar as she stared down at him. "What? How do you know I even have one?"

"You seem like the kind of person to prepare enough to have one fully charged for a trip. I'm right, aren't I?" The self-satisfied look on Leo's face made her want to say no just to spite him. Instead, her confidence went out the window as she clambered off him.

"I thought men hated using them," she muttered, digging around for a condom in Leo's duffel. When she retrieved the foil packet, she rolled her lips over her teeth and rocked back on her heels, trying to regain some of her control.

"Why would I hate using something that helps get you off?" Leo, for what it was worth, seemed genuinely confused by her question and her reluctance at the idea. She was starting to realize just how bad her previous sexual partners had been. If Leo freaking Diaz was more obsessed with getting her off than any of the previous men she'd dated, then what did that say about her? "It's a tool, not a competition, Piper," he continued. "I could use a manual screwdriver or an electric screwdriver to drive a screw into a wall. Both work. I'm still doing the screwing. Even if I'm not the person working the screwdriver, I'm the freaking foreman. Just grab it, and we can use it if you want to in the moment."

"Okay." She nodded, still feeling extremely exposed, half-covering her naked body with her hands and thankful for the darkness of the room.

Leo's logic made sense. She wasn't sure how exactly he was planning on using her vibrator, but they'd cross that bridge when they got there. Blushing furiously, she bent down, unzipped her suitcase, and pulled out the hot pink wand she had fully charged before packing it away, just like he had guessed. She brought it over to the bed, where Leo was sprawled out with his arms still above his head and what looked like zero cares in the world, nude body on full display. It was the first time Piper had gotten a good look at all of him. The thick length of his cock stood on end between his legs, and the sight of it made her swallow. Occasionally, sex was painful for her, not just mediocre. She had learned to tune out the pain completely and breathe through it when her body wasn't feeling up to the task, but this time, she really just wanted to feel good for once.

"We don't have to do this if you don't want to," Leo said. His eyes were still hungry as he dragged them down her body, and it sent a bolt of courage through her.

"I want to," Piper decided, climbing on top of him again and straddling his knees. Leo's eyes flicked to the thighs she always worried were a little too stocky, up to the breasts she feared were too small, and then finally landed on her mouth as she ripped open the condom wrapper with her teeth, tossing her vibrator to the side of his body and then the foil wrappings to the floor.

"Qué hermosura." It was barely a whisper, like Leo was mumbling to himself or thought he hadn't said it aloud, but she heard it well enough and couldn't help the smile from blooming across her face. She was fairly certain he'd called her pretty, and it was shocking how much she wanted him to think that. "Is that smile for me, princesa?" He grinned back at her. "You never smile at me. Bet it's not fake this time, huh?"

"Shut up," Piper scoffed. Leo's mouth snapped shut along with his eyes when she slowly rolled the condom down his cock.

The opportunity presented itself, so Piper leaned forward and met his lips, sinking into it when she saw the veins in his tied wrists strain to hold back. Their tongues twined. Their bodies pressed together with his cock pinned between them. She liked the sounds Leo made when she started to rub herself recklessly against his shaft. The power of being the one to make Leo beg and plead for more made the heat build in her stomach as she moved against his beckoning hips.

"Piper," Leo cried out. "This is fucking torture. I want to be inside you. *Please.*" There was that word again. The one word she could hear him say on repeat until forever. It was so wrong that it felt so right to reach between their bodies and guide him to her slick entrance. They didn't belong together, especially like this, but at that moment, what she needed and what she should need were two entirely different things, and she no longer cared about the latter.

Piper whipped her hips downward hard, sinking onto his cock. The timid girl who only gave in the bedroom was no more. The soft moan that Leo buried in her neck when she pressed her forehead into the pillow beside him made her release a moan of her own. And then they moved. Slow at first, so she could get used to him stretching her so much. They breathed together as Leo whispered incantations under his breath in Spanish. She liked that Leo's speech was free and unrestrained, delivering lines she couldn't translate but could instinctually understand by how desperate and reverent they sounded. He was so responsive, bucking with her and pressing at all the right moments.

When he found that perfect spot inside her, Piper laced her fingers in Leo's hair and pressed her fingers into his scalp, trying to ride him directly into the fire.

"Fuck, it feels so good," Piper gasped. "Want to be untied, Leo?" The question came with a firm buck of her hips, eliciting another groan from deep in his throat.

"Sí. Yes. Please, princesa. Whatever you want," he begged. Piper smiled, pushing up on her knees as she pulled his arms down to his chest. She continued rolling her hips as she made quick work of untying her underwear and tossed it to the side. Once released, Leo's hands grabbed at her hips to help her thrust. "I liked being tied up, but I really love touching you," Leo admitted and shifted a little under her, hitting that spot again that made her lose the plot for a second.

"Leo, that's—don't stop." Her broken speech was good enough.

Leo kept his rhythm as the corners of Piper's vision went hazy with unshed tears of pleasure. It was so extreme that she was sure she would tip over the edge soon enough, but they kept going, fucking each other so hard they were losing steam. Leo seemed to be holding back his release. His jaw clenched when he backed off a little, and every time he did, it was just enough for her to lose a little momentum before it built back up again, edging her when she just wanted to come.

"Dammit, Leo!" Piper's aggravation came out when he backed off once more. The timings of each of their releases were battling one another, and if that wasn't a perfect metaphor for their entire relationship, she didn't know what was.

"I'm gonna get you there," Leo promised. His hands flew to his sides, feeling around until he found what he was looking for. A flash of pink and the glow at the top when he clicked the button let her know it was her vibrator. She was so keyed up and desperate to release that she would do just about anything to tip over, earlier hesitation aside. He slid the toy between their bodies and held it in place as he clicked the top again with his thumb. The vibration hit her like a tidal wave when she rocked him into her on another thrust.

Piper couldn't speak. Instead, she sucked in choppy breath as Leo used the hand not currently pinning her toy to the base of his cock to guide her to lift again with a firm press of his fingertips under her ass. She released her inhale when he slammed her back down onto him. The vibrator knocked hard into her clit, and... pure euphoria. Nothing had to build anymore. Her orgasm detonated, exploding through her core and shaking every muscle in her body in waves. Below her, Leo was slowly pumping out his own release, stiff fingers digging into her hips as he let go with a strangled sob.

When the last of Piper's orgasm finally left her limp and lifeless, she pulled the vibrator away from her sensitive flesh and rolled off Leo. And there they stayed for an inordinate amount of time, staring up at the ceiling, not speaking, and breathing like they'd both gotten the wind knocked out of them.

Nothing had ever felt so terrifying. The replays of the way they had locked eyes when they both released solved nothing. The memory of how Leo had called her pretty sent Piper's heart treacherously fluttering. This was supposed to be nothing but sex, and really good sex at that, but she couldn't help the nagging panic rising in her that said that wasn't at all what they had just done. Maybe she was a coward, but she didn't want to risk a glance in Leo's direction to find he didn't feel anything remotely as groundbreaking, so she rolled onto her side with her back turned to him, burrowed under the bedding, and shut her eyes.

The pretense of sleep did nothing to quell how hyperaware Piper was when she felt the bed dip and lift beside her, but she kept her eyes shut even as she heard the padding of Leo's footfalls against the carpeted floors, the distinct sound of a zipper, and the front door shutting. She shouldn't feel hurt that he had left her bed immediately after, and yet, she did. It was just one more reason to hate him. He'd literally left the room to get away from her. And so, she stewed for a few minutes, got up to use the bathroom, then angrily got back in bed, chastising herself for sleeping with the enemy until the bed dipped beside her again.

"Hey," Leo whispered. "Are you awake?"

Confused, Piper rolled onto her side and slowly opened her eyes to Leo holding up a cheap clear waste bin liner filled with ice. She sat up, pulled the covers with her, and blinked back into existence, her body still worn and naked.

"You got me ice for my...?"

"Ankle, princesita." Leo smirked. "You didn't think this was for your—"

"No! Of course not." She yanked the bag out of his hand, wiggled her foot out from under the covers, and carefully set the ice on it. The shock of the draft coupled with the ice made her even more awake. Alert enough to see Leo strip off his pants and go for his underwear. "What are you doing?"

"What's it look like I'm doing?" Leo scoffed. "I'm taking my clothes back off."

"Why?"

"I sleep naked." It was simple enough, and yet she found she couldn't help but stare at all of his rippling muscles as he shed his clothes again. "I figured we've already done the worst, so sleeping next to each other won't be a huge deal. I'd rather not waste what little time I have left to sleep figuring out a way to not be violated by the springs of that couch."

"Right," she agreed. It was a sound argument. "I guess good night, then?"

"Night." Leo slipped under the covers, rolling onto his side.

Piper gave her ankle another minute or two under the ice before she set the bag to the side and settled in. The heat from Leo's body made her want to curl into him, but she refrained, forcefully shutting her eyes.

Twenty-Six

LEO

Light poured in from the window, and Leo rolled over, finding only empty sheets next to him. He wasn't surprised. This wasn't a lay in bed naked all morning cuddling kind of affair. This was a one and done. Sure, they had slept in the same bed, but he wasn't about to assume that meant anything. Nor would he read into the fact that Piper had ended up spooning his backside in a sleepy haze, and he'd somehow ended up facing her and pulling her into his chest. It was still freezing in the room, so he wagered they'd both needed the warmth to avoid hypothermia.

When Piper wasn't using every available breath she had to bite his head off or playing into the world's desperate need for perfection, Leo thought she was kind of cute. She smiled in her sleep, and it wasn't the peppy sunshine-and-rainbows smile she slapped on her face to fake perfection. This was a sated smile, one she seemed unaware she was making. Satisfaction. He had given that to her. She had finally released her good-girl bullshit for long enough to make him crawl to her. Piper thought she had been in control last night, but Leo had held her every sigh of pleasure in his hands and his mouth. Making her say every single thing she wanted and delivering on her every desire gave him a strange sense of dominance. And maybe she was a little right about how much he craved power. Piper, on the other hand, had confirmed that a lot of her personality was an act last night, and he was never going to let her live it down. Thinking about fucking with her already had his cock standing on end again.

The next time Piper said something sickeningly sweet to someone or pretended to be innocent, Leo would be there to remind her that she had demanded his fingers to do obscene things to her body. She had tied his wrists together with her underwear so he couldn't move other than to lift his hips to go deeper.

The shower was running, so Leo figured now was as good a time as any to fix the quickly-hardening problem between his legs. How he had any energy left was a mystery considering when Piper had fallen asleep beside him, it was already four a.m., and he'd fallen asleep much later. He would never admit to himself that he'd spent most of the time he should have been sleeping replaying every touch and glancing at the dozing heap next to him. Leo adjusted the pillows at the headboard and stroked himself twice, closing his eyes. The images from the night before flashed through his head yet again. He could almost hear Piper moaning in his ears, so breathless and pissed off that he could pretend it was real.

"*Oh, God, yes!*"

Leo's eyes snapped open, his cock still encircled by his needy fingers. Then he heard another moan. The sound was real, and it was coming directly from the bathroom. He knew those noises— some of them were going to be permanently etched in his brain. She had to know he could hear her. Maybe she wanted him to hear. Without another thought, Leo jumped off the bed and barged into the bathroom. Piper's body was hazy behind the glass shower pane, the steam billowing out into the room through the open door, but he could see where her hand was well enough, in between her legs. The other hand was pressed into the glass as if she had to physically hold herself up while she touched herself.

"*Leo?* What the hell?" Piper squeaked, covering herself with both hands. Leo flipped around so his bare ass was turned to her, breathing like the wall of steam he'd hit on the way in had knocked the wind out of him.

"You're thinking about me, aren't you?" The words came out rough as sandpaper.

"What? No, I'm not!" Panic laced Piper's voice, and it was several octaves higher than normal, coming out in soprano when after hours of having to listen to her, Leo knew she was a mezzo.

"Don't lie, princesita," he crooned. The idea of her thinking about him while she touched herself in the shower had him so turned on that he couldn't even pretend to not be. "If you're going to think about me, I might as well be here for it. You didn't lock the door. Can I turn around now?"

"It's 'may I turn around now,'" Piper huffed.

"*Déjame,*" Leo bit off. *Let me* seemed more appropriate because he flat-out refused to do a damned thing she didn't ask for.

The water hitting the tiles was the only sound for several long seconds, and he imagined it running off her slick breasts before hitting the floor. Then Piper finally spoke.

"Turn around," she whispered. He slowly turned over one shoulder and peered through the glass at her before shutting the door behind him to let the humidity build up again. She had swiped her hand over the glass so there was a window into the shower that let him see her clear as day. Her piercing blue eyes bore into his, and her long, wet eyelashes fluttered as she flicked her gaze down to his erection. A smirk tilted her mouth. "Maybe you're the one thinking of me."

"*Cállate,*" Leo barked out as he reached down to stroke himself again. Piper's eyes went even wider, but she let her arms fall to her sides, exposing all her intimate parts as she watched him. "Please touch yourself, Piper. I'm not touching you, so this isn't against our one-night rule, I promise." He didn't even know what the hell kind of a promise that was considering what he was doing had to be pretty damn close to crossing that line, if not completely over it.

"Leo..." Piper's voice drifted off before she gave in, and he could see her hand return between her legs. A soft moan escaped her lips again, which had him gripping himself harder as he watched through the veil of fog separating them. "*Leo.*" This time, when she said his name, it was the way he had heard it the night before. A demand. "You're thinking of me, aren't you?"

"S-sí," he huffed out, groaning. Leo stepped forward to press his hand into the glass wall. The desire to touch her was all-consuming. Piper's blurred body arched behind his palm, her full breasts smashing against the unwelcome wall between them so he could see them in all their glory. She was just out of reach behind a thin, *evil* pane of glass he wished he could shatter with his fist to get to her. He wanted her breasts in his mouth like they had been night before, so he stroked himself harder. "God, Piper." Her body rolled against the glass, all the way down to where her hand was swirling at the apex of her thighs.

"You want to touch me, but you can't," she taunted in a low drawl with a buck of her hips against the pane. "We said only once."

"Careful," Leo warned. "Or I might come in there."

She started to stroke herself faster, and he followed suit, pressing his hairline into the glass to watch her as she thrust into her hand. "Oh, you're going to come," her muffled voice called out.

"Fuck." Leo snapped, dropping his cock and reaching for the handle of the shower.

"What are you doing?" Piper jumped away from him as he stepped inside, the water hitting him head-on and dripping down from his dark curls over his face.

"I'm not going to touch you, but, fuck, Piper. I don't want to come all over the floor. You can't expect me to watch you smash your tits into the glass and not want to see them up close." He sounded pathetically desperate, and he wanted to smack himself upside the head for coming into the bathroom in the first place. Everything about this screamed danger, and he was already way too in over his head with her. One night with her had altered his brain chemistry.

Piper's glare turned from anger to confidence as her finger returned between her legs. "You're right, Leo. I want you to be able to see me. Back up against the wall," she ordered. He almost tripped as he fumbled backward, hitting the cold tile of the shower and letting his now-wet head fall back against it as goosebumps sprung up on his arms. The water hit his groin, the perfect lubricant as he started to slowly rub himself again. He watched Piper and ran his tongue along his lower lip as she moved into the middle of the shower and lay back against the wall, arching into her hand.

"Do you want me to do anything?" Leo asked.

"I want you to pretend you're fucking me." Piper shoved a few fingers inside herself, and Leo let out another curse in Spanish under his breath. Her slick body glistened under the water, her round breasts bobbing as her fingers pumped inside her. It took every morsel of his self-restraint to not touch her. To not slip his hand over every place the water caressed her body. To not bury himself inside where water couldn't reach.

"Already done. Is that what you were doing before I came in here?" Leo synced the timing of his hand over his cock to Piper's fingers, remembering how it felt to bottom out inside her.

Piper closed her eyes and gasped. "You were fucking me with your fingers."

"And my tongue," he encouraged. She bit back a strangled moan, the perfect response. "Now you know how it feels to be constantly haunted by someone's body." Leo picked up his pace when she did, both of them frantically chasing an orgasm. "It's going to be worse for me now that I know what you look like when you lose yourself. I know what you look like when you're wet in a hot tub. Wet in the shower. And wet on top of me."

"I'm going to pretend you're on your knees next time I do this to myself. You'll be doing everything I tell you to." Piper's hips bucked against her hand. Leo had to restrain himself from dropping to his knees right then. She hadn't explicitly asked for it, though, and he'd only do it if she asked. If she wanted it enough, she would demand it, none of that walking on eggshells bullshit she must have done with all her exes.

"Even in your thoughts, I'll be doing what you want, Piper," he panted. "No one's ever given you what I did. And for the rest of your life, I'll be in your head, in your fingers when you stroke your clit just right. In your toys when they're vibrating inside you. It'll be me, every time."

Piper let out a choked sob. The sound made Leo's eyes snap shut. He wanted that noise to seep into his skin along with the steam. God, he wanted to touch her so bad he was two seconds away from just doing it. "Look at me, Leo." His eyes snapped open on command. "Don't touch me, but get on your knees."

Por fin.

Leo's knees hit the shower floor with a thud, and the water splashed around his thighs. If the pain that jolted through his kneecaps was any indication, there would probably be bruises on his legs tomorrow, but he didn't care. His line of sight was right at her waist now, a perfect view of her fingers plunging into her heat, over and over and over again.

"*Gracias.*" The thanks slipped out of his mouth by accident, and he felt a little stupid until he looked up to see the devilish smile on Piper's face. God, she was pretty when she truly smiled, even when it was done with malice. "Am I allowed to touch myself?" he panted, falling right back into submission.

"I'll tell you when."

Leo set his hands on his legs, his fingers digging into his thighs in the hope of relieving some of the pressure as he watched her. Her breathing picked up as her chest heaved above him. He had already adjusted himself to make sure a stream of water was hitting his cock more directly. It was almost painful how badly he wanted to touch her or himself, literally anything beyond the water trickling down over him. But that wasn't what she wanted, and he refused to be another man who didn't give her what she wanted. He was better than them. Eventually, though, he would come, whether he was touching himself or not.

"Por favor, *please*, Piper. I'm so hard, I need to—"

"I'm close. Finish with me."

"Yes." Leo snatched up his cock, stroking it harshly.

It didn't take either of them much longer. Piper's hand slowed its movements near his face, and Leo almost drowned as he choked on the water pelting him from above while he came on the tile below. When he finished and regained his faculties, he slowly stood up, his mouth hanging open. How the fuck was he going to keep his hands off her for the foreseeable future? He couldn't even keep out of the bathroom while she was showering. Piper's cheeks were flaming red as she took one giant step away from him like he was a ticking time bomb. Her chest was still heaving to catch air, and his traitorous eyes took in the sight of her body after orgasm. Her wet hair was clumped into thick strands, the lavender tips turned a darker purple he wanted to run his fingers through. He could smell her lemon and sugar-scented shampoo invading his nose. Now that she had backed out of the stream of water, goosebumps sprung up on her arms, and her nipples were hard with the cold instead of with arousal.

"I, um," Piper started, the words falling away into the steam and water crashing between them.

Her eyes flicked away from him as her hands draped over her body again, whether from the chill or to hide from him. He hoped it was the former, but her body language said otherwise. What they had just done bordered pretty damn close on what they had done the night before, and they both knew it. It technically didn't break their agreement, but the way he was looking at her now felt way too intimate. It was terrifying. Foreplay and even sex didn't require this level of obsession, one person taking over his every thought. It shouldn't make him suddenly desperate for her to smile. She just looked guilty, and that thought sucked the air out of his lungs.

"Sorry," Leo swallowed.

"No, I'm—I didn't mean to—"

"You didn't do anything I didn't want you to. If I made you—"

"No, it's my fault." Piper blinked like she was surprised by her statement.

Leo opted to play it off. "If you want to take credit for this, I am totally fine with that."

"Okay, we're equally at fault." Piper scoffed, and the color returned to her face as she pointed to the handle of the shower door. "Get out."

Like someone had lit a fire under his ass, Leo sprinted from the bathroom in a way that would have made Usain Bolt proud, panting when he made it to the bed as he flopped, wet and face-down into the mess of sheets. He was in trouble. This couldn't keep happening, and sex was only part of the problem. It shouldn't feel so good to watch Piper succumb to her own fingers while thinking about him. He shouldn't be watching her sleep like some weird-ass stalker. She was *Piper*! The girl who had so wrongly misinterpreted him from the moment they had met. Who was a fake. Emotionless. Who purposely smiled at everyone but him.

The same girl who had a breathtaking smile when it was real and looked like a dream when she came.

Twenty-Seven

PIPER

The *tap tap* of Leo's finger against the steering wheel was setting Piper's teeth on edge. Beyond the extremely uncomfortable reality of having to road-trip the rest of the way to Archwood with someone she both hated and had now hooked up with, Leo was blasting the *Jaws* soundtrack through her stereo. The chances she was in the car with a serial killer or someone equally horrendous, like a person who didn't use their blinker to switch lanes, were low, but never zero. The song wasn't the stereotypical insidious shark attack song that everyone knew, thank God, but it was still eerie.

"What's next? 'Baby Shark'?" Piper grumbled.

"Not a fan of extremely popular and universally liked movie scores?" Leo asked, his voice laced with condescension.

"You're right, I should one hundred percent be constantly listening to the soundtrack my brother sings when sneaking up on me in a pool," she deadpanned.

"I am happy to change it to *Gladiator*," Leo offered. Piper knew he was joking, but she also didn't feel like testing him given that he probably really did have the score to a battle scene queued up on his phone. How fitting. *Gladiator* might actually be the perfect soundtrack to their entire relationship.

"What about *Titanic*?" Finding a middle ground was one of her best skills when it came to mediating for other people—she'd even solved a few of Thea and Yuri's spats that way over the last two years—but when it came to battles of her own, she typically found herself backing down. Unless it was Leo.

"I didn't know you were such a Céline Dion fan. Or maybe you just want to be painted like a French girl." He switched lanes, and Piper's back went ramrod straight as she jabbed her finger in his direction in horror.

"Oh my God! Use your blinker!"

"There's no one on the road," he argued.

"Can you see the future? Do you have eyes on all four sides of your head? No. You do not. There could always be a car that you don't see. And how hard is it, really?" Piper repeatedly flicked the air up and down with her hand to simulate how easy it would be to just turn a blinker on and off.

Leo chuckled. "Is that how you like to touch yourself?"

The car went dead silent except for the famous shark theme song that decided to make its debut through the car stereo at the exact inopportune time of Leo's comment. He quickly tapped the pause button on the dashboard screen and cleared his throat, gripping and ungripping the steering wheel. Piper's face heated, and she refused to look in his direction, choosing instead to look out the window at the excessive amount of trees that made up the Oregon landscape.

"I, uh, you—" Another clear of his throat, and Leo seemed no closer to relieving them of this painful conversation.

"Use your blinker," Piper said under her breath.

"Yeah." Leo bobbed his head with excess enthusiasm. "Absolutely. You're right. Sorry."

Instead of responding, Piper hit the play button to drown out the silence between them. As the *Jaws* theme played through her speakers once more, all it did was make everything more uncomfortable. She was held hostage by thoughts of Leo on his knees, looking up at her from the floor through dark eyelashes. Maybe she was the real shark in this car, but Leo was something worse—someone who made her lose control of her emotions. Every inch of her skin felt branded by his touch even then, just sitting beside him. That cliché phrase in romance novels where someone let out the breath they didn't know they had been holding—that was her, except she had let out some inner vixen she wasn't aware had been dormant for, well, *forever*. Whatever it was, it needed to go back where it had come from.

"What's the play here?" Leo had reverted to his normal confidence, and she turned her head in his direction, furrowing her brow.

"What?"

He gave an exaggerated sigh. "Are we pretending we didn't hook up, or are we going to be mature adults about this?" She should have known he wouldn't just stay quiet.

"I don't know," was the only thing she could think to say. "You seem to have a plan."

"My plan was to pretend it didn't happen. Fuck being mature." Leo chuckled lightly and caught her eyes for a second before turning back to the road. She could feel the corners of her mouth tipping up. Occasionally, he was funny. She'd give him that.

"Or maybe it is mature to call it a mistake, move on, and never speak of it again?" The crack in her voice said that the statement was a load of bullshit, but she was grasping at straws.

"No." The word was uttered through gritted teeth.

"No?" Repeating it back at him did nothing to help Piper understand.

"Never speak of it again? Yes. Move on? Already done. Mistake? No." Leo's jaw ticked like he was legitimately angry.

"Well, what would you call something that we never should have done and we both regret?" Irritation pricked the back of Piper's neck as she shifted in her seat.

"I regret nothing, Piper. Nada. I'm not going to sit here and pretend that I didn't enjoy every fucking second of it and that I wish it didn't happen. I'm not a liar."

Piper seethed at the last word. "You're calling me a liar now?"

"What do you call someone who commanded the room last night and this morning, *smiled* about it, and now is acting like it was the worst thing that ever happened to her?"

"Someone who had a brief lapse in judgment—"

"We went at it for forty-five minutes! That wasn't brief."

"Fine! An *extended* lapse in judgment," Piper admitted with a hiss and a flail of her hand. "I regret it because it wasn't me. We were out of our minds. Since when do you take orders from anyone? You have no problem bossing me around on stage—"

"It's literally my job to do that," Leo interrupted again. "What the fuck do you think directors do? Sit on their hands?"

"No, I just didn't think you'd let me tie up your hands with my freaking *underwear*!" Piper snapped. Once she realized what she had said, the image of Leo with his wrists pinned together flashed in her head, and a red heat battled with the freckles dusting her cheeks.

"Here's what I think." Leo's voice was calm, soft but sure. "I think you liked it so much that it terrifies you. It scares you that you could be anything like me."

"I'm nothing like you. I'm not rude, or demanding, or..." She trailed off when she saw the smirk on Leo's face, and she knew exactly what he was thinking. She had been every single one of those things last night.

"You want me to lay it all out for you? I'm happy to repeat back everything you said to me last night."

"What about you, huh? You're a lot like me, then," Piper challenged. Two could play at this game, and there were several things Leo had said last night that were out of character for him. "You were saying 'please' like that was your job."

"I can be polite," Leo grumbled. "Sometimes. It doesn't mean I'm like you."

"You weren't just polite, Leo. You did everything I told you to."

"So, you're saying that you let people walk all over you?"

"No, I'm saying that you did things you didn't want to do because it got you laid."

"Oh, I wanted to, Piper." The low, throaty tone of his voice made her squirm.

"Well, sex is sex," she mumbled.

Leo cocked his head to the side. "Is it?"

No. It really isn't, Piper thought. "Yep," she said.

"Did you already forget that you told me that no one's ever made you finish?"

"Can we just stop talking about this, please?" Piper dug through her purse just for something to do and came up with a tube of Chapstick. She wanted to ask Leo if he felt like he was shattered in pieces, too. But he was good in bed and probably had the same experiences with everyone as he'd had with her. He had liked it, sure, but did it feel like he had to rebuild himself this morning, carefully placing the pieces back together to cover up the contents of his soul?

"Only if you admit you liked it." The arrogance with which Leo lifted his chin made Piper's application of her Chapstick more of a frustrated swipe.

"Fine. I liked it." She shoved the cap back on and snapped it hard before tossing it back into her purse. "Happy?"

Leo flashed his teeth at her. "Very."

"It will never happen again. We got it out of our systems, and we'll forget about it." The nagging thought in the back of her head reminded her that her body was insatiable now. This desire Leo had unlocked was never going to be fulfilled. He was wrong about one thing, though. She did regret it, because now she was stuck like this, thinking about how thoroughly undone she could be if only it were Leo's hands doing the undoing. She'd have to find someone else now. Someone who could do the same things to her that he did. But she already knew she would never be comfortable enough to demand what she wanted like that again.

"Exactly. It never happened." Leo zipped his lips and twisted the key before tossing it out the closed window. "And, to be very clear, I won't tell Sam, and you won't tell Thea. I really can't have Sam finding out about this."

"Find out about what?" Piper asked, fluttering her eyelashes in feigned confusion.

Leo chuckled, catching on. "No idea."

Twenty-Eight

PIPER

The sight of the olive green house at four-three-six Juniper Street made Piper's muscles relax. Leo had driven the rest of the way to Archwood in what would probably go down as the strangest car ride ever, but when he pulled up to his house, Piper was so tense from just the idea of driving a mile or two to her childhood home that Leo repeatedly offered to just walk the distance from her house to his instead of making her drive. She was still feeling a bit stubborn from everything that had happened, so she refused. Out of everything that had gone down on the trip, driving for five minutes wouldn't kill her. And yet, when she got behind the wheel, every bone in her body locked up, and she wished she would have listened to Leo. After accidentally yard-sailing an entire bag of sunflower seeds across the passenger seat and console and squeezing the steering wheel until the blood left her fingers, Piper finally made it home.

The noise coming from behind the front door didn't surprise her in the least. It was two in the afternoon. Piper would be more shocked if there wasn't any commotion inside. Judging from the other car parked on the street, the Winstons were over. She twisted the knob and gave it a hard push. The front door always stuck on the way in due to the paint that had built up from how many times Piper's mother had repainted the door, and no one had bothered to fix it.

"Suck it, losers!"

A wide smile broke out across Piper's face. She'd know that voice anywhere. Jayla, the Winstons' oldest kid and her little brother Cooper's constant accomplice, was on her feet in the living room dancing a little jig with a remote control in her hand while Cooper and his other best friend, Camden, stared up at her.

"Dammit," Camden yelled, tossing his controller onto the couch beside him.

"Language!" Walker's voice called from somewhere beyond.

"Sorry!" Camden shouted back.

"You're cheating." Cooper stood up and went toe to toe with Jayla. Piper's little brother was right in the middle of his awkward teenage phase and looked like he'd grown an entire foot since the last time she had seen him. His voice was starting to do that cracking thing that said he would soon have the voice of a man. "How do you always win?"

"You should be asking why you two always *lose*." Jayla grinned and continued her victorious hip swivels.

"Well, I know why I lost. I fucking suck at this game!" Camden groaned and then quickly corrected himself. "I mean, uh, *freaking*."

"Piper!" The sound of her sister's squeal made Piper perk up in the doorway as she heard heavy footfalls down the back hallway and then saw a blur of long black hair whip across the room. Then Piper was engulfed in the smell of strawberries as she leaned into her sister's embrace. Pearl always smelled like fresh fruit and home. It was morphing into something more mature now, but it was still the same comforting scent. When Pearl pulled out of her arms, Piper stared in awe. Pearl was still just as petite as the last time Piper had seen her, but there were hints of a more womanly figure filling in.

"You got new glasses." Piper reached up to tap the rim of Pearl's circular frames, and the glasses slid down a little on the bridge of her sister's nose. The sight made Piper smile again. She might miss it if Pearl ever stopped having to push her glasses back up.

"I did! I also got my doubles pierced because I'm a cool bitch now." Pearl brushed her hair off to the sides to show off the new silver heart-shaped studs above her familiar dangly heart-shaped earrings.

"Language!" Camden called out as he, Cooper, and Jayla closed the distance between the living room and the Hartrick sisters. Pearl rolled her eyes and barely gave Camden a second glance.

"Anyway, I've turned over a new leaf. New car, new me. I'm edgy now," Pearl declared, shaking her shoulders back and forth in a shimmy, her sleek hair brushing back over her shoulders as she did. Piper giggled because "edgy" was the exact opposite of what Pearl was. Her sister might dress in a little more black than before and frequently wear combat boots, but Pearl's favorite color still was and always would be pink, the color of love and romance and all things cute. That was why the mauve sheets Piper had picked out for her sister—which she now would *not* be giving her—looked both mature and romantic at the same time.

"Um... Piper?" Cooper's hesitant voice broke the attention off of Pearl, and everyone turned to look at him.

"Coop!" Piper tossed her arms around her little brother, and he stiffened underneath her, gangly arms hanging at his sides as she crushed him. "Hug me back, you dingus!"

"You should really go to the bathroom," he said into her ear. Piper pulled back from his embrace in confusion just as her oldest brother, Colin, along with her aunt and uncle and their best friends, Amala and Roscoe Winston, rounded the corner from the kitchen.

"The college girl is back." Walker beamed and then came to a halting stop in front of Piper, eyes wide in horror, before whirling on his wife with a finger jabbed in Piper's direction. "I told you this would happen!"

"What are you—oh." Talia blinked at Piper, who shifted on her feet, nervously looking down at herself and wondering what the hell everyone's problem was.

"Jesus, do I have something in my teeth?" Piper asked. She covered her mouth with one hand. Amala burst into laughter beside Talia, who had her lips curled over her teeth to hold back her own laughter.

"This is not fucking funny," Walker snapped.

"Let's just..." Roscoe, decked out in his police uniform, started to herd Walker away from the door.

"Will someone tell me what the hell is going on?" Piper threw up her hands in exasperation.

As always, Colin, the resident expert on everything, was the one to finally explain. He took a step forward, looking rather amused as he pointed below her head. "The massive hickey on your neck gives away the fact that you probably had sex with Leo."

Piper's head snapped backward, and her mouth fell open as she flung a hand up to her neck to frantically cover the mark. She was going to fucking murder Leo.

"Other side, sis," Pearl giggled, and Piper transferred her hand over as she stared down at the floor.

"No, that's not—" Piper sputtered, trying to find some way around the obvious mark Leo had left on her. How the hell had she not noticed it at the hotel that morning? It was on the side Leo would have seen the entire three-hour drive, too, which only confirmed what a giant asshole he was.

"Let's go talk, shall we?" Talia latched onto Piper's wrist and pulled.

"I'm coming!" Pearl singsonged.

"Same. I absolutely need to hear this," Amala said with glee, trailing on Piper's heels and stopping with a hand out when Jayla followed. "Not you."

"Mom, I know what sex is." Jayla rolled her eyes. Piper darted her eyes to Cooper, who took one giant and frantic step away from Jayla, yanking on Camden's arm to drag him away from the conversation, too. "I'm thirteen, not four."

"Still too young to be doing anything." Roscoe narrowed his eyes at Cooper, who took another giant step backward and flinched when he ran into Walker's chest. Cooper and Jayla had been friends since they were eight. Camden had also befriended the both of them back then, too, but no one gave him the same look her brother was getting. Camden seemed too focused on eyeing Pearl to pay any attention to the conversation at all. It was a new development, but not at all surprising given how stunning Piper's sister was. Pearl never gave Camden the time of day, though. Whether it was because she was oblivious or just grossed out by her little brother's best friend liking her, Pearl never said a word.

A loud clearing of Walker's throat and a hard press of his hands into Camden's shoulders broke the kid out of whatever Pearl-obsessed trance he was in. Cooper and Camden both looked the picture of guilt, although if Piper had to bet, neither of them actually was. There was a fog of hormonal teenage weirdness in the air, and it was wildly amusing. "C-Squared," the nickname given to the boys by Jayla herself, were both in that weird stage where sex seemed equal parts terrifying and enticing. Currently, it seemed like they were taking the terrified route, slowly backing away from the group of adults. While Piper was thankful for the turn in the conversation, it reminded her she was the only person in the room who was truly guilty, hand still pressed over where Leo's mouth had been.

Jayla should have also been in her awkward teen phase, but she had skipped over any embarrassment at all and steamrolled right back into the conversation with a loud snap of her fingers. "Calm down, everyone. I haven't done the nasty yet." She laughed and tossed her golden box braids over her shoulder. "C-Squared haven't, either. Sidney did kiss Cooper once, though."

"I told you that in confidence," Cooper hissed.

"Sidney? *Ooooh*," Piper crooned. She had absolutely no idea who Sidney was, and if she had to bet, Cooper didn't even kind of care about Sidney. He'd never admit it, but Piper was fairly certain that Cooper had liked Jayla from moment one. Carter had tried to bet Walker once that Cooper and Jayla would end up together, and Walker refused to take the bet—that was how aware everyone else was of their bond.

"You never told me that." Camden's mouth dropped open, and he glared at Cooper.

"You were... busy," Cooper finished lamely. "Did Jayla tell you that Theo kissed her?"

"I'm going to murder you, Cooper Dale Hartrick!" Jayla shouted. Piper held back a laugh at the made-up middle name that was nowhere near Cooper's legal one. She was starting to think that maybe her own love life wasn't as screwed up as she had thought it was. This entire ordeal felt like a soap opera.

"You started it, Jayla Eleanor Winston," Cooper shot back. Also not Jayla's middle name.

"What in the ever-loving fuck is going on?" Roscoe whirled on his daughter and then locked eyes with his wife. "Tell me you didn't know about this. Who the hell is Theo?"

"I plead the fifth." Amala grinned.

"Theo," Cooper mumbled. "Is a dick."

"Language!" Walker huffed on cue.

"He really is a dick, though," Camden agreed and waved a hand over his face in a circular motion. "Huge nose, too. It feels like you're talking to his second ego. Maybe Jayla should break it for him. We all know she has a mean right hook."

"She taught me how to throw a punch once." Pearl smiled sweetly.

"Really?" Camden bounced and gestured to himself. "Punch me in the face."

"Why the hell would you want that?" Colin furrowed his

brow. "I think if we want to test her punching capabilities, you should hold a pillow."

"I think it's time we leave all the men to stew, don't you?" Amala turned to Talia conversationally.

"Probably best if we don't want Walker and Roscoe to go on a tirade and Jayla and Pearl to start a boxing club owned by Colin." Talia tipped her head in the direction of the stairs.

"Coincidentally, our butcher at Lydia's is a boxing instructor." Amala gave a cheeky grin to Piper over her shoulder. "And Leo's father."

Piper followed reluctantly, still clutching onto her neck. She'd much rather all the focus be off her, but Leo had made that impossible. Even as she made her way up the stairs, she could feel every eye in the foyer following her, her uncle's searing glare stronger than anyone else's. Walker had always maintained extremely unreasonable expectations about her love life, and she wasn't sure why she thought that would stop after she was out of the house and on her own. Adults had sex, and while Walker was making up for her lack of a father figure, it didn't change the fact that she wasn't a baby anymore. She'd probably forever be sixteen in her uncle's eyes, the age she had been when he'd lost his brother and sister-in-law and she'd lost her parents. Sometimes she felt like she was right back there in the aftermath, unable to control her emotions and living on the edge of tears. Being locked in the stone-faced smile she had curated as an adult was easier.

Twenty-Nine

PIPER

The childhood bedroom Piper had left behind when she went to college looked the same. A large antique wooden dresser sat in the corner of the room beside the arched window and white chiffon drapes. The queen-sized bed with its fluffy floral comforter had just enough space for all the women in her close-knit family to pile atop it, leaving her no room to sit with them. Piper pulled the chair from her vanity and set it beside the bed as four sets of eyes eagerly locked on her. It felt like children's story time, though the subject was for mature audiences.

"Did your tire really pop, or was that just an excuse?" Talia's eyebrows were raised in accusation, but there was no real threat behind the look.

"My tire really popped. We spent the whole morning getting it fixed, and Leo chewed the mechanic out for trying to sell me the wrong size tire." Piper folded her arms over her chest, feeling a bit defensive.

"And?" Pearl waved her hand for Piper to elaborate.

"What do you want to know? I needed to stay with my car, and it was late. Or early, depending on how you look at it." She was deliberately skirting around the main event, and everyone knew it.

"Yes, getting my car towed often leads to my husband and I sucking face." Amala's voice dripped with sarcasm.

"Gross, Mom!" Jayla objected.

"How do you think you and your brother were made? I'm sure Piper can explain. Take it away." Amala gestured to Piper wildly.

"I..." Piper groaned. "Okay, we got a hotel room, and the entire point of traveling together was so that Leo could afford it, so I suggested he just sleep on the pull-out couch."

"I take it he did not sleep on the pull-out couch," Talia said with dry amusement.

"Well, first we snuck into the hot tub area, I tried to jump the fence, rolled my ankle, and he kinda had to half-drag, half-carry me everywhere, and we didn't have any swimsuits, so we were just wearing underwear, and I was wearing a shirt, but..." Piper cringed and looked away while she said the next part. "Then we accidentally started making out."

Talia tipped her head to the side, narrowing her eyes. "That's it?"

"No." Piper bit her lip and blushed furiously. "Then it started dumping rain on us, and he had to carry me back to the room because of my ankle, and then it just kind of happened."

"Just to clarify," Pearl raised her hand, "Leo? The guy you repeatedly told me you hated?"

"I still hate him. He's a jerk! I mean," Piper gestured to her neck as proof, "he sat next to me the entire car ride back and said nothing about this monstrosity he gave me."

"He didn't force you into anything, did he?" Amala's face softened.

"No." Piper adamantly shook her head, feeling suddenly very obligated to defend Leo despite not being his biggest fan at the moment. "He got consent. Multiple times. I promise. I don't know why I wanted to, but I did. But it'll never happen again."

"That bad?" Amala inquired as Piper looked down at the floor. Did she even want to explain that it was the best sex she'd ever had? Or did she want them to think it was the worst so they would stop questioning her? The second option was appealing, but it wasn't the truth.

"It was, um... he knows what he's doing." Piper cringed. "And we might have taken a weirdly sexual shower this morning. But that's it! It's done." She karate-chopped the air with finality.

"Are we taking bets?" Amala turned to Talia.

"I think Walker would kill me if I took bets on this," Talia said. "He was so convinced that something would happen with Leo on the way here to begin with, and I assured him a billion times that he was being dramatic, but apparently, he was not."

"Well, they already made out once before the trip, so even I could have told you something was going to happen," Pearl droned.

"True," Jayla agreed. "Coop's phone popped off when that news came out."

"Excuse me?" Talia gaped.

"Carter's a freaking snitch," Piper groaned.

"I would think, as your sister, that I would get to know first and have the honor of snitching, but yeah, Carter can't keep a secret to save his life." Pearl giggled.

"I was going to tell you, but Carter read me like a book." Piper sighed and then turned to her aunt for more explanation. "We got into it at the library once, fighting about—I don't even know." She technically did know, but she wasn't about to bring up their entire discussion about love or how she'd practically dared Leo to kiss her. "Then he kissed me, and we both kinda freaked out. We had successfully avoided each other outside of rehearsals up until you decided to plan this whole trip behind our backs."

The corner of Talia's mouth twitched, holding back some sort of smile. "It seems like you like him more than you're letting on."

"I don't. Liking his dick and thinking that he *is* a dick don't have to be mutually exclusive." Piper neglected to mention that just *liking* it was the understatement of the century. Leo's body had sent her mind into the gutter too many times to count on the way home, and just recounting the night was making her face flush with the memory of how he looked thrusting into her with deep, deliberate strokes. If anyone ever wondered if they could be attracted to that small notch in between clavicles, Piper was living proof that it was possible.

"How was it really?" Jayla asked eagerly, propping her chin up on her knees as she hugged her legs to her chest. Pearl was hanging on Piper's every word, too. The pang of guilt for not behaving like a role model with a good representation of love for her sister and Jayla made Piper's face fall. She knew she avoided love like the plague, but she didn't want that for them.

"It wasn't exactly romantic," Piper said.

"Scale of one to ten?" Amala asked.

"Eleven," Piper replied and then buried her face in her hands. "I don't know. Maybe I've just had really bad sex up until now?"

"Both can be true," Talia said softly. "When you're with the person you're supposed to be with, it's better."

"Ugh." Piper adamantly shook her head. "I'm not supposed to be with Leo. I promise. We already decided this was never happening again."

"Why does it have to never happen again if you liked it?" Pearl asked.

"Because we still hate each other," Piper argued.

"I just don't get why you hate him," Jayla chimed in. "Coop said it's because he told you what to do in high school. I tell everyone what to do all the time, and you still like me."

"Leo's a prick about it. You're not," Piper said simply.

"How could it possibly be that good if you don't like him?" said Pearl, once again coming in with the hard-hitting questions.

"I don't know." Piper groaned. "We were kinda pissed off the whole time, and he made me... explicitly say things... in a mean way?"

"Oh." Amala's eyes went wide, and she looked at Talia. "So, the opposite of you and Walker."

"I mean, he's not *mean*, per se." Talia grinned sheepishly at her hands.

Piper was about to voice her complaint about having to hear about her aunt and uncle's sex life when Pearl made a loud, disgusted sound.

"*Gross*," Pearl gagged.

"Mom, old people don't get to talk about sex," Jayla complained.

"You wanted to join this conversation," Amala pointed out. "Fuck around and find out. I can start talking about your dad and—"

"I'm out!" Jayla got up from the bed, and Pearl seemed to match her embarrassment as she, too, bolted toward the door.

Pearl paused just before the doorway and looked back at Piper with a glint of excitement in her wide doe eyes. "Come find me later, and we'll put the new sheets on my bed?"

"Um... yes to the first part." Piper grimaced. It seemed to dawn on Pearl's face a second later when she gasped loudly.

"You didn't!"

"I already ordered new ones. They'll be here in three days." Piper's voice cracked.

All she got in response from her sister was a look of disgust before Pearl made a quick exit.

Amala waited patiently for Pearl to disappear safely behind the door before she folded her hands in her lap and looked over at Talia. "Now that I got rid of them, advice time?"

"Advice time," Talia parroted.

The air in the room suddenly grew serious, and Piper wondered what advice they thought she needed and why they couldn't give it with Jayla and Pearl in the room.

"I don't need advice. We're done. It's not going to happen again." Piper tried to get up from her seat to leave when her aunt hit her with a glare.

"Sit down," Talia said in her parenting voice and pointed to Piper's chair.

Amala hummed thoughtfully and nodded, and Piper felt like she was about to get an earful as she slowly dropped back into her seat.

The sudden urge to cry caught in Piper's throat. This felt so much like what her mother would do. Like a deep discussion was on the rise in the same way Paisley used to meet Piper eye to eye when she was disappointed in her. As a grown-ass woman, Piper could stand up to the two mother figures in her life easily enough, but the knowledge that she would never again get to sit down with her mother to work out her problems was a cold slap to the face.

"Frankly, Piper, you have been dating the absolute scum of the earth," Talia said bluntly.

Piper's eyes blew wide. "What? I—"

"Don't interrupt," Amala cut Piper off with a raise of her hand before she could give a rebuttal.

"As someone who loves you, I'm no longer comfortable supporting you when you date people who are beneath you." Talia crossed her arms over her chest.

"You're mad that I slept with Leo?" Piper balked. Whatever she was expecting, it hadn't been this.

"Leo?" Amala scoffed. "No. We adore his family, and I can't imagine that his parents would ever raise someone as awful as you seem to think he is."

"Every other person you've dated? Yes," Talia said. "I know you, and I know that you didn't even like them. You barely mentioned Todd when I came down after your breakup. You didn't care, so I can't for the life of me figure out why you do this. Is it that you don't know your worth? Do you need someone to tell you what you're worth? Because I will."

"*We* will," Amala chimed in.

"I—" Piper swallowed and felt her face go hot as tears started to crest her eyes and fall down her face. "I don't know."

"Why is it that Leo seems to make you feel something, and that's when you decide you don't want to take things further?" Talia asked. Her voice was still stern, but her face had softened a bit.

"I don't like the way he makes me feel, okay?" Piper wiped frantically at her face.

"And how is that?" Amala's eyebrows rose.

"Out of control!" Piper yelled. "I can't control my emotions around him. Usually, I'm pissed because he's being a jerk, but on the way here, when the tire popped, I couldn't even stop myself from sobbing about my dead fucking parents in front of him. So, no. I don't want to be in a relationship with someone who makes me feel like that."

"Oh, honey," Amala whispered, her face twisting into sadness.

"Piper." Talia's nose twitched like she was going to cry, too. "It's not wrong to feel."

"It is, the way I do it," Piper murmured and let her face go cold and emotionless. "It consumes me when I let it. So I don't let it. I will never again be that sixteen-year-old girl who was so sad she could barely breathe."

"You're too hard on yourself." Talia shook her head. "You suffered a huge loss, Piper. It's okay to not be okay sometimes. I'd even wager that it's healthy. You are so much like your uncle. I don't even know how I didn't realize just how much pressure you put on yourself to be strong when you don't have to be."

"It's been years, Talia. It's time for me to stop wallowing. I don't want to invite more pain into my life. My dream is gone, but I can make other people's dreams happen for them. I can support other people. I don't need that for myself." Piper calmly got up from her seat, steeling herself as she tucked her hair behind her ears.

"You can have a new dream, Piper." Talia swallowed, and a single tear tracked down her face. She was holding onto Amala's hand like she needed strength for the conversation.

"I have what's left of my family, and that's good enough. I

don't need more people." The bitterness of her own voice caught Piper off guard. The little girl hiding in the back corner of her mind screamed that Piper was a liar, but at that point, the voice was just screaming into an empty void.

"Closing yourself off from new people and new dreams doesn't make you strong, Piper," Amala said. "It makes you scared."

"I'd rather be scared forever than desolate," Piper whispered and pointed to the door, hoping they'd leave. "I'm sorry if that makes you both disappointed in me. I'm going to take a nap now."

"Piper," Talia croaked.

"I love you, but I'm tired," Piper replied. "I barely got any sleep, so I'm gonna rest. I don't want to talk about this anymore." She could see every fraught crease on the faces of the two women who were as close as she'd ever get to having a mom again, but as much as she knew they cared, they were wrong.

"We love you. All of you," Talia said, Amala nodding solemnly beside her. "Even the broken parts. I know, despite never getting to meet them, that your parents would not want this for you. This is not over. Have a good nap."

The door swung open, and the two women stepped through, giving Piper silent but sad looks as they left, Amala shutting the door behind them. It took Piper a while to do anything but stand there, staring at where they'd left, and when she finally moved, it was only to crawl into her bed, still wearing Leo's hoodie. She pulled her knees into her chest and let one last tear fall before she swiped it away and closed her eyes to dream. The one place she allowed herself to play out a life she would never have. The one place where that little girl she had closed herself off to wasn't scared or hardened to loss.

Thirty

LEO

> PIPER <SUNFLOWER EMOJI> 7:23 PM
> You're an asshole.

LEO 7:24 PM
You spoil me with your flattery

> PIPER <SUNFLOWER EMOJI> 7:32 PM
> You marked me.

LEO 7:33 PM
You mean the mark of the devil? You got that on your own <smiling devil emoji>

> PIPER <SUNFLOWER EMOJI> 7:52 PM
> You sat 1 ft away from me for 3 hrs and failed to mention the giant hickey on my neck. I know you like to suck the life out of things, but there's no need to take it out on me. <vampire emoji>

> LEO 7:53 PM
> You said nothing happened, therefore, by your own account, I didn't do anything. I hope you find the real culprit. I bet he's fantastic in the sack.

> PIPER <SUNFLOWER EMOJI> 8:48 PM
> Eh, he was alright. He spent most of his time begging, poor thing.

Whenever Leo spent time with his family, he could expect a rapid fire of invasive questions. His first two nights in the house, with only his parents and grandmother around, he was the focus of everyone's attention and had to sneak away repeatedly to respond to Piper's texts so no one would read over his shoulder. He had already answered a series of questions about the drive down from his family, giving placating answers in order to avoid what felt like a giant glowing arrow above his head that read "I had sex." And, sure, he might have been a bit of an asshole for giving Piper her own glowing sign on the side of her neck, but her reaction was worth it. Besides, even though Piper hadn't given him a matching hickey, his grandmother had been staring at him since he had arrived like she knew, and the woman looked even more terrifying with her silk headscarf covering her bald head. Leo had gotten most of his looks from his parents, but his attitude was straight from Abuelita. It was a shame that the breast cancer hadn't run screaming from her body yet, but he figured she must be close to scaring it off if she was able to immediately scare Leo with a single look.

When Thanksgiving finally rolled around, Leo's sister, his brothers and their wives, and the lone grandbaby were around to help field the brunt of the questions. He could finally take a small breather from his mother constantly telling him how wonderful Piper was for driving him down.

"Antonio, ¿y por qué no esta tomando Saanvi?" Lucia, Leo's

formidable mamá, was already starting off strong the second they sat down at their table full of food. "Saanvi, please tell me it's because you're pregnant. Necesito más nietos." Leo's brother and his wife Saanvi's firstborn was in Mariana's lap chewing on a spoon, barely one year old, and Leo's mother was already demanding more babies.

"Mamá," Antonio scolded. "Can't we just relax with the one kid for now?"

"Relax? What's that like?" Saanvi scoffed and pointed to her spawn. "That one doesn't know what relaxing is. And I'm not drinking the wine because I have a headache." Saanvi didn't speak Spanish, but since marrying Antonio, she was starting to pick up a lot from being around his family's special brand of Spanglish.

"You know," Lucia elongated the last word in a way that hinted she was about to say something probing. Leo waited for the punchline. "I used to get headaches all the time when I was pregnant with Antonio, Marcos, Alvaro, and Leonardo. Maybe you are pregnant with a boy?" Leo chuckled and shook his head. "What are you laughing at, mijo? You think it's funny that you gave me pains?"

"No, mamá, lo siento." Leo sighed and admitted defeat immediately, as if he had any control over what the fetus version of himself had done in the womb.

"Ooo, Leo's in trouble!" Alvaro called out. Alvaro was a year older than him, but Leo always maintained that he was more mature than his brother.

"You gave me pains, too, Alvaro." Lucia pointed at Alvaro and then at the last remaining son at the table, who was too busy making eyes at his wife to pay attention. "Marcos gave me the most pain, though. I thought we were going to have to get the priest when you came out." The fact that Leo's parents hadn't been to a sermon or a midnight mass in at least fifteen years made no difference. If any of them ever did something wrong growing up, his mother always threatened to call the priest from Our Lady of the Mountain to come down and exorcize the devil from them.

"You still might have to call him." Harper, Marcos' wife, grinned from her place beside her husband. "He gives me headaches all the time."

"Maybe you're just dehydrated." Marcos gave Harper a playful shove with his shoulder.

"I've had lots of fluids today, actually." Harper lifted a prideful finger.

"Coffee does not count, mi amor." Marcos laughed and swept a strand of hair out of her face. The newlyweds that they were, Marcos and Harper always had some sort of physical contact going on. One time, Leo had accidentally walked in on them heavily making out in a back room, so he didn't want to know where their hands were under the table.

"I say it counts," Saanvi decided. Both of Leo's sisters-in-law fit right in with the Diaz family. It made sense considering Saanvi and Harper had been best friends long before either of them had gotten married. Leo's oldest brothers were happily coupled up, while Alvaro stayed vehemently single and seemed to not give two shakes about marriage at all. There was a bit of pressure on Leo's end to get it right when he eventually did marry. Growing up a Diaz meant it was ingrained in him to start a family. While it might be annoying to some, he had always loved the prospect. His family, though chaotic, were his people, and he had always wanted to add a wife and kids into the fold. It was why Alejandro Moreno was his idol. The man had it all: a career, a love life, and now a third kid on the way. Moreno's life proved that Leo could also have it all if he tried hard enough.

"Leo, when are you getting a girlfriend?" Mariana asked from her seat. His sister knew exactly what she was doing when she asked the question, because all eyes immediately trained on him.

Leo opened his mouth to respond and was cut off by Abuelita. "That girl you drove down here with es muy bonita, no?"

Leo held back a groan of annoyance. He could barely even get a word in with his family. By the time he'd backed them down from this particular ledge, there would be a wedding date waiting for him with half the linens picked out. He was still trying to figure out a way to deny that he wanted to date Piper without altogether disagreeing with his grandmother's obvious observation that Piper was attractive when Mariana butted in again.

"Piper?" she squeaked with enthusiasm. "I love her!"

Alvaro cinched his eyebrows together. "I thought he hated Piper?"

"No, no. Aquí no se odia." Mateo, Leo's father, who was usually quiet unless he had something profound to say—in this case, an adamant declaration that the Diaz family weren't the hating kind—finally spoke up. Although Mateo looked slightly menacing and both his jobs, butcher and boxing instructor, involved cutting or punching things, out of everyone in Leo's family, his father was the teddy bear. His laugh boomed like thunder, and he often cried over touching commercials on the TV. "Mari, Varo, let the poor boy speak, will you?"

"Gracias." Leo sighed and massaged his temples. "No tengo novia, y Piper is *definitely* not my girlfriend."

"¿Por qué no?" Abuelita's eyebrows were raised in a way that said she might smack Leo with the nearest utensil or shoe if he didn't answer correctly. He wouldn't put it past her to whack him in the back of the head with the ear of elote on her plate.

"Porque... no le caigo para nada bien," Leo answered carefully. 'Dislike' didn't quite cover Piper's true feelings considering she had blatantly said she hated him, but he didn't want his family to dive too deep into the details.

"Maybe you should be nicer," his mother declared with a slap of her palm on the table. "She drove you here. You should be grateful." Lucia gestured to the table between them topped with a half-carved turkey as if to say *it's Thanksgiving, after all*.

"She only did that because you and her aunt planned the whole thing. If I asked, she would have said no." Leo was glad that he had gotten most of his food down while the attention was on his brothers, or he would never have gotten to eat. As it was, his mother and his grandmother began to list off all the things he should be doing to gain Piper's affections, and he was now the one with the headache. He sat quietly and let them ramble on as his cell phone buzzed in his pocket. In the most discreet way possible, he pulled it free and glanced down at a new text message from Piper. He'd changed her name in his phone out of some weird compulsion after the last few days of back-and-forth texts.

PRINCESA <SUNFLOWER EMOJI> 5:22 PM
It's still there. I will never forgive you.

He made sure no one was looking when he sent a quick response back.

LEO 5:23 PM
I'm not sure what you're referring to.

He grinned down at the lie he had sent and followed it up with another text.

LEO 5:23 PM
I think my abuelita is onto me. Did you do something to me?

PRINCESA <SUNFLOWER EMOJI> 5:24 PM
I did many things to you. You're going to have to be more specific.

The chortle that came out of Leo's mouth was a mistake, a grave error he realized immediately when it interrupted whatever conversation his mother and grandmother were having. Once again, all eyes were on him.

"Who are you texting?" Marcos leaned over his shoulder to try to sneak a peek at his phone.

Leo quickly locked it. "No one."

"Princesa?" Marcos teased. Leo cursed himself for not having faster reflexes. "I'm gonna assume that's Piper."

"Leonardo Rafael Diaz, ¿que les he dicho de celulares en la

mesa?" Leo's mother pointed at him, and he quickly pocketed his phone with a glare at his brother for drawing attention to him. She had full-named him, so she meant business.

"Wait, hold on." Harper leaned over the table to look at Leo. "This is Piper Hartrick, right? As in Walker and Talia's niece? Colin Hartrick's sister?"

Intrigued, Leo peered around Marcos to speak with his sister-in-law. "You know her brother?"

"I know of him. I met him a total of one time when I walked in on him and my sister, Scarlett, doing *things*." Her voice was low, like she was sharing a secret.

"I assume those were adult things." Leo chuckled. Given what he knew of Colin's exploits and Piper's other brother—thanks to Piper's fifteen-minute rant on the second leg of the trip about how Carter wouldn't be joining her family for Thanksgiving—the Hartricks seemed to be a clusterfuck when it came to their love lives.

"She was depressed for a solid year after they graduated high school because of him." The tone said that Harper was not Colin's biggest fan, and for some reason, Leo felt oddly defensive of the guy he didn't even know.

"I mean, people can change, though, right?" Leo argued. "Piper said he just got an internship at a cancer research lab, and he was the top of his class at Johns Hopkins. He knows an extreme amount about sunflower seeds. Maybe he's not so bad anymore?" He didn't know what the sunflower seed bit had to do with anything, but he couldn't imagine it worked against his argument.

"Their aunt and uncle are good people," Leo's mother agreed. "So were their parents. It's a shame what happened to them."

That statement put a damper on the conversation, and everyone went painfully silent. It had been big news in town back when the accident happened. Leo's family had just moved to Archwood six months prior so his grandmother could get into the oncology center one city over. His parents had felt guilty for being employed at Lydia's Grocery at the time because though the man who'd caused the accident had barely touched his own business before his death, they had still legally been his employees. There seemed to be a mass community of guilt associated with Cole and Paisley Hartrick's death because Jeff Cohen had always been a drunk, and no one had stopped him from doing the unthinkable.

"You should invite her for dinner." Leo's mom finally broke the silence, plaguing the table with the absolute last thing Leo wanted to do.

He dropped his fork. "¿Pero por qué?"

"As a thank you for driving you down." Now that his mom had gotten started, Leo could see that her eyes were backlit with the spark of an idea she wasn't going to let go easily. "She has no mother or father, Leonardo, and everyone could use más familia."

"Mamá, no creo—"

"I will make tamales!" Abuelita chimed in with a level of excitement Leo knew he couldn't curb.

"No, no," Leo waved his hands around. "Mira, she hates me. Really, *really* hates me."

"Mm-hmm. ¿Por qué? ¿Qué hiciste?" Abuelita cocked her head with her eyebrows arched. The fact that she thought he had done something to deserve Piper's torment wasn't surprising, but her next question said she knew exactly the nature of his and Piper's weird relationship, and that terrified him. "You had no fun on the drive?"

Leo swallowed. "It wasn't... no fue tan malo." It was far from horrible. He'd never come so hard before, and he would probably use the memories from that one night alone to fuel all his sexual fantasies for the rest of his life. The horrible part was that he couldn't stop thinking about it or about Piper, and inviting her anywhere near him while he tried to tamp down his thoughts was a bad idea.

"It's settled, then." His mother smiled. "Text her and let her know to come tomorrow." Leo just stared back at her, still trying to find a way out of this. "¡Ya!" Lucia pointed her finger at him in a direct command to get the ball rolling.

"You said no phones at the table, and—"

"*Leo*," his father warned.

"Fine," Leo muttered, whipping his phone back out of his pocket. He tapped out a message to Piper somewhat aggressively.

> LEO 5:58 PM
>
> Dinner tomorrow at 6. My house. I'll pick you up so you don't have to drive. Cover up.

The three little dots indicating Piper was typing popped up immediately, and Leo held his breath, waiting for her response. Meanwhile, his family had moved on to harassing Alvaro about his grades in college, and no one noticed that Leo's life was flashing before his eyes. The text bubble disappeared and reappeared three times before he finally got a response.

> PRINCESA <SUNFLOWER EMOJI> 6:00 PM
>
> Excuse me?

Leo scrunched his eyes shut, then peeled them back open to stare down at the message for several long seconds before tapping out a follow-up.

> LEO 6:01 PM
>
> My mom decided you needed a thank you dinner. Cover the mark before I pick you up.

> PRINCESA <SUNFLOWER EMOJI> 6:02 PM
>
> Oh, you mean the hickey you didn't give me? I think I'll leave it uncovered.

> LEO 6:02 PM
>
> I'm sorry, okay? I got a little carried away. Please cover it.

PRINCESA <SUNFLOWER EMOJI> 6:03 PM
See you at 6.

Leo had enough mental forethought to recognize that Piper did not altogether agree to his terms, and he let out a long, anxiety-ridden sigh.

Thirty-One

LEO

At first glance, the olive green house looked like every rich person's house, matching the neighboring ones and so clean it looked like a show house for a realty company. That was what rich people were always good at, anyway—showing off their wealth. Leo's impression morphed into curiosity with each step he took closer to Piper Hartrick's childhood home. There were seemingly random, yet cohesive pops of colorful flowers lining the yard and lanterns hanging from poles that lit the way to the front door. On the contrary, when Leo used to tutor in high school, other rich people's homes seemed to showboat their immaculately cut grass and clean lines. This house let some of the colors overflow from the flowerbeds and climb the railing to the covered patio. Everything seemed to point directly to the front door, as if to tell the world that comfort and joy were waiting inside.

The concrete slab step landing by the door had two large handprints above five smaller ones, where each of the Hatrick siblings' names were scrawled permanently into the concrete. Piper's father Cole's handprint had a smiley face drawn into the palm. Leo found Piper's tiny hand and couldn't help but smile down at it before he brushed over it with an oddly gentle slide of his shoe. The tattered doormat below the black door was something straight out of a dad joke manual, reading, "Hello, I'm Mat." Leo let out a small chuckle before lifting his fist to the door to knock.

The door opened soon after to Piper's tattooed and grumpy-looking uncle. Leo's only prior interaction with the man had been an entertaining one, but he could now see why Piper's ex-boyfriend, Harden, had basically run for the hills when Walker had confronted him back in high school, because the way he was staring at Leo now said he was not his biggest fan.

"*You*," Walker said.

"Me." Leo nodded, unsure of what else to say. Wordlessly, Walker widened the door for Leo to step inside but barely moved out of the way, so Leo had to do an awkward side-shuffle to get in without touching him.

"Piper will be down in a second," Walker grumbled and waved him farther into the foyer.

The pointillist painting of the open book Piper had mentioned hung over a long wooden shelf lined with multiple copies of the same five books. Instead of following Walker into the kitchen, Leo stopped in front of the painting. Piper was right—it felt exactly like how his brain worked.

"I got that for my wife at the coffee house down the way." Walker stayed in the foyer with him, tone sharp, but Leo wasn't one to get intimidated.

"Piper told me. I've never been inside, but my sister-in-law manages it, and she gets a lot of art from her sister's shop." Leo took a step closer to the painting, his narrowing field of vision separating the pieces and showing him the dots that made up the whole picture.

"Harper." Walker nodded. "She hangs out with Talia and Amala sometimes."

Leo dragged his finger along the spines of the matching books and quirked an eyebrow at the author's name. "You wrote these?"

"Mm-hmm."

"*The Dating Brigade*." Leo read a spine aloud. "What's the genre?"

"Romantic suspense," Walker replied shortly. The conversation was going absolutely nowhere, so Leo buckled down. In the blunt way in which he did everything, he turned on his heel to face the man directly.

"Clearly, you don't like me, so let's hear it." Leo waved a hand out to Walker.

"What makes you say that?" Walker asked.

"The extremely warm welcome," Leo deadpanned.

"I don't really make a habit of liking anyone Piper dates because they tend to be—"

"Assholes?" Leo finished for him. "Completely agree on that front, but I think we've previously established that. To your other point, we aren't dating and won't ever be."

"Then I already know you aren't treating her with respect." Walker folded his arms over his broad chest.

Leo knew he should be embarrassed about the hickey if that was what Walker was alluding to, but Piper was a full-ass adult, and Leo wasn't about to apologize to her protective uncle for something she had consented to. "Did she *say* she was disrespected?"

Walker blinked but said nothing, and that was all the response Leo needed. There was no way Piper had said anything because, out of the two of them, Leo was the one who had been disrespected—not that he was complaining, but he unfortunately seemed to be very into degradation when Piper wasn't wearing any clothes. "I'd never force a woman to do anything. Ever. Now that we've gotten that over with, how much romance is in this book, exactly?" Leo pulled *The Dating Brigade* off the shelf and stared down at the blue cover. A feminine hand held a bouquet of flowers down on a cutting board while a large block knife, like the one Leo's dad used at the butcher counter, sliced through the flowers. At the cut, a pool of blood seeped from the stems. The cover alone sold the book.

"You got a problem with romance novels?" Walker questioned.

"On the contrary." Leo thumbed through the pages. "I don't really read anything that's not a script, but my roommate, Sam, is obsessed with smutty books. I was trying to see if I should tell him to read it. Is this one mostly romance or mostly suspense?"

Walker shifted, his mood seeming to lighten a little. "It's really hard to explain. The back cover description was probably the hardest part of the book to write. Romance is a big element of the book, and there's plenty of smut, but it's not just about the romance. The suspense part of it feels a bit like the Hardy Boys or Nancy Drew but more adult, with higher stakes and a psychological element to it."

"Does it have an ambiguous ending? Because Sam will kill me if I tell him to read something that doesn't end with a happily ever after."

"It has a happily ever after." Walker chuckled. "You can just take that one. I hate that my wife displays my books in the front of the house like some sort of weird altar, anyway. Maybe if I keep handing them out for free, she'll put them back on the bookshelf in the living room."

"We've been over this, honey." Piper's aunt strode into the foyer, and Walker's posture relaxed even more as she came to stand beside him. "I'm proud of you, and those are staying right there." Talia turned to Leo conversationally. "I assume he tried to threaten you?"

"Hey!" Walker complained and reached up to tug on Talia's ponytail.

"I told you to leave him alone. But, fair warning to you," Talia swiveled to look at Leo, "Piper's feeling a bit murderous about the stunt you pulled, so I'd watch out for her."

"I can handle her." Leo shrugged.

"No *handling* anything." Walker mean-mugged Leo.

"She's upstairs in her room if you feel like knocking on death's door." Talia grinned. "Feel free to piss her off. She could use a bit of a fight."

Leo looked up the stairs and gave a quick jerk of his head in confirmation before scaling the steps.

"And Leo?" Walker called out.

"Yeah?"

"Leave the door open, or Piper won't need to kill you."

"Fantastic," Leo huffed under his breath as he reached the top step.

"First door on the right!" Talia shouted. Leo found the door easy enough and knocked gently on it.

"Come in!" Piper's voice called out. When Leo pushed open the door, Piper sat up abruptly in her bed, blue eyes locked on him in surprise. "Leo? Shit, what time is it?"

"It's five-thirty." He wandered in and scanned his surroundings, attempting to act casual about the way he needed to fill in this gap in his brain, to know what her room had looked like in high school after she came home from a long day of getting on his nerves. It was simple and clean, but there were pieces of Piper that said this was her space. The whiteboard calendar sitting on her wooden desk was blank except for the week of Thanksgiving, filled with color-coded descriptions and times, like she had come home and immediately sat down to schedule her next few days. *Dinner w/ Leo 6 PM* was written on today's date. "I'm early, and I figured I should make sure that you weren't serious about leaving my gift on your neck."

"It's almost gone." Piper rolled off the bed haphazardly, stumbling up to her feet. She gestured to her neck, and Leo stepped closer, lifting his hand. The urge to touch her sparked in his fingertips.

"Can I see?" he asked. He tried to make his voice sound teasing, but it came out breathy. "I think it's best if my family doesn't ask any questions."

Piper rolled her eyes and brushed her hair to the side, exposing more of her neck to him, and he remembered why he had originally wanted to suck on it so badly. She had made a little gasping sound when he did it the first time, and he imagined he could have her making the same sound again. His thumb brushed over the spot he knew was there but was now barely visible.

"Good enough for your standards?" Piper whispered.

"I can't see it." If he was being honest, the fact that he couldn't was disappointing. Some strange part of him wanted her body marked by what they did the other night forever, and maybe that was why his hand traveled to cup the back of her head. Piper's breathing grew shallow as her eyes met his, and that electric feeling that had taken over the last time pooled at his spine.

"Piper, do you have a pen somewhere?" A tall blond man with large wire-rimmed glasses stepped into the room and immediately went to Piper's desk without taking notice of Leo and Piper's proximity. Leo dropped his hand away from Piper and took a large step back. Colin had been a year ahead of him in school, but Leo still recognized him.

"The good ones are in the drawer," Piper said. Her previously shaky voice went right back to normal, as if the moment they'd just had never existed.

"Black ink?" Colin asked. "I'm taking notes on apartment listings."

"Yeah, there should be some in there."

"Colin, right?" Leo asked when Colin came out of the drawer victoriously with a black-inked pen. Leo stuck out his hand. "I'm Leo."

"Oh, I know who you are." Colin hesitated for a moment, then shook Leo's hand. "You slept with Piper, and she used to complain about you all the time in high school."

Leo choked on his spit. "Right to the point, I guess."

"*Colin,*" Piper drew out her brother's name in an embarrassed whine and pressed her fingers into her forehead.

It didn't seem like Colin was put off by any of the reasons he stated for knowing who Leo was, so Leo continued. "I know who you are, too. My sisters-in-law don't seem to like you very much. You seem all right to me, though. Did you use to date Scarlett Wallace?"

Colin's face lost all its color, then flipped to worry. "Does Scarlett hate me? We didn't date. We—she made that very clear."

"I'm sure she doesn't hate you, Col," Piper soothed and then glared at Leo like he'd just purposely walked into a field of landmines.

"So, apartment hunting?" Leo's segue into a new topic of conversation wasn't great, but it would have to do. "Where are you moving?"

"Back to Archwood. The research facility I got into is in Merrick," Colin explained.

"Plus, you love us and want to see us more," Piper teased.

"Everyone I love is here," Colin agreed.

"Ah." Leo nodded. "My family moved here for the oncology center in Merrick, so that makes sense that the research center is close."

Piper jerked her head toward Leo. "Why? Who—?"

"My abuelita," Leo explained. He was a bit surprised by her reaction. It was almost like she had thought for a second it could be him who was sick.

"What's her diagnosis?" Colin asked.

"Adenoid cystic carcinoma," Leo recited. Medical jargon was not his forte, but Wes had helped him a bit with learning what some of it meant when Abuelita had started chemo again. There was a moment after she was diagnosed when the same focus Leo had for film had gone directly into researching cancer, as if he could magically change any outcome with a Google search. His brothers had had to forcibly pull him out of that rabbit hole at the time because WebMD had him convinced that the world was burning and everything was a deep, dark pit of despair.

Colin tipped his head to the side. "That's rare. I assume it metastasized?"

It took Leo a second to remember what that meant, but then

he nodded. "She had surgery for it a while back, and then it came back with a vengeance. She's doing pretty well right now, though."

"Good," Colin murmured and got a far-off look in his eyes, like he was searching for information in his brain. Behind his thick glasses, Colin's eyes were the same color as Piper's, and Leo wondered which one of their parents had given them such a daunting shade of blue. While Piper's eyes were bright and happy, with a hidden layer of sadness, Colin's held wisdom and also some discomfort under the surface. His posture was perfect, but it looked forced, and he kept fiddling with his hands like he was unsure what to do with them. "My work will be centered around acute myeloid leukemia in children, but, if I recall correctly, adenoid cystic carcinoma has a fairly long life expectancy with chemotherapy, even at stage four."

"That's what I've been told," Leo said. "She's at stage four, but it's been seven years since she was diagnosed, and she's still kicking cancer's ass." Something squeezed his bicep, and he looked down to find Piper's hand there. He had no idea how long she had been massaging her thumb into his arm in slow strokes, or if she even knew she was doing it, but it was strangely comforting, so he leaned into her touch. Colin said nothing, just started to tap the pen he was holding against his thigh in a nervous tic. His eyes kept flicking to Piper as if he were looking for permission to be done with the conversation. "Anyway, we have to get going," Leo said, giving Colin an out.

"Right." Colin saluted him with the pen, then stalked out of the room, looking relieved.

Leo turned to Piper as soon as Colin was out of earshot and glanced down at her hand, still holding his arm. "So, I'm a household name? How often do you talk about me, princesita?"

Piper ripped her hand back. "This is what I get for trying to be nice to you." Each word was laced with poison, and she trudged out of her room without a second glance. Her reaction made Leo inwardly smile as he followed her down the stairs. It was a bit of a sport to him now to get her riled up. The last time she had been so confident, he was kneeling between her legs and craving every order that passed through her lips.

Piper pushed past her aunt and uncle to get to the front door when she reached the bottom of the staircase. Walker stumbled back out of her way, muttering "Jesus" under his breath as Leo passed beside an extremely amused Talia. Leo caught the door just in time with his shoe before Piper was able to slam it in his face. With a dramatic bow in Walker and Talia's direction, Leo stepped through the doorway and closed the door behind him, his eyes locking on the angry blonde leaning against the passenger side of his parents' car. Dinner was either going to be a blast or an absolute disaster.

Thirty-Two

PIPER

As much as she could, Piper stayed vehemently silent on the way to Leo's house. The cold shoulder treatment was working out well for her. Leo was a worthy adversary, shooting her antagonistic looks the entire drive to see if she would crack. Truthfully, she was worried that if they spoke, she would end up straddling him on a back road instead of making it to dinner. The stalled moment they had shared in her room was not doing much to make her think that this night was going to end the way it should.

When they pulled up to the curb in front of the house, Piper couldn't help but smile at the cozy one-story tucked into the cul-de-sac. There was an old red truck with chipping paint parked in the driveway, its hood popped as a man leaned over the engine. He was yanking on something with a tool, his muscles taut with tension. Leo parked and unbuckled, practically throwing himself out of the car.

"Yo te ayudo," Leo said before slamming his door and jogging over to his dad. Piper watched him for a moment before she opened the passenger door just in time to hear the back half of Mateo's response.

"¡—que falta de respeto!" He sounded mildly angry, which was odd considering every time Piper had ever been inside Lydia's, Mateo had been the epitome of kindness—nothing like his son. She was even more surprised when Mateo turned to call out to her over Leo's shoulder. "I apologize for my son's rudeness. He should have opened your door."

"Oh." Piper blinked. "Uh, no problem. I can open my own door."

"You are our guest, and we treat our guests better than that." Mateo smiled kindly and then tossed a scolding look at Leo.

"You looked like you were struggling," Leo huffed, his shoulders shrinking a bit.

"Mira, you think you could do better?" Mateo's tone turned teasing as Piper met them by the rusted truck.

"I know I could." Leo set his shoulders back. "You've got a lot of gray hair now, viejo."

"Who are you calling old man? I'll be stronger than you on my deathbed. But since you want to show off, toma." Mateo tossed a wrench at Leo, who caught it easily and grinned as he bent over the hood. Piper had exactly zero mechanic skills and had no idea what Leo was doing, but he seemed to be unscrewing something. As Leo frustratedly yanked on the wrench, Mateo leaned conspiratorially toward her and murmured, "He thinks he's so strong, but he forgets that I'm the one who taught him how to get all that strength."

Piper giggled as Leo grunted and finally pulled the bolt loose. He rose to his full height with a cocky grin. "What was that?"

Mateo scoffed and shook his head as Leo passed the wrench back. "Go inside and help your mother. And introduce your girl this time. You are lucky I already know who she is."

"I'm not his girl." The words shot out of Piper's mouth like a cannonball at the same time Leo groaned, "¡No es mi novia!"

Mateo whistled and lifted both hands, wrench included. "My mistake. Go inside and introduce your not-girlfriend to everyone, then."

Leo blew out an aggravated breath through his nose, and Piper couldn't help but wonder what conversations Leo had had about her when she wasn't present. Maybe she was a household name in his home. A warm hand pressed into the small of her back to guide her to the front door, and it felt so intimate that it made her consider telling everyone she was sick and running home. The hand placement was exactly where it had been in the hotel room when Leo wanted to push into her deeper. She stuttered a step at the thought, and he seemed to think better of touching her, the warmth of his palm leaving a second later as they walked the rest of the way to the front door.

Tall shrubbery had blocked most of Piper's view of the house when they'd shown up, but she could see it all now. The light blue siding and white door had new paint, but it did nothing to hide the weathered, lived-in look of the house. She loved it. As an interior designer, houses and rooms looked better when they evoked good feelings and memories instead of making you feel like you had to take your shoes off for fear of dirtying anything up. Her mom used to say a house was not a home unless you could see yourself living in it. Things could both be orderly and hold meaning. While the color combinations were outdated, and the unstained oak light fixture above the door looked to be from the seventies, everything about Leo's home screamed family, or "familia," as the tattered doormat at her feet read.

Leo turned the knob and threw his shoulder into the door to pop it open. Piper held back a smile at the knowledge that he seemed to have a sticky front door, too. "We're here!" he yelled.

"En la cocina!" a woman's voice called back.

No one was in the living room, but Piper barely got a glance at the brown sofa and carpeting and the oak end tables before Leo pushed her into the kitchen. Beside Leo's sister, Mariana, who Piper knew from her soccer days, was Lucia, Leo's mom, hovering over a giant metal bowl filled with water and corn husks that sat on the tan laminate countertop. An older woman with a sunflower-patterned headscarf sat in a wheelchair at the rectangular dining table with an even bigger bowl of white batter that looked to have the consistency of smooth peanut butter.

"Everyone, this is Piper," Leo announced with a wave of his hand in her direction. "Piper, this is my m—"

"Piper! So good to see you again." Lucia beamed and wiped her hands off on a nearby towel before throwing her arms out to hug Piper. Piper leaned into it with a smile. While Mateo was mostly quiet behind the butcher counter at Lydia's, Lucia was always outgoing and never hesitated to hug her when Piper ventured into the grocery store. Talia had told Piper several stories about the bull-headed way Lucia had challenged a few of the store's vendors that had failed to deliver shipments on time or in good condition. She was a powerhouse of a woman and fully deserving of the managerial position.

"I don't know if you remember me." Mariana raised her hand shyly and stepped toward Piper as she pulled out of the embrace with Lucia.

"Of course I remember you," Piper said. "You were a machine on the soccer field. Do you still play?" Mariana was a few years younger than Piper and Leo but had made the varsity team at Archwood High her freshman year. She and Scarlett Wallace were the forward duo of everyone's dreams. Piper, on the other hand, was a defender and often benched for not being aggressive enough. Being a klutz didn't help, either. Mariana was quiet but could easily throw a shoulder to toss an opposing player to the ground and come out with the ball in her possession.

"Yeah, I got a scholarship to play at Oregon State." Mariana beamed.

"That's awesome, but I'm not surprised. You deserve it," Piper said.

Leo had the same dark eyes and thick eyelashes as Mariana. Her hair was wavy, a few escaped strands coiling around her face and the rest pulled back into a French braid just like Lucia beside her, but Lucia's hair had strands and sections that were washed out and shining silver against the yellow kitchen lighting. While

Mariana's features had the same intensity as Leo's, hers were feminine in their sharpness. She could have been Leo's twin with how beautiful she was. If Piper recalled correctly, Alvaro, one of Leo's older brothers who had been a year ahead of her in school, was more of the same. It was the strangest thing to know how all those curls must feel, soft and thick, just like Leo's had felt when she had tangled her fingers in them.

"And this is my abuelita, Isabel." Leo made the introduction as if Isabel were the most highly esteemed person in the family, and when she wheeled out from under the table, Piper knew why. The confidence in her mannerisms was the same as Leo's.

"Ah, so you are the woman my grandson is secretly pining after?" Isabel asked.

Piper's mouth dropped open as she twisted her head to Leo, who practically leaped forward to set a hand on Isabel's shoulder. "No, Abuelita, this is Piper. The one I don't like. At all. In any way, shape, or form."

"Wow," Piper scoffed. "I'm so flattered. Would you like to insult anything else while you're at it?" Leo legitimately looked her up and down like he might do just that.

"Mmm," Isabel snorted and gave Leo a wry smile. "Eres igual de terco que tu abuelo. El amor no respeta la ley, ni obedece a rey." Piper looked to Leo to translate, catching none of Isabel's quick-off-the-tongue remark, but Leo just clenched his jaw and folded his arms over his chest, glaring at his grandmother. Isabel ignored him and made eye contact with Piper again, raising her thin hand to gesture to a large bowl on the table. "Would you like to learn how to make tamales?"

For the next hour, Piper sat at the table watching Isabel carefully craft tamales out of the masa mixture. Isabel's veiny hands shook a bit as she formed the right shape in the damp corn husks and spooned in the seasoned pork, but she swatted away Leo's hands any time he tried to help her. Piper had no qualms about this woman's capabilities—cancer clearly had nothing on Isabel's strong will. Out of everyone Piper had met that day, it was blatantly obvious where Leo got his attitude from, in addition to his confidence. Everything Isabel said was either blunt or teasing. She had a laugh that defied her sickly appearance, and the longer Piper sat at the table, the less Isabel looked frail and breakable. Isabel wasn't fighting for her life; she was bursting with it.

Thirty-Three

LEO

By the time the tamales were done and all of his brothers and their wives had shown up for dinner, it was pitch-black outside, and Leo's stomach was eating itself. The smell that wafted from the steamer made him groan with impatience. Piper, for what it was worth, hadn't complained once about just how long it took his family to sit their asses down at the dinner table. Between his desire for food and his brothers' constant underhanded remarks about the nature of his and Piper's relationship, Leo was about ready to bite someone's head off. He had gotten so used to eating something unheated out of a can for ninety-nine cents, it was pathetic how much his stomach was clawing at him to eat something real.

"So, Piper, what are you in school for?" Alvaro asked when they all finally made it to the table. His tone was a bit on the flirty side, and Leo didn't care for it.

"Interior design," Leo answered for her and shot Alvaro an indignant look that screamed *keep it in your pants, asshole*. Alvaro just grinned and shoved half a tamal in his mouth.

"I'm double majoring in business, too," Piper added from

Leo's right. Sitting next to her was a terrible decision he had made out of some misguided attempt to keep her away from his intrusive brothers. His fingers itched to touch her. She was wearing a purple cable-knit dress that matched her lavender-tipped hair and white knee-high socks with brown riding boots. He wanted to see her wearing only the socks, like something straight out of a schoolgirl fantasy.

"Ah, so you're smart *and* beautiful," Alvaro cooed.

"Maybe she could tutor you so you don't fail another course, Varo," their mother chimed in. Leo bit back a smirk at Lucia's comment, which immediately killed Alvaro's game.

"Piper's mom actually did the design for the whole coffee shop," Harper said.

"We'll have to have you over to the house soon to look at our third bedroom," Saanvi said to Piper, then turned to Leo's brother. "Right, Antonio?"

Antonio had just taken a large bite of tamal and choked it back quickly to answer. "Right." He nodded, then looked fondly at his wife. "We have a bit of an idea, but it'd be cool to have a professional take a look."

"Really?" Piper wasn't hiding her excitement well, leaning over the table with eager eyes. "I-I mean, yeah. That'd be cool. I'm working on building up my portfolio right now, so I'd be happy to do it for free." Leo frowned but kept his mouth shut. Piper was always undercutting herself and devaluing her work, and it was starting to grate on his nerves. "You don't even have to take my advice if you don't like it. It's not a big deal."

"Piper," Leo snapped. His entire family swiveled their heads away from their separate conversations. Piper shrunk, folding her arms over her chest, her obvious tell that she was now uncomfortable. "I—sorry." Leo swallowed, dividing his eye contact between Antonio and Saanvi. "You should definitely take her advice and pay her for it. She's helping with the set design for the musical. I've seen her work, and she's really good. And *you*," his gaze landed on Piper, who had a dazed expression on her face. "I know you're capable of standing up for yourself, so stop selling yourself short. It's irritating."

Piper dropped her fork onto her plate with a clank and glared at him. "I was being nice, Leo. Not that you would know what that's like."

"Damn," Marcos whispered, trying to hold back a laugh. "I think you've met your match, Leo."

Then, because his family was ruthless, they all hopped on the Piper train and ganged up on him.

"Yeah, Leo, lighten up! You're such a sourpuss." Mariana grinned.

"You know, if you keep frowning like that, your face is going to stay that way permanently," Alvaro warned in his best fatherly tone.

"What he needs is a woman to keep him in line." Abuelita pointed a bony finger in the air.

"He is capable of smiling, I swear." Leo's mother looked right past him to Piper, who was cackling at everyone's antics. Lucia then turned to Leo. "Where did I fail you? Did you not receive enough attention as a baby?"

"I dropped him once," Mateo offered.

Lucia shook her head. "No, that was Alvaro."

"So that's why I failed that one class," Alvaro cut in and then winked at Piper.

The fork Leo was gripping hard enough to bend dug into his palm. "No, it's because you didn't study and you were too busy screwing around with whoever you were seeing at the time." It might have been in poor taste for Leo to bring up Alvaro's propensity to bounce around from relationship to relationship, but he wanted to take an ax to his brother's flirtation and chop it off at the knees. Alvaro wasn't good enough for Piper. No one was, but Alvaro especially, because Leo couldn't stomach the idea of his brother touching someone who was his, even if Piper had only been his for one night.

The teasing atmosphere at the table died off with Leo's biting remark, and Alvaro looked pissed. "Do you need help taking that stick out of your ass?" he asked.

"¡Se calman o los calmo!" Their mother snapped her fingers and jabbed one at Alvaro.

"You two can have it out in the ring tomorrow, but for now, you will apologize to our guest for being so rude." Leo's father was calm, but Leo could easily see the fury written behind his eyes as he flicked his gaze between Leo and Alvaro.

"Sorry." Alvaro's apology to Piper was less than enthusiastic, with a sidelong glance at Leo for getting him into the mess in the first place.

Out of all his siblings, Leo sparred with Alvaro the most. They had shared a room for seventeen years. They were also complete opposites. Alvaro was charismatic, made friends with everyone, and wore bright colors. Leo had a select few friends and preferred black. Despite all of that, Alvaro was still the person Leo confided in the most, so when his brother looked his way, Leo took a deep breath and set his hand on the back of Piper's chair. It was the most truth he could offer at that moment. He had no idea what this thing was with Piper, and she still frustrated him to no end, but there was something magnetic about the way his body wanted to touch her. Something ferocious about the jealousy that gnawed at his insides when someone much more in line with Piper's characteristics also noticed how beautiful she was.

Alvaro gave him an almost imperceivable nod, the corner of his mouth twitching slightly. Leo turned to Piper next. She was shyly folding her napkin into a perfect triangle and not looking at him.

"Hey," Leo murmured and tucked a finger under her chin so she'd meet his gaze. Her eyes were large pools of blue he wanted to drown in, and guilt clawed up his chest for making dinner so uncomfortable for her. "I'm sorry for being a," he paused for a second and opted for appropriate phrasing in front of his parents, "jerk." Realizing that his fingers were still propped under her chin, he quickly dropped them and avoided every single one of his family members' gazes.

"It's fine." Piper traded her discomfort for the fake smile she always wore, and Leo's stomach dropped. Unless it was on stage, he fucking hated that smile.

"I'm gonna use the restroom," Leo announced, yanking his chair back from the table. His entire family watched him with rapt attention, mouths all slightly parted except Abuelita. She sat in her wheelchair at the other end of the table with a knowing smirk as Leo stomped off toward the bathroom.

Thirty-Four

PIPER

Soon after Leo abandoned Piper at the table, the Diaz family started to clean up dinner. They were adamant that she not lift a finger to help, so she sat with her hands in her lap, stewing over her dispute with Leo. She wished she were allowed to help with the cleanup just so she would have something to do to stop her unraveling thoughts. Leo's abrupt exit seemed to be more of an excuse to get away from her than anything else, and she couldn't place whether he was rethinking holding his hand to her face or if he was pissed about her reaction to his apology.

Instead of doing anything productive, Piper did what she did best and overthought everything. What was bothering her most was not Leo's apology—that seemed genuine enough—it was that he had been right in the first place, even if he had said it in his usual bark. She had taken a budding opportunity to create and do something she loved and snuffed out the embers. Interior design was not just her hobby, and yet, she had acted like it was some side gig she wasn't good at or capable of. If she kept this up, none of her employees would ever respect her. She had the talent, she knew she did, but she found herself always trying her best to make sure no one knew about it.

A thump against the table beside Piper had her looking up from her fidgeting hands. Isabel's wheelchair had hit one of the legs of the table, rattling the dirty dishes still atop it. She offered Piper a warm smile.

"You'd think after the last three years of wheeling myself around I would know how to use it." Isabel wheeled back a bit from where the tire had connected with the table.

"Well, I've had my legs for twenty-one years, and that doesn't stop me from running into every coffee table I can find." Piper chuckled.

Isabel's strong laugh surprised Piper, though it shouldn't have, considering how strong Isabel's personality was. When her laughter died down, she yanked out the chair Leo had been sitting earlier in to make space for her wheelchair and pulled up beside Piper. "What are you thinking about over here?" Isabel asked. Her accent was thick, and her voice had a motherly tone to it.

"Is it that obvious?" Piper sighed and ran a hand through her hair, tactfully avoiding eye contact.

"About as obvious as Leo leaving the table to definitely not use the bathroom," Isabel said. "Are you rethinking what he said?"

"As much as he annoys me—" Piper blanched, realizing it was rude to say that to one of his family members, and tried to backtrack. "Sorry, I just mean..."

"Psh, he *is* annoying," Isabel scoffed, unoffended. With a secret smile, Isabel leaned toward Piper a bit. "He's as stubborn as an ox, and he frequently puts his foot in his mouth. You don't have to take it back when it's the truth."

The nerves fell away when Piper smiled back at her. "I guess you know him better than I do. But... I think, for once, even though he was a brute about it, he's right. I do tend to undersell my work. I wouldn't mind a portfolio boost, but I acted like I'm not good at what I do, and that's not true. I helped my mom with that coffee shop when I was thirteen, and they kept some of my original ideas in the final design." Piper sighed and shrugged her shoulders.

"Why do you think you do that?" Isabel cocked her head in a gesture of curiosity more than pity.

"I didn't always. I'm sure you know that my parents aren't around?" Piper asked. Isabel nodded. "People were constantly asking me how I felt right after it happened or blaming any of my reactions to things on the fact that my mom and dad died. I started to notice pretty quickly that people were only looking for one answer, so I gave them that answer. That I was fine. And I get it, because who wants to talk about an uncomfortable subject like that?" It was oddly comforting to share a small piece of herself with Leo's grandmother. Despite the stern facial features and harsh lines, Isabel had a calmness that radiated off her like a warm blanket. She was listening intently and hadn't interrupted Piper once, not even to continually bob her head in the usual way people did when they were pretending to listen. She didn't need to outwardly prove she was listening because Piper could tell she was. "I lost friends pretty quickly when everyone realized that I wasn't fun to be around, so I changed that. My brother told me that brains can be tricked into being happy if you practice smiling, and a lot of the time, it works. But I started to wonder what other things I was annoying people with, and I guess I got so far out of control with trying to not be a burden that I constantly feel the need to discount all my achievements so people know that they don't have to show up for me."

"Mmm," Isabel gave Piper a considerate look and seemed to ponder something before she spoke again. In the background, Leo's family had started up some salsa music, and they cleaned and talked over it to each other. Despite the background noise, Piper felt like she was in a quiet bubble with Isabel. "I've been a burden for seven years now," she finally said, and reached up to touch the sunflower-patterned scarf covering her head. "I was usually the person who helped others. I was loud and proud about my accomplishments because someone needed to be. But then I got sick, and for years I didn't allow anyone to coddle me or help me. I wanted to do it all myself because I knew I could, and I didn't need anyone telling me I was weak. I got out of my abusive childhood home on my own. I taught myself English for work. I raised a family on pennies. I survived the loss of my husband. I can still make the damn tamales." Isabel laughed, and Piper giggled with her at the thought of Leo repeatedly getting his hands slapped away when he had tried to help her earlier. "I *can* do everything on my own, but I don't have to. I've learned that the people who help me when my body or my spirit are weak don't find me to be a burden. My daughter once told me that my stubbornness to not take the help was the real burden." Piper considered that for a moment before Isabel continued.

"My body is weak, but my soul is strong. Your body is strong, Piper, but your soul is suffering. There are people in your life who see that and who won't find you to be a burden. If you don't already have them—and I know there is at least one person who seems to care so much that he had to leave the table—then you find them. The world tells us not to take up space, but if we don't, then we don't exist. You are allowed to be sad or angry or proud, and the right people will value you no matter what you feel." Isabel rolled out from under the table, grabbed Leo's dirty dish that he had left in his exit, and set it on her lap. Piper watched as she pushed toward the kitchen and looked back over her shoulder. "We are only here for a little while. Take up the space, Piper." And with that, Isabel wheeled into the chaos unfolding in the kitchen.

A fast-paced Spanish song blared through an old speaker sitting on the counter, and when Piper finally tuned in to her surroundings, she smiled at the scene. Leo's parents were spinning around in the small space between the countertops, swinging their hips in a salsa dance while Alvaro scrubbed at a dish in the sink. Mariana was dancing on her own in the small open space where the hallway turned into the living room, where Leo's remaining two brothers and their wives were talking animatedly in the corner.

"At some point, we're going to need to get you a dishwasher," Alvaro groaned to his mother as he aggressively scrubbed at the dish Isabel had handed him. Lucia moved away from her husband, still flicking her hips back and forth as she danced over to her son.

"I already have two dishwashers." Lucia smiled, then grabbed Alvaro's soapy wrists, holding his hands in the air. "They're right here."

"Ha. Ha." Alvaro rolled his eyes as Lucia snickered and danced back to her husband.

The whole scene felt familiar to Piper. It was equal parts lovely and agonizing to watch. Like a fond memory clouded with something painful. Mateo spun Lucia under his arm and grinned at her as she twirled, like she was the sun and he couldn't help but stare directly into it. It was too late to stop the tears before they came, so Piper rose from her seat and made a swift exit.

Thirty-Five

LEO

Water dripped off Leo's nose and coated his eyelashes as he stared at his reflection in the bathroom mirror. His blood was pumping in his ears like one of those pivotal moments in a movie where they edited in the sound of a beating heart so viewers knew just how serious the scene was. His anger was different this time. He was pissed at himself for his inability to make Piper smile. Her real smile was reserved for special occasions, and he desperately wanted to be a special occasion instead of a bystander.

With a swipe of a towel over his face, Leo took a deep breath and set his shoulders back, his hand hovering over the doorknob. He could do this. He could go back to only craving her body. He didn't need anything else. They weren't friends. They didn't even like each other, so there was no reason he should need every piece of her.

Just be normal, he thought before he twisted the knob and wandered back out to the kitchen.

As usual, El Caballero de la Salsa, Gilberto Santa Rosa, rang out in the front rooms as Leo's parents and sister shook out their limbs and moved their feet about in quick steps. He automatically scanned the kitchen area for Piper. When he didn't find her, he moved out to the living room. She was nowhere to be found, and he wondered if his behavior had run her off.

"Afuera," his grandmother murmured as she rolled up beside him, nodding her head toward the front door.

Leo didn't try to pretend he wasn't looking for Piper because Abuelita could always see directly through his bullshit. Instead, he bent and kissed the top of her head, the soft fabric of her headscarf brushing his lips. "Gracias."

The front door was a bit tricky, but Leo had it down to a science: twist the knob all the way to the right, push in, then pull out. When he yanked to pull it open, he didn't have to search for Piper at all. She was sitting on the stoop with her knees tucked into her chest. Her head turned to look at him, and his heart plummeted at the sight of the red splotches down her cheeks, where tear tracks were still damp on her face. He slowly shut the door behind him and sank down beside her.

"Did I do this?" Leo choked out.

"No," Piper whispered, wiping at her face. She released her legs and set them on the cracked concrete, angling her body toward him. "I'm going to tell you, but you don't get to make fun of me."

Leo shook his head, hurt that she would assume he would kick her while she was down but remembering that her take on what had happened in high school was that he'd done exactly that. "I won't," he reassured her.

"Do you remember when we were talking in the library about how we could see love in other people?"

"Before I kissed you?" Leo asked with a sheepish smile. "Of course I remember that."

Piper gave a small nod of acknowledgment and then sighed deeply. "My parents used to dance in the kitchen when they were making dinner. When they were cleaning up. For no reason at all."

"Oh," Leo whispered. Understanding hit him square in the

chest. He scooted closer to her and wrapped one arm over her shoulder, pulling her into his side.

"It's not the same, of course." Piper let out a short, unhappy laugh, her tears building speed and falling heavily down her face, as if speaking her memories aloud were further dredging up her pain. She continued despite all of it. "The songs were all in English, and my dad was a horrendous dancer, but your dad looked at your mom the way my dad used to look at my mom, and I just couldn't..."

A sob escaped her lips, and Leo's other arm flew up to pull her in tighter until her head was against his chest and his arms were cocooning her. He was surprised at how easily his body molded into her. He was seldom the person people turned to when they needed soft words. Sam usually came to him when he needed a black-and-white answer to a question. It felt like Leo had been missing out on an important piece of life up until then, sitting in front of his parents' house with Piper wrapped up in him like a blanket. He didn't enjoy that she was crying—his impulse was to do something ridiculous to fix it like running around his parents' yard and ripping flowers from the beds to cheer her up—but, somehow, he knew sitting with her was exactly what he should be doing.

"I'm sorry," Leo murmured. "You deserve to watch them dance again." *And for someone to look at you that way*, he thought.

"No, I'm sorry. I didn't mean to do this." Piper's head popped off his shoulder, and she wiped harshly at her cheeks.

"How many times do I have to tell you to stop apologizing for feeling things, princesa?" He brushed a strand of hair away from her wet cheek.

"One more time, I guess." Piper sniffled. "We don't even like each other, and you're here consoling me. Why?"

"Because I want to," Leo said. He wanted to tell her more. To say that he was starting to realize just how much he did like her, but there was a time and a place for that, and it wasn't when she was finally telling him something real about her parents. "I like to think I'm a good person." Piper curled her lips over her teeth. "If a bit blunt," he added. She let out the laugh, and he rolled his eyes. "Jesus, tough crowd tonight. Fine. I'm a *decent* guy. I do what's right, regardless of how I feel about anyone." And he felt a hell of a lot for her.

"Is this where you tell me that you may be rough around the edges, but you're really just a softie on the inside?"

"No." Leo chuckled. "But I'm not heartless. I'm loyal. You won't catch me staying silent on hard topics or standing by while people get bullied. And I guess I have a soft spot for a select few."

"Sam," Piper said, lifting a finger to count. "Your family." Piper stared down at her fingers for a moment before lifting all of them, and Leo chuckled.

And you, he reluctantly thought.

Instead of saying it, Leo let his hands fall away from her body and rose to his feet, dusting off his pants before he held out a hand. "Dance with me, Piper."

She gaped up at him and shook her head erratically. "What? No. I can't do that."

"Why not? I didn't know them, but something tells me that your parents would have wanted you to dance. Dance with me, princesa. You know you want to." That got her attention. He stretched his hand out farther in invitation, and she gave in, rising to her feet as he pulled her up.

"Okay." Piper sniffed and swiped the dust off her clothes before reaching for the door, twisting the knob, and throwing her shoulder into it. Leo held back his amusement at how easily she'd learned the trick to getting it open and followed in after her. After countless hours of rehearsals, he should no longer be surprised by how quickly Piper picked up anything. He only hoped that she wouldn't pick up on his developing fondness for her as quickly as she did other things.

Everyone was in the living room now, twiddling their thumbs and looking around in a failed attempt at innocence. If Leo had to bet, they'd all been staring out the blinds and through the glass portions of the front door to get a glimpse of his and Piper's conversation. His family was too nosy to do anything less.

"Where's the music?" Leo raised his eyebrows, knowing that they had turned it off in an attempt to eavesdrop.

"We were just taking a break!" His mother frantically reached for the remote on the end table and hit play. Everyone flinched as the music started up in the middle of a loud salsa song, but Leo ignored them all, again stretching his arm out to Piper.

Piper lifted her hand warily. "We really don't have t—" He reached for her hand and tugged her into his chest. "Oof."

"We're dancing." Leo said it loud enough for his whole family to hear, and they all kicked into gear, grabbing onto their partners as he set his hand on Piper's waist and positioned her hand a little off to the side. He stepped, and Piper followed, swaying with the motion, her hips moving under his fingers in a tantalizing swing. She had learned how to salsa a bit from the Havana scene in the musical, and he liked that he'd been the one to teach her how to dance again.

When Leo managed to take his eyes off Piper, he scanned the room to find the exact look Piper had described on his father's face when he had looked at Leo's mother earlier. It was mirrored in Antonio and Marcos as they danced with their wives. Leo spun Piper under his arm and watched as the purple and blond of her hair floated through the air. The cable-knit dress fanned out from her waist as she moved, and he was so mesmerized by how beautiful she looked that he twirled her under his arm just so he could see it again. Piper threw her head back with laughter, her nose scrunched and her eyes squinted from the strain of how wide her smile was. He had the ridiculous thought that she looked like an actual sunflower before she stumbled over her own feet. He maneuvered quickly to catch her around her middle before she faceplanted.

"My bad." Leo grinned. "I forgot you can't walk, let alone spin."

"Oh, shut up." Piper shoved his chest and then jogged over to his grandmother, who was observing the dancing from a corner of the room. "You have to take up space!" Piper shouted over the music. Next thing Leo knew, Piper was spinning his grandmother around in circles and wheeling her in and out to the music. Abuelita let out a boom of laughter when Piper sashayed around the entire wheelchair, dramatically swinging her hips and shaking her shoulders as her arms flailed about. Leo stood still and watched, rooted to the spot as Piper gripped his heart like a vise and tugged.

"Your staring is about to get creepy," Alvaro said as he pulled up beside him. Leo blinked out of his trance and jerked his head toward his brother, who was smirking at him.

"I'm taking your dance partner," Leo announced as retribution for Alvaro's observation. "Mari?" Leo held out a hand, and his little sister grinned maniacally as she folded into his embrace. "Say nothing," he warned.

"I didn't speak," Mariana whispered.

"You're going to talk behind my back later, though." Leo looked down at his sister, and she just offered him a shrug, not denying it. This fucking family.

Unlike Piper, Mariana spun effortlessly under Leo's arm, and he flicked her around with ease. Her laughter filled his chest with contentment as he dipped her back over his arm. It had gotten easier to be away from his family the longer the stretches of time in between visits. Despite how annoying they could be sometimes, he loved them. Coming back to his roots reminded Leo how badly he missed being a part of his family's shenanigans and just how painful it would be when he went away to film school. He wouldn't be able to make treks back to Archwood from LA like he could from Fletcher. And, for some reason, that knowledge made him look across the room to where Piper was spinning Abuelita in a slow circle. He contemplated what it would be like to no longer see her, and he frowned when he didn't like how desolate it made him feel.

It wasn't an immediate realization, but, rather, a slow creeping of consecutive thoughts that climbed up his spine and into his head.

You'd miss sparring with her.
You'd have to stop thinking about her body.
And her laughter.
Who's going to call you out on your shit if she's not there to do it?
You'll have to stop wanting to kiss her.
Or wanting to be around her.

It sounded like half a life. Even worse than not having Piper at all would be the memory of having her. The memory of her dancing in the living room with his grandmother. Only the memory of her lips pressed into his in a hungry dance of passion to keep him warm at night. Her smooth skin moving on top of him. The wrinkle in her nose when she smiled deeply. The freckles that charted her face like constellations. The storm behind her usually soft eyes when she warred with him. Would he ever stop wondering what color she'd dye her hair next or wanting to be the one who held her when she broke down? There wasn't a way to say yes to those questions without lying.

El amor no respeta la ley, ni obedece a rey. Love does not respect the law, nor does it obey the king.

Thirty-Six

LEO

Leo's fists hit the boxing pads connected to Alvaro's hands in a rapid series of jabs and crosses before he ducked under the swing of his brother's right arm. The drill he had done thousands of times usually calmed his nerves, but it was doing nothing to stop the restlessness of his body today. Boxing and work were the two things that usually gave him tunnel vision, but ever since the hotel, he was consistently using his fighting skills to talk his brain down from its hyperfixation on Piper.

"Turn your punches, Leo!" his father shouted from the sidelines.

Leo obeyed, adjusting his hands to match his target as Alvaro transitioned him to a few uppercuts. He stayed on track for a few rounds until a flash of blond hair in his peripherals caught his attention, and his focus was thrown off. It was just for a second, but it was long enough. Alvaro's training pad connected with the side of his head. Fumbling a bit, Leo sidestepped before regaining his composure. When he did, he fought the urge to look over his shoulder and failed. There was no surprise at all when the blond hair he had spotted was just some random lady gearing up for her own workout.

"Güey," Alvaro dropped the training pads, "you into women twice your age now?"

Leo cringed and shook his head. The woman who had caught his attention was at least forty, and she looked nothing like Piper. He might like older women, but not *that* much older, even though the woman was going to town on a punching bag like it had personally offended her, which did kind of feel like a Piper thing to do. Or, rather, it felt like something Piper would do to *him*. Truthfully, he was about ready to throw himself at the older woman's feet and pretend to be interested to avoid the look Alvaro was giving him. Maybe the woman would take pity on him. The last time Leo had been at someone's feet, though, had been in that damned hotel room, and he could almost taste Piper's essence on his tongue like a long-lasting bite of Listerine.

"Where's your head at, mijo?" His father stepped toward them.

"I have a guess." Alvaro grinned.

"Ya no jodas," Leo spat. "Do you want to get in the ring? I'll wipe the floor with you."

"I bet you're just dying to get in the ring with me after last night." Alvaro pulled the training pads off his hands and stretched his fingers tauntingly.

The drill Antonio and Marcos were performing a few feet away was still ongoing as Marcos shouted over, "Just ask her out, Leo."

"Says the guy who went to a coffee shop every day for three months instead of asking Harper out," Antonio teased. Marcos swung at his head, but Antonio blocked it easily. "I'm just saying. I asked Saanvi out a few days after I started working at the mechanic shop."

"She said no," Leo pointed out. Antonio was usually a chipper guy, but getting rejected had made him a grumpy bastard for months until he got Saanvi to change her mind. Leo's brothers paused their drill and made their way over to him.

"Is that what you're worried about?" Antonio asked. "Saanvi only said no because she was worried about dating someone she worked with again. She used to date the guy I replaced at the shop, and he was a grade-A douchebag."

"You're also a grade-A douchebag," Alvaro said.

"Says the guy wearing a muscle tank," Antonio retorted.

Alvaro folded his arms over his chest. "They're comfortable."

"You look like you go to the gym just to stare at yourself in the mirror," Leo scoffed.

"And I'm a saint compared to who my wife used to date," Antonio said. "That guy got fired after someone caught him signing off on work he didn't actually do." Their father gasped beside Leo as if genuinely shocked that someone would slack off on their work. Despite Alvaro's one failed college course and general class-clown attitude, even he had the tenacity of a workhorse; the side hustle he had been working at since high school was still going strong, and he could often be found in the shed at their parents' house welding together tiny pieces of metal to create his next trinket. The tiny metal director's chair Alvaro had made him for graduation was still sitting atop Leo's desk in his apartment.

Before his father could start a lecture about due diligence in the workplace, Leo switched the subject, hoping to curb everyone's desire to get into his love life. "I'm not worried about Piper saying no because I'm not asking her out. She hates me. I hate her. That's the way it's always been."

"Ay!" Their father smacked his shoulder hard, and it took all of Leo's faculties not to react. Sometimes he forgot just how strong his father was, and it had been a while since Mateo had gone up against any of his family members in the ring.

"*Strongly* dislike," Leo self-corrected.

Alvaro called his bluff. "If you hate her so much, why'd you get so pissed when I was flirting with her?"

Leo shifted on his feet. "Because she was there for a thank-you dinner, not to get hit on by someone who'd flirt with an inanimate object if it looked at him sideways."

"Nah." Marcos shook his head at Leo. "You were looking at her like you wanted to eat her. Varo's a flirt, but you know he's harmless."

"You seemed close enough when you were dancing," their father agreed.

Leo sputtered. "It's salsa! Was I supposed to leave room pa Jesucristo?"

"What exactly happened when you had to stay overnight?" Antonio asked. "I can't imagine your broke ass could afford a separate hotel room."

"There was a pull-out couch." Technically, it wasn't a lie. There *had* been a pull-out bed. Leo just hadn't used it or even made it far enough to see what it looked like pulled out.

Alvaro scoffed. "Did *you* also pull out?"

"Niños respeten," their father warned with a raise of his eyebrows at Alvaro. Alvaro just stared at his younger brother with smug satisfaction while Leo floundered for a response.

No, I very much stayed in, came to mind, along with *and it was the best night of my life.*

"No," he opted for the simpler version, hoping his family would take it as a declaration that he hadn't hooked up with Piper. Leo knew his father was under no illusions that his children didn't have premarital sex, and given that Lucia had given birth to Antonio six months after the honeymoon, Mateo didn't exactly have room to talk. It wasn't necessary to lie about it, but this time, more than all the other times Leo had slept with someone, it felt personal. He didn't kiss and tell, so he wasn't sure why his brothers were so adamant that he spill his deep, dark secrets.

"So, you won't mind if I do give it a shot, then?" Alvaro asked.

"She's not your type," Leo said. He was playing right into his brother's hand, but he couldn't help it. If Alvaro and Piper started dating, he'd pull his own hair out.

"What's it to you if she is or isn't my type?"

"Varo's type is everyone." Marcos laughed. "You gotta come up with a better excuse, Leo."

"Fine," Leo huffed. "I mind."

"Why?" Alvaro pried further. He clearly already knew the answer but wanted to hear it straight from Leo's mouth.

"We..." Leo looked away. He didn't even know what the answer was. The hotel was supposed to be a one-time thing. It was supposed to relieve the sexual tension indefinitely. Instead, he was thinking about Piper more than he ever had, and not just about the way she moved under the sheets, but the way she had cried on the porch. How desperately those tears had made him want to hold her. The way it felt to have her in his arms laughing and smiling at him as they danced. Her real smile. He had cataloged her freckles and the delicious shade of pink her cheeks turned when she blushed. The way her lips felt and tasted sliding over his. Frankly, he was both terrified that the hotel room might actually be the last time he would get to kiss her and terrified that he didn't want it to be the last time. And so, Leo listed off all the other reasons he shouldn't be interested in Piper Hartrick like it would solve the heart palpitations in his chest when he thought about her.

"Mira, we fight constantly. We disagree on so many things that I don't see how it would ever work. She lets people walk all over her under the guise of being nice, and I can't stand it. Half the time when she walks into a room she's putting on some sort of perfectionist act, yet I seem to be the only person she doesn't mind openly hating. Not to mention, I'll be leaving for film school in LA after graduation, and she has a business to take over in Merrick. We don't want the same things. I've never seen her date anyone who wants a family, and you all know that's what I want eventually, so it doesn't matter if I like her. It doesn't matter what happened in the hotel room, because she and I? There is no way I can come out of that unscathed. So, no, Varo. You can't ask her out, because she's mine. And no, I won't ask her out because she'll never *be* mine," Leo bit off.

His brothers and his dad were all staring at him open-mouthed like he had just told them he'd been abducted by aliens and commanded to build Devil's Tower out of mashed potatoes. *Close Encounters of the Third Kind* aside, he was done with any and all conversation regarding Piper, so he fisted his hands in his gloves and held them up. "Now, which one of you do I get to take my anger out on before I lose my damn mind?"

Alvaro stepped forward, raising one wrapped hand to volunteer. "This should be good."

Sweat dripped down Leo's face as he panted and dropped his hands to his knees. The only one who had given him a run for his money all morning had been his father. Leo could punch harder, but his dad's technical capabilities far outreached his own. The years of experience and almost daily training his father had on him compared to Leo's sporadic sessions in his room with one punching bag showed. Offense had always been Leo's strong suit —he was quick on his feet to spot the perfect time his opponents opened themselves up to take a hit. Given that his father was an extremely defensive boxer and, along with Floyd Mayweather, believed in the longevity of not getting hit at all, it felt nearly impossible to get a punch in. Leo still managed to get a few good hits in, but there was a clear winner when they called it quits, and it wasn't him.

"Finally!" Antonio shouted from the sidelines. "I think he's worn out."

If Leo wanted to, he could blame his clear loss on his exhaustion from going several rounds with all three of his brothers prior to his father, but it wasn't the truth. He *was* exhausted, but his skill level was inferior, and he knew it. And despite being tired, he still wanted to keep going. He couldn't rest for fear of thinking. Thinking led to thoughts of Piper, and he couldn't take any more of the torment.

"Who's next?" he called out, taking off his mitts to adjust the sweat-soaked wraps on his hands. His brothers and his father all stared at him like he was insane. "Varo?"

"You already beat me once." Alvaro shook his head, and his usual playful expression sobered. "I promise I'm not actually interested in Piper. I just wanted you to admit *you* are."

Leo ignored him. "Marcos?"

"Uh, I told Harper I'd bring her lunch in a bit. I'm trying out a new recipe, so I gotta head out."

Marcos was a line chef at a local local restaurant, gunning for the main chef position. It seemed like a valid enough excuse to Leo, but the mention of Harper only reminded him that in two hours he was meeting Piper at Harper's coffee shop, Roaster's Republic, before they started their road trip back to Fletcher. He knew she had chosen that location specifically because he had said he'd never been inside before. When she suggested it, he tried to argue again on the front that he couldn't afford a six-dollar coffee, and Piper had waved him off, reminding him that *she* needed coffee and she'd buy him one to shut him up for at least part of the drive. It was just a way for her to buy him that coffee he'd never had. They both knew it, but she'd delivered it in a way that made it sound like he was doing her a favor by accepting the freebie. The thoughtfulness of it all had his stomach somersaulting again, and that pissed him off.

Leo locked eyes with Antonio, still searching for an opponent. Antonio shook his head. "I gotta get home. Saanvi's not feeling so hot."

"Yo me encargo." Leo's father gave all his brothers a short nod toward the locker room, giving them the go-ahead to leave. The way he'd said it sounded more like he was going to "take care of" Leo than take the next round. Once all three of his brothers had slinked off to the showers, his father turned toward him slowly, face calm and unreadable. "Siéntate." He pointed to a bench off to the side. Leo hesitated before he let out a puff of air through his nose and stomped over to the bench.

"¿Qué?" He sat down abruptly on the bench and started to rip off his gloves and wraps, frustration backing every movement in his hands. He didn't feel like listening to whatever lecture his old man was about to lay on him.

"Don't give up," his father said simply. Everyone knew that Mateo Diaz was a man of few words, but Leo was at a loss for what the hell he meant by that.

"I didn't." Leo's reply felt more like a question. "You're just better at defense than I am. You won fair and square."

His father grinned. "That's nice to hear, but I'm talking about your girl."

"She's not my—"

"Don't play that with me. She may not be your girl, pero quieres que lo sea." *You want her to be.* Leo couldn't argue with that, but it still didn't change any of the facts he had stated earlier for why it wouldn't work. As if he could read his mind, his father continued. "All those reasons you listed aren't good enough. Nada podría evitar que amara a tu mamá."

"Pero mamá también te ama," Leo argued. It didn't matter if he loved Piper to the ends of the earth, reason be damned. His father seemed to forget that it took two people to make a relationship, and Piper vehemently hating him was a problem. "Piper has made it very clear that she doesn't like me, papá. I'm still wrapping my head around the fact that I *do* like her." Leo emphasized the word "like" so his father would understand. This weird infatuation he had with Piper had to be temporary. It wasn't love. There was no way he had flipped the script so drastically from hate to love. How could he love someone who still did so many things he hated? He wasn't about to change his personality to better fit what she was looking for. He wasn't going to change his mind about the way he lived his life.

"I saw the way she looked at you. It might have been just lust, but I doubt it." His father folded his hands in his lap with an air of confidence that said he knew exactly what had happened at the hotel.

"Porfa, I don't want 'the talk' again. It was bad enough the first time." Leo groaned and refused to make eye contact.

His father chuckled. "I won't tell your mother, or she'll threaten to call the priest again. Between you and me, though, we all like Piper."

"Yeah, she's..." Leo waved his hand around in an all-encompassing gesture to signify everything he couldn't put words to. "She's also infuriating."

"Compromise is a beautiful thing, mijo. You could learn a thing or two from her. And she could learn some things from you. Don't give up so easily." With that, his father rose from his seat and winked at him before heading to the locker room.

Leo offhandedly wondered what his father had been like when he was younger. Playful and bright-eyed like Alvaro? Or maybe reserved and shy like Marcos? Something told Leo his father had been more bull-headed like him but had softened as he got older. Compromise seemed to be woven into the fabric of Mateo's being. Not that he would give up easily in a fight, but that wisdom had changed him at his core. Like he knew exactly what was worth fighting for and what didn't need to be fought at all. Leo wanted that. Wanted to know when he could lay down his arms without displacing his values. Wanted to know if Piper was someone he should fight for instead of fight against. When was it time to pull a Kat Stratford from *10 Things I Hate About You* and dramatically declare that the worst part about hating her was that he didn't?

Not even close, not even a little bit, not even at all.

Thirty-Seven

PIPER

"This is so much better than Folgers." Leo was practically chugging the coffee Piper had gotten him as he pulled out of the Roaster's Republic parking lot. He hadn't even questioned it when he assumed the driver's position, and Piper was more than happy to be the passenger princess.

"And the caramel drizzle Harper suggested that you were so adamant you didn't need?" Piper asked.

"Delicious. I can admit when I'm wrong. I want that shit in my veins." He licked his lips, and she followed the motion of his tongue.

It was nearly impossible to stop thinking about all the things Leo's wicked mouth was capable of. Piper's entire coffee plan had utterly failed to stifle the sexual tension, at least on her end. She had thought starting their day in a public area would start them off strong. It was a truce of sorts. Or a "we hooked up and we can't do it again, so here's a consolation coffee" idea that utterly failed the moment Leo wrapped his soft lips around the rim of his lid and sucked, like he'd done all over her body.

"What should we listen to today? My aunt has me hooked on a serial killer podcast," Piper suggested.

"We could compromise and listen to the score of *The Shining*?" Leo asked.

Piper looked at him to confirm he was legitimately serious and found he was. "Ew! No. Why?"

Leo frowned. "What's the difference between listening to that and a serial killer podcast?"

"One is listening to a story about people who got murdered and the hunt to track them down. The other one makes me feel like I'm the one who's about to be murdered."

"I feel like out of the two of us, you're more likely to be a murderer."

"How do you figure?"

"You have that depraved look about you." Leo was obviously trying to keep a straight face, but his mouth hitched up on one side, threatening to unravel. Making the grump crack a smile always made her feel like she'd been given some kind of award. "Plus, all the really depraved serial killers we make movies about are all white."

"They're also men," Piper noted. "When you get into that field, will you make me a serial killer movie about a woman just absolutely slaughtering a bunch of people? You can make her Latina and bilingual, too. Maybe a revenge plot? That would be badass."

"Tri," he said.

"Try what? Making the movie myself? I wouldn't even know where to start." She shook her head, dismissing the idea.

"No," Leo said. "You directing a movie sounds like a terrible idea. You'd just let everyone do what they want, and nothing would get done. I meant I'm trilingual, so if I was going to make a serial killer that resembled us both, I'd make her trilingual."

Piper turned to him, eyebrows raised. "What other language do you speak?" With a flurry of one-handed motions, he answered her question. "You know ASL? When did you learn that?"

"High school. I thought it would be cool to silently use behind a camera someday to keep quiet on the set, but still give small directions."

"You took two language courses in high school?"

"No," Leo drew out the word. "I took one language course in high school."

"I'm not following," Piper screwed up her face in thought. "You mean you took an online class for sign language? And then Spanish class sitting down in an actual classroom?"

"I didn't take Spanish in high school," he said, looking slightly uncomfortable. "I already speak Spanish, so that would have been an easy A. I learned American Sign Language instead. I'll be the interpreter at all of our shows when we finally get to opening night."

"Are my wires crossed? We were partners in Spanish class, Leo. You corrected me every chance you could. We competed for the top grade in the class." Piper was starting to think she was going crazy.

"I wasn't taking the class, Piper."

"So, what? You were there for fun?"

Leo let out a long sigh before answering. "I was there as a teacher's aide. I got credit for the class, but I didn't really need the credit. You were the one who made it a competition and assumed I was in the class."

"No. You're lying," she decided. "We were partnered up like everyone else. And when we weren't partnered, you *still* corrected me."

"I corrected you because I was a TA, Piper. I'm not lying." His voice was calm, but there was a slight edge to it.

Piper adamantly shook her head. She didn't know why this new information made her want to break into tears, but knowing that the foundation of how she knew Leo was false felt like the ground was being ripped out from under her. "Then, what, you just pretended to be in the class for most of the year because you wanted to make fun of me? You only corrected me and no one else, Leo."

"You would turn this around into some sort of character assassination," Leo snapped. "I had an out that period. Señora Bracamontes requested that I come in as a TA because your grade was slipping after your parents died. She said you needed help, and she didn't think you wanted to ask for it, so," he waved his hand in the air in exasperation, and Piper's face heated, "silly me thought 'yes, of course, I'll help her, she's going through a rough time.' I didn't know Señora Bracamontes didn't tell you I was a TA. Then you assumed I was in the class, got offended when I corrected you, and improved your fucking grade. So, as far as I'm concerned, I did my job and got jack shit out of it other than you calling me an asshole all year."

"So, let me get this straight," Piper seethed. "You wanted an award for your one charitable deed? You wanted me to be thrilled that you were there continually calling me and no one else out every time I did something wrong because you were a TA? And, on top of that, you wanted me to magically know that you were there to help and be grateful for it even though I didn't ask for help and I also didn't *want* anyone's fucking pity? Calling me Perfect Piper was just part of the deal, huh?"

"You couldn't take a single correction from me because it screwed up your perfect persona. I didn't even come up with that nickname, Piper. Your ex-boyfriend did. I was just the one who said it to your face and the only one who cared to help you, even when you made it your personal goal to be hostile. I know I'm not the best teacher in the world, but you were nice to every single person but me. Why?"

"Because," she whispered. "Do you get how humiliating it is to be the only one you focused your attention on? There were so many people in that class, and the majority of them were worse at Spanish than I was, but you singled me out. I was so tired of everyone looking at me like there was something wrong with me, so I made sure they had no flaws to look at. Then you showed up one day and started calling out my flaws like it was your job. Like you were my goddamn director. And I didn't know that you were literally there to direct me." Silent tears were sliding down her face now, and she swiped at them angrily.

"Hey." Leo's voice lost all its anger, falling into a soft plea. One hand on the wheel, his other hand reached up to her face, his eyes flicking between her and the freeway. The warmth of his palm made Piper's lashes flutter as Leo swept a thumb under her eye. It felt good despite the betrayal. He was right—he was the one person who shot her straight about how he felt, which made this news feel even worse. "I should have told you I was a TA. It was childish and petty. I'm sorry." His hand fell away from her face.

"I know that you telling me I was doing something wrong isn't a good enough reason to be a bitch," Piper murmured and let out a choked laugh. "You just... you really know how to get on my nerves."

"The feeling is mutual."

"It worked, though, huh? I aced that class." Piper cackled and watched as Leo's mouth turned into a half-smile.

"I like to think I aced it, too." He glanced over at her, eyes dancing with humor. "We were neck and neck for that highest grade, but ultimately I won because, well, I speak fluent Spanish."

"Smartass." She rolled her eyes with another laugh, smacking his arm.

"For what it's worth," Leo's tone grew serious, "I never would have judged you for needing help. I actually judged you for acting like you didn't."

"I did try to get help once." Piper sighed. "Not in Spanish, obviously."

"What happened?"

"My uncle kinda forced all of us kids into therapy. It was a good idea in theory, I just didn't have the heart to tell him or my aunt that my therapist wasn't a good fit. It was hard enough being seen as anything but perfect without adding more of a burden to their load. So I just kept enduring it. I felt like another thing to check off my therapist's list, so I made sure I fit into the box she wanted me in. Said all the right things until she believed me and thought I was improving. It's not her fault that she couldn't read my mind, but," Piper shrugged, "we never built up enough of a rapport for me to tell her the truth."

"And what's the truth?" Leo asked.

"That I was broken. I'm still broken, but I'm better at controlling it now. Except around you, apparently. Sorry I keep crying in front of you. It's really embarrassing." Piper's face heated again, and she was sure it was already red from the tear tracks, so the blush had to be doing wonders for her complexion.

"You never have to apologize to me for feeling, Piper. I'll say that however many times you need to hear it."

Leo's hand was resting on the center console, and with no warning at all, Piper reached out and squeezed it. His eyes went wide as he jerked his head away from the road to look at their entwined hands, and the shocked expression on his face made Piper immediately retreat. The impulse to hold his hand had come out of left field, so she couldn't blame him for his reaction. It wasn't like they were anything to each other than travel companions, reluctant co-workers, and a one-night stand. She couldn't imagine a world where Leonardo Diaz liked her enough to actually hold her hand.

Thirty-Eight

PIPER

"Emma, you're flat! From the top!"

"Emma, that's not your mark. Run it back!"

"That's your line, Emma."

"Now you're too sharp!"

"If we have to do this one more time, I'm going to lose my goddamn mind."

"How did you forget every single one of your lines over the break?"

"Focus, Emma, I'm begging."

"Well, we have to get this scene down, so I guess run it again."

Each new remark that came out of Leo's mouth got harsher and grumpier as their first rehearsal back from break turned into a breeding ground for mistakes. Piper had watched Emma repeat the same scene so many times she was starting to wince every time Leo called a restart. Emma was botching lines left and right. Her usually flawless voice cracked with strain, and she looked weak and tired, like the very last thing she wanted to do was to be in rehearsal, keeping face. Piper could read it easily. Whatever vibrant and magnetic energy Emma had had before, when she had pulled people in through song and personality—she was barely a shadow of that person now.

After studying with her several times, Piper thought she knew Emma's character pretty well. She wasn't scatterbrained. She didn't come to rehearsal with anything but her best, which meant today, with her failed notes and failed acting, *was* her best. That thought made Piper catalog Emma's appearance next. She was dressed in the same grunge wear as normal, but she was more buttoned-up than usual, as if she were cold or sick. The way Leo's grandmother had thrown on a knitted cardigan at one point during dinner because her body couldn't quite warm up on its own. The thought made Piper's stomach drop.

As rehearsal continued, Piper watched Leo fret and huff over Emma's performance, constantly dragging his fingers through his hair in frustration. The more time passed, the more Piper was getting irritated that Leo couldn't stop for one second to regroup and notice that something was clearly wrong. Moreno had called out of today's rehearsal when his wife had ended up in the hospital over the break, and that could have in part been why everyone seemed on edge, but it didn't justify Leo's inability to have nuance. He couldn't read the room. He was too focused on the show and on getting every detail right to pay attention to the facts. The ones that seemed so glaringly obvious that Piper could pick up on Emma's turmoil from the last row of the theatre. Whatever was going on, it wasn't good, and Leo was not helping.

And so, Piper held her tongue. She would wait for the opportune moment to tell Leo that he had his head so far up his ass that he couldn't see what was right in front of him.

The holidays were a special time of year for a lot of people, but the season could also bring about sorrow and heartbreak. After her parents' deaths, birthdays, Thanksgiving, and Christmas always felt more sad than celebratory, and Piper still had a family that cared about her. She wasn't sure exactly what Emma's home situation was, but Piper was already reeling through endless possible Thanksgiving fiascos that could have snuffed out Emma's spark.

Apology after apology spewed from Emma's mouth every time she did something wrong, and while Piper knew the mistakes weren't intentional, Leo seemed to be taking them as a personal affront to his very being. When Leo finally called it quits at the end of their rehearsal, furiously scratching a note onto his clipboard with a heavy hand, Piper collected her anger and shoved it into a box in the back of her mind before approaching Emma.

"Hey." Emma nodded in her direction, and Piper gave her a smile back.

"Hey, how was your Thanksgiving?" Piper sat down beside her on the edge of the stairs.

"Pretty good. My family already has the tree up for Christmas because they're all a bunch of hoes for the holidays. I think I'm still filled to the brim with cider and turkey," Emma said. Her tone was bland, like she was saying something that would normally make her laugh or smile, but without the feeling behind it.

"Nice." Piper nodded and searched for a follow-up question. If it wasn't her family, then maybe Emma really was sick. "Are you cold?"

"No. Are you?" Emma asked. "They finally fixed the heating in here, thank God."

"Oh." Piper shook her head. "No, I'm good."

"Look… I'm sorry I was a shit show today." Emma looked up at the ceiling. "I promise I'll do better next time. I guess I just wasn't feeling it."

"We all have our days." Piper shrugged. The way Emma was avoiding eye contact solidified it for her. Something was very wrong, and while Emma didn't seem open to telling her, Piper could at least fix one problem. "Well, I gotta go talk to Leo about one of my scenes. See you tomorrow for our usual study session?" Emma turned her head even farther from Piper as she nodded. No words. No agreement. No anything.

Leo was standing with Sam, looking as furious as ever as Piper stomped over to him.

"I need to talk to you," Piper said sharply.

"Okay, talk," Leo sighed. He was patently irritated by her interruption of whatever ruthless notes he was making on his clipboard, and she could not give less of a fuck.

"Alone," she hissed.

"Whatever it is," he said slowly. "I'm sure it can wait a minute while I talk to Emma."

"Now, Leo." Piper folded her arms over her chest and stared him down.

Leo cocked his head and narrowed his eyes at her before sighing in exasperation and calling out across the stage, "Emma, stay put. I need to talk to Piper, and then we need to have a chat."

"All right," Emma's voice called back.

Immediately, Piper started toward the closest room that had enough privacy and, hopefully, soundproofing for her to yell at her director.

Thirty-Nine

LEO

The door slammed shut behind Leo as he followed a very pissed-off Piper into the dressing room. She whirled around to face him, and he caught a glimpse of her hair whipping around in the reflection of the vanity mirror. The scowl she wore said what he already knew.

"You're mad at me," Leo stated. "What is it this time?" Despite her theatrics, he couldn't tell just from looking at her what had her panties in a twist.

"I'm not surprised that you don't seem to know why," Piper said.

"And I'm not surprised you want to make this some kind of guessing game, princesita," he retorted. "Spit it out."

"It's fucking obvious! You were a dick to Emma." She jabbed at his chest like she had before their first kiss, and the memory of that had him wanting to bite her finger... or suck it into his mouth. Either one.

"Emma botched half of her lines and was pitchy on all her songs today. I don't know if you know this, but I'm the director, so it's kinda my job to tell her when she's not doing it right." Leo folded his arms over his chest, feeling a bit defensive.

"Oh, I'm very aware you're the director, hotshot." The words came out of Piper's mouth like they were laced with poison. "Let me ask you this: since you're the almighty ruler and will know the answer to my measly peasant question—"

"Oh, come on, that's not what I—"

"Has Emma ever fucked up her lines or songs this badly?"

"No, which is why it was disappointing that she came to rehearsal today and barely put in any effort."

"*Barely put in any effort*," Piper mimicked him with the most insulting impression imaginable. "Would you listen to yourself? You can't be this dense. People don't just have mass talent and work ethic one day and then nothing the next. There's obviously something going on with her outside of the show, and it's causing her lack of focus."

"If something is going on outside of the musical, then she shouldn't have brought it to rehearsal," Leo snapped. It seemed like no one understood the concept of basic professionalism. "She was failing our business class before we helped her, and she was still killing in rehearsals. The second any of you walk out on stage, you should leave whatever bullshit is happening in your lives out of it."

"That's impossible sometimes, and you know it!" Piper stepped toward him, meeting him toe to toe. The wrinkle in her nose displaced the dusting of freckles across the bridge. That usually only happened when she smiled, and he wished that was the reason for it now.

"I always keep my personal life and my work life separate." He hadn't realized they were both shouting until he punctuated his last sentence with a little more volume. His chest was rising and falling in rapid succession, and maybe it was because he wanted the argument to be over or because it felt like a lie the second it came out of his mouth, but he fell silent. As if to prove him wrong, his eyes dropped to Piper's chest, her breasts expanding and releasing under the top seam of her plush maroon sweater dress.

"I don't think you do," she whispered. Leo scrunched his eyes shut to avoid looking at her, and his brain unhelpfully played back the memory of her riding him at the hotel, bouncing on top of him. His cock thickened in his jeans, and he knew he was fucked before he said it out loud.

"Eres mi debilidad," Leo mumbled, shaking his head.

"I'm deliberate?" Piper asked.

"Jesus, you're so bad at Spanish."

"I had a really bad teacher's aide." Piper smirked.

"You're my weakness, princesa," Leo translated before he slammed his mouth down on hers, rules be damned.

Piper fisted Leo's shirt as her lips clashed with his in both desperation and anger. With the hungry way her mouth devoured his, she might have been pissed, but she didn't seem to care that he had broken their one-night-only agreement. One hand pressed into the small of her back, he leaned into her and walked her backward into the vanity, his mouth still nipping and biting at hers.

When Piper's backside hit the wooden chair wedged partially under vanity, he reached behind her and maneuvered the chair off to the side before pushing her against the table. The various brushes and makeup containers rattled atop the vanity when he had her flush up against the edge. In one forceful swoop, his hands cupped under her ass and lifted, slamming her down on top of the counter, and he stepped between her legs.

"Can you be quiet?" Leo's voice was hoarse as he dragged his tongue down her throat, reveling in every roll of Piper's chest.

"I'm not going to shut up just because you want me to," Piper snarled. "I—" Whatever she was going to say was cut off by an airy gasp when he bit her neck.

"Everyone is still out there," he murmured against her skin. "They'll hear what I'm doing to you if you don't shut up."

"It'll be more suspicious if we're quiet. We came in here to fight." She said it in a whisper anyway. Leo trailed harsh, sucking kisses up her neck, and he peered up to watch her head loll backward.

"Then we'll continue our fight while I fuck you in the dressing room like the dirty temptress you are." Leo's fingers slid under Piper's dress and over her polka-dot tights. "You think Sarah Brown was just as filthy as you are?" His hands continued their trek up to the hem of her underwear and yanked both them and her tights down.

In the responsive way her body always seemed to react to his, Piper's hips tipped up to help Leo drag the garments down her legs as she panted her agreement. "Yes." Apparently, the one thing that he and Piper would ever agree on was that if a fictional character were a real person, she'd be dirty in the bedroom… or the dressing room. Once he finally had her relieved of everything from her waist down, she made quick work of unclasping his belt. "Adelaide would be a sweetheart in the bedroom. Which is why Emma is perfect for the role."

"She may be a sweetheart, but if she can't get her act together, I'm going to have to get her understudy to swap with her," Leo bit off as he helped her pull his pants down.

"Why don't you stop being a dick?" Piper said, grabbing onto *his* and yanking when she said the word. He muffled his moan by burying his face in her hair. "Just ask her what's wrong instead of tossing her out with the trash!" she shouted. She was fully jacking him off now, and he had to grip the edge of the vanity and clench his jaw to continue.

"I'm not doing this to make friends, princesita. We've been over this." He dragged his fingers over her slit, happy to find that she was already wet for him. To an outsider, his voice had to have sounded incredibly strained and strange. He wasn't quite nailing the performance. Being pissed off at her only made his cock harder in her hand, which in turn made him almost lose the ability to speak. "If people can't *enter*," he shoved two fingers deep inside her and slanted his mouth quickly over hers to smother her gasping moan in a kiss before continuing on. "If people can't enter the theatre and leave their personal shit behind, then they aren't very good at acting."

Piper's hips canted when he pressed his thumb hard into her clit. "*Ohhh*—you, you asshole!"

"Nice recovery," Leo praised in a low voice. She glared at him but rolled her hips into his fingers as she squeezed his erection harder.

"I actually do think you're an asshole, so it wasn't hard," she hissed.

"Oh, I'm *very* hard," Leo murmured, still aware that he was pistoning his hips to fuck into her hand.

"Condom?" Piper whispered.

"Dammit!" he yelled when he realized he didn't have one, then did his best to salvage the swear into something for their argument. "Why is it that every time I'm trying to do my job, you act like there's some way I could be doing it better? Am I really that fucking bad at it?" That one might have leaned a little further into his insecurities than he would have liked.

"Sometimes it's good to be tested at work, and—" Piper cut herself off with a shake of her head then abandoned the loud voice for a soft whisper, "—screw this. I'm on birth control, and I'm all clear. I'm good to keep going as long as you've been tested recently, and—"

"Yes." Leo cut her off and yanked her hips forward so she was balancing on the very edge of the table. "All clear." He'd never had sex without protection in his life, but the sheer excitement of it had his cock already weeping precum. Then again, he'd never had sex in the dressing room of a theatre with half the cast outside before, either.

"I don't think you're bad at your job," Piper continued their argument where they left off and dragged his swelled tip over her wet entrance. "I think you need more compassion."

"Compassion," he repeated, letting his eyes fall shut as he slowed their pace.

"Maybe ask what she wants?" Piper breathed, still dragging his cock up and down her center. "I mean, ask her what's wrong."

"What do *you* want, princesa?" Leo's voice wasn't loud enough for anyone to hear but her. He was beyond the entire argument by then and could barely see straight, he was so desperate to jerk forward. She had already proved her point, and he'd lost. He clearly couldn't keep his work life and personal life separate at all. "Rough? Soft? Please say rough."

"I want you to fuck me like you mean it."

"I always mean it." He whipped his hips forward and sank into her with one damning thrust. Piper let out a moan that he had to smother with his mouth again. "Shh, shh, shh," he scolded, replacing his lips with his hand to cover the noise when he started to rock. "That's it, Piper. Suck on my fingers." The pleasure was already starting to build, his balls hanging heavy between his legs as he thrust. The vanity kept making a smacking sound against the wall, and it was enough to make him a bit paranoid that someone would find them like this. Someone would know he had broken all of his professional boundaries because he couldn't resist the feeling of Piper's naked legs hooked around his thighs or the way her lavender-tipped hair swayed with each chase of his hips.

"Mmm," Piper's hot tongue pulsed against his fingers. "Harder," she said around her mouthful.

Leo threw his head back with eyes closed as the rhythmic slap of skin and wood hitting drywall filled his ears like the devil and angel on his shoulders. One told him to do what she said, and the other told him that if they made any more noise, the entire cast would be apprised of their twisted way of dealing with an argument.

"Floor," he decided. Piper gave a quick nod before he was scooping her up, hands splayed under her ass as he turned to squat and lay her back, one hand cradling her head so it wouldn't hurt when he thrust home again. With no assistance from him, Piper frantically lined up his cock, and they were connected again. His thrusts were harder this time. Piper let out a small gasp. "Okay?" he asked. The ground was glazed concrete, so he couldn't imagine it felt great on her back.

"Yes," she whispered. "Break me."

On command, Leo bottomed out, and Piper let out a soft groan that made him feral. Each frantic push and pull made him that much more desperate. The sounds she made were the same ones he had been dreaming about since the hotel and getting off to for over a week, but they were also what would get them caught if she kept it up. "Please, Piper, you have to be quiet." He reverted back to begging for her compliance. "We can't get caught. I don't do shit like this. But you... God, you're so wet, and you feel so fucking good. You either need to keep yelling at me or find a way to stop making all of those sexy little noises."

Instead of responding, Piper pulled up the hem of her dress, exposing more of her bare stomach, and shoved a wad of the fabric into her mouth, biting down. He took that as his opportunity to sink into her as hard as he could. When it was confirmed that Piper's cry of pleasure was muffled by her dress enough, he kept his thrusts deep and demanding, so hard that Piper's legs were bucking off the ground with each push.

"I don't want this to stop, princesa." He was gasping for air, but still managed to keep his voice quiet. "One night wasn't enough. Two won't be enough. I can't stop craving you. *Please.*"

The repeated bob of Piper's head was enough agreement to make him tip over the edge. Her fingers dug into his hips as she jerked and writhed underneath him. His muscles spasmed and his vision went hazy with abandon as he poured into her. They had gotten the timing exactly right this time, he thought, but he still felt a wave of insecurity. She was good at lying and had even told him point-blank that she knew how to fake an orgasm. Carefully, he rolled off her, his arms flopping around to pull his pants up. His limbs felt even more like jello than after a long workout with his punching bag.

When Leo finally managed to clear the fog from his brain and get enough air back into his lungs, he tilted his head to look at Piper. She had her eyes closed, her long eyelashes fanning across her flushed cheeks, and her dress was back in its original position. "Did I hurt you? I'm sorry." He lifted himself up on his forearms to scan her for injury.

Piper's eyes blinked open. "No. You didn't hurt me. I'm just contemplating my existence and wondering when my self-respect went out the window."

"Yours left in high school. Mine left the second you told me to get on my knees." Leo shrugged. "Self-respect is overrated anyway."

"Well, you're still a dick, so there's that." She chuckled.

"And you're still all rose-colored glasses and fake smiles," Leo countered.

"I'm starting to think you're really obsessed with seeing me smile, Leo." Her teasing came with a genuine smile and a laugh that he would stash away for a rainy day if he could. Because she was right: he was becoming addicted to the way her face lit up when she was truly happy. "So... you said you wanted to keep—"

"Yes," he said without hesitation. Denying how badly he wanted her had gotten him nowhere the past week except constantly in his room letting off steam with his punching bag or his cock in his hand. Every day since having her, all he had been able to think about was Piper's hot mouth against his and how soft her skin felt. "I meant it. As much and as often as possible, I want it."

"I do, too." The sigh Piper let out made his eyebrows rise.

Leo grimaced. "If you don't want to, then just say so." He jumped up from the floor, his eyes landing on a packet of baby wipes in the corner of the room. "I'm not forcing you to do anything. You're acting like it's a hardship for you."

"I just said I *do* want to." She got up from the floor, too, and took the wipes from his hand. "As long as we keep it a secret and it's just sex."

"What else would it be?" He wasn't sure if he was asking

himself or Piper that question, but he suspected the former. His brothers were right to flick him shit. The need for her body came with so many things other than just basic attraction now.

"Nothing, I guess, as long as we both know that," Piper said.

"We both know that." Leo nodded. Falling for her was a bad idea on so many levels. If he went down that rabbit hole, she would end up breaking his heart. He knew it. "And I'll talk to Emma."

"You will?" The smile that broke out across Piper's face made his heart clench in his chest. Her nose crinkled, and her dimples popped with deep indents. "I won."

"I feel like *I* won, but yes, I'll talk to Emma. I'm not going to dive deep into her personal life, but you're right. She's never been this off before. Something's gotta be wrong." The smile on Piper's face was replaced with a look of concern. "Do you need help with that?" He pointed to the wipes in her hand, his mind whirring with the idea of what helping would entail.

"I got it, Casanova." She rolled her eyes. "Go talk to Emma."

"All right." He nodded and moved toward the door. "And Piper?"

"Yeah?"

"Sam will be at Wes's tonight. Come over?" Leo choked down the frog in his throat. "I, uh—can't make food or anything, unless you want a can of black beans or Top Ramen, which is what I was planning on eating, but…"

"Sex?"

"Yeah, I mean, I could eat something else." He winked.

"I'll be there at seven." Piper laughed, shaking her head. He grinned like an idiot as he twisted the knob and barged out into the hallway with a little more pep in his step, already pulling out his phone to text her his address.

Forty

LEO

The theatre was mostly empty by the time Leo found who he was looking for. Emma sat on the very edge of the stage, directly in the center, looking out at the empty rows of seating. Unhappiness was written so clearly on her face that the lingering warmth he felt from his tryst with Piper dissipated on the spot, replaced by a sinking feeling. One that said that Piper was right, and he had been completely remiss and self-absorbed earlier to not have noticed that something was wrong with Emma. He approached her as one would a skittish horse, slowly so as not to scare her, when he took a seat beside her.

"Sorry," Emma said. "I know I was bad today."

"We all have our off days," Leo reassured her. "I'm sorry I was an ass."

"I didn't bring my best today." She swallowed and looked away.

"But why didn't you?" He leaned forward to try to catch her eyes. "I've never seen you rehearse like that before. In the three years I've watched you on stage, I've never seen you... " He trailed off.

"Be complete dog shit?" Emma gave him a sad smile. "You can say it, you know. I don't think you're a dick for calling me on it when I wasted this entire rehearsal."

"Piper may have needed to spell it out for me, but something feels really wrong," Leo said.

Emma curled her lips over her teeth, her black eyeliner smeared a bit at the corner of her eyes. "Noticed that, did she? I thought I was hiding it pretty well."

"You weren't. Are you okay?"

"N-no," Emma choked, shaking her head.

"Is it something I can help with?"

"I can't tell you." She sniffed, wiping at her eyes. "No one can know. I'm embarrassed, and I should have known better."

"Are you... in danger?" Leo asked carefully. When his question had a tear rolling down her face, his blood ran cold. Emma was usually like him. She didn't give a fuck what anyone thought, and she got by with sheer determination. "Life or death? Please tell me you aren't dying."

Emma reined in a wayward tear with her thumb and sat up straighter. "I'm not dying, and I don't think I'm in danger."

"That's not very reassuring." He sighed. "God, I feel like such an asshole. You could have told me you needed a day off. I know I'm a bit harsh, but if you needed it, I would have given it to you."

"No offense, Leo, but I don't think one day will help me." She let out a small chuckle that was wholly unfunny.

"Can I do anything?" Leo floundered. His brain immediately jumped to all the reasons he might be out of sorts, usually having to do with money or lack thereof. "Do you need somewhere to stay? My apartment is shit, but I could ask Piper maybe, and—"

"I have an apartment, Leo. It's fine."

"What about a secret for a secret? I tell you a secret, and you tell me one in return," he suggested.

"How good is your secret?" she asked.

"I'll tell you, and if you decide it's not enough, then you don't have to tell me yours." When Emma nodded, Leo sucked in a breath. "I... fuck." He cringed. "I like Piper."

"No shit." Emma laughed, a genuine one this time. Despite the lack of enthusiasm for his secret, he was happy she was cheering up a bit. "It's either that, or you just really want to hook up with her."

"Well..."

"Oh." Her eyes lit up. "You *did* hook up with her."

"Please don't tell her," Leo groaned.

"Was she not there when you had sex with her?" Emma gave him a coy smile.

"Jesus, where did the sass come from?" Leo knocked his shoulder against hers. "I mean don't tell her that I like her. This is supposed to be casual, and she hates me."

"Sure, I'll keep your really lame secret, Leo."

"I take it that wasn't enough of a secret to tell me yours?" He kept his tone hopeful, but Emma immediately shook her head and buried her face in her hands. "Will you tell someone who's not me? I'm really worried about you. Is it... do you want to talk to someone who's not a dude? Maybe I'm not the right person to tell." He got a nod in response, so he kept on. "Piper? Maybe she hasn't left yet." He already had his phone out and was dialing her number before Emma had a chance to respond.

"Have you come to your senses and decided tonight is a bad idea already?" Piper answered immediately.

"What? No." Leo blinked. "Did you?"

"No." Her response made him drop his shoulders in relief. "Why are you calling me?"

Emma was still quietly crying beside him, so he got right to the point. "Did you leave already? Can you come back? Emma needs you."

"She needs me?" The flirtatious way she had answered his call fell away, replaced with urgency.

"Yes. You were right. Something's wrong." The beeping indicating that the call had ended startled Leo until he heard loud footfalls coming from backstage. "That was fast," he called out.

"I was still here." Piper made her way out onto the stage and plopped down on Emma's other side. "The dressing room needed a little cleaning. It was a bit disorganized."

"Right." Leo made furtive eye contact with Piper behind Emma's back and started to rise from his sitting position. "So, I think I'll leave so you two can talk?"

"No!" Emma yanked on Leo's arm and pulled him back down. He sat obediently.

"You want me to stay?" he asked.

"C-can you?" Emma's voice cracked. Piper's wide blue eyes were flicking between the two of them, trying to read between the lines. Leo wished he could prepare Piper, but he had a feeling that whatever Emma was about to say, it wasn't something anyone could prepare for.

"Of course." Leo nodded. "I'll just be here for moral support."

"I'm here," Piper said in a soothing voice. She grabbed Emma's hand and waited quietly while Emma took a few deep breaths.

"My... my grades are still not where I would like them to be in our business management class," Emma sputtered. Leo exhaled. He could help with that. Piper could help with that.

"Okay," Piper said. Whatever relief Leo felt, it was clear to him that Piper did not feel the same.

"So, like I told you before the break, I scheduled a meeting with Professor Hornbill. But it was just to see how I could improve my grade, I swear." The defensive tone Emma took on made Leo's stomach drop. He suddenly knew exactly where this was going.

"What did he do to you?" That sickening feeling he always had around Hornbill might not have had any merit before, but his hunches had never been wrong.

"Leo, let her tell her story at her own pace," Piper scolded.

He snapped his mouth shut and gave a quick jerk of his head. "Sorry."

"He..." Emma trailed off, and the tears started to come down harder.

"It's okay." Piper tucked herself closer into Emma's side. "Right now, you're safe."

"I think I gave him the wrong impression," Emma sobbed. Leo wanted to scream or blurt something resembling *no, you absolutely did not*, but instead, he clenched his jaw and both fists in his lap and took Piper's advice to stay silent.

"And what impression is that?" Piper asked. Leo had no doubt that Piper was on the same page as him. He hadn't realized it before then, but Piper knew, too. Piper had never once swooned over the cunning professor. If anything, she always looked uncomfortable in that class. In the last few weeks, she hadn't even sat in the first row.

"That I wanted something more than help with my grades," Emma croaked. "Please don't tell anyone. He said he'd drop my grade more if I told anyone."

Fucking bastard. Leo couldn't sit any longer. He got up from beside Emma and started to pace, wearing a path into the floorboards of the stage. He needed to hit something—Waylen Hornbill, to be exact.

"Okay." Piper nodded slowly. "I won't tell anyone unless you want me to. Neither will Leo, right?"

Leo didn't respond. He wanted to tell everyone. He wanted to fix it, to bring it straight to the administration and get Hornbill fired. No, fuck being fired—he wanted to set fire to Hornbill's classroom and bring the bastard down with it.

"Right, Leo?" Piper reiterated with a scowl.

Leo cleared his throat and steeled himself against his anger. Sitting on his hands was a skill he would have to learn. "I won't tell a soul."

"Whatever he did is not a reflection on you," Piper stated, turning back to Emma. Piper's voice was calming enough to draw

Leo back from his tumultuous thoughts. She only ever allowed her true emotions to show when she wanted them to, and up until then, he had thought the skill was more deceitful than useful. But while Emma cried and he fumed, Piper kept her kind face and soothing tone. "You did nothing wrong, Emma."

"But maybe I—"

"No," Leo interrupted. "People in positions of power don't use their power to scare or threaten unless they know they did something wrong."

"He's right." Piper gave Emma a sullen smile. "Now, I have to ask, do you need medical attention? Are you physically okay?" The question made Leo want to upchuck the entire contents of his stomach.

"No—I mean, yes, I'm okay. He didn't get far enough to... do anything like that. It's stupid that I'm even bringing this up. Nothing even happened." Emma let out a harsh laugh and flicked her hand in the air as if to dismiss the whole thing.

"You are *not* stupid," Piper enunciated clearly. "He crossed a boundary, and that's not nothing."

"He made you cry, Emma." Leo's voice wavered as he sat back down beside her. He was still restless, every thought bouncing around in his head, but he didn't want to spook Emma by wandering anxiously behind her.

"Okay." Emma wiped under her eyes. "I promise I'll do better at rehearsal."

"Don't worry about that," Leo said. A pang of guilt stabbed through his heart. "I am so sorry about today. You are extremely talented, and having one bad day doesn't mean anything."

"What do you need right now?" Piper asked Emma.

"I want to not think about going to class tomorrow, just for two seconds." Emma sniffed. "I'm *so* tired of thinking about it."

"Okay." Piper clapped her hands together the way Leo did when he was calling order to the stage. "Here's what we're going to do. I'm going to call my roommate and tell her to stay in for the night. We're going to stop by Target on the way to my apartment and get an excessive amount of spa things and probably something for Thea to bake because baking's her love and her stress language. Then we're going to wear those sheet masks that make us look like horror villains while we watch movies and eat an obscene amount of pizza and ice cream till we want to vomit. Sound good?"

"God, yes." Emma's shoulders sagged in relief for the first time since Leo had sat down with her. Piper peeked over Emma's shoulder at him, and he knew exactly what her apologetic look meant. Any plans they had made were now canceled. The pang of longing in his chest was inexplicably not about the lack of sex he would be having that night, but rather that he liked the idea of Piper blowing him off to help a friend. And knowing that only made him want to touch her more.

"Have fun tonight." Leo forced a smile and got up from the floor, dusting his hands off on his thighs. He still felt useless and was definitely going home to relieve some of his anger with a punching bag, but at least Emma would feel better. He had exactly twelve hours to figure out how to control himself enough to sit in a classroom while Hornbill pompously explained business practices like he wasn't a wolf in sheep's clothing.

If Leo made it out of the classroom without breaking every bone in Hornbill's body, he would consider it a win.

Forty-One

PIPER

"It's so cute that it's gross. I need a toaster bath," Emma sighed. They had just made it past the scandalous library scene in *The Promenade*, which had Piper flashing back to her first kiss with Leo and blushing furiously. Now, Quinn German was bathing in a large copper tub while her co-star intimately washed her hair.

"Stop moving!" Thea scolded as she put the finishing touches on Emma's toes with black nail polish. "Have either of you ever done it in a bathroom?" Her tone was wistful, as if she were remembering fond times, and Piper's brain immediately jumped to wondering when the last time she had cleaned their bathroom was.

Piper wrinkled her nose. "I swear, if you were fooling around in the bathroom with Yuri—"

"Answer the question." Thea smirked and capped the jar of polish.

"I haven't," Piper grumbled, then tactfully looked away in case someone could read the guilty look on her face. Showers didn't count, as far as she was concerned. Especially because she hadn't technically touched Leo during that encounter. It wasn't an outright lie so much as an omission of mutual masturbation. Dressing rooms, though Thea might consider them bathroom-adjacent, didn't count, either.

"I haven't, either, but I don't date much. Most men either think I'm terrifying, or they think I'm into really freaky stuff. It's probably the fishnets and the choker." Emma pulled on the close-fitting elastic necklace around her throat.

"Your entire vibe is hot," Thea praised. "I wish I could pull that off."

"I tried it once. My hair was dyed black at the tips in high school, and I wore fishnets everywhere. My uncle was not a fan. I wasn't really, either, but I was trying to be cool. You," Piper pointed at Emma, "actually *are* cool."

"Thanks," Emma said through a bite of crust. The coffee table was covered in pizza and breadstick boxes, a plate of freshly baked cookies already half-devoured between them. The excessive amount of food made Piper remember Leo's comment about the lack of food in his apartment.

"So... I have an idea." Piper curled her lips over her teeth, feeling a bit sheepish.

"And what is that, Pipes?" Thea lifted her eyebrows suggestively.

"Okay, hear me out." Piper sat up straighter. "Whatever's left of the food, we package it up and drop it by Leo and Sam's." She could already tell that Thea wanted to read into her suggestion more than Piper wanted her to, but Emma was the first to speak up.

"Leo, huh? Are you into him?"

Piper adamantly shook her head. "It's not like that. I just..." She sighed. "He said he was literally going to eat a can of beans as a meal tonight. Not only is that gross, but it just feels wrong to not share with them."

"Are they really going to want our half-eaten pizza, though?" Thea asked.

"They're college boys, so probably. I've seen Sam eat plenty of questionable things," Emma said.

"Good point." Thea nodded. "Yuri would eat a full horse if it was offered to him."

Piper tapped her lips with her finger, thinking. "We could just go back to Target and get them real groceries instead of our leftover pizza. Or is that even weirder than the pizza idea?"

"I like it." Thea slapped her thighs decisively.

"Okay, but can we do it in a way where they don't know it's us, then? I don't want either of them to think I'm being... what's the word?" Piper asked.

"Elitist? Stuck-up? A spoiled brat? Better than everyone else?" Emma suggested.

"Jesus," Piper huffed out. "Yes. Those things. Am I—"

"I don't think so, no." Emma's mouth broke into a small smile that felt almost secret in nature. "And I don't think Leo does, either."

"I'm pretty sure he's called me every single one of those things." Piper scoffed.

"And *I'm* pretty sure he's drastically changed his mind since then." Emma gave a cavalier shrug.

"Drastically?" Thea narrowed her eyes, and Piper felt her gaze like a magnifying glass, ready to uncover every single illicit affair Piper had had with Leo just by inspecting her.

"So, we get them groceries, and we leave them on their porch." Piper quickly took the reins of the conversation, eager for Thea's focus to be elsewhere.

"Sounds good to me," Thea said. "Do not let me forget laundry detergent while we're there this time." Thoughts of Leo's scent wafted into Piper's head at the mere mention of laundry. His clothes always smelled intoxicatingly clean, like he rinsed all his shirts in rainwater and washed them in a mountain breeze. The hoodie she had stolen no longer smelled like him, and she was surprisingly disappointed by that fact.

"I should get my lemon custard shampoo while we're there,

too," Piper considered. She had almost used the last of her current bottle. "Need anything while we're there, Emma? I'm buying."

"You're both so... nice." Emma gave a halfhearted smile.

"Hey." Piper softened her voice. "This night is about you. If you don't want to, then we don't have to do anything but sit here."

"No, I want to, I just wasn't really expecting to have fun or for you to be on my side. On *everyone's* side." It had not been necessary for Emma and Piper to explain much before their girls' night for Thea to intuitively know why they needed one. And, like everything else she did, Thea had thrown herself into a supportive role right beside Piper. "I told my roommates what he did, right down to where we were in his office when he put his hand on my thigh and what he did while it was there." Emma swallowed and gave a short shake of her head. "They either didn't believe me, or they didn't care. I can't decide which is worse."

"That says more about them than it ever will say about you," Thea stated.

"I keep thinking I'm crazy, like maybe I'm the one overreacting," Emma whispered.

"You're not overreacting," Piper said earnestly. "I don't have to know about the logistics of what happened to know it was wrong."

"I don't know what to do." Emma fell back against the couch. "And I'm pissed I have to do fucking *anything*. I didn't ask to be in this position, but what the hell am I supposed to do? Say nothing? What if he does this to someone else, but worse? Then I have to be the one who feels guilty because I didn't say anything?"

"You should never feel guilty about someone else's wrongs," Thea said. She was using her therapist voice, the soothing sound of which Piper was convinced could heal many people's problems. "That being said, if you do want to say something, it will not be easy. There will be people who don't believe you. They'll say you're being dramatic or that you must have read the situation wrong. Some people will even say that you should be appreciative of attention like that. And he'll either deny it entirely or blame it on you, and that's if he gets reprimanded. All of that sucks. All of it is unfair. You should not have to beg for people to care about this or about you. Some women find peace after speaking up, and some women think it would have been better if they kept silent. That's a decision you're going to have to make, but whatever you decide, I will be there. I am on your side."

"*We're* on your side. Whether you want to report it, whether you want to slash his tires, whether all you want to do is to move on, I'm there." Piper nodded.

Emma took one choppy breath before responding. "I think the worst part is that he seemed so concerned at first. He had me telling him all the things I was struggling with in school and even in my personal life and acting like he genuinely gave a shit. And I was eating it up, thinking he was actually going to help me."

"The patterns for these types of people are usually the same. I've been studying psychology for a while, and it's still hard to see when someone is genuine. Manipulative people prey on vulnerability. They want you to feel obligated to them so they can get what they want," Thea said.

Each word sank into Piper's chest. The fear of being used was so ingrained in her. Her high school boyfriend was the textbook definition of manipulative, along with most of the men she had dated after. The problem—for her, at least—along with identifying the manipulators, was her very real fear of the genuine connections on the complete opposite side of the spectrum. The people who didn't manipulate, but, rather, loved her regardless of her faults would end up hurting her, too. She could never decide if losing the good people in her life was worse than dealing with the bad ones. There didn't seem to be an in-between she could balance on.

Emma slowly bobbed her head, considering. "I have no idea what to do, so for now, I just want to go ding-dong-ditch Leo and Sam's apartment and scream loud music in the car."

Piper lit up and jumped to her feet. "We need angry girl music immediately."

The hardest part about dropping the stuff off on Leo and Sam's porch was not the act itself, but how to escape without Leo noticing. The parking lot that belonged to the apartment complex was wide open, with nowhere to hide three girls who couldn't stop giggling to save their lives. And so, Piper sat in the passenger seat of Thea's car with an assortment of packaged food on her lap. The clementines peeking out the top of the bag were a little green and definitely not in season. Emma was in the backseat holding another full bag of college meal essentials, ranging from frozen chicken nuggets to a secret item that Thea had gone on a solo mission for at the store. Knowing her, it was probably some sort of baking ingredient that Piper couldn't imagine Sam or Leo would ever use. Thea liked to leave random bags of flour everywhere she went on the off chance she needed to compulsively bake at someone's house. There was no need to leave baking products at Leo's apartment, though, and Piper had said as much, but Thea had just brushed her off and gone about her business.

"Okay, so, what if we don't ring the doorbell at all?" Emma suggested.

"But then the food will just be sitting there all night unless one of them decides to go out," Thea retorted.

Piper hummed in agreement. "Well, Sam is staying at Wes's, so we only need to worry about Leo. We could call him? He has my number, so it can't be me."

"He's got mine, too," Emma said.

"That leaves me. I don't think he has my number." Thea stroked her chin like a conspiratorial villain.

"Perfect." Piper grinned. "So, we very stealthily put the items on their porch, drive away, and then Thea calls Leo."

"And no one will see us when we look like this." Emma tossed her hair over her shoulder triumphantly.

All of them were clad in fully black outfits, and Piper had the genius idea to mix one of Thea's black eyeshadows with water to swipe under their eyes. They looked like criminals straight out of a Charlie Chaplin film, but the hysterical laughter that ensued after they got a good look at themselves in the mirror was worth it. Emma was having fun, and that was all that mattered.

"On three?" Piper asked. When Emma and Thea both bobbed their heads, she started the count. "One... Two..."

"Wait!" Emma interrupted, jabbing her finger toward the opposite end of the parking lot. Piper looked out her window to see Leo in black joggers and without a shirt on, running along the sidewalk. Her mouth parted slightly as she watched him swipe his fingers through his hair and slow his run as he got closer to his apartment. He was just close enough for her to see the glistening sweat coating his skin as he passed under a street light.

"Jesus," Piper whispered, entranced by the way Leo's muscles worked, imagining the way they had moved earlier that day when he was on top of her and begging her to keep quiet. The rustling in the back of the car snapped her attention to the present, and she realized just how close to the car Leo was. Thea and Emma had already both ducked so he wouldn't see them. "Shit!" Piper frantically pulled on the lever to throw the back of her seat down and ducked under the window while clutching at the food on her lap.

"See something you like?" Thea snickered beside her.

"Shut up," Piper hissed. Emma had completely lost it in the back seat, covering her mouth and wheezing with every breath. "He's attractive, okay? Leave me alone."

"Is he," Emma gasped for air, her face red and contorted with laughter, "gone?"

"I refuse to look again," Piper grumbled.

"Don't worry," Thea announced with an air of importance. "I'll save you from objectifying him." She poked her head up from where she was hunched over and made the static noise of a walkie-talkie with her mouth. "The sex god has entered the building, I repeat, the sex god has entered the building." Emma wheezed harder as Piper reached for her door handle.

"I hate you both."

Forty-Two

PIPER

The night spent gorging herself on pizza and Thea's baked goods made Piper feel almost hungover the next day. She needed coffee before she died. Judging from the way Thea and Emma were still sprawled out on the couch and out cold when Piper snuck out of the apartment that morning, they were both going to need something to fix the kinks in their necks when they woke up. Piper's solution to that was also coffee. After leaving the sleeping beauties a note to meet her in front of the Condor Building before class, she drove straight to the coffee house on campus.

"Piper?" The barista called out her name, and Piper stepped forward to grab the carrier full of coffees and the sack of breakfast sandwiches she had ordered, pinning the bag under her arm so she could hold the drinks with two hands. If she ended up spilling a drop of coffee, her morning mission would be all for naught. Liquid gold was not to be wasted.

"Thank you!" Piper smiled and tipped her head to the side in lieu of a wave.

Everyone seemed to avoid Piper on the way to the Condor Building, as though word had gotten around that she was a klutz and they were worried she would take them down with her. Her careful balancing act succeeded all the way to the front steps before someone slid their hand under hers and the drink carrier. Fight or flight kicked in, and she thought about dumping one of the coffees on the thief before she realized the warm hands cupping her own were helping, not hindering.

"Do you want me to hold some of this?" Leo asked when Piper met his eyes.

"Actually," she adjusted her grip, "one of the coffees and a breakfast sandwich is for you."

Surprise sparked behind Leo's expression. "Really?"

"Yeah." Piper gave an awkward shrug. "I was already picking stuff up for Emma and Thea, and I get coffee there every day, so. Have you eaten breakfast yet?"

"I haven't eaten anything this morning. Thanks for thinking of me. Which coffee's mine? Where's your sugar-infused frap thingy?"

"Oh, they're all peppermint lattes," Piper explained as Leo took one of the to-go cups out of the carrier. "I didn't know what Emma wanted, but I know Thea's order by heart. They were really busy at the cafe, so I thought it'd be easier for them to make a bunch of the same thing. Plus, my order is a little more complicated, so I didn't want to take up even more of their time."

"Do you like Thea's order?" Leo narrowed his eyes on her as he took a sip.

"It's all right. Mint in coffee is a bit weird to me." Piper shrugged and carefully held out the paper bag for him to take his sandwich.

He did, then took the entire drink carrier off her hands, holding it out so she could take her own drink. "So, you just ordered something you didn't really want because it was easier for someone else?"

"I don't dislike the drink. It's still pretty good," Piper argued.

"But it's not what you wanted," Leo countered.

"It's coffee."

"Can I go with you tomorrow to get coffee?" he asked.

"Trying to rope me into buying you more?" Piper teased.

Leo took a deep sip of his drink. "I'm addicted now, and it's your fault for introducing me to it."

"Fair point. We could all use a little extra caffeine after yesterday." Her comment felt like a weight dropped between them. Their good-natured conversation was no more.

Leo frowned. "I barely slept at all last night. How is Emma?"

Piper knew exactly what he meant because she had tossed and turned all night, too, sick with disgust over Emma's situation. "I don't know how she's doing. I assume not great."

"What's the plan?"

"Plan?" Piper repeated back.

"Yeah. What are we going to do? He can't just get away with it." Leo was vibrating with energy. She could practically see it with the way he couldn't stand still. Not even Thea the fixer had been this adamant about taking action against Hornbill. But Thea was also a woman, so she knew just how nuanced the whole thing was.

Figuring it was best to chop Leo's burn-the-world energy off at the knees, Piper got right to the point. "*We* are doing absolutely nothing."

His mouth dropped open. "You can't be serious."

"We will not do a thing until Emma tells us otherwise." If Piper had to body-check Leo to stop him from confronting Professor Hornbill, she would. "If she wants to do something, we will. If she wants to do nothing, we will keep our mouths shut."

"But—"

"*No.*" Piper shook her head. "I know what you're thinking, and I agree that Professor Hornbill deserves to go down, but you know who doesn't deserve to be taken down with him? Emma. Regardless of the truth, the world will pin her as the problem. If she wants to take him on, she can decide that. We don't get to decide it for her."

"Moreno can help us, though. He trusts me implicitly. If I tell him what happened, then he'll believe her. She can win this," Leo argued. "We can help her."

"There's no way we can protect her from how cruel the world will be about this, Leo, and I will not let you tell one single person about this until Emma says otherwise." Piper's tone was firm. Leo might have thought that she never stood up for herself, and maybe she didn't, but she had zero problems fighting for other people. "She trusted us with this information, and you don't get to start a war on her behalf when she hasn't told you to do so. You don't get to make her feel guilty for not turning him in if she chooses that, either."

Leo set the coffee carrier on the landing and started to pace. Piper half regretted getting him coffee now that she saw how wired he was and was about to inquire where his head was at when he came to an abrupt stop in front of her and let out a long sigh. "Okay."

"Okay?"

"Yes, okay." Leo groaned. "You're right. I wasn't thinking about the repercussions. I just really wanted Hornbill to pay. I want to watch him go down in flames. He deserves to have his life ruined, and, vindictively, I want to be the one to do it. I want to break his fucking face, Piper. I stayed up most of the night going for the longest run of my life and then beating the shit out of my punching bag, and it didn't help. I *hate* it. I *hate* him. I can't stand the thought of him manipulating other people or the idea that he's done this before. I've noticed how he looks at the girls in our class, how he looks at *you*, but I had no real proof, so I didn't do anything. Maybe if I trusted my instincts, this wouldn't have happened to Emma."

Piper watched as Leo's chest rose and fell, anger curling his hands into fists. She set the remaining breakfast sandwiches next to the drink carrier on the ground and reached up to place one palm against his chest. The action came out of some unfounded notion that she could slow his heart rate just by touching him. It was ridiculous, but she did it anyway. Leo reached up and encircled her wrist with one hand, not seeming to mind the contact.

"I had the same feeling about him," Piper said. "It's no one's fault but his. We can only hope that justice will bite him in the ass eventually, but, if it helps, I'd love to watch you break his nose."

"How do we just go in there and sit down in his class like nothing is wrong?" Leo's hand gripped Piper's wrist a little harder. "He's teaching us about fucking ethics, Piper. I don't know what I'll do if he looks at Emma or you or any other girl sideways."

"Sit with me. I don't know if Emma's coming today. I wouldn't blame her if she didn't come to class, but if she does, she can sit with us. We do the things that we *can* control."

"Oh, Emma's coming," Emma's voice said from behind Piper. She dropped her hand from Leo's chest and turned to welcome Emma and Thea into the discussion. Piper didn't miss Thea's raised eyebrows and her cursory glances between Leo and Piper. "Where's the coffee you promised me? My head feels like it's going to crack in two."

Eager to do something that would get Thea's observing eyes off her, Piper stooped down to grab the bag of sandwiches at the same time Leo bent to grab the drink carrier. Drinks and sandwiches were passed out, and everyone fell into a prolonged silence.

"Wow, don't everyone talk at once," Emma said dryly.

"Are you okay?" Leo asked first. "We can leave right now. We don't have to go in."

"Please don't start coddling me now, Diaz. Where's the guy that gave me shit yesterday for botching all my lines? I want that guy back." Emma took a sip of her coffee.

"He'll be back when you botch your lines at rehearsal later. Right now, I'm just a friend," Leo said and then turned to Piper with a smirk. "Told you she doesn't want me to go easy on her."

"You could have been less of an ass, and you know it," Piper shot back. She also didn't miss that Leo had called Emma a friend even though he had insisted several times before that he wasn't directing to make friends.

"I do know it, but I'm sure you'd be happy to tell me again," Leo said, and he wasn't wrong, especially if Piper told him the same way she did last time. If she was freely admitting it, part of the reason she had gotten zero sleep, on top of tossing and turning over Emma's predicament, was because she kept reliving her time with Leo in the dressing room. It wasn't the fighting she was reliving, either—it was the way he had taken her on the floor like he had lost all control. Like they were wild animals incapable of holding back their desire. Pure, unadulterated lust.

"I'll tell you however many times it takes," Piper mused. Leo's eyes flicked over her face as if searching for more meaning behind the statement. He must have found it because she was no longer talking about whether he was an asshole, and he knew it, considering the corner of his mouth was tipped up in a coy smile.

Then, seemingly out of nowhere, Leo reached his hand up to her cheek and brushed his thumb just under her eye. "You had a streak of dirt or something on your face," he explained.

There was no way Leo could telepathically know what the streak was from and link it to the groceries left on his doorstep, but paranoia kicked in anyway. "Weird," Piper said and cleared her throat a little too forcefully. "Thanks for getting that."

"Sure. Anytime." Leo's hand clenched and unclenched at his side.

"Okay, what the fuck is going on here?" Thea twiddled a finger between Leo and Piper.

"Nothing," they replied simultaneously.

Thea scoffed. "You two are hooking up, aren't you?"

"Thea!" Piper gasped, her face heating. She glanced at Leo, who looked unbothered by Thea's outburst. "No, we aren't!" The lie filled her mouth with a bitter taste, and she hated it. She could feel Leo's eyes on her, but she was terrified to look. The idea of Leo having a real reason to hate her made her insides churn. She snuck a peek at him and found him taking a massive bite of his breakfast sandwich, effectively ignoring her, which felt worse than his disappointment.

"You look like you got caught stealing cookies out of the cookie jar," Emma said.

"Okay, fine, we are, but it's not a big deal. It's just to let off steam," Piper said, shooting an urgent look in Leo's direction for him to corroborate her story.

"What? I was just trying to mess with you." Thea gaped at Piper. "I didn't know you were actually having sex with Leo! What the fuck, Piper?"

Piper opened her mouth like a fish several times before looking to Leo for help. He finally swallowed his bite and said, "I told Piper I didn't want anyone to know."

There was no way Leo had just saved her. He would never do that. And he *had* technically agreed that they shouldn't tell anyone.

"Right, we still hate each other. We're just, I don't know, having a little fun." Piper brushed it off.

Emma coughed and shot Leo a look Piper couldn't quite read, and he pointedly took another sip of coffee as Thea berated him, "I don't count as *anyone*. I'm the one person who when someone says 'don't tell anyone,' she's still supposed to tell!"

"Well, apparently not," Leo shot back.

Piper lowered her gaze to the floor. Thea always told Piper everything—sometimes, a little too much—and while Piper shared enough to give the illusion that she was vulnerable with Thea, she always kept some things close to her chest. There were levels to her vulnerability, and out of anyone standing outside the Condor Building, Leo was the one who had gotten the furthest down her ladder. Before the several breakdowns Piper had had in Leo's presence, Thea was the person she'd opened up to the most, but now, for some inexplicable reason, it was Leo, a guy she didn't even like, who knew her pain the best. It both terrified Piper and made her feel like shit. She was a horrible friend, and she knew it. Not everyone was as brave as Emma was.

"I'll tell you everything later tomorrow when you get back from Yuri's," Piper said to Thea. "I promise."

"You better." Thea grumpily took a sip of her coffee. "I have to go to class now, but if you want to do literally anything else, I'm happy to skip with you," she said, directing the invitation at Emma. Unlike Piper, Emma had told Thea everything the night before, and that reminder was enough to make Piper feel like she had been punched in the gut.

"I can't." Emma's face fell. "It'll hurt my grade in the class. I don't want to give him an excuse to make everything worse. He can't win."

"He's not going to do shit," Leo ground out. "Are you going to turn Hornbill in?"

"And say what, exactly?" Emma scoffed and dove headfirst into sarcasm. "He touched my leg a little bit and breathed on me? What exactly do you think anyone is going to do about that, Leo? There's no proof. No one is going to see that as what it was."

"But maybe—" Leo started, but Piper cut him off with one hand on his arm. He sighed, but stopped talking.

"Unfortunately, she's right," Thea said. "She can make a complaint to the administration, but the likelihood that any real repercussions will come from it is low."

"It's my word against his." Emma sighed. "I just want to get through class. That's my goal today."

"Okay." Piper nodded and turned to Leo with her eyebrows raised. "We can do that. Right?"

All four of their gazes swung to the front door of the Condor Building, where students were starting to file inside. Piper dry-swallowed and looked between Emma and Leo, her eyes finally landing on Leo and pleading for him to harness all his self-control. His chest inflated and deflated once before he responded.

"We can do that."

Forty-Three

LEO

When Waylen Hornbill entered the classroom with the same casual ease of someone who always got what he wanted, Leo shifted in his chair, Emma on one side of him and Piper on the other. He had planted himself there on purpose, searching for some amount of control in a situation where he couldn't take any action at all. The frown he was wearing would have made his mother or Abuelita say, "if you don't stop, your face is going to stay that way," but Leo could not have cared less whether he would end up with permanent frown lines. He was on high alert, watching Hornbill as he wrote out their business ethics topic on the whiteboard at the front of the classroom. If he had permission, Leo would love to shove his textbook right up Hornbill's ass where it belonged.

"Welcome back, everyone," Professor Hornbill finally deigned to address the class with a smile most people found disarming, maybe even charming. As soon as the wool had been fully pulled from Leo's eyes, that weird feeling he always got around Hornbill intensified. The smile wasn't just discomforting anymore; it was blatantly manipulative. Leo frowned harder. Emma didn't look up from where she was drawing something on a sketch pad, no doubt trying to do anything to get through the class. Piper's hand twitched beside Leo when Hornbill turned his attention to their table. They had sat near the back, and Hornbill still made sure to single them out. "Emma, put that away, will you? You can finish your little art project later."

Leo leaned forward and opened his mouth, ready to tell Hornbill that he was going to *become* a little art project if his show of superiority didn't end soon. His knee-jerk reaction stopped abruptly when Piper's hand found his leg under the table and squeezed. Instead, he took a deep breath and focused on tamping down his anger. Nothing good would come out of an explosion. Leo looked at Emma beside him, folding her hands on her sketch pad to comply, and was surprised to hear Piper speak up from his other side. "Actually, my brother said Harvard did a study on it, and doodling is proven to help students stay alert and retain more information." The frown on Leo's face broke. Piper was fucking brilliant. Her attack was calculated and factual, and given the dumbstruck look on Hornbill's face, she had won the argument.

"Is that so?" Leo chimed in, slapping a notepad down in front of himself with gusto and turning to Emma conversationally. "Can I borrow one of your colored pencils?"

"Of course." Emma nodded and passed three of them over.

"I guess as long as it's not a distraction," Hornbill said with another fake smile, one that wasn't pleasant or cute like Piper's. The intention behind it changed everything.

"You usually look at your phone thirty times during class, so maybe *you* should try doodling, too." Leo cocked his head and attempted to give Hornbill a good-natured look, but it probably looked more menacing. He was better at telling other people how to act than doing the acting himself.

Luckily, Leo had never been particularly nice to Hornbill, so the man just chuckled and said, "Just don't let your grades suffer."

Leo might have been imagining it, but he thought he caught a brief glance at Emma before Hornbill walked away. He knew he hadn't imagined it when Emma took a shaky breath beside him and went back to drawing. Instilling fear. That was the entire purpose of Hornbill's agenda, and his statement about grades was a warning. Not to Leo, but to Emma. The warning? *Tell no one.*

Leo scrawled out a note onto his pad before sliding it subtly closer to Emma. Not close enough that anyone could see it was for her, but close enough that she would know it was.

You okay?

On Leo's other side, Piper was getting out her note-taking stuff and trying not to look over at him and Emma. He could tell by the way she had positioned her body away from them, but her eyes kept shifting down like she wanted to read the note. Emma didn't respond, but a minute later, he could see the word *fine* drawn into the patterned flowers she was doodling.

The rest of the class passed without incident as Hornbill laid out what Leo was sure the man thought was the most scintillating stump speech on the nature of the corporation and its relationship to society. All of Leo's attention was on his drawing, and contrary to what Hornbill had tried to spout earlier, he *was* paying attention, but the sunflower he was drawing seemed to spell out exactly who he was paying attention to, even with his total lack of drawing skills. He stole a peek at Piper's paper at one point to see that she was taking notes on the lesson but had also made aggressive comments beside some of her notes targeting Hornbill, a small act of rebellion that made Leo unreasonably happy. Nothing might come of Piper writing "asshole" or "hypocrite" on her notepad, but Leo found solace in the fact that they both had found things to do while feeling helpless.

Emma was much more skilled at sketching than Leo and had

drawn a rose with drooping petals and jagged thorns, the tips of her fingers black from where she had smudged the graphite. When Hornbill finally dismissed the class, she carefully flipped her sketch pad closed, rose from her seat, and left without a word. She did what she had set out to do. She had made it through class.

Forty-Four

PIPER

The line to the front counter stretched to the back of the on-campus coffee house, and Piper shuffled forward a few inches to make a little more room for the person behind her. Leo, standing at her side, didn't move with her, a stone statue declaring his territory right where he was standing and not a millimeter farther. She still had zero idea why he was coming with her at all. If he wanted coffee, she could have just brought it to him. The smooth surface of the apatite stone in her palm was her best calming tactic not to overthink his presence.

"Next," the heavily tattooed barista, a dark-haired guy with a septum piercing, called out.

"Hey, man." Leo stepped up to the counter and set his hand on Piper's lower back to guide her forward. Piper, marveling at how relaxed and cool the barista looked and how ridiculously plain she must have looked in comparison, had decided that he would take one look at her and immediately be annoyed by her drink order.

"What can I get you two?" The barista's voice was chipper

enough, but it didn't stop Piper's inner monologue from echoing in her mind.

"I'll have a small peppermint latte," Leo said and then looked at Piper with his eyebrows raised.

She was still reeling from the fact that he had ordered the exact thing she'd bought him the day before when she finally spoke up. "Yeah, make that two—"

"No," Leo interrupted with a firm shake of his head. Piper blinked, confusion pulling her eyebrows together as Leo turned back to the barista. "Sorry. Piper, tell him what you really want."

Piper looked behind her at the long line, feeling her anxiety flip in her stomach. "It's fine, Leo. I'll just get—"

"Piper, for fuck's sake, order what you want," Leo intoned in a low voice. He stared at her, his dark, defiant eyes piercing through her indecision like he could somehow burn it away with the intensity of his stare.

"We're holding up the line," Piper hissed, rubbing her thumb over the apatite stone again.

Leo bristled and spun around on his heel, spine straight and confident as he called out, "Does anyone have a problem with this girl ordering the drink she actually wants?" The line looked mostly confused and somewhat terrified of Leo's menacing presence. Piper's face heated with embarrassment.

"Leo, what the hell?" she whispered.

"You're paying, so order that frilly-ass drink I know you want, and stop making yourself smaller on behalf of other people. If anyone gives a shit about how much chocolate syrup you want, then they live a bitter existence and should check themselves."

"Hell yeah!" The girl behind fist-pumped the air in solidarity.

Leo turned back toward the barista and pointed at his name tag. "As long as you tip Jared appropriately, I'm pretty sure he doesn't give a shit if you want extra syrup in your drink. Am I right?"

"Yep." Jared nodded, looking bored.

"Fine. I'll get a medium iced vanilla macchiato with two

pumps of caramel drizzle and cold foam." Piper slammed her card down on the counter with a dramatic flourish of her hand.

"Card reader," Jared said boredly. Flustered, Piper picked her card back up and tapped the chip against the reader she had used hundreds of times at that exact coffee shop, then tipped him thirty percent for the inconvenience of having to deal with her. "What's the name on the order?"

"Leo and Piper," she replied, this time without a stutter. Their names paired together didn't sound as weird as they should have. They rolled over her tongue naturally despite how aggravated she was with Leo for forcing her hand.

They moved to wait for their drinks off to the side and stood in silence for a moment before Piper finally spoke up.

"You didn't have to make a scene," she grumbled, knocking her shoulder against Leo's.

"Making a scene is quite literally in my job description." Leo, as usual, wore a smug expression.

Piper rolled her eyes. "You know what I mean. Was that the entire reason you came with me?"

Something flashed behind Leo's eyes before whatever it was vanished, and he gave her a curt nod. "Yeah. No one should make you feel like the things you want for yourself are an inconvenience, not even yourself."

"I don't get it. It's just coffee. It's not a big deal," Piper said, even though it felt very big. Like a strange sort of turning point where she was starting to agree with Leo on some small front.

"Maybe not, but the little things add up, Piper." Leo shrugged. "You order what you think will be easy for someone else one minute, and the next thing you know, you're pushed to the back of every room, and no one can hear you when you're ordering at all."

"That seems extreme." Piper grimaced and folded her arms over her chest, pinching the apatite between her thumb and forefinger.

"Tell me this, then." Leo tapped his finger against her arm.

"Why do you do it, princesa? When you had dinner with my family, you seemed genuinely excited to work on Antonio and Saanvi's room, and then you diminished your skill immediately. You said nothing about your brother not coming home for Thanksgiving. The other day, you had an idea about your scene, you let Sam talk over you, and then you didn't bring it up again until I asked you. You cross your arms over your chest when you feel uncomfortable, like you're trying to make yourself smaller. You let me steamroll over you when I asked you to join the show. When—"

"Leo, stop," Piper pleaded, her hands shaking as her thumb pressed harder into the stone. The way he had laid it out in front of her felt like a road map to how she had become weak and spineless, and it made her want to vomit.

"Piper? Leo?" a barista called out their drink orders, and Piper practically bolted to the counter to grab them. She lodged the apatite stone between two fingers, took a cup in each hand, and walked straight out of the crowded cafe. Leo followed her step for step, meeting her at the bottom of the staircase outside, where she sheepishly passed over his coffee.

"I'll probably spill this everywhere if I'm holding both," she muttered. Leo didn't respond, just wordlessly took his coffee and watched her fumble with the delivery as the apatite stone slid through her fingers. It fell from her grasp and to the ground, bouncing across the pavement. In a matter of seconds, the stone had slipped into the shadows and out of sight. Piper's head began to whip back and forth in a panicked search. If she lost the stone, she would never forgive herself. Her mom had given it to her after the first time Piper had helped on a design project, and while painting the kitchen cabinets in her childhood home wouldn't usually seem like a big deal, to a six-year-old, being entrusted with choosing the right shade of blue felt like magic. The important memory was practically bottled up and stored in the stone she had so carelessly dropped. Before her anxiety turned into a full-blown attack, Leo reached down and picked something up from behind his foot, handing her the blue stone a moment later. Piper exhaled with relief. "Thank you."

Leo raised his eyebrows, apparently waiting for her to say something in response to his earlier demand to know why she constantly undercut herself.

"What do you want me to say?" she asked.

"What do *you* want to say, Piper?" Leo retorted. The black rims around his irises seemed to intensify as he waited for her to speak.

"I know I'm practically invisible now, and I know I made it that way, but I feel like when I try to be visible, people think I'm a burden. People don't like it when I'm sad, Leo. I'm not allowed to be sad." Piper looked down at her feet and slid one of her tennis shoes along the ground to side-kick a pine cone.

"You could never be invisible." Leo shook his head. "Even when you're sad, you're so... bright."

"I know I'm smart, but that doesn't mean anything, apparently, because I still can't figure myself out."

"You are smart, but that's not what I meant. I mean you're a light. It's hard to be invisible when you shine that brightly. Happiness isn't the only valuable emotion, Piper. I think you should stop letting people turn you off just because you want to save them from how you feel," Leo said in earnest, his mouth twitching at the end. The double entendre was clearly not lost on him.

Piper let out a long-held breath and slowly let a playful smile take over her face. "So, you'd prefer if I let people turn me on, then?"

"People? No." Leo stepped closer to her and dropped his mouth to her ear. "Just me. What are you doing right now?"

A shiver ran down Piper's spine, and a warm, coiling feeling in her stomach replaced the knots of anxiety and panic she had been feeling before. Leo's breath whispered across her ear, and her body screamed for more pressure—to dominate him and show him exactly how sure of herself she could be.

And suddenly, her plans were set.

Forty-Five

LEO

The front door to Leo's apartment had barely shut before he had Piper pressed against it, kissing down her neck. They'd hustled to get to her car, and Leo hadn't touched his coffee since he knew from the look in her eyes that she wanted this just as badly as he did. The sound of her soft whimper as he sucked at her pulse point made him that much more desperate to rid her of her clothes and feel her silk skin sliding against him again.

"Where's Sam?" Piper breathed.

"Class," Leo managed before covering her mouth with his. He knew why she was asking—she didn't want anyone else to know about them, and it felt like a slap to the face. But any hesitation he had quickly disappeared when Piper's tongue slid between his lips. How the fuck she always tasted so sweet, he would never understand. One drink of her, and he was intoxicated with the scent of her lemon shampoo and the feeling of her soft lips. The hard jerk of her hips into his tented pants as she tugged on his bottom lip with her teeth reminded Leo how much he liked when she took control. "Use me to practice saying what you want," he murmured against her mouth. "Boss me around, princesa. Take up space."

"Your grandma told me that same thing." Piper sucked in a breath as she thrust her hips forward again.

He groaned, shaking his head. "Please don't bring up Abuelita when we're about to have sex."

"Good point," Piper chuckled. With a swift push of her hands against his chest, she stood up straighter. "Take me to your room. Now."

The demand was like a thickening agent for Leo's cock and had his heart hammering behind his ribcage so hard he could hear it in his ears. His body instantly knew what to do, latching onto her hand and pulling her down the hallway to his bedroom. He opened the door and tugged Piper inside without a second thought, and hesitated only when she paused to look around.

Leo's room was nothing special: just four white walls, his boxing stuff crammed into one corner, a bed, and a shitty particle board desk he had bought at a garage sale with a folding metal chair to accompany it. He had all sorts of papers strewn atop the desk and a dusty mason jar holding half of his pens, pencils, and highlighters. The others, of course, were scattered on top and underneath his school and script work. He could see now that he had left the cap off a highlighter, which was probably dried out at this point. The black cloth hamper in the corner had a shirt dangling off the side, and his bed was just a simple metal frame with no headboard, a mattress with jet-black sheets, and a dark green comforter. Compared to whatever interior design perfection Piper's room must look like, Leo imagined his room must scream "poor person chic" or "jail cell."

"You're probably used to something a bit more posh," Leo said. Piper's childhood bedroom—which he had committed to memory the second he stepped inside—had a mattress that probably felt like laying on a bed of clouds, while he avoided a certain corner of his own mattress because the springs had broken through most of the padding, and he could feel them trying to dig their way through the final layer if he sat directly on top of it. Most everything in his room was disposable, and yet, Piper's eyes found the few things that weren't.

Piper looked back over her shoulder as she picked up the small metal director's chair off his desk. "This is exactly how I imagined your room would look like."

"Cheap?" Leo mused.

"Temporary. You're always moving on to bigger and better things." Piper thumbed the metal figurine in her palm and turned to face him, holding it up. "Except this."

"Varo made that." Leo nodded. It had more sentimental value than monetary despite how good Alvaro was at making tiny metal masterpieces.

"Mmm." Piper placed the chair back on his desk and pulled the handcrafted, leather-bound journal propped against the wall to her chest. "And this?"

"Moreno gave it to me when I got the scholarship," Leo said. It was currently blank because he had had grandiose ideas of using it for something important and had no idea what exactly that would be.

Piper set the journal back down and leaned against the desk, her palms pressed into the fake wood behind her as she looked him over, her blue eyes still hungry. "Take your shirt off, Leo," she directed. Leo obeyed, reaching behind his neck with one hand and dragging his black T-shirt over his head as Piper pointed to the boxing equipment in the corner. "Show me how you use that."

The anticipation was clawing at his insides, but Leo moved toward the small black duffel hanging off the hook on his closet door and pulled out his wraps. Slowly, he bound his hands with material in the way his father had taught him to do and let his gaze wander over Piper's body as he did so. She was watching him like a hawk, and he had half a mind to redo the wraps when he was finished because Piper looked as though she was about to grade his participation. He only moved on because he needed to touch her at some point soon.

Once his boxing gloves were on, Leo yanked the punching bag out from the corner, bear-hugging it into submission away from the wall. He gave Piper a cocky grin before taking his first set of punches, landing his blows with strength. He hadn't thought to try impressing anyone but his own family or his opponent before, and, as far as he knew, Piper had zero idea how proper boxing technique should look, but he refused to be sloppy about it. She told him to show her, so he not only needed to do it, but he needed to do it well.

Sweat started to percolate on Leo's forehead as his muscles worked, continuing the drills he had been using for the last month to get his libido under control every time he thought of Piper. This time, with her watching, it was only ramping him up. He only stopped when he saw Piper moving in his periphery, coming to stand beside him.

"Show me?" Piper's voice was small again, like she thought he would say no, but she should have realized by now that Leo could never say no if she was asking.

~

"Harder."

"I'm trying!" Piper heaved out a sigh and swung at the punching bag he was holding.

"Put some weight behind your swing." Leo gave her the go-ahead again and gripped the bag, hoping he would feel it when she punched this time. Piper's face screwed up in concentration as she bounced on her feet, arms held up in a fighting stance. Her face said she was serious, but Leo had to bite back a smile because she looked like more of an angry Tinker Bell than a stone-cold killer. She swung again, but it still didn't have much heat. "You're not breathing. Breathe with your punches." Piper moved again, and Leo chuckled. "Elbows in... tuck your chin, too—

nope, your chin is tucked now, but your elbows are chicken-winging."

"This was supposed to be sexy and empowering. I just look stupid," Piper sighed in defeat, her arms going limp at her sides.

"Everyone looks stupid when they start because it takes practice. Plus, my mitts aren't your size. Here." Leo maneuvered behind Piper and grabbed her hand, pulling her around to face him with her back to the punching bag before he knelt on the floor at her feet. Piper looked down at him, her eyes giving away that she was remembering the same thing he was: the last time he had been kneeling below her. "This leg," Leo curled his fingers around her left calf and pulled forward, "should be in front and parallel to your back leg." He slid his hand up the inseam of her pants and watched as Piper squirmed under his touch. He took his time drawing out the tension, waiting for her to snap.

When Leo finished adjusting Piper from the waist down, he rose slowly in front of her, so close that his front brushed all the way up her body. Piper had to be aware of the game he was playing given the way she was leaning into each touch. His head at her eye level now, he gently set his pointer finger under her chin and used his thumb to tuck it into her shoulder, the way he would to protect himself from a painful blow to the face. She looked up at him through her eyelashes and watched with a heavy gaze as he slid his hands over her shoulders, down her biceps, and to her wrists, where he pulled one hand close to her face, making sure her forearm was straight, and set the other out from her chest.

"That's good, right there. That's the stance," Leo finished and stepped back. He was pleasantly surprised to see the brief flash of disappointment on Piper's face when he stopped touching her, but he proceeded with the instruction. This wasn't just foreplay, but a lesson about confidence and feeling strong in both body and mind. He wanted Piper to feel the same way he felt when he boxed, so he held up his cupped hands in front of himself like makeshift pads. "All right. Hit me, and make sure to follow through."

"Okay." Piper nodded and took a deep breath. A calm seemed to settle over the room as her focus went steady. When her fist swung and connected with his hand, Leo absorbed the punch easily, but he could feel how much more power was behind it.

"Better," he assured Piper when her gaze met him for approval.

"That felt good," she said.

By now, Leo was so turned on by the entire show that the only thing that came out of his mouth was, "Mm-hmm."

"Leo?"

"Yeah?" He stepped a bit closer.

"Get on your knees again." Piper's stern voice was back, and that alone made Leo's cock strain harder against his zipper. He slowly bent back down to the floor and assumed his position. Piper removed his boxing gloves from her hands but left the wraps on as she slid her jeans down over her ass in a tantalizing shimmy to the floor. He didn't touch or offer assistance, waiting for her to give him exact instructions. Her underwear came next, but the pace was so torturous that he envisioned himself going feral and ripping them off her body with his teeth.

"Please, Piper." Leo was back to begging again, and he couldn't care less how demeaning it was. Or, rather, he *did* care, and he liked it.

"I love it when you say that word. Say it again," Piper demanded.

"*Please.*" Leo licked his lips in preparation for what he hoped she was going to ask. She lifted her bare thigh and set one hand on him for stability as she rested her knee on his shoulder.

"You want me to tell you what I want?" Piper asked. When he nodded, his head rubbed against the inside of her thigh, and he groaned. "I want you to go down on me like you're dying, Leo. Do that thing that you did with your tongue in the hotel room. Get me off, and then fuck me in your bed."

"Yes, ma'am," Leo rasped as Piper draped her calf over his shoulder, and he bent his head to taste. She was already so wet that his tongue slid easily over her, and he reveled in the soft moan she let out, determined to have her making more crude sounds.

"Harder," Piper instructed in a firm tone. Leo made his second pass with so much pressure that he was practically suffocating himself between her legs.

Drowned and smothered in Piper Hartrick's arousal would be the absolute best way to die, he decided. His tombstone would read, "Here lies a man who died in heaven." He had never thought himself someone who was into breath play before, but if it had to do with Piper's thigh wrapped around his head, he was definitely into it. He had also never thought of himself as submissive before, either, but somehow, he felt more powerful than ever with his knees aching from the hard floor, feeling Piper succumbing to his mouth at her own request.

A few more swipes, and Leo found what he was looking for with the tip of his tongue. His signature move was to vibrate the roof of his mouth like he did with rolling R's. It wasn't exactly the same—his tongue never needed to vibrate so forcefully when he spoke Spanish—but he'd tried it once on his first college girlfriend, and the response was enthusiastic enough that he continued to keep the trick in his back pocket. The response he was getting now from Piper was wild, and he basked in every second of it.

Piper's hips bucked as she let out a moan. "Fuck, that's so good. Do it again." He did, and her body thrusted hard against his face in response, chasing his tongue. Leo gripped her harder at the waist to keep her steady as he licked and sucked and flicked her clit in a persistent pattern so as not to ruin her momentum. Piper's breathing was erratic as she repeatedly offered him praise. He took each desperate cry of his name and used it as fuel to keep going, to keep listening to the sounds she made that were all for him and all because of him. "I'm—holy shit, Leo!" He could feel it when Piper came, her body tightened furiously with excess ripples of tension as she rode his tongue for several long seconds. Her head and her back were arched against his punching bag, but he had her firmly gripped at the waist, knowing her well enough to know she wouldn't realize the punching bag wasn't sturdy enough to lean against and would end up falling over if he didn't hold her up himself.

When Piper's leg finally slid off his shoulder, she wobbled a bit, a dreamy expression taking over as he rose to his feet.

"Good?" Leo couldn't help but ask.

Piper's chest rose and fell once before she gave him a sated smile. A real one that threatened to send him to his knees again. "You're very good at that."

"I told you I was." He still wasn't wearing a shirt, so he reached for the hem of Piper's and smirked at her as he pulled it up to wipe his wet face. She said nothing but bit her lip, and her blue eyes swam with warmth and something mildly sheepish underneath it all. A strand of hair fell over her face, so Leo did what he probably shouldn't have and reached up to tuck it behind her ear. Then he took it a step further when he brushed his thumb over the apple of her cheek, her face still flushed from her orgasm and warm to the touch. He should be fearful that she would find out just how much he loved touching her, and not just for sex, but because being around her was the highlight of his day, even when they were fighting.

"You were so sure of yourself when you said it. I thought it was just overconfidence," Piper said.

Leo tipped his head and moved her hair away from her neck to press soft kisses against the skin there, one hand holding her waist and the other on the small of her back, gently pressing with his fingertips and coaxing a sigh out of her. "And now?"

Piper lifted her arms to rest her palms against his bare chest. "I think it's warranted."

"Am I overconfident with anything else?" Leo asked. He genuinely wanted to know, but his mouth had other ideas as he continued dragging his lips over the column of her throat.

"Yes, but I can't think when you're doing that." She huffed out a laugh.

He kept traveling downward, leaving open-mouthed kisses across her collarbone. "Do you want me to stop?"

In response, Piper moved to unbutton his pants and pull his fly down. "No, and you don't want to, either." She palmed his cock, and he buried his face in her neck, letting out a shaky breath. "You're so hard, Leo."

"You tend to have that effect on me."

"Just recently," Piper teased, and she dropped his pants and underwear at the same time, his cock bobbing heavily between his legs. He had just enough forethought not to respond to Piper's comment. *Recently* was so wrong it was almost laughable. He hadn't always liked her the way he did now, but his body had always had this reaction to her. Even in high school, as a horny teenager, it hadn't taken much for him to picture her naked. The real Piper was so much better than his adolescent fantasies, and he itched to remove her top and see her. As if she could read his mind, she lifted her arms and shot him a look.

"Use your words, princesa." Leo set his hands on his hips, displaying himself in all his glory. "Be *mean*."

Piper's eyes narrowed in a glare. "Take my shirt off, asshole."

He grinned, feeling his body go hot all over as he reached for her. "How do you want me to take it off?"

"In a way that makes me shirtless. Don't be a fucking snail about it." Piper snapped her fingers together.

"Fuck." Leo let out a chuckle at how insanely turned on he was, and he ripped her shirt over her head, disposing of it on the ground. "What about your bra?"

"You want me to be mean?" Piper bit her lip, seeming to retract a bit from her earlier venom.

"Not if you don't want to, but if you're feeling bad for my sake, don't. I am very into this." He reached behind her and flicked at the clasps to her bra, releasing it to the floor. His eyes roved over her breasts. "The only reason I haven't hauled you to the bed yet is because you haven't told me to. I like hearing you order me around."

"I didn't tell you you could take my bra off yet, so you aren't very good at following directions," Piper said.

Leo let out a shaky breath. "Punish me, please."

"Gladly." Piper reached her hand out in one succinct and fluid motion. With a yank, she had him by his cock and started pulling him toward the bed. He obeyed, groaning when she got impatient with the speed of his walking and gripped him harder. He expected her to be on top like last time, but instead, she flopped down onto his singular pillow and pulled him on top of her. "I think we're good without condoms." She raised both her eyebrows at him, clearly waiting for a confirmation, which he gave with an overly eager bob of his head. "And you're going to do all the work."

"So, not a group project, then?" Leo mused.

"Don't talk back to me," Piper sniped.

"Yes, ma'am." He positioned himself between her legs and waited.

"You want to fuck me?" she teased.

"God, yes," he murmured.

She gave him a conniving smile. "You can put the tip in, but only the tip."

Leo huffed out a complaint as he moved to comply, gently pressing through her barrier with a level of self-control he hadn't known he possessed. "This is fucking torture." One hand strained to hold himself up as he palmed his cock to hold himself back with the other.

"Don't move another inch." Piper's voice was still strong, but he could tell it was torture for her, too. Her hips seemed to want to urge him inside, even as she told him not to. "Beg first."

"I can't take this anymore." Leo rocked and felt himself slide in just a bit more, so he pulled back with extreme reluctance, still wanting to obey. "I can feel how wet you are. I'd fit so well, Piper. You know I would. I'll do anything you want, and I promise I won't stop until you get off again, and if you don't want me to come, I won't. I just want to fill you."

Piper hummed in disapproval and grinned. "Not good enough."

The pained groan Leo let out was pathetic. "Piper, I'm desperate. I'm begging. I can't stand it. Put me out of my misery. Please."

"There it is." Her eyelashes fluttered shut before opening and piercing him with the sea of chaos behind her eyes. "Fuck me, Leo."

"*Finally*. Thank you." He dropped his vice grip and sank slowly into her, reveling in the feeling of her walls squeezing his cock inch by inch and the way she whimpered beneath him. "Fuck, you're so tight."

"Maybe you're just really big," Piper countered, her hips freely tipping to help him sink farther.

"Don't tell me that. I'll get a big head." Leo lay down on top of her to reach as far as he could inside. "Please don't tell me to stop, either. It feels too good."

"Don't you dare stop," Piper said, low and breathy. "But I'm gonna need you to start moving before I lose my mind."

"Gladly," he mimicked her earlier retort back at her and started to thrust forward. Her breasts swayed and bounced each time he slammed home, and each buck of her legs had him gripping her hips harder.

"That's perfect," she panted. "I can come just like this."

Leo was purposely grinding down harder to hopefully hit her clit when he bottomed out, so her praise made him feel on top of the world. He was doing everything right. All of the world's problems—all of his problems—could be solved by rutting into Piper and listening to her tell him how good it was.

"I could do this a million times just to watch you come," Leo murmured, rocking forward. "Give me another one, princesa. I've done everything you wanted. I deserve another one."

"You do." Piper nodded and gasped with another roll of his hips. "Don't come yet, Leo. I'll tell you when, okay?" Her voice had lost all of its bite. She was just Piper now—sweet and sunny, and so pretty as he slipped into her. Whatever this stage was, where she became the truest form of herself, telling him what she wanted without having to play a character, he was obsessed with it. However many times he had to be submissive just for Piper to get used to being herself and asking what she wanted, he would. He would do just about anything for her.

And right then, with Piper unraveling beneath him, Leo realized that his affection for her had spiraled into dangerous territory. There was no way he could be casual about taking her to bed. He was so in love with her that the world seemed to snap into place. A missing piece to the equation of his life had finally been discovered, and everything made sense now. Piper challenged him. Her opposition made him better, and he had smiled more than he ever had since realizing just how wonderful she was.

"Leo," Piper moaned. "Come with me."

"I'll go anywhere with you."

And he did, until they were lying beside each other and all he had left were the thoughts that hadn't left like he thought they would.

Brushing off something Leo's body had thought up in the heat of the moment would have been easy enough. He could see himself falling victim to a chemical reaction to Piper and believing it was love. But, even in the euphoria, his body hadn't been the one telling him he had fallen—it had been his heart. After his thirst had been quenched, he still felt every bit as in love with Piper as he did during.

"I want to know," Leo murmured.

"Hm?" Piper had her eyes closed next to him as he smiled and pulled her in closer to his chest. The lack of sleep was probably getting to her, and he could feel it deep in his bones, too, as the warmth of her body and the smell of lemon flooded his senses.

"You said I was overconfident in some areas, and I want to know where," he explained. She had called him out for numerous things over the years, and even if she had been wrong on some accounts, she hadn't been when it came to Emma or how his management tactics could use some TLC. The only way to improve and to find out how to be someone she could love was to ask her.

"Your music taste." Piper yawned.

Leo snickered. "That's it? You don't like my movie scores?"

"I don't." Piper prodded his ribs, and he wiggled slightly away from her. "We need to get you into some female rage music."

"Female rage music," he recited.

"Exactly." Piper scooted closer to him like she was seeking warmth, so he wrapped his arm around her back and set his chin on top of her head.

"Anything else, mi vida?" Leo had just enough self-control not to jump out of his skin when he used the nickname, but Piper just sighed, oblivious, as her warm breath whispered over his chest.

"On a more serious note, I think with you, it's overconfidence in what you think is right. It's not even that you're wrong, but the way you go about it is wrong," Piper said. Leo opened his mouth to argue, but she continued, "I think you believe everything is black and white, and you lack nuance. You're right when you tell me that I bend to people's will, but you won't bend to anyone's will, and I think that's equally bad."

"So we both suck?" Leo asked. "Maybe it's time for a compromise."

"Compromise," Piper considered. "I need some of your self-assurance, and you need my..."

"Awareness?" he offered. "You're more aware of other people's needs than your own."

"And you know how to deliver on yours and other people's needs."

He couldn't help the playful smile that crossed his face. "I like delivering on your needs, specifically." Piper shoved his chest and cackled. "But can I ask a question?"

"You just did."

"Piper," Leo said sternly.

"Okay, fine. Ask away."

"You seem to know other people well. You noticed Hornbill, and there's no way that you didn't notice that all your ex-boyfriends were assholes."

"That's not a question." Piper pulled her head back to look up at him, and Leo could see it in the depth of her eyes that she did know. That she had purposely entangled herself with these people.

"Why?" he asked.

Piper moved to sit up, pulling the covers up to her chest as Leo followed beside her. "This is going to sound ridiculous to you."

"Try me."

"You know how you said you're always calculating in your head how much you can spend or how to make things work financially?" He nodded. "Well, I calculate the amount of myself I can give to someone before I end up loving them. And then I calculate how much I love someone by how much it would hurt to lose them."

"And..." Leo paused to work it out in his head. "When you don't love them, you don't have to worry about losing them?" he guessed. Piper gave him a somber nod. "But what's the point of dating if not to find love?"

"Companionship." Piper lifted one shoulder. "Sex, if it's good? I don't know. It sucks to be on your own with no one to want you, but I also don't want to be in love with someone."

Leo's heart clenched. "Because you're scared?"

"I'm beyond being scared, Leo." Piper's voice was serious, and he felt stalled in time, waiting for a punchline that would never come. She was never going to love him back because she didn't want to love at all. "I never recovered from my parents' death, and I know I won't recover from when or if anyone else in my family dies before I do. And even Thea, who I promised myself I wouldn't get close to, just... got in anyway, and now I'm stuck here. I don't know how to stop loving people when they're gone. I don't know where to put that love when there's no person to pour it into anymore, so I don't go there to begin with, especially with guys. I see the way people look at each other when they're in love. I see the way it alters their lives. It's different from family and even friendship because it's the deepest and most vulnerable kind. The kind that will be the hardest to lose. If you think I'm a shell of a person now, Leo, I would be dust in the wind if I lost someone like that."

"That sounds..." Leo swallowed. It didn't sound like any way to live, but he could understand it. Losing Piper now would feel like an insurmountable thing to get over.

"Selfish?" Piper rolled her lips over her teeth. "Yeah, it probably is. I do my best to make sure I'm not a burden to other people, though. I try not to use people."

"I don't feel used," Leo said, his voice cracking. All he felt around her was desperation to know more, the exact opposite of what she wanted to give.

"You don't?" she asked, locking eyes with him.

He shook his head and leaned forward. "And I was going to say that that sounds really lonely, princesa."

"Sometimes it is." Her blue eyes met his, and he could see right through them to the depth of pain behind them, to where the sad person lived just behind the happy front.

"Use me, Piper," Leo whispered. "You don't have to feel alone when you're with me."

"We can do this without love being in the equation?" Piper asked.

The way her gaze pleaded with him and softened when he reached out to hold her hand was damning. She wanted hope when all he could give her was false confidence. Leo's thoughts warred with one another, one telling him he needed whatever piece of her he could have because unlike her, he *was* selfish, and the other saying it would be wrong to agree to something he had already broken. They had agreed to be honest with one another. Being in love with Piper made him the bad guy. It made him that person she so adamantly proclaimed he was at the beginning of the year. The one who took what he wanted and didn't care who he hurt in the process. The one who would, no doubt, end up hurting himself.

Leo gave a microscopic nod of his head and finally became someone she should hate. "Yes."

Piper could now add *liar* to her list of reasons he would never be good enough for her.

Part Three
Try with me

Forty-Six

PIPER

Piper slipped in through the front door of the bungalow, hoping she could somehow get to her room unscathed and without an altercation. She majorly owed Thea an explanation, so she shouldn't have been surprised when she turned on the lights to walk through the darkened living room only to find Thea sitting in their leather accent chair, facing the doorway with a stern expression and her arms folded over her chest.

Piper jumped and clutched at her heart. "You scared the shit out of me! Why were you sitting in the dark?"

"I was going for 'disappointed parent waiting for their kid to get home from illicit activities,'" Thea said dryly. "How'd I do?"

"I'm having flashbacks to that one time senior year when Walker and Talia were sitting on my bed and waiting when I climbed in through my window." Piper moved to set her keys and purse on the decorative wall hooks she had measured a thousand times to get level and perfectly spaced when they had moved in.

"Wasn't your window on the second story?" Thea asked.

"Yep. I think they should have given me an award for managing to climb in and out in the first place." Piper gave a cursory glance at Thea's posture to see how pissed she was before sitting down on the large maroon sofa kitty-corner to her.

"Hm, can't say I'd give you an award, either." *Ah, so, she's very mad*, Piper thought. "Where were you just now?"

Piper swallowed and looked down at her hands as she answered truthfully, "I spent most of the day with Leo."

"Are you two together now?" Thea's eyes were wide as she leaned forward on her forearms.

"No." Piper shook her head. "We agreed that this is just for fun and we're using each other. And I know that sounds bad, but he agreed to it, and—"

"Piper," Thea cut her off with her hand up in a stop position. "Why didn't you tell me any of this? Is it me? Did I do something to make you not trust me?"

"You have never made me feel that way. It's the opposite, actually. I know I could tell you anything, and you'd still be here." Piper bit her lip and looked away. She had mistakenly thought that telling Leo why she was so closed off would make it easier to tell Thea, but, for whatever reason, this was harder. When Piper was with Leo, it was almost as if she told him things involuntarily, too sucked in by the warmth of his skin and his clean laundry scent to notice when they were so far deep into the conversation that she was spilling all her secrets. With Thea, she only shared things on purpose. Piper knew she owed her friend something, or she would be exactly what she always feared she was: selfish.

"Then why?" Thea's voice choked, and Piper could see the hurt on her face.

"It has nothing to do with you," Piper pleaded. "I promise. I just—I have a hard time letting people in, and you specifically because I know you'll understand. You'll love me no matter what I do."

Thea's eyebrows cinched together. "And that's a bad thing?"

"For me? Yes. I have this..." Piper searched for the right words, the ones that had come so easily when she had been in Leo's arms earlier. She remembered the look in his eyes when he asked if she was scared—soft and earnest. "I have a fear of losing people. It feels much worse than a fear at this point, like a reality. Like the more I let people in, the more I realize how painful it would be if they were to leave or die."

"Because of your parents," Thea said. It wasn't a question, but more of an acknowledgment that Piper wasn't crazy for feeling that way.

"Yes." Piper let out a long sigh. "And I know it's not healthy to shut people out to protect myself, but I don't let you see how much I'm still not okay after my parents' deaths. I don't think I'll ever be okay, and adding more people I love to my life just feels so reckless."

"You think I don't notice?" Thea's voice was calm but pained. "I *know*, Piper. I bake your favorite desserts when I notice you're crying in your room. I see the way you hesitate every time you get in your car, and I know why. I see when you take out your inspiration box for comfort. And I know why you choose who you date. It doesn't hurt you much when it ends because you never truly liked them in the first place. I think I even know why you were so secretive about Leo."

A tear threatened to slip down Piper's face as she slowly started to realize the magnitude of what Thea was saying. Every time she had woken up after a long night and Thea had been there with scones, every time Thea had offered to use her car to drive them wherever they were going. The understanding look Thea had given her when Piper had started dating Todd, and the one after things with Todd had ended. What she didn't understand was Thea's last statement.

"Why do you think I'm so secretive about Leo?" Piper asked.

Thea sat back in her chair and met Piper's eyes directly. "Because he's not like the others. This isn't someone you just allow yourself to be around. He wasn't chosen, he just happened. He gets under your skin and is there whether you want him to be or not. I think it feels real to you, and you didn't want me to know because then you'd have to face some stuff you don't want to face."

Piper's chest flipped as she shoved down her rising panic. Real was the exact opposite of what she wanted. "No. That's not it, I just—I told you a billion times that I hated him, and I was embarrassed by my lack of self-control. You and Yuri are just so perfect and loving that I thought it'd be weird for me to tell you that Leo and I are fucked up. I mean, who settles an argument by hooking up in the dressing room after rehearsal? That can't be normal."

Thea's eyes went wide, and she jolted forward to the edge of her chair. "Oh my God, you have *seriously* been holding out on me! You think I would judge you for doing extremely hot things? Have you met me? Sex is literally my favorite thing to talk about, and you, finally having good sex? I'm here for it. Also, Yuri and I got into an argument about a literal potato chip the other day, so clearly we aren't perfect."

"It doesn't matter with Leo, really, because it's not like we're in a relationship. It's purely physical. We agreed to keep real feelings out of it."

"What was the argument about?" Thea narrowed her eyes, and Piper suddenly felt the room shrink as if she were in the middle of an interrogation.

"Emma. Leo was getting frustrated at rehearsal because she kept missing her lines and singing her songs all pitchy. He didn't notice that she was clearly having a bad day and just assumed she was being lazy about her work, so I pulled him aside and told him to get his head out of his ass and open his eyes." Piper folded her arms over her chest.

"And then you hooked up, and?" Thea rolled her hands over one another.

"Then he said he would talk to Emma, and when he realized I was right, he called me to come talk to her." Piper covered her face with her hands and groaned into her palms. "And then I basically canceled our plans to do it again at his apartment later that night by inviting Emma over, and he didn't even blink."

"So... he's clearly listening to you," Thea said, a secret smile dancing behind her eyes that Piper wanted to put an end to immediately. "What did you two do today besides rail each other into oblivion?"

"He got all irritated that I didn't buy the coffee I wanted the other day when I just got your order for everyone and demanded to come to the coffee shop with me this morning. I didn't know that was why he was there till we got up to the counter and he made me ask for my stupid fancy drink." Piper saw the wry smile play across Thea's lips and quickly added, "Then we went back to his apartment and agreed that this is casual."

"Look, I know you're terrified and you don't think love is worth it, but this is far from casual."

"We *agreed* on it, Thea." Piper lifted her chin to get her point across.

Thea scoffed. "I hate to break it to you, but nothing about what you just said is casual. And maybe he doesn't even realize it yet, but Leo is into you. I'm sorry, but he is, and I think he's valid for feeling that way."

"No, he's not." Piper shook her head. "Why would he agree to our entire deal if he was?"

"Same reason I'm friends with you. Some Piper is way better than none."

Some is better than none. The sentiment made Piper feel like she had been struck down by lightning. And maybe she didn't believe that Leo felt that way, but she knew Thea did.

"We can agree to disagree on Leo." Piper choked back the emotion in her throat. "But I don't want you to feel like you're only getting part of me anymore. I already love you, so there's no use in hiding anymore."

"I love you, too." Thea reached out and squeezed her hand.

A tear slipped down Piper's face as she said, "I'll brave the pain for you."

Thea moved over beside Piper on the couch and pulled her into a hug, her wild curls whipping Piper in the face before she pulled her in tighter. "Can you make it up to me by telling me every filthy detail of your sex life?" Piper cackled and wiped at her face. Thea practically bounced from excitement in her seat. "Oh my God, you're blushing. Tell me everything!"

For the next hour, as Thea baked scones, Piper endured every squeal and raunchy comment from her best friend as she laid out how exactly she had begun sleeping with the enemy. That was followed by a slightly mortifying reciprocity of information where Thea laid out the details of the potato chip incident that had ended with Yuri eating potato chips off her body until both of them were in hysterics, giggling and frantically blowing on the hot scones so they could eat them before they cooled. Then, when there were simply too many scones to eat on their own, they invited Emma over to down the rest.

Forty-Seven

LEO

A harsh glow from the porch light reflected off the window as Leo peered into his apartment from the front stoop. The long run he had taken to get his mind off things had the exact opposite effect. It had been a long day of meetings with Moreno and the lighting and staging crew, and sitting across from Piper as she and Elliot explained their set design drawings had been torture. Elliot's engineering of Piper's ideas was flawless, and Leo had to shove down the green monster inside him to give Elliot the praise he deserved. Even the breakaway chairs Elliot had drawn up for the Havana scene with spring-activated pieces were nothing short of genius. The folding set design that Elliot and Piper had developed pulled out to reveal the inside of the mission. It had a folding layer within that transformed it into the Havana club, and then the entire thing folded back out to make an outdoor street scene, all of which had Piper's meticulous design work. The thick file Piper had smacked onto the table full of research she had done on 1950s Manhattan and previous productions of the show made Leo unreasonably turned on. That was how, along with Leo's desire to claim Piper after the way Elliot had been looking at her, they had ended up in the backseat of her car in the empty parking lot of the theatre.

Leo had never been more fucked, both physically and mentally, before. In the weeks that followed his lie, Piper had spent every available second in his bed, tangling with him under his sheets until eventually she left to avoid Sam.

It was all too much—the lying and sneaking around. Besides the lie that Leo had told Piper, he felt just as awful lying to his best friend.

Through the window, Leo could see Sam was still up, sitting on the couch and watching *The Promenade* for the billionth time. Sam was a dreamer and frequently liked to imagine himself as an A-list actor and America's next heartthrob. He had the acting chops to get there someday, and if Leo had any say in it, he'd drag Sam by his collar into stardom along with him.

When Leo finally decided to brave Sam's presence, he walked in through the front door and threw his backpack on the ground. Sam slowly popped his head up from where he was sprawled out with a fuzzy blanket and gave a mild wave at Leo, and the pit in Leo's stomach grew three sizes like the Grinch's heart. But while the Grinch was becoming a better person, Leo was just becoming better at being a lying asshole.

"I need to tell you something," Leo word-vomited and stomped his way over to the couch. Sam lifted his head higher and looked at Leo with questioning eyes. "I slept with Piper."

"I already knew that, you dick," Sam huffed. "I came back early once, and the walls are thin, so I left. Plus, you looked guilty as fuck when Piper and I were doing the kissing scene, like, forever ago. I just wasn't going to make you tell me if you didn't want to."

"Oh." Leo cringed. "Sorry." He rubbed the heels of his hands into his forehead. He didn't have a headache, but it felt like there should be a way to massage out the thoughts stuck in his head that wouldn't leave him alone.

"Why are you telling me now?" Sam reached for a roll of toilet paper on the floor below him.

"Are you sick?" Leo asked, and Sam confirmed it by blowing an entire noseful into a few sheets he had ripped off the roll.

"Yes," Sam said simply, though his stuffy nose made it come out more like "des."

"I should let you sleep, then." Leo turned to walk away, but Sam lobbed the toilet paper roll at the back of his head with surprising force. Leo turned around to find Sam looking extremely dizzy from the exertion as his torso fell back onto the couch.

"Tell me first, then I'll sleep," Sam bartered.

Leo let out an exasperated sigh. "Fine. I, uh..."

"Hurry up, I'm tired," Sam whined.

"Okay, okay, Jesus." Leo raised his hands in defeat. "I'm telling you because I'm in love with her."

Sam transformed into the human embodiment of a heart-eye emoji. "You're in love?" The look immediately depleted, replaced by a sickly grimace.

"Are you going to throw up?" Leo stepped back.

"Maybe," Sam admitted.

Leo made quick work of running to the kitchen to grab a large bowl and set it in front of Sam, who lazily bobbed his head thank-you. Now that Leo was really looking, he noticed Sam's hair fell in clumps of sweat-soaked strands, and he wasn't just under one blanket, but four. "Are you two finally dating?" Sam asked.

"No. This was supposed to be casual, and she told me she doesn't want to be in love with anyone ever. She doesn't exactly know I'm in love with her," Leo explained.

"So what are you doing, then?" Sam gained a little more levity. "If she doesn't want what you want, then you can't sit around scrapbooking pictures of your future children together."

"I haven't met a single person who's done that." Leo rolled his eyes.

"True. I'm gay, but not an organized, scrapbooking gay. That seems like a lot of work." Sam yawned then hit Leo with a low-energy stare. "You can't keep torturing yourself."

Leo's whole body stiffened as he said everything aloud. "I'm telling you as a friend, not because I want you to give me sound advice that I already know. I have a limited amount of time to be around her before I go to film school and she goes back to Archwood to run her parents' business, so I'm taking every single second I can. I don't care that I'm screwing myself over, because she's worth it. I don't care that I'll probably regret it. I don't care that she's never going to know how I feel about her. I just don't care about anything other than being around her. No me importa."

Sam gave an exasperated sigh, longingly looking over at the roll of toilet paper on the ground. Leo walked over to pick it up and handed it to him. "Thanks." Sam began to rip pieces off. "This is not going to make you happy, Leo. Maybe if you tell her that you're in love with her, she'll feel the same way."

Leo pulled his fingers through his hair. "Stop trying to give me hope, Sam. She's never going to be in love with me. She basically told me that point-blank."

"But you didn't tell her how you feel!" Sam must have found a little strength within himself because his voice had turned loud and irritated. "So how do you know that it wouldn't change everything?"

"Not everything is a rom-com!" Leo shouted back. "This won't end well for me, and I already know that."

"I have never known you to be this dumb." The sick version of Sam had no qualms about telling it to Leo straight. "If you're not planning on telling her, then the whole thing is a bad fucking idea."

"Stop reminding me it's a bad idea," Leo snapped. "I know it is, and I don't give a fuck. La amo." He punctuated his Spanish with a flick of his hand. "End of story."

"I just want you to be happy." Sam shivered and pulled the blankets up around his shoulders.

"I'm happy when I'm with her," Leo murmured. In response, Sam lurched over the bowl and upchucked, like the statement was the grossest thing he had ever heard. "Shit!" Leo jumped backward and waited for Sam to stop emptying his stomach, then asked, "Have you taken anything yet?"

Sam's sickly moan echoed in the bowl. "What exactly would I take? It's not like we have anything."

Leo started toward the kitchen, where he already knew he wouldn't find anything to help. He looked through all of their cabinets, muttering to himself when he couldn't find even a bottle of ibuprofen. The fridge was his next bet, but he didn't find lemon or honey in the cabinets to make the hot water concoction his mom always used to make when he or his siblings were sick.

"Does Wes have drugs?" Leo called out over his shoulder. "Can we call him?"

"He's not awake. Who do you think I got this shit from?" Sam called back weakly. "Sorry, I don't think I can rehearse tomorrow."

Leo trudged back over to the sofa and crouched down to Sam's eye level. "You really think I'm worried about that right now?" He reached out a tentative hand and held the back of it against Sam's clammy forehead, another thing Lucia used to do. With one touch, she always seemed to know just how sick Leo or one of his siblings was. He didn't know how to gauge a fever, but the blazing heat against his hand said that Sam probably had one. Resigned, he stood up and pulled out his phone. "I'm going to call someone."

A quiet knock finally came on the front door an hour later, and Leo flew up from the arm of the couch to open it. Piper stood on his doorstep holding a reusable Lydia's Grocery bag and wearing his black hoodie that she had never seen fit to give back. It looked better on her anyway. Without preamble, she barged into the apartment.

"Where's Sam?"

"He's asleep on the couch," Leo said. "You didn't need to come over. I just wanted to borrow some stuff and then never return it. I could have come by."

Piper heaved the nearly full bag onto the countertop, the contents rattling inside. The items Leo had requested shouldn't have taken up much space, so he wasn't sure what was actually in the bag until she started pulling things out one by one. Along with the supplies he had requested for Sam—honey, lemon, Vicks VapoRub, and Tylenol—she'd brought what looked like the ingredients for chicken noodle soup, those lotion-infused tissues his family never bought, and a stockpile of other drugs and products. Leo reached for one of the boxes and held it up, confused.

"Why does he need Imodium A-D? He has a fever. I don't think he's shitting himself just yet." Leo craned his head to look at the sleeping lump on the couch just to verify that Sam hadn't soiled himself without his knowledge.

"Oh, um..." Piper's cheeks tinged with pink as she pulled a larger box containing a small humidifier from the bag, and she looked away. "You said you didn't have any medicine, so I just picked up some other basic things while I was at the store. I was grocery shopping when you called, so it wasn't a huge deal."

"You were grocery shopping at one in the morning?" Leo narrowed his eyes.

"Yep." Piper nodded a little too aggressively. "It's nice when there's no one there."

He knew she was lying, but felt the need to deter any future trips to the grocery store at an ungodly hour. "If you do that again, invite me. Biston's is the only place open that late at night, and it's where my freshman year roommate got mugged once."

"Thea went with me."

Leo shook his head. Two of them might be able to do some

damage, but he doubted it. He'd seen the way Piper punched, and while she was learning more each time he gave her another lesson, it wasn't enough. "I don't like it, Piper. For either of you. It's not safe, and I know you don't like driving at night, so just call me next time."

The defiant look in her eyes fell away, and she gave him a curt nod. "Okay."

"Thank you," he murmured and gestured to the slew of medications she had brought. "And thank you for all of this."

"I got washcloths, too. For his forehead. You said he had a fever, right? My dad used to put a cool cloth on my head when I was sick." Piper shrugged, but Leo saw the twinge of sadness behind her eyes, and his heart clenched. "But you probably have washcloths, so it was a stupid idea."

"We do have washcloths, but it's not stupid." Leo gave Piper a soft smile and took the washcloths from her hand, ripping open the packaging. He handed one cloth back to her and set the rest on the counter. "You do this, and I'll get the other stuff ready. And then it looks like we're making soup?"

Piper nodded. "My mom's recipe."

For the next several minutes, they worked in silence, prepping every element of the home remedy they mutually decided would heal Sam. Leo grabbed a pair of clean socks from Sam's room and made the hot lemon and honey tea. Piper rolled the cool, wet rag and woke Sam up by pressing it to his forehead.

"What's happening?" Sam moaned, his eyes blinking slowly into awareness.

"We're taking care of you. Can you sit up? You need to take this." Leo held out the assortment of cold and flu pills and vitamin C tablets.

"Piper?" Sam groaned but sat up a bit. "I love your uncle."

"What?" Piper screwed up her face. "I think that's the fever talking. He's very taken, and I think Wes might have a problem with you saying that."

Leo laughed and shook his head. "He probably does have a

fever, but I think he means Walker's book. Walker gave me a copy of *The Dating Brigade*, and Sam's already read it twice."

"Oh. That makes more sense." Piper held up a thermometer. "Open up."

"I want a matchmaking empire like Landon and Cora." Sam looked incredibly dizzy as he spoke his gibberish. "I want a big choppy knife." Sam's pointer finger sliced through the air and made a few lazy stabbing motions.

"Okay, buddy," Leo sighed. "You're losing it."

"I assume that has to do with the book?" Piper asked. "I haven't read it."

"No clue," Leo said. "Sam, shut up and do what she says." Sam mumbled a protest but opened his mouth obediently. When the thermometer beeped and Piper pulled it out from under Sam's tongue, Leo leaned over to clock the temperature at one hundred two point six. "Fuck. Okay, take this." He shoved the pills he had prepared into Sam's hand and grabbed the lemon honey tea from their shitty chipped coffee table.

"Yes, Dad." Sam's joke lacked enthusiasm, his entire body drooping with exhaustion as he dropped a pill into his mouth and chased it with a sip of tea.

Leo reached for the VapoRub and watched Sam's throat bob slowly on a swallow. "Okay." He held up the jar and the clean pair of plaid socks he had retrieved from Sam's room. "This goes on the bottom of your feet and your chest so you can breathe better." Leo was a good friend, but he wasn't about to slather Sam's feet for him.

An hour later, Sam was passed out on the couch again, and Leo and Piper had a full container of chicken noodle soup cooling in the fridge for when he woke up. In the kitchen, Leo had learned that Piper's lack of spatial awareness wasn't limited to walking and balance. By the time they had finished the soup, he had blocked at least three open cabinet doors from hitting her head. When they moved on to Sam's room, stripping the bed of its sheets to wash them, she had managed to smack her shin on his bed frame. She finally agreed to get her eyes tested at Leo's insistence despite her multiple proclamations that she was simply tired.

Leo wadded up Sam's laundry and wandered out to the tiny closet in the hallway that housed their washer and dryer. Piper yawned and wordlessly pulled open the door for him, then lifted the washing machine lid, anticipating all of his requests before he voiced them. He shouldn't have been surprised given the way Piper took to the stage at rehearsal. Leo tossed the sheets into the machine and then reached for the massive canister on the shelf above it.

"What's that?" Piper asked.

Leo unclasped the side, releasing the rubber seal, and held it open for her to look. The contents were murky white and looked a bit like milky pond water or the whey on top of an unmixed tub of sour cream. "I make my own laundry detergent. It's my abuelita's recipe. It looks gross, but it works better than the normal stuff, and it's cheaper. It's basically a fuck ton of Jabón-Zote, borax, and Arm and Hammer." He pulled out the plastic measuring cup and slopped some of the stuff into the washing machine as Piper looked on in interest.

"That's so cool," she said. He figured she was joking, but he looked over to her and found she was leaning toward the canister he had set on the dryer to breathe in the scent. "This is why you always smell so good."

"Oh, yeah?" Leo smirked and stepped toward her. "You can smell me any time."

Piper shoved at his chest with a small laugh before she took a cursory glance at the front door. "I should probably go."

"No." Leo shook his head. "It's late, Piper. Just stay with me."

"I don't know." Piper bit her lip. "What about Sam?"

"He already knows. He came back early once, and you're very vocal." Leo winked.

Piper scoffed, then looked thoughtful. "I don't want to impose. I can just suck it up and drive home."

"Princesa, I imposed on *you*. It's three in the morning. You're not driving home." Leo could see the moment Piper broke her facade of trying to stay strong right before she flung her arms around his neck.

"Thank you. I had a shitty dinner with my brother, and I really don't want to drive this late."

"With Carter, you mean? What happened?" Leo pulled away and tucked his hand at the nape of her neck.

"He said he's not coming home for Christmas. I guess his girlfriend's family decided they were going skiing, and she pretty much forced his hand into going to see her family instead of ours." Piper shrugged sadly, then started to walk toward Leo's bedroom. "They got in a huge fight about it, apparently, and Carter just gave up. He kinda shuts down when it comes to conflict." Piper paused for a minute to pull back Leo's covers, and he watched with rapt attention as she stripped out of her jeans and crawled into his bed in her underwear and his hoodie. It looked so domestic. So natural. "Anyway, we've already missed Hanukkah with Talia every year we've been away from home, so it sucks that we can't all be together for Christmas, at least, you know?" When she noticed he was just standing in the doorway, watching her, she patted the spot beside her in bed.

"Yeah." Leo nodded and started to strip down to his underwear. "I get making sacrifices for the people you love, but I don't think it should be all one person all the time. That seems unhealthy." He flicked the lights off and crawled under the covers beside Piper, meeting her face to face. "I think if I was dating you, I wouldn't just insist on Christmas with my family every year when I know how much your family means to you and why you need to go home sometimes."

"Exactly," Piper agreed, and Leo felt his heart skip a beat. She hadn't completely discounted the idea of them being together, and, because he was a complete fool, it gave him a glimmer of hope. "I was actually going to ask if you wanted to ride back together for Christmas?"

"Yeah," Leo said. He took a deep breath and leaned forward to kiss her forehead. It was probably crossing a line, but he didn't care anymore. "I'll drive, and you can be a passenger princess. Buenas noches, mi vida."

"Good night, Leo." Piper rolled away from him, and his heart sank until she wiggled back into him, her ass spooning his crotch. He was thankful she couldn't see him, or the smile that crossed his face when she came in close would have been a dead giveaway. The arm that he draped over her was still probably a giveaway, but, again, he no longer cared. He would play house with Piper for however long she let him.

Forty-Eight

LEO

A fresh shower and a few classes down, Leo sat in the office he shared with Moreno, scouring the day's script and making notations so he wouldn't easily forget his ideas when they came up in rehearsal. Sticky notes with his chicken scratch handwriting lined the desk, ranging from a sick-Sam-level fever dream of half-thought-out ideas to structured and competent plans. He picked through the notes to find the ones that applied to the upcoming rehearsal and stuck them to his clipboard. A lot of this night's rehearsal would be reliant on Emma, and although she had been doing great in rehearsals lately, he shot her a text to make sure she was up for it after their business class that morning. Her response made him chuckle.

> EMMA 4:56 PM
>
> I'm fine, Mom. I drew a picture of Professor Pervert with his head chopped off and I feel great.

The text Leo sent back, demanding to see said drawing so he could frame it, was followed up with a question from Emma about his status with Piper. He patently ignored it in favor of confirming with Moreno that he could use some of the theatre budget to buy donuts for the whole cast as a morale boost after the plight of sickness everyone had experienced the week before. Thanks to Piper's contributions to the set, the usually tight musical budget had a little wiggle room for higher-quality costumes and props along the way. The last stretch of mapping out scenes and musical numbers had finally come, and they were well into performing large chunks of the show and working out only the small details. Details Leo had obsessed over for the last few months and was happy to throw himself into again before everyone arrived on set.

An hour passed before Leo decided a break was in order, and he pulled out the book Sam had practically shoved into his hands before he left their apartment. The name "Hartrick" stood out on the cover like a swift jab to his heart. Getting even more involved with Piper and her family was a terrible idea, but Leo opened the paperback to the first page anyway, pulled in by the intriguing cover art and Sam's repeated declarations that it was the best book ever written. The prologue wasn't much of anything at all. Just a date, a time, and two sentences.

October 15th, 1:42 AM
A pivotal moment for some meant buying a new house or getting married. For Landon Cole, it meant helping his girlfriend slide a bloodied knife out of a soon-to-be corpse.

It was one hell of a hook, and Leo no longer had any qualms about reading further because he *needed* to know what happened. Sam was onto something. Leo could practically picture the descriptions and the imagery playing out in his head. For a while, he lost the plot of his own life in favor of the fictional one in his hands. It was that same spark he had when he watched a good movie or when he was directing the musical.

Before Leo knew it, the leather-bound journal Moreno had given him was open on the desk, and his hand was flying over the pages as he took notes. Sam was going to be pissed that Leo was underlining lines in the book, but he'd just buy a new copy from Walker when he went home for Christmas.

Donuts in hand, Leo wandered out to the stage humming Taylor Swift under his breath because, to his surprise, Piper's suggestion about female rage music had been a good one. The *reputation* album had fueled a few of his boxing sessions so far, and when Taylor Swift was pissed off in his knockoff AirPods, he could perfectly imagine Hornbill's face as his target.

"Donuts?" Leo raised the box into the air like Simba in *The Lion King* when he found a few cast members on stage. "I'm going to be hard on all of you today, so I'm buttering you up with sweets."

"When are you not hard on us?" Wes eagerly reached for the box, whipping out a glazed donut as people started to flock to Leo.

"I expect everyone to give me their all." Leo shrugged. "I don't think that's asking too much."

"Well, I think donuts are an excellent way to sweeten the pot." Elliot walked out on the stage and gave everyone a wide smile before reaching the donut box and pulling out an iced bear claw. Leo tamped down his gut reaction to say something snide. Jealousy was not a good look on him. Elliot had done nothing wrong, and yet, every fiber of Leo's being wanted to scream every time he was in the guy's presence. He had never been overly territorial before, but he had also never been in love before, and his heart constantly wanted to lay claim to Piper like he was a caveman.

Leo cleared his throat. "Thanks, Elliot. You and Piper working on the set today?"

"Yeah." Elliot swallowed a bite of his donut. "We're taking some measurements today so I can start building since we've finally narrowed down the perfect design for the Hot Box. She's a genius."

"Yeah, she's talented in lots of ways," Leo said.

Emma cut in with a sideways glance at Leo that said to cool it. "And I'm sure your architecture and engineering majors are coming in handy."

"You know me, I love to work with my hands." Elliot lifted them for show, and Leo had the brutal thought of chopping those same hands off at the wrists so Elliot could never touch Piper with them. That thought was quickly followed up with a more sane one: *okay, Jigsaw. What the fuck is wrong with you?*

"You're doing great." Leo mustered some fake enthusiasm because, really, Elliot *was* doing a good job and did not deserve the vitriol Leo's brain was conjuring up. Piper was turning him into a fucking psychopath, and, truly, if Elliot was what she wanted, then Leo should be happy for her.

Elliot beamed. "Thanks, boss."

Leo opened his mouth to offer another compliment to backtrack on his previously unhinged thoughts when his cell phone started ringing in his pocket. "Uh, one sec." When he pulled it out, his mom's caller ID glared up at him, and he furrowed his brow. He thought about declining it and calling her back later, but it felt a bit odd for her to be calling at a time when she was usually at work, so he picked up. "Mamá." And that was when he heard it: the unmistakable sound of crying.

"Leo," his mom sniffed on the other line. His heart stalled and then started beating out of his chest. Something was very, *very* wrong.

"¿Mamá? ¿Qué pasó?" The frantic tone he used must have alerted everyone because Sam quickly stepped forward, eyes emblazoned with concern.

"Abuelita—"

His mother's crying intensified, and she barely got the words out before Leo found himself sitting on the floor, head spinning and nausea roiling in his stomach as Sam held him upright.

Forty-Nine

PIPER

The orchestra pit was dimly lit when Piper finally found a way inside after dragging information out of a tear-streaked Sam. Showing up to rehearsal to find Leo missing and everyone looking forlorn was a punch to her gut. Even more so when she learned of Isabel, the woman who had told Piper to take up space and with whom she'd laughed in Leo's living room. More than anything, the urgency to find Leo came first. The bone-deep need to sit beside him as his world came crashing down. She would hold him to the earth and ground him because she was starting to think that being alone was always worse.

When Piper found him, Leo was sitting on the first violinist's chair amidst the half moon facing the conductor's podium. His face was buried in both hands, back hunched over, and hair even messier and more unkempt than usual. He had never looked so small before. That commanding presence Piper was so used to had vanquished in the face of Leo's grief. With any luck, he would get his confidence back, unlike the way she had allowed herself to dwindle away when her parents died.

"I knew you'd come," Leo whispered. His voice was hoarse

and pained, the kind that splintered Piper's heart and sat deep in her chest next to her own grief. He didn't look up from his hands at all to meet her gaze as she sat down beside him, but she knew that he meant the words for her. Somehow, he had known that out of anyone, she'd be there. Maybe it was because of her parents, or maybe it was the strangely emotional connection they seemed to share. The one she had been trying to fight off since meeting him all those years ago.

"Of course I did," Piper said. She hesitated for only a second before reaching out to take one of the hands Leo had covering his face, pulling it into her lap for comfort. It was almost indecent the way she was desperate to piece his heart back together.

"I'm not okay, Piper. You don't have to be here if you don't want to be." Leo let out a short, pathetic excuse for a laugh.

The pad of her thumb brushed over his palm with reassuring strokes. Leo finally dropped his other hand from his face and looked over at her with tear-streaked cheeks. "Someone I know keeps telling me that it's okay to feel," Piper teased with a soft smile.

"He seems intelligent." Leo wiped at his face. "And extremely attractive."

"He's okay." Piper gave him a shrug and playfully bumped her shoulder against his before steering the conversation back to the present. "She was wonderful, Leo. She really was."

Fresh tears rolled down Leo's face as he bobbed his head. "I should've visited her more."

Piper shook her head. "You couldn't have."

"I could have worked harder. Maybe got a second job so I could afford trips back to Archwood more often. I used to wait tables before I got the job as Moreno's assistant here." Leo sniffed. "Hell, if I wasn't so stubborn, I could have asked to drive down with you every time you went to visit your family."

"We would have killed each other, and I would have thought that you had to have hit your head on something to even propose that idea," Piper argued.

"But I could have figured it out!" Leo's voice turned frantic. "I don't see them enough. My family hasn't been enough of a priority. I'm missing every important milestone in everyone's lives. Antonio and Saanvi announced they're having another kid, and I wasn't there to congratulate them. Mariana has a boyfriend now, and I missed that, too. Mira, Abuelita had cancer, and I *still* didn't make her a priority. Maybe you were right about me, Piper. Maybe I'm just selfish."

Piper didn't realize it until she went to speak, but she was crying, too, all while adamantly shaking her head with each of his statements. "You aren't selfish, Leo. I saw how you were with your family. You love them. You care about them. You're always FaceTiming them and bringing them up in conversation. You danced with your sister in the living room. You made sure your mom got flowers when she got her promotion. You're a lot of things, Leo. You're too blunt with people when it comes to the truth. You're constantly grumpy. You steamroll your way into getting what you want, sure, but no, you aren't selfish. Not even close. Half of the shit you do is for other people, even when it's tactless."

"You hide yourself so you don't hurt or burden people. That's unselfish," Leo murmured.

"Or maybe it's selfish not to let people in." Piper gave a small lift of her shoulders. Since her discussion with Thea, she had only felt lighter. "Maybe it's wrong to think that I deserve friendships when I don't give myself over fully to anyone. I protect myself from love and expect other people to be vulnerable with me while I give them nothing in return."

Leo squeezed her hand where she was still holding it. "Being scared and calculating risks is a part of life." He sniffed and wiped his face. "But not taking any risks is lonely. You deserve love, Piper. You deserve everything real and wonderful about love. You deserve someone who makes you smile for real. Someone who wants every part of you without making you feel like you're a burden."

You do that. The thought came so quickly to her mind that

Piper couldn't combat it if she tried. It was shocking, but it was still true. She never felt like a burden for letting her emotions out when she was with Leo. Sure, a lot of the time the emotion she felt around him was anger, but even then, sitting with tears streaming down her face, there wasn't some invisible force telling her to hold it together for him. For the first time, she thought she might believe him and that love wasn't so far out of reach.

Piper's chest tightened as she stared into Leo's glistening, regretful eyes, seeing past his words to the heart of his problem. Despite his confidence, he still teetered on the edge of believing he wasn't good enough for his family. "You deserve your dream, Leo. You deserve every bit of praise for the work you put out into the world, and I think your family understands why you can't drop everything all the time to come home.

"If I recall, your grandma was one of your biggest fans. She loved that you were pursuing your passion. You're the living embodiment of your parents' devotion. They see that. I know they do. What you're doing is showing Mariana that she can be anything she wants to be. You're proving that being a part of your family emboldened you enough to go out and get everything you and they deserve. You're proving that you are every bit the man your grandmother helped raise. So what if you aren't home every four seconds? You are doing something important. You being here *is* giving them your time. And anytime you need to physically be with your family to remind you why you're doing what you're doing, all you need to do is ask, and I promise to not kill you when you insist on exclusively playing movie scores the entire way there."

There was no response for a long moment as Leo stared at her until he finally jerked forward. His arms wrapped around Piper's neck as he pulled her head into his chest. She could feel him shaking as a sob wracked his body, and she clutched onto his torso harder, burying her face in his shirt while he buried his in her hair. They stayed that way for an inordinate amount of time, holding onto each other like Rose and Jack held onto that door in *Titanic*, except there was room for both of them on the plywood because *fuck that.*

Finally, when Leo pulled back, Piper wiped under her eyes and gave a choked laugh at how ridiculous it was that the most real conversation she'd had in years was with someone she thought she hated.

"If I ask you a question, will you give me an honest answer?" Leo asked.

Piper didn't think before responding, "Yes."

"What did you do when they died?"

"I wallowed." Piper toyed with her hands. "I thought about them constantly until I got so tired of thinking about them that I tried to drown the pain with really mediocre sex with 'Harden-Can't-Get-a-Hard-on.' And then I got drunk at a few parties."

Leo nodded, and not in a way that made her feel like he was judging her life choices, just a small acknowledgment that said he understood. "So, is it true, then?"

"Is what true?"

"Harden really can't get a hard-on?" A real smile blossomed across Leo's face, and Piper let out a short cackle in return.

"Who do you think started that rumor?" she asked. Leo grinned even wider, the tears still staining his cheeks but gaining a little levity. "Technically, he can, but he was such a dickwit that I felt obligated to deter other women from sleeping with him."

"Was he your first?" Leo asked.

"Unfortunately." She cringed.

"My first sucked, too. Jenny Applebee. She was really… spirited?" He chuckled. "I normally don't kiss and tell, but she literally told everyone the next day."

"She gave you rave reviews," Piper recalled. She remembered being very annoyed by the information while also wanting to know how exactly the sex had been so good when Harden made her feel nothing but uncomfortable.

"It was truly awful, so I don't know why she lied. I didn't ask her to, I swear."

"I think you're the only one I'd give a rave review for," Piper admitted, biting her lip at the admission.

"I have an idea." Leo leaned forward and thumbed her bottom lip, pulling it free from her teeth. "What if we skip the mediocre part of your coping strategy?" Warmth licked up her spine, and she shifted in her seat in a poor attempt to tamp down any inappropriate desire. She was surprised at how easily he could flip the script. Her emotions felt like a loose cannon around him, going from crying to laughing and then lusting in a matter of minutes.

"I'm not sure that sex is a good coping strategy at all," Piper said. All the times they had already slept together didn't change the fact that she didn't want Leo to regret a decision he made in the thick of grief.

"I know it's not a good idea on paper, and maybe this proves that I am selfish, but I want a break from how awful I feel right now. You make me feel good." Leo sighed and shook his head. "But I shouldn't drag you into my misery. Sorry."

"I know exactly what you mean." Piper sucked in a contemplative breath and tapped her fingers against her thighs. "Well, maybe it's not so bad to take a little break."

Leo, whose head had previously hung low, staring at his feet, snapped his gaze up to look at her with hopeful and watery eyes. "Yeah?"

"Yeah," she decided.

Leo leaned forward tentatively and met her lips with a slow press of his own. It wasn't like their usual carnal passion. Both their faces were still wet with tears, and instead of begging for sex, it felt like he was begging for something else entirely. *Take the pain away*, he pleaded in the soft brush of his thumb against her arm. Piper's fingers stroked the nape of his neck and responded in kind with desperation. His lips were dredging up her own grief that she kept stowed away in the back corner of her brain. Nothing was enough to quell the pain, even when she moved to straddle him, her legs dangling off the back of the first violinist's chair. Leo groaned when she rolled into his groin, and she felt the destruction of their decision waiting for them like a phantom symphony in the orchestra pit was playing the *Jaws* theme.

"Please," Leo whispered against her lips. Her favorite word to ever leave his mouth sounded different this time. They both knew the plan wasn't working. Instead of masking the pain, this was heightening it, soaking into her bones as she sought out her pleasure. Neither of them seemed willing to stop, though. She could feel it in the way he moved, hopelessly asking for her to give him something to be happy about. And she tried, she really did, but the connection was too... too *everything*. Her nerves were pricked with emotion like she was sixteen again and looking for any way to dull the pain that losing her parents had caused. It didn't matter that pleasure was a part of it this time, unlike when she'd tried to drown it out in high school. Sorrow was right under her skin. Right below the surface of Leo's mouth and fingers, searching for release.

And so, Piper continued despite knowing it would be raw and vulnerable for them both. It would rip her limb from limb, split her down the middle until she was flayed open to the core. The very thing she didn't want to happen with Leo.

Piper unclasped his belt with shaky hands and adjusted on his lap so he could pull his cock free from his underwear and pants. Between slow and deliberate kisses, his warm fingers pulled her underwear to the side under her flannel dress, and he helped lift her long enough for Piper to sink onto him with an agonizingly slow drop of her hips. When he was fully seated inside, they both let out a simultaneous gasp and nothing more before they were moving, chasing a high that was sure to only be a low when they reached it.

"Fuck," Leo panted, squeezing his eyes shut hard. "This feels—"

"Do you want to stop?" Piper moved through choppy breaths as she tried to hold back the grief lodged in her throat and chest. Each shift of her hips made the pleasure rise in her stomach, and it was only a matter of time until the grief and pleasure collided inside her in what was sure to be a disastrous upheaval of emotion.

"No, keep going," he breathed, chest heaving as his eyebrows pulled together in concentration. His eyes were pools of darkness until the tears finally dropped past his waterline to roll down his face in clear tracks of misery. "Make it stop, Piper, *please*."

"I can't," she choked out and canted her hips to try to get a better angle. When he hit the spot that usually made her cry out in pleasure, a broken sob escaped her lips instead. Leo clutched onto her harder, scooting out to the edge of his chair so her legs could wrap around him. Urgent thrusts had her underwear hitting her clit as they jerked forward, and the warmth coiling in her stomach started to rise quicker than she wanted it to. One look at Leo's desperate face, and she knew he was terrified to tip over the ledge, too. They were both hanging on for dear life.

Leo heaved air into his lungs and kissed her in a blind panic. Piper kissed him back hard, feeling his wet lips tremble against hers as her nostrils burned with the bite of incoming sorrow. She dipped her tongue into his mouth as if that could solve what was about to pour out of them, but all she could taste was the salt of Leo's tears. Everything they did was futile. Her sanity hung in the teetering balance between them, an object just barely out of grasp. No matter how far she wanted to toss her grief aside, it was rising like a destructive tidal wave. Leo was her anchor, but instead of grounding her, he was tied around her waist and pulling her to the bottom of the ocean.

"Damn." Leo's curse as he bucked against her felt prophetic. The dam was about to break. They both knew it, and yet they chased release anyway. Their bodies demanded it. Sought it out. Begged to break. "I'm gonna come."

"Me too." Piper groaned, closing her eyes as the first set of tears began to fall onto her cheeks. "I can't stop."

"Oh, God," Leo croaked. There was no stopping it now. A wave of misery descended on them, ready to eat them alive. His muscles tightened and jerked forward underneath her, his hands pressing into her back like she could save him from the onslaught of grief when she couldn't even save herself. The culmination of everything she had held back during the last five years poured out with the quivering of her legs and an aggressive tingle up her spine. She wasn't soaring into an orgasm, but dropping into a bottomless pit.

When it was over, the hysterics started. They were still connected, falling into each other, broken and choked with grief. Leo's face was sopping wet, and Piper tried to help by wiping at it. It was a fruitless attempt for both of them. He was doing the same to her, running his thumb under her eyes to no avail. There was no point in cleaning up a mess when they were still in the middle of a shared mental breakdown.

"They're gone," Piper finally whimpered as her eyes fell shut.

"Why did she have to leave?" Leo's thick lashes, damp and clumped together, fluttered to let more tears drop down his face. "She was so healthy when I saw her last. You were there. You saw how she was." Piper bobbed her head in agreement, making her tears fall faster. "She was only sixty-seven. That's too young. Your parents?"

"Thirty-eight," Piper sniffed. "It's not fucking fair." Death didn't care how lively or wonderful someone was. It just took.

"*It's not fucking fair,*" Leo repeated in barely a whisper, leaning in and holding onto her tighter. "Don't ever leave early, okay?"

"You either." She buried her face in his neck.

"Piper." His hand cupped the back of her head as his body shook with another sob. "I'm sorry I ever judged you for how you dealt with it."

"You were right." Her voice trembled. "I hide. I don't let people see until the grief overflows like—"

"This," Leo finished for her, sniffling. "I get it, though. This..."

"Sucks," Piper whispered.

"Yeah." A few deep breaths seemed to calm him a bit as his hands brushed up and down her spine with a gentle touch. "Will you go to her funeral with me?"

The last time Piper had gone to a funeral, she had stood next to her siblings, uncle, and grandfather as they stared at a framed photo of her parents. They were smiling and happy in the picture, and she remembered believing that she would never feel that way again. She could still hear Carter's sob beside her. She could feel her sister's fingers entwined in hers as Pearl cried into her shoulder. Cooper's tears were quiet, while Colin and Walker wore matching stone-faced expressions. Her grandfather had reeked of alcohol and swayed on his feet. And maybe she had internalized that at the time, thinking that alcohol would somehow mask the pain. It hadn't. Sex hadn't, either. This time, however, even though the sex didn't heal her, she felt almost relieved to let the pain out. It was excruciating, but she didn't feel like she had to put on a smile for the first time in a very long time. Leo had given her that, so the least she could do was attend another funeral.

"Yes," Piper nodded. "I'll be there."

Fifty

PIPER

In the rainy-day funerals of TV and film, everyone had a black umbrella to hold above their head. At Isabel's funeral, no one had protection while they huddled together in the frigid December rain. Colin and Carter had flanked either side of Piper like twin pillars, partially protecting her from the cold, but now, standing in her bedroom before everyone arrived for the funeral reception, she was soaked to the bone, her black dress clinging to her body as her tights put up a fight to peel away from her legs.

The weather that day felt like the direct antithesis of the day they had buried Piper's parents. At the time, she had thought that it *should* be raining. That the birds shouldn't be chirping and the sun shouldn't be shining down on her as she stared at her parents' caskets. In the end, it was all the same. She and Leo both had lost people. They both wanted to succeed in their careers. They both cared about their family and friends deeply and constantly wondered if they were doing the right thing.

For the entire ceremony, as the priest from Our Lady of the Mountain gave Isabel a proper Catholic burial, Piper had been elsewhere. Her eyes found Leo standing in the grass across from her, and she hadn't looked away once. His face was downcast, but he hadn't cried like his mother or Alvaro beside him. Leo had retreated in on himself. The entire drive down to Archwood, even with Sam, Emma, and Carter to liven up the road trip, Leo's face had shown barely any emotion at all. She remembered it well, the numbness after loss, where it felt like she had expelled every ounce of emotion inside her until there was nothing left. Sometimes she wondered if she had ever really recovered from that place. She could trick herself into being happy now and had even experienced real joy, but the gray blanket of grief always seemed to linger just under the surface.

Still, over the last few months, Piper had felt a little lighter as she unraveled pieces of the grief she had kept hidden. When she allowed herself the grace to feel pain, it was a weight lifted from her shoulders. The grief blanket was heavy, and she didn't realize just how heavy until someone else took some of the weight. And maybe that was why she had had the urge to touch Leo during the ceremony. To be the one at his side the way Walker's arm had been wrapped around Talia's waist or the way Leo's brother, Antonio, had clutched onto his wife's hand.

Before, Piper could ignore her secret dreams regarding relationships because she knew they would be too painful in the end. Now, she found herself wondering if maybe even the pain of loss was worth the reward of love. The most terrifying thought of all was that the one thing that had truly changed in the last few months was Leo. She wanted to still hate him because it felt safe to stay in that bubble, not knowing how wonderful he was. Not knowing the way his skin felt or how the sound of his laugh eased the tension in her shoulders, how much he would sacrifice for the people he loved. She wanted to still believe he was a jerk, but the comfort she now got from his ability to make decisions and be a natural-born leader told a different story. The way he allowed her to speak her mind—not only allowed, but demanded to know her thoughts and opinions.

After Piper had changed into a dark purple dress she hoped

could pass as black since her only black dress was now sopping wet, she stared at herself in the mirror. Her hair was clumped together, and the drying strands were starting to frizz. It looked the way it had the night she had first slept with Leo. Even when the only thing they had going was an alarming attraction to each other, he had told her she was beautiful. It was easy to believe he meant it because he had had no reason to lie. Leo touched the parts of herself she thought she hated and turned everything good.

A knock on the door interrupted Piper's scan of her body, and she called out "come in" as she gathered her soaked clothes from the floor. The door creaked open, and she was surprised when it wasn't one of her siblings who stepped through the doorway, but Leo, wearing a black T-shirt and pants that replaced his dress wear from earlier.

"Hi." He shut the door behind him.

"You're early," Piper noted.

"I thought I could help set up just for something to do, but Talia and Amala told me to get lost." Leo huffed out a laugh. "So I figured I'd come see what you were doing. I still think it's weird that they're holding the mercy meal for us."

"That was actually Walker's idea," Piper said. She sat down on her bed and patted the spot beside her. Leo followed her cue and sat next to her, his warm body brushing against hers. She leaned into his heat, a welcome force against the leftover chill from the rain. "He said one of the shittiest things about having to bury my parents was that everyone expected him to entertain guests after the funeral." She didn't elaborate on how Talia and Amala had found Leo's mom crying in the employee bathroom at Lydia's after they had already told her and Leo's dad to take some paid time off. Or that Piper's family had seemed to unanimously decide that they would be the ones to rally around the Diazes. Even Carter had forfeited his ski trip and gotten into a massive fight with his girlfriend so he could come home this year. Piper's family knew what it was to lose someone. They knew what was important, and they knew what it felt like to have help because Amala and Talia had been that for them the year Piper's parents had died.

"And now you all get to experience the thousand primos and tías I have," Leo joked. "Not the way I pictured you meeting my entire extended family."

"You pictured me meeting your extended family?" Piper turned her body to face him, hoping that she didn't look too eager.

He leaned forward, resting his forearms on his thighs, and met her eyes with an expression she couldn't read. "I picture you doing lots of things, Piper."

"Oh." She swallowed, her heart fluttering in her chest.

Leo's hand swiped through the tangled, damp curls on his head before he flopped back onto her bed. "A lot of them said they wanted to come to opening night, so if not for Abuelita, you would have met them at some point."

"Right," Piper reasoned. She fell back beside him, still trying to make sense of how exactly he pictured her. Was it just sexual? Or did he feel the pull of connection past that like she did, too?

He turned his head to look at her so their faces were only a few inches apart. "Thank you for being here."

"This is my house," she whispered back.

The corner of Leo's mouth quirked in slight amusement, which Piper counted as a win. "You know what I mean."

"I wish..." Piper grimaced and shifted on the mattress to get comfortable with the admission she wanted to share. "I wish I would have stood next to you at the funeral. I wanted to, but I didn't know if that was appropriate."

"I would have liked that," Leo said. The reply was simple enough, but it squeezed her chest nonetheless. If he wanted her there, then that was where she should have been. She should have taken up space. Should have let her heart feel everything she was supposed to feel. That was what Isabel would have done. "Whatever you're thinking right now, stop it." Leo's hand reached up and gently brushed her cheek.

"I stopped myself from doing something I wanted to do again." Piper's voice was barely a murmur as Leo scooted closer, pressing his forehead into hers.

"I'm never going to expect you to be perfect, mi vida."

Her mind whirred from the nickname he had used a few times now. She had translated it easily enough, but she couldn't place exactly what he meant by it. It could be something friends called friends, or something mothers called their children.

Piper could barely make out any of Leo's features, but she could almost taste his mint toothpaste. That distinct laundry scent of his clothes mixed with the rain and a faintly spiced cologne overwhelmed her senses. Before she could allow herself to breathe him in more or to get the full recipe for his laundry detergent, he was kissing her. It was just a soft press of his lips, but her mouth didn't hesitate to return it, leaning into him and closing her eyes.

When Leo pulled back, her head swam. "What was that for?" she asked.

"I wanted to." Leo shrugged. "So I did."

"I wish I could be like you. Just do what I want and not worry so much about it."

Leo's eyes softened. "You don't want to be me. There are several things I want that I'm scared to go after. I like you the way you are, beautiful and perfectly flawed."

Piper blinked, taken aback. "Perfectly flawed? That sounds like more of an insult."

Leo propped himself up on his forearms, and his eyes traveled from her head down to her thighs before her legs disappeared over the edge of the bed. "Perfect isn't real. You are. Everyone has flaws, and I think what people do with those flaws is what truly determines their character. I used to think you blatantly ignored all of yours, which is why your very existence pissed me off." Piper rolled her eyes with a scoff, and Leo broke out into a grin. "But you don't do that at all, do you? You're constantly striving to be better. When you find one of your blind spots, you admit when you're wrong, and you move forward. You don't always get it right, but the fact that you constantly try is what makes you so beautiful. In a lot of ways, you're better than me. I'm learning to accept defeat, but sometimes when I want something, I have a hard time letting go of it even when I know it's not mine to have."

"I don't think you give yourself enough credit. There's a balance between trying to be better and letting things go versus letting everything overshadow you. I have the balance all wrong." Piper turned to lay on her back, staring at the ceiling. "I used to think that you ignored all your flaws, too, but you don't. You not only admit when you're wrong, but you take on the wrongs of other people, and you're incredibly hard on yourself about them."

"Sometimes I feel like I'm doing the right thing in the moment, and then afterward I see how wrong I was. Like with Emma. Some problems can't be solved with sheer force."

"Some problems can't be solved by watering myself down for people." Piper bit her lip.

"So we both suck." Leo huffed out a small laugh. "Should we high five on it?"

She couldn't help but smile back at him, and it gave her a small amount of pride that she was the one bringing out his personality again. Leo had seemed so small in the weeks that followed Isabel's death, just going through the motions. The only times there had been a spark of his usual fire were on stage and any time he had to sit in their business class with Professor Hornbill. Leo couldn't seem to contain the passion he felt about his work, even when he was sad, nor was he any good at holding back anger.

They hadn't been together since that night in the orchestra pit, and Piper was terrified to touch him again after the emotions they had set loose the last time. It took her a while to calm the hurt her heart had dredged up, and the way she had done it was by helping Leo. She had barely spent any time at her apartment since that day in the orchestra pit. When Leo wanted to work outside of rehearsals, Piper would be there with Emma, letting him critique their acting and singing. When he wanted to do nothing at all, Piper would bring him ice cream and junk food, and she and Sam would sit with Leo on the couch, watching his favorite movies. She pretended she had never seen *The Sixth Sense* so Leo could be excited about the prospect of her watching it for the first time. She loved that he was the absolute worst person to watch movies with because he murmured lines along with the actors and paused every few minutes to share a tidbit about the filming of the scene. His obsession with plot twists ranged all the way from cult classics like *Fight Club* to the uncovering of Prince Hans's true motivations in *Frozen*. Her first time ever watching *Interstellar*, Leo had adamantly told her when to focus, as if he really thought she would suss out the twist from the scenes that alluded to it before the big reveal. He had spent more time watching her reactions than watching the actual movie, and when she had audibly gasped at the black hole conundrum, she saw the spark of joy behind his eyes again.

And now, laying next to Leo on her bed, Piper wanted to bring back some of his spark.

"I think I'd rather do something else," she said, sitting up.

Leo sat up too, his brow furrowed. "What's that?"

She leaned forward and cupped the nape of his neck. "I'm going to kiss you because I want to." She didn't give him a chance to respond before her lips met Leo's, soft and searching. He pressed one hand on the small of her back as the other curled under her thigh, pulling her in. It wasn't the way they usually kissed, heated and desperate. This time her lips seemed to say *this isn't for fun anymore*. She was kissing him because it felt like healing, not because of lust.

"I am knocking," Walker's voice declared from behind the door with three loud booms on the wood. Piper pulled away from Leo and righted her outfit as the doorknob twisted, and Walker walked in with his hand covering his eyes.

"Don't be dramatic," Piper sighed. Walker let his hand fall

away from his eyes as Piper snuck a look at Leo, who seemed entirely too amused.

"You," Walker pointed at Leo, and Piper scooted to the edge of the bed, ready to defend him, "should go downstairs. Your family's here. And your tall friend with the blond hair won't stop badgering me about my book. He's freaking me out."

Leo chuckled and got up from the bed. "Sam's... enthusiastic."

Piper got up with Leo, ready to follow him downstairs. "Are you up here hiding from him?" she asked her uncle.

"I don't like attention," Walker muttered.

"Probably shouldn't tell you that I read it, too," Leo said.

"Ugh, people reading the book that I wrote for people to read. Gross." Walker made his way out into the hallway.

"I was not expecting that twist. I read the ending in my office, and I almost spilled my coffee all over myself," Leo said. "And the sex scenes were definitely—"

"Do not finish that sentence," Walker interrupted, his eyes flicking over to Piper. "I do not even kind of want to know what *you* specifically think of the smut in my book. Nope. No, thank you. Piper's not even allowed to read it."

"Walker, I'm not sixteen anymore." Piper sighed. "You can't accost my sexual partners in cars and threaten to tell everyone they have a small dick anymore."

Walker and Leo both froze in the hallway. Eyes wide, Walker whipped his head toward her. "You know about that?"

"Of course I know about it. And I know that Leo was there." Piper turned an accusatory look on Leo.

"I was an innocent bystander. And I'd appreciate it if you didn't refer to Harden as one of your sexual partners ever again," Leo grumbled.

Walker folded his arms over his chest and leaned against the wall. "We are in complete agreement on that."

"You're both idiots," Piper said.

"So." Walker raised his eyebrows at Leo. "I've always wanted to know, did you—"

"Tell the whole school that Harden has a tiny penis? Please," Leo scoffed. "Of course I did." Walker broke out into a wide smile. "I think Piper did more damage, though. She told everyone he couldn't get a hard-on."

"Fantastic." Walker nodded at Piper. "Good work."

"I'm still pissed that Talia told you about him." Piper started down the steps as both men trailed behind her. The noise of the wake got louder with each step she took toward the bottom floor.

"We don't keep secrets from each other," Walker said. "Although sometimes I wish she wouldn't tell me certain things." The look he tossed between Piper and Leo made her cheeks heat. She was going to kill her aunt.

"There you are!" Lucia sidled up to her son and yanked on his arm. "*Ya llegaron todos.*" *Everyone... is here*? Piper half-translated in her head. The app she had been using recently to brush up on her high school Spanish could at least get her that far. Leo's mom paused briefly to look over her shoulder at Piper before steering Leo into the living room, where most of the same people from the funeral were crowded and chattering. "Piper, you look lovely as always." Lucia stopped and elbowed her son. "Doesn't she look pretty, mijo?" Leo's eyes locked with Piper's, and she felt the pang of vulnerability. It was one thing to call her pretty in private, but it was another thing entirely to say it out loud in front of his family.

But Leo didn't hesitate. "She's always beautiful," he stated before turning to greet one of his aunts.

Piper could feel her uncle's eyes boring into the side of her head. She fidgeted with her dress under his scrutiny and didn't make eye contact, but she knew what was coming. Everyone could say what they wanted about Walker—that he was a terrible cook despite Talia's frequent attempts to train him, that he cursed like a sailor, and that he was often way too hard on himself—but he was hyper-observant when it came to Piper and her siblings.

"You like him more than whatever temporary thing Talia said you were doing," Walker stated as fact. Piper's mouth opened and closed several times, trying to work up the words to contradict him. "For what it's worth, he clearly likes you more than that, too. I don't know your exact reasons for staying far away from genuine relationships, but I have a pretty good guess."

"Walker," Piper warned. She didn't want this conversation—not because he wasn't right, but because it was still easier to hide from it.

"No," Walker said simply. "I've been your parent for six years of your life, and I've earned the right to call you on your bullshit. Your mom and dad did not want this for you. They did not want you to hold yourself back from relationships just because you're scared to lose people. We survived, Piper. It was and is terrible every day we wake up without them, but we survive. People like Leo help make surviving that loss easier. Am I terrified of losing Talia? Absolutely fucking petrified. Why do you think I obsessively call her when she takes long trips to come see you? Leo's brother and sister-in-law at the dealership have assured me ten thousand times that her car is fully operational, and I *still* get paranoid about it. I walk into rooms and immediately search for her and all of you because I need that physical proof you're all safe."

Walker gave Piper a sheepish look. "I'm working on it. But you know what I'm not going to do? I'm not going to hold myself back from loving more people just because I'm scared. I'm not going to stop hoping that the fucking adoption agency will call Talia and me with good news. I'm not going to stop hoping that my dad won't relapse again." Walker squeezed her shoulder, and Piper finally looked at him, her eyes watering. Everything in her heart said he was right, but her brain was still telling her the opposite: that she would never truly survive unless she never went there. "Some things are worth being terrified over. Taking on all of you was worth being terrified over. Being in love with my wife is worth being terrified over. And I don't care if you decide that it's Leo that you want or someone else entirely as long as you know you can have it all. Be scared, Piper, but don't be inflexible with your heart."

"I—" The tears started to fall down her face, and she wiped at them with a quick hand, hoping no one from Leo's family would notice. "I don't want to love him. It was so much easier to hate him. I don't know what to do."

"Your mom was a huge pros and cons list fan. You could try that? She made a pros and cons list on whether to date your father."

"She did?" Piper let out a soft laugh.

"Oh, yeah. Your dad found it at one point and kept doing things so she'd add to the pros column." Walker smiled. "You exist, so I bet you can guess which side won out. And something tells me you already know which side would win out if you made one yourself."

Piper gave him a slow nod, biting her lip before she said, "I'm not convinced he likes me back."

Walker chuckled and rolled his eyes. "Yeah, okay. Sure. I'll let you two figure that one out. When you do, don't tell me about it." He mimicked gagging before he started to walk away. "And tell him to stop reading my books!"

Fifty-One

LEO

The quiet mumbling of the room was getting on Leo's last nerve. Abuelita was not at all quiet, so he didn't know why everyone insisted on hushed tones as they meandered about the Hartricks' living room and kitchen. His loud extended family were all silencing their children from running around and offering condoling glances to one another like that alone would soothe the loss.

"¿Mijo?" Leo's father set a firm hand on his shoulder. "¿Te encuentras bien?"

Leo's frown deepened. "I hate this."

"Lo sé."

"No, you don't know. I'm talking about *this*." Leo waved his hand out to the living room. "Why the fuck are we all just standing here like sitting ducks?"

"¿Y qué quieres que hagamos? Hm?" Leo's mother came to his other side, her expression angry as she folded her arms over her chest. "You think you can do better?"

Leo let out a puff of air through his nose. "It's not the mercy meal I have a problem with, Mamá, but Abuelita wouldn't want everyone just standing around feeling sorry for themselves. I'm gonna get some air." He turned on his heel and started for the sliding glass door he hoped led somewhere where people weren't.

The backyard of the Hartrick house was pristine. No rusting tools were lying around. The lawn itself was free of crabgrass, and the large deck decorated with fairy lights was picture-perfect. The cool breeze should have made Leo feel better, but as he sat down on the edge of the deck, he couldn't help but feel like Piper's life had no room for someone like him. Success was an elusive thing that oftentimes felt a bit too out of reach even for Leo's ambition, but for Piper, it was right there. She could live a somewhat carefree life without him.

"I'm out here," a voice said from the corner of the deck. Leo jerked toward the sound and found Piper's brother Colin sitting in a chair and looking up at the sky. "Sorry, I just thought it'd be weird if I didn't announce myself and you thought no one else was back here."

"Yeah, that would have been weird," Leo confirmed. "What are you doing back here?"

"Avoiding Scarlett," Colin said simply. Leo bobbed his head and looked toward the sliding glass door that led back inside to where he'd seen his sister-in-law Harper and her younger sister Scarlett in the living room earlier.

"Ah, makes sense," Leo replied.

"I tried to talk to her, and she told me to go away, so here I am," Colin sighed. "She doesn't like funerals, so I thought I could cheer her up. Apparently not."

"Her brother, right?" Leo asked.

"Yeah." Colin nodded. "He died when he was eleven."

"What was your plan to cheer her up?" Leo's eyebrows raised.

"Paints and brushes," Colin said. "She's an artist. She paints when she's sad or happy or stressed." The way Colin spoke was always so to the point, and Leo appreciated his ability to get right down to business.

"I think you should give them to her anyway. If she won't talk to you, just give them to her sister, and she can pass them on," Leo suggested.

"Okay." Colin got up from his seat, immediately taking to Leo's idea.

"All right." Leo blinked. He was used to people following his orders, but a Hartrick listening to his suggestion and rolling with it off the bat? Unheard of. "Good luck," Leo called back as Colin slid the glass door open to leave the backyard on a mission.

"Do you want space, or someone to sit with?" Piper's voice called out from behind Leo as she passed by her brother in the doorway.

Leo turned around to tell her he wanted to be alone, but the second he saw her, he knew that wasn't true. "Sit with me." Once Piper was safely seated beside him, he let out a slow breath, unsure of what to say. "I don't like that it doesn't feel like Abuelita's spirit is in there. Your family's nice for throwing this for us, and I'm sure it would have had the same result at our house, but I can't stand it. She was the life of every party, you know? I just hate that she's not here to yell at everyone for being so sad."

"What if we changed it?" Piper asked.

He turned his torso to face her, finding her ocean eyes full of compassion. For once, he had hope that she might feel the same way about him. "What did you have in mind?"

Piper skipped down the aisle of Lydia's Grocery holding up a bouquet of sunflowers wrapped in brown paper.

"I feel like we're getting sidetracked. Why do we need flowers?" Emma asked and reached up to smack Sam's hand away from a shelf stocked with toaster pastries "Focus! You don't need Pop-Tarts."

"Walker said that he eats Pop-Tarts when he's writing, and he's a literary genius," Sam proclaimed. "Maybe I need Pop-Tarts to give me that edge of brilliance."

Leo chuckled. "Sam, you're a great actor. You don't need Pop-Tarts. And you need to chill with Piper's uncle before he kills you off like one of the characters in his book." He wrapped one arm around Piper's waist as she came to stand beside him. "Emma's right. We're here for tamal ingredients and enough massive bowls to make said tamales. Why do we need flowers, princesa?"

"Sunflowers are your mom's favorite flower, so I thought they'd cheer her up. Plus, your grandma had sunflowers on her headscarf the first time I met her, and I'm buying, so." Piper gave her shoulders a happy little shimmy, looking genuinely delighted by her reasoning. She was entirely too adorable for her own good, and Leo didn't want to break that, but he had promised her complete honesty during their drive back from Archwood after Thanksgiving. After already breaking that promise by not admitting his feelings, he felt he owed her the truth.

"Sunflowers aren't my mom's favorite flower." Leo watched Piper's face fall and quickly added, "But the second part is true. I bought that headscarf for Abuelita's birthday in high school. We should get the flowers."

"No." Piper shook her head, pulling her eyebrows together. "I distinctly remember you texting me to tell Talia to get your mom sunflowers." She reached for her phone in her pocket as if she were going to go back through their texts to prove him wrong, though he already knew what she'd find there. He had, in fact, told her that.

"Yeah, uh, I don't know, I must've just been thinking about sunflowers at the time. It's not a big deal." Leo shrugged and looked away, realizing suddenly that even back when he hated Piper he'd still subconsciously thought about her and the dress she wore at the karaoke bar. And the headscarf... had Piper been subconsciously stuck in his head then, too?

Piper touched his arm with a gentle brush of her fingers to draw his attention back to her. "Sunflowers are *my* favorite flower, Leo."

Emma coughed, and both she and Sam strategically began

inspecting the Pop-Tarts when Leo jerked his head in their direction. Their acting was subpar at best.

"I didn't know that, of course," Leo started, his shoulders stiff. "But I probably could have guessed. You have a sunflower dress, the earrings you're wearing right now are little sunflowers, you have that sunflower in your inspiration box from your mom, and you're... sunny." He was going to die on the spot from mortification.

"Oh." Piper blushed and reached up to touch one of her earrings. He could see on her face that she must have been considering what all of that meant when they were rudely interrupted.

"Piper?" a man's voice called out from behind them, and Leo's back immediately went ramrod straight. His body always had an instant reaction of disgust to that voice, and he hoped he was hearing it wrong, but he found his ears were dead on as usual when he turned around.

"Harden," Piper replied when she met her ex-boyfriend face to face. Her tone was ice-cold, and it only made Leo love her more.

Leave that sunshine for me, princesa, he thought.

"You're back in town?" Harden came to stand directly in front of Piper, entirely too close for Leo's comfort. With his hand still on Piper's waist, Leo took a step back, and she followed.

"Just for a funeral and for Christmas." Piper's answer was so short and to the point, Leo thought that might be the end of the conversation. Unfortunately, not only could Harden not get a hard-on, but he also couldn't read a room.

"You're doing another funeral for your parents? That's weird," Harden said. Piper stiffened under Leo's arm, and the immediate anger that coursed through his veins made him want to throw punches first and ask questions later. His fist balled up at his side.

"No, you dick." The first person to speak was surprisingly neither Leo nor Piper, but Sam. "But Pipes, if you want to throw your parents another funeral, I'll go because *I'm* not an asshole."

"Damn," Emma chortled next to Sam.

"Jesus, who died?" Harden scoffed and pointed between Emma and Sam. "And who's the witch and the beanstalk?"

"God, you're exactly the same person you were in high school," Leo grumbled. "My abuelita died, and Sam and Emma are our friends."

"And the witch would be happy to conjure up a spell for *you*," Emma pointed her finger like she was already spellcasting, "to swap with Leo's grandma."

Harden laughed like Emma was joking, though everyone else knew there wasn't an ounce of humor behind her statement.

When Piper finally spoke up, her voice was so small that it felt like a blow to Leo's heart. "Harden, we have a lot to do, so if you could—"

"So, what? You two are dating now? You hated each other in high school." Harden questioned Leo only, gesturing to his hand around Piper's waist and leaning forward to touch her shoulder. "Don't you want a real man?"

The red plaguing Leo's vision was just calm enough for his fist to not meet Harden's face as each word slipped out of his mouth with deadly precision. "Get your fucking hands off her. And if you interrupt her again, I won't be nice about it." Thankfully, Harden let his hand fall to his side as Piper started to speak.

"I changed my mind about Leo because he's not a bad person. You are. And we don't have time for your bullshit, Harden, so please fuck off to whatever swamp you crawled out of." Piper stood taller, and Leo was proud of her for holding her ground but completely taken aback by her not outright declining that they were together. He liked it way too much, and he wished she would have just drawn a line in the sand again instead of leaving open a window he wanted to crawl right through.

"At least I'm not five foot nothing," Harden said. Leo rolled his eyes. He was five-seven on a good day. Back in high school, Leo might have cared more about a barb at his height from a taller guy, and yes, Harden was at least six-one, but Leo could still flatten him like a pancake. Harden didn't look like he used his arms for anything but swinging his daddy's golf clubs. Piper was still several inches shorter than Leo, but he didn't mind that he didn't have to stoop too far to reach her lips.

"I'm way taller than Leo," Sam chimed in. "But ask me if I want to go against someone I've watched beat the shit out of their punching bag for the last four years."

Meanwhile, Emma had started murmuring an incantation under her breath like she was legitimately casting a spell, hands slowly rising as if to summon a demon. She most certainly would have been burned at the stake at the Salem Witch Trials. It should have been a dead giveaway that she was fucking with Harden given her raised hands both proudly displayed middle fingers, but he looked like he was going to piss himself. All the anger fell away from Leo's muscles, and humor replaced it. By the time Sam joined in on the chant, Leo was desperately trying to hold back his laughter. Theatre kids were nuts, and he loved them.

Piper carried on with the conversation like nothing at all was happening behind them. "Besides, I don't think you should be talking about the length of anything, Harden." Leo finally let his laughter slip out in a breathy cackle that he tamped down by smiling and kissing Piper's forehead.

"Whatever. You're all freaks," Harden snapped and turned around to leave. When the aisle was finally relieved of his presence, Emma and Sam broke out into cheers as Piper smiled and leaned into Leo's hold.

"Finally! I seriously thought we were going to be stuck in frat boy purgatory forever," Emma groaned.

"Dude does *not* know how to read the room," Sam agreed. "What was that nonsense you were chanting?"

"It's from *Hocus Pocus*," Leo answered for her. He'd know lines from a classic movie like that anywhere.

"My parents used to make me watch that every Halloween." Piper giggled, her nose wrinkling and eyes squinting from how wide her smile was. Leo had never seen her mention her parents and follow it up with a real smile before.

"I memorized it when I was little because I'm a freak." Emma took a step toward the shelf and pulled down a box of strawberry Pop-Tarts. "It felt good to fight back against someone like that." She lifted the box in the air, her shoulders held back in determination. "But I might need a little extra edge if I'm going to turn in Professor Hornbill."

Fifty-Two

LEO

Christmas didn't feel as destitute as Leo thought it would. After Abuelita's wake, which they had successfully turned into a celebration of life—in his grandmother's case, a tamalada with loud music and card games that lasted until well into the night—the holidays felt lighter. Even when they weren't together, knowing he was just a ten-minute drive from Piper's house relaxed him. And when December thirty-first rolled around and she showed up to be his New Year's kiss a little after midnight, Leo had been ready to argue his case again on why she shouldn't be out driving that late until he saw Colin's round glasses and the wave of his hand out the car window before he drove away. They had spent an hour under the stars and another hour outside her house, kissing in Leo's brother's conversion van, until she finally dragged herself from the bed, much to Leo's chagrin, when someone—probably Walker—flicked the front lights on outside her house.

Piper made everything better. That was why when they returned to campus and Emma's sexual harassment report garnered zero response from the administration, Piper was the one to come up with an idea to speed up the process. Leo shouldn't have been shocked by her ingenuity, but with Emma's and then Moreno's permission, the plan was formulated, and safety in numbers became the new play.

"This is fucking insane." Emma held a stack of fliers in her hand with their show poster printed on the front. The entire cast and crew of *Guys and Dolls* was spread throughout Fletcher's campus in the most high-traffic areas. The four headliners and Leo stood in front of the Condor Building on campus where the main stone path split in two. Canvassing wasn't necessary considering Moreno's wife posted to her socials that she was attending the opening, but it was a good excuse to start a war.

"We don't have to do it if you don't want to," Piper reiterated to Emma for the millionth time. "Maybe it's not a good idea."

"It's a *great* idea," Leo said.

"What if we get Moreno fired?" Emma bit her lip.

"Moreno said he'd go down with this ship. Teaching isn't his long-term profession, and he's well off enough that it won't hurt him. Plus, think about the shitstorm of bad press Fletcher would get if they did fire Moreno. All he or his wife would have to do would be to speak out about the reason, and Fletcher's reputation would be destroyed by the media," Leo pointed out.

"What if I'm the only one?" Emma's voice came out timid, and Leo felt the anger rise in his chest toward the person who had made the powerhouse he'd cast as Adelaide afraid. But it would all change soon. Waylen Hornbill was going to pay for scaring Emma and anyone else he had threatened with his power.

"Predators typically don't do things just once. Even if no one fills out the form, it doesn't mean he hasn't done this to someone else," Piper said and turned the flier on top of her stack over to the backside. Leo flipped one, too, so he could read it over. It wasn't like they could change anything unless they reprinted one thousand fliers, but he knew Piper's perfectionist brain was rereading over the blank sexual assault and harassment form for any errors. The one they had created had been embellished a bit from the original that Moreno had had Emma fill out.

"We'll start when you're ready." Sam held his phone at the ready to shoot off a text to the masses to start canvassing.

Emma took a deep breath and looked up and down the path before nodding. "Let's do this."

Leo watched as Piper set her shoulders back, put on a straight face, and made her way to her designated spot on his right.

And so it began.

The first fliers they passed out were to a group of sorority girls who barely looked at the paper before they moved along. After that, Leo could tell that Emma and Piper were getting more comfortable with the idea. No one was stopping to talk about the backside of the flier. They were all just trying to get to their next class or the nearest dining hall, so there was a slim chance they would find out what exactly they were holding until they were far down the path.

Partway through the day, Leo had gotten rid of most of his stack and only had a few fliers left. "Our first show is Saturday night. Tickets are going fast, so make sure to get yours," he said, holding out a flier to a shy girl he had seen idling nearby, staring but not approaching.

"Uh, one of my friends said you're passing out... forms?" The girl's voice quieted to a nervous whisper at the end, and Leo carefully flipped the page over and handed it to her. "Oh. Great, thank you," she mumbled. Before Leo could even respond, the girl raced off, and the pit in his stomach dropped further. It wasn't the first time someone had come specifically for the form that day. Word was spreading throughout campus like wildfire, and he knew that a lot of the other cast members were having similar experiences.

"What is this?" The voice made Leo's blood boil as he turned to see Professor Hornbill standing directly in front of Emma. Leo had never moved so fast in his life, crossing the distance and sidling up to Emma's side just as Piper moved in.

"We're spreading the word about our show." Leo spat out an answer as he stepped in front of Emma. Piper quietly pulled her over to Wes and Sam on the path, putting several feet of distance between Emma and Hornbill. Leo didn't look their way for fear that he would absolutely lose it if he saw the fear on Emma's face again. Instead, he pulled out the packing tape from under his arm that they had used to tape up fliers and ripped off a piece. He stuck it to the top of a new page, harassment form side up, and gave Hornbill a conniving smile as he reached up on his tiptoes, asking, "Want one?" before he stuck it to the professor's forehead out of pure spite. It was an absolute joy to watch Hornbill rip the flier down as Leo started his spiel in a monotone voice. "Our first show is Saturday. If you show up, Professor Moreno has advised security that you're not welcome, and you will be escorted from the building, hopefully by force. Also, if you have been sexually harassed by a student or faculty member at Fletcher University, please fill out this form. As you can see, we have provided directions on how to fill it out properly. For example," Leo drawled. "Under the perpetrator, we've listed Professor Waylen Hornbill, but you can list any name on that line."

"You think this is funny?" Hornbill snarled.

"The opposite." The look Leo gave him was nothing short of deadly. "I think sexual harassment and assault should be punished by the full extent of the law and then some. Don't you agree?"

"I—of course I agree." Hornbill's face turned sheet white as he looked in Emma's direction before he blinked and quickly turned away, his fist clenching at his side.

"Your body language is giving you away, Professor." Leo cocked his head.

"Putting my name down is entirely inappropriate," Hornbill said.

"Oh, okay, so you *do* know what's inappropriate. Good to know." Leo shrugged. "If you've done nothing wrong, then you have nothing to worry about. It's just an example. Hypothetically, though, if in the future you did decide to do anything without someone's express consent, I would gladly end your miserable existence."

Hornbill seethed. "Is that a threat, Mr. Diaz?"

"Hypothetically? Yes. Now, if you'll move along, we have show fliers to pass out. Have a fantastic day!" Leo gave Hornbill a fake grin and then patently ignored him, moving around his side to hand fliers to two students passing by.

Hornbill stutter-stepped before stopping in front of Emma again. "I just wanted to say that I'm so sorry if you misconstrued anything between us." His tone had a sick sweetness to it, like he was practicing his sincere and caring voice—the one he probably used to manipulate people on the regular. Emma stiffened beside Piper, and Leo halted his canvassing efforts.

"Do. Not. Speak to her," Piper seethed.

Leo had been about to step in again when Emma set a hand on Piper's arm and spoke. "I misconstrued nothing, and you know it. Go to hell."

Hornbill's eyes widened before the mask fell away, replaced with a cruel look. "Nothing will happen to me. I have tenure."

"We'll see," Emma countered.

With that, Hornbill turned over his shoulder to leave, and it felt like Emma had won the battle. But it was high time to win the war.

Fifty-Three

LEO

The energy backstage was so palpable Leo could feel it vibrating through his veins like an electric current. The cast of *Guys and Dolls* was all huddled together in costume, quietly whispering their anxieties to each other. It would be easier after opening night, but the first show was always nerve-racking.

Moreno came to Leo's side and patted his back with a grin. "Full house tonight, huh?"

"Sold out." Leo cracked his knuckles to expel some of his pent-up energy, and his eyes automatically scanned the room for their Sarah Brown.

"She's in the bathroom puking," Emma called out from beside Wes.

Leo anxiously tapped his fingers against his legs and glanced at Moreno.

"You want to go get her?" Moreno smirked.

"I'll be right back," Leo promised with a sheepish smile before he scurried off toward the dressing room for a short pit stop before the bathroom. Besides the obvious need for Piper to be backstage with the show starting in the next fifteen minutes, the real reason he wanted to see her had nothing to do with the show and everything to do with needing to touch her. To feel her presence steady him. He would see her, and everything would be okay.

Leo knocked on the door to the women's bathroom with two quick raps of his knuckles before walking in. "Piper?"

She was standing at the sink in her maroon mission uniform —a blazer with shoulder pads and gold buttons fastened up to the collar at her neck, a pencil skirt, pantyhose, and her brunette wig hanging around her heavily made-up face—as she white-knuckled the sink. "Hi," she whispered. He immediately went to her side and set a hand on her back, rubbing up and down her spine.

"Did you throw up?"

"Yep." Piper stood up straighter to face him. "I'm trying not to do it again."

"Did you bring a toothbrush?" The glare she shot him made him chuckle. "Sam has to kiss you several times, so I'm just looking out for him."

"Yes, asshole, I used the mouthwash I keep in my purse."

"So prepared," Leo teased and held out her inspiration box. Piper took it wordlessly and dug inside for the apatite stone. He reached up to cup her face and looked into her eyes, which were the same color blue. "Are you okay?"

"I don't know if I can do this." She blew out a shaky breath, the clean mint scent hitting his nose.

"Yes, you can. I know you can." He reached his other hand up so her head was cradled in his palms, careful not to mess up her stage makeup. "I chose you for the part, and I'm never wrong." Piper's eyebrows lifted, and Leo grinned, tilting his head to the side. "Okay, I'm wrong some of the time, but I'm not wrong about this. I'm not wrong about you, princesa." He wasn't talking about the show anymore, but she never did seem to notice when he took things a little further. Or, if she did notice, she never said anything.

"But what if you are?" Piper countered.

"I'm not."

"I'm terrified," she whispered.

"I am, too," Leo said. His eyes searched her face, and he could see that familiar anxiety of hers there. He wondered if she was still terrified of love, too. Still scared to be his. "We did everything we could have possibly done to make this show everything it needs to be. You have your lines and your songs down. Your set is beautiful." *Everything you touch is beautiful*, he wanted to say, but right before the biggest moment of his career thus far when everything hinged on having their heads straight probably wasn't the best time to confess how in love with her he was. "I'm the ASL interpreter, so I'll be out there the whole time. If something happens, you can glare at the back of my head."

Piper sucked in a breath through her nose and let it out slowly while bobbing her head, her thumb brushing over the stone in her hand. "Okay."

"Okay," Leo mimicked. And then, because he couldn't resist, he leaned forward and brushed his lips against hers, just one small press before he pulled away and let his hands drop from her face. Instead of questioning him, Piper threw her arms around his torso, the inspiration box contents rattling behind his back, and leaned her head into his chest. His arms embraced her, and his thumbs traced circles into the maroon wool. "You look so strange as a brunette," he mumbled.

Piper laughed as she pulled away and reached her hand up to wipe at his mouth. "And you look so strange with lipstick."

"Good to know." Leo thought, for a moment, that he might just say *fuck it* and tell Piper how he felt right there in the women's bathroom, but she interrupted that train of thought.

"We should probably get back."

Leo nodded and puffed out his chest. "It's showtime."

"Have you been waiting the whole time just to say that?" The light cackle Piper let out made his smile even wider.

"Of course I have."

The stage lights were always too bright to see a damn thing in the audience, and Leo wasn't sure if that made things worse or better. It was hard to imagine anyone in their underwear when you couldn't even see them, but as Moreno took the stage and Leo waited in the wings, he figured he would find out soon enough whether he was meant for the spotlight.

"Good evening," Moreno spoke into the microphone in his hand and beamed out at the audience. "Thank you all for coming. If you'll all join me in giving a warm welcome to our director, my protégé, and the hardest working young man I've ever met, Leonardo Diaz."

The applause from the house was more thunderous than Leo expected. He only took a brief moment to look back over his shoulder at Piper, who was giving him one of her rare, nose-scrunching smiles. These days, her smiles came less and less rarely, but they were no less special. He winked back at her before his feet carried him to center stage, taking the mic from Moreno on his way in.

"Thank you all for coming to Fletcher University's production of *Guys and Dolls*. We are thrilled to have you here celebrating our opening night in the great Olson Theatre." Leo's practiced speech continued as he signed and explained the safety protocol, directing everyone's attention to the glowing exit signs in case of emergency. Once he finished explaining that refreshments and treats would be sold during intermission, he had fully regained his confidence. "Flash photography is strictly prohibited, and we ask that you stay seated during the performance except in the case of an emergency. And I regret to inform you that if you're tired of me already, you're in luck, because I'll be your sign language interpreter for the evening, so you're stuck with me." The crowd laughed at his joke, and his plan to lighten them up from the boring announcements worked. "With that," he paused for dramatic effect, "welcome to nineteen-fifties Manhattan."

The lights dimmed on stage as another round of applause sounded in the theatre. Leo made his way down the side steps to the floor seats at the very corner of the stage, where a dimmed spotlight shone on his music stand with a printed copy of the script for his ASL interpretation. Mouth pursed, he took a big swig from his bottled water and a deep breath as the introduction song, "Runyonland," started up in the orchestra pit.

Leo kept his eyes on the crowd as he signed the lyrics when the music transitioned into "Fugue for Tinhorns," his heart beating out of his chest. From what he could hear, everyone was executing their roles to perfection. The hard thing about being the interpreter was that he couldn't see what was happening on stage, but Moreno promised to take notes, and Leo's desire to make his show accessible was more important than seeing the performances he had seen a thousand times already. Watching the audience was almost more fun because he could clock their reactions when the show got to his favorite scenes.

When the Mission Band entered from stage right, Leo broke his unspoken rule to not look back and watched as Piper took the stage and stepped onto a small box for her stump speech song. The song was a berating of sorts, a holier-than-thou tune about telling drunkards to lay down their bottles and to "Follow the Fold" by resisting the devil and coming to Jesus.

Before, Leo had never gotten to just enjoy the sound of Piper's voice. He always had his ears tuned in to any detail that needed altering. Now, he listened intently to how her voice blended with the air in a soft yet demanding way. It was fitting that the song called for people to come to church and lay down their sins because hearing her voice felt that way. Like he was in a house of worship where all he wanted to do was drop to his knees and praise the ground she walked on. She sounded confident. The way she did when she was with him, in the bedroom or otherwise. Tonight would be the night he would tell her how much he loved her, because she had to feel it, too. The pull of his heart to hers. It didn't feel like a game anymore. It hadn't been casual for him in a long time, and he didn't think it ever would feel that way.

It took Leo a second to realize he had gotten distracted and failed at his sign language duties before his hands jumped into action, and he positioned his back to the stage and followed the lyrics, heart full and dizzy from nerves.

Fifty-Four

LEO

The post-show chatter made Leo's pride soar. He could hear bits and pieces of conversations as he made his way through the packed lobby.

"The fight scene was hilarious, and..."

"Who wouldn't want to marry Adelaide?"

"The club scene with the neon lights and cigar smoke..."

"Do we know if the guy playing Sky is single? Because..."

Leo didn't have the heart to stop and tell the group of girls wondering about Sam's relationship status that Sam was much more interested in the man playing Nathan Detroit than in any of them, but he pocketed the information to tease Sam with later. Sam's performance was flawless from his vocals alone, and he was well on his way to becoming an elusive heartthrob just like he had planned.

When Leo's eyes landed on his family corralled in the corner, they were all gesticulating ecstatically with their hands as they talked. His mother led the pack in a discussion with Piper's aunt and uncle. He smiled to himself as he watched his father sidestep one of her flailing arms while she elaborated on whatever she was talking about. His father was so used to the way his mother moved that he could spot one of her accidental backhands from a mile away. Leo's eyes skipped over to Piper's aunt and uncle. Walker's hand was pressed into Talia's back, and he was looking more at her than he was paying attention to the conversation. And, God, Leo wanted all of that and more with Piper.

Beside Walker and Talia, Leo's siblings and their significant others all stood chatting with Piper's siblings, their families already so woven together that it felt like a natural progression to make everything official. Pearl and Cooper, the two youngest of Piper's siblings, were practically bouncing with excitement as they carried on a conversation with Mariana. Carter was in an animated discussion with Alvaro, and Leo made a mental note to check on that duo later. The two of them doing anything together sounded like a nightmare of practical jokes and included the possibility of burning down buildings. Colin stood like an awkward gargoyle, avoiding Harper and Saanvi's pointed glares as they whispered to one another.

"There he is!" Antonio called out from the wings. "The big director man!" Leo crossed the distance between them and stuck out his hand to shake his brother's. "Don't be an idiot." Antonio latched onto him and yanked Leo into a bear hug instead of returning his handshake. "You know I'm shit when it comes to theatre, but I thought it was fantastic," Antonio said.

"Phenomenal," Saanvi chirped from beside them, her hand resting on her stomach.

"Except for that time in the beginning when you forgot to do the interpretation," Alvaro called out. Leo should have known he could always count on one of his brothers to point out his mistake.

"A little distracted?" Carter chimed in with a coy smile. Yeah, Leo was absolutely going to have to separate Alvaro and Carter before they became thick as thieves.

Leo rolled his eyes. "Funny." He had barely gotten the words out before his mom was mauling him from the side and practically weeping on his shoulder about the performance, his dad giving him a fatherly pat on the back that said "bien hecho, mijo" without having to say anything at all.

All of the commotion and praise, however, failed to keep Leo's attention when Piper walked out into the lobby, free of her stage makeup and costume. The long-sleeve green satin dress she was wearing had a deep V in the front that he wanted to bury his face into and a slit he followed with his eyes that stopped high up on her thigh. Her closed-toe black heels ribboned around her ankles and tied in bows. Best of all, she was wearing a real fucking smile. He had to hold himself back from murmuring something entirely indecent under his breath in present company. She was walking sex, and it felt like her wavy hair was moving in slow motion as she swayed around a few guests and stopped to hug Emma, who was, to no one's surprise, wearing all black.

A loud clearing of a throat made Leo jump back to reality from the place in his head where he had been stripping Piper naked. He jerked his head to the sound and found Piper's disgruntled uncle glaring at him. Leo wasn't afraid of Walker in the least, but the entire sleeve of tattoos and menacing stare was enough to get him to stop undressing Piper in his mind.

"I'm gonna go meet with the cast," Leo decided, already angling his body toward Piper. "Thank you all for coming."

"I see how it is." Marcos chortled if that was explanation enough and tucked Harper into his side, kissing the side of her head. And it was. Leo gave him a quick nod before he escaped through a crack between his parents and beelined for Piper.

When Leo came up behind her, he pressed his front gently against Piper's backside and dropped his mouth to her ear, his voice low so no one else could hear, but he suspected by Emma's amused facial expression that she knew exactly what Piper's dress was doing to him. "You're trying to torture me."

A knowing smile pulled on Piper's red-painted lips. "I have no idea what you're talking about." Her tone was sultry and lacking any innocence at all. He moved around her side, his fingertips brushing the slit at her thigh in what might have looked like an accident to anyone else but was far from it. Piper let out a choppy breath, and Leo snuck a glance at her backside, quickly admiring it before he noticed the ribbon on one of her heels had unraveled.

"Your shoe," he muttered before dropping down on one knee and patting his thigh. Piper's eyes went wide in alarm, and so did Leo's when he realized how ridiculous it must look for him to be on his knees in the middle of the lobby. Half of the conversations around them quieted, and Leo could feel the entire cast searing holes into his head as whispers started. He and Piper weren't in the bedroom, and he wasn't supposed to be on his knees at all. He wondered if the heat creeping up his face was showing. Besides the select few, they had kept their relationship—if that was even what he could call it—a secret from the cast, and this was one hell of a way to out them. He cleared his throat and attempted to sound as confident and nonchalant as possible. "Your shoe is untied."

"Right," Piper squeaked, lifting her heel to press it into his thigh. He looked up at her and couldn't help but remember all the times that he had tasted her from this exact position as he slowly tied a bow at her ankle. Then, he gripped her calf and slowly guided her leg to the floor, another maneuver that was not at all necessary, before he rose to his feet. "Thanks." Piper had left all of her acting on the stage. The crimson stain splashed across her cheeks was so revealing it had him breaking eye contact.

Unfortunately, the eyes Leo met first were Moreno's, trained on him with his eyebrows lifted in a way that Leo could only assume was some sort of a reprimand.

"Find me later," Leo whispered to Piper before scurrying off in the direction of Moreno and his stunning wife, whom everyone had their eyes on. Quinn German was beautiful, of course, and Leo had technically seen her naked, too—albeit onscreen—but regardless, Leo thought that if people were searching for the most beautiful woman in the room, it would be Piper, hands down.

For the next hour and a half, Leo and Piper circled each other like starving vultures. Even when his eyes weren't on her, he was watching the way Piper's dress moved like water in his periphery. When she passed in front of him once, her hand grazed his groin, and he had to get himself a refreshment to cool down. It was a game of cat and mouse. He would shoot her a heated look from across the room, she would turn back to her conversation with a smirk and a lick of her lips. Both of them knew exactly what would happen the second they were alone together.

Fifty-Five

PIPER

The hallway was empty except for two cast members passing by, whispering and clinging to each other with secretive smiles, and it was clear that Piper and Leo weren't the only ones feeling the pull of lust after the exhilaration of opening night. Her family had finally taken off for Archwood again, and as much as Piper loved them and loved talking the head off the interim CEO of Hartrick Designs about the design concepts for the show, all she could think about was getting Leo's hands on her. The secret looks they had shared all night had her on edge. When she finally figured out where he had run off to, she headed straight there.

Piper knocked twice with her knuckles on the office door and opened it to find the culprit of every longing ache in her body sitting behind his desk. His white dress shirt was partially unbuttoned, the sleeves pushed up on his veiny forearms, and his hair was disheveled from where she was sure he had been running his hands through it.

"Working on directors' notes already?" Piper asked, shutting the door behind her and locking it. Leo looked up from where he was writing something on the clipboard that was always glued to his hands. His gaze liquefied, and he tossed his pen on the desk, leaning back casually in his chair, his eyes freely trailing up and down her body.

"You're in big trouble," Leo said.

"I've never been to the principal's office before. How much trouble am I in, sir?" Piper swung her hips a little more than necessary as she ventured farther into the untidy office space. Leo had papers strewn across the desk in a disorganized chaos. She itched to tidy everything up but knew Leo probably had some sort of method to his madness. A place for everything, and everything in its place.

"So much trouble. Both our families are here, and you thought it was okay to wear *that* dress?" A strangled groan slipped through Leo's lips as his thick eyelashes fluttered shut.

"Mine left, so technically it's just yours now." Piper shrugged. "And Carter."

When Piper had slipped the dress on after the show, she only hoped it would have some effect on him. The way the black smoke of his eyes roamed her face, heavy with salacious implication, said they were stuck here until they both had their fill of each other. She wished the dress had some magical capability to make Leo fall for her, too. Not just her body, but everything else. She was starting to think that she would never have her fill of him.

Leo rose from his seat slowly like a predatory lion stalking his prey, and, God, did she want to be the prey. The dress clothes he was wearing had her wanting to pull something out of *The Promenade* and rip open his shirt, buttons flying everywhere. She always liked it when his hair was in disarray. It looked like he had been doing something illicit already, and his rakish appearance had her ready to debauch him further. His arm reached out for her, and she took it, pulling him to her and pressing her chest into his as his sturdy hands found her hips.

"Fuck, princesa. I'm trying to control myself," Leo said, his hand tightening on her waist.

"Don't," Piper ordered. "I don't want you in control."

He bent his head forward and trailed deep, sucking kisses up her throat as Piper wiggled to press her pelvic bone into his hardening erection. He was holding back, and she hated it. She wanted him unraveled, so desperate that he said everything that came to his mind. Maybe then she would know exactly how he felt and if she was crazy for thinking they could be something more.

"Here? In the office?" His hand slid up to her breast, and he massaged it as his mouth found her ear. "Moreno would kill me if he found out."

"He just left with his wife. He never has to know." She kissed him, hard and needy. Leo met her mouth with equal force, finally unraveling a bit of control. The high of the night did not have to end yet, and she would be damned if she didn't relieve some of the pressure coiling in her belly.

"You're a terrible influence on me. The library. The hot tub. The dressing room. Your car." Leo punctuated each location with a harder press of his lips and slid his hand under where her dress split on her thigh, his fingers finding her silky underwear. Then, in a motion that made her dizzy, he jerked away with a gasp. "No." Leo shook his head, one of his dark curls flopping over his forehead. Piper's heart sank in her chest. The part of herself that specialized in self-preservation said to book it and never look back. If he was rejecting her for sex, there was no way he wouldn't reject her if she asked for more. She was just about to reach for the door to leave when Leo stepped an inch forward, both his hands raised. "Don't go. Fuck, this is not how I planned on this going. I just meant to stop for a second. Long enough for me to give you this." He grabbed a small box sitting on the end of the desk and flipped open the top. His fingers reached in and pulled out something dangling from a thin gold chain.

Piper stepped toward him and reached her hand out, still confused. A small sunflower pendant swayed in the air between them. Her fingers traced over the petals, feeling the coolness of the metal. "You got me a necklace?" It wasn't so much a question as a statement of awe. The necklace looked expensive, and she immediately wondered how much it had set him back. The invisible calculations Leo said he always made started up in her brain.

"I didn't buy it," Leo replied, reading her mind. "The chain was my abuelita's, and Varo makes metal trinkets, so I had him make the sunflower. It cost me a favor that he gets to call in whenever he wants, though, which is mildly terrifying."

"It's beautiful," Piper whispered as he dropped it into her outstretched palm. She turned the charm over in her hand, admiring all the tiny petals welded together.

"He does good work," Leo agreed and shifted on his feet. "I just thought you deserved an opening night gift. I saw one on a billboard the other day, and I couldn't afford to get you one studded with diamonds, so I—"

"This is better," Piper cut him off and looked up into his eyes. She would have cherished a flower that he had cut out of a gum wrapper, but this—this was beyond anything she could have expected. "I..." *I love you.* The words almost slipped out, but she caught them before she embarrassed herself. An opening night gift didn't mean that Leo felt anything other than gratitude for her role in keeping the show alive. "I wish I got you something."

"You've bought me like ten coffees over the past few months" He grinned. "And a wide range of medications, along with the groceries you dropped off on my porch that you think I don't know were from you, Emma, and Thea."

"W-what? How did you know?" Piper's heart jolted in her chest.

"You put Thea down as your emergency contact for the show." Leo grinned. "I might have broken a rule by programming it into my phone because you tend to injure yourself a lot, and I got worried I'd need to call her."

"Oh." Piper bit her lip.

"That, and Thea didn't quite hang up the phone before I could hear you all giggling."

"God, we're so stupid," Piper groaned. "You're not mad?"

"No, I'm not mad. I have several questions about some of the groceries you three decided on, but I'm not complaining." Leo shrugged.

"It was the children's applesauce pouches, wasn't it?" Piper covered her face with her hand. "I just really love them, and they're an easy snack to pack away."

"Actually, it was more the bottle of strawberry-flavored lube that I was confused about."

Her mouth fell open. "What? I'm going to kill Thea! I didn't put that in there, I swear."

"Oh, I know *you* didn't." He stepped toward her and pressed a languid kiss into her shoulder. "I don't think you need it, princesa. You're *very* responsive. Can I put it on you?"

"Your... body?" Piper's voice cracked.

"The necklace." Leo met her eyes with a smirk.

"Oh." Piper bobbed her head. "Yes, please." She flipped around in a hurry, shoving the necklace into Leo's hands as she intrusively peeked at the stuff on the desk. Any more silence, and she would inevitably fill it with things she was scared to say. Things she wondered if Leo ever thought. If he did think about her that way, she imagined it was fleeting. They were going in different directions after graduation. While she was starting to believe that their never-ending debate on management styles was challenging her to be more confident, he probably still thought her arguments a nuisance.

"Do you know how many times I've thought about this?" Leo's husky voice said in Piper's ear. The tips of his fingers slid up her spine to her hairline, where she was holding her loosely curled locks out of the way.

"Thought about what?" Piper shivered at his touch, wondering if she had spoken aloud all her imaginings of them together.

Leo finished clasping the necklace, and his hand dragged down her backside. "You. In my office. Ask me how many times I've thought of you bent over this exact desk in one of those little dresses you wear."

The air whooshed from her lungs in a flurry of desire. "How many times?"

"Daily," Leo rasped, his warm breath ghosting over her neck. The outside of his loafer met the inside of one of her heels, and he slowly scooted her foot along the floor, widening her stance. He repeated the motion on the other side until her legs were stretching the fabric of her dress and hiking the slit to the crease where her hip met her leg. "Just like this," he whispered.

Piper bent at the hips, leaning her chest and arms down to the surface of the desk as she shuffled some scraps of paper out of the way. The edge of the desk dug into her stomach as she stuck her ass out in search of Leo before brazenly dragging the bottom hem of her dress up her thighs and to the small of her back, exposing her underwear. "Like this?"

"That's perfect," Leo murmured. She could feel his erection press into her a moment later, partially hitting the spot where she was desperate to grind into him. She let out a small gasp of gratitude and braced her palms more solidly on the desk to gain leverage to push her ass harder into him. He let out a groan. "It feels like I'm taking advantage of you like this, but we both know who's really taking advantage of who, don't we?"

The confidence that made her feel powerful every time they were together filled her to the brim. "Yes."

"Tell me what you want, princesa. Use me. I'll kneel at your feet and lick you until you alert the entire building of how fucking gone I am if that's what you want." Leo yanked her underwear to the side, and she moaned at the slide of his fingers over her wet seam.

How fucking gone I am. The words reverberated in Piper's head, begging her to ask a follow-up question. Had he fallen as hard as she had?

"I want you," That was the real truth. She didn't just want his body, though that was probably the way it sounded. "Drop your pants."

"Yes, ma'am," Leo breathed. She heard the sound of his belt

unclasping and the zipper sliding down his slacks before his hand pressed into her lower back, steadying her as she felt his hand guiding his cock right where she wanted him.

They didn't speak. Piper's breathing synced with Leo's in a way that made it feel as though they were one body as he nudged the crown of his cock past her barrier. She unabashedly angled her hips to help him slide in, but she was so wet from all his teasing that despite how much he always stretched her, he slid in easily with one slow and torturous press of his hips. One hand pressed harder into her spine as the other cradled her hip, his fingers sliding underneath the strap of her underwear. Each rolling pump of his hips made her feel impossibly full and achingly empty each time his cock left before sliding back in.

It had become second nature the way their bodies slipped and fit together. Like the mechanics of a clock, gears turning and interlocked for one common goal. Leo's legs began to slap against her thighs as he went deeper and harder, a fervent demand she had asked for as she fumbled and searched for something to hold onto. He sensed her struggle and pulled on her hips, dragging her backward until she could grip the edge of the desk, her knuckles turning white, and she moaned his name the way she knew he liked it.

Something about not being face to face and still Leo knowing exactly what Piper needed felt intimate. Like he had studied her reactions enough to know when she needed more and when she needed less, though she never needed less. His body spoke in a way only she understood. He would sink a little deeper, then back off as if to ask her if she wanted that, and then she would speak it into existence as a command. She imagined for Leo it felt good to let go of the power he usually held. For her, it felt like she finally didn't need to be perfect or polite. She picked up his power and used it as a talisman to take what she wanted, what she needed, without fear and without shame.

"A little to the left," Piper said. She barely got the words out before he had eagerly shifted to exactly the right spot. "Oh, *yes.* Right there."

"Good?" he panted, fucking into her faster. "Is this what you want?"

She nodded and gasped with each thrust. "You're so good at following directions, Leo."

"Yeah?" The pride in his voice made her almost finish, hearing how thrilled he was to listen. "I love you like this."

I love you like this. It was so close to what she wanted to hear that she closed her eyes and pretended the last two words weren't there at all. Then her head did what she did best and overanalyzed them.

"When you can't see me?" Piper asked. She wanted to take the question back, but it was already out there, a weight of insecurity dropped between them like a bucket of ice water.

Leo pulled out, and Piper whimpered at the way her body felt like an aching chasm without him. He moved his hands under her and pulled her up, turning her around and sitting her down on the desk instead of bending her over.

"I see you," Leo said. His index finger curled under her chin before his mouth landed on hers. His lips and his tongue were slow and searching until the heat picked up again and her core was begging for his cock. "You don't even know how much I see you."

With her head tipped back so Leo could kiss down her throat, Piper pulled her arms from the sleeves of her dress and let the material fall down her torso. When it pooled at her hips, she got exactly what she wanted—for Leo to see more of her. She had gone without a bra, so her breasts were bare and already getting attention from Leo's hot mouth as he sucked at a taut nipple. She liked being bent over the desk, but her naked skin against Leo's hands and tongue felt freeing, warm, and loving, even if he didn't mean for his body to love her.

"I see you, too." She moved out to the very edge of the desk and reached for his cock, pulling him to where he belonged.

They rocked together slowly at first, Piper with her eyes closed. The underwear that was still pushed to the side hit her clit perfectly as he pushed home.

"Piper, fuck—just like this."

"Wait for me," Piper whispered. Leo jerked his head in a nod and took several shaky breaths as he drew back and forward. She could tell how hard he was holding back, his muscles shaking with the strain of it before she joined him, and her body ached with a building release. "Leo." His name was the only thing she could think to say as her orgasm crested and washed over her, but he knew what she meant and only had to thrust one more time before he followed her. Their breaths were ragged as he pulled her up to a sitting position again and pressed his forehead into hers, eyelashes fanned and fluttering against his cheeks. "Good boy," she praised.

A smile spread across Leo's face as he slowly shook his head, chuckling. "Woof," he joked and bent to kiss her slowly until she was smiling against his lips, too.

A giggle escaped her throat when they broke apart.

Leo shook his head as he tucked himself back into his pants. "You're so demeaning." The devilish glint in his eye said it didn't bother him at all, and his words immediately after confirmed it. "Feel free to boss me around and reward me for being good anytime."

"You should say 'during sex,' or I'll start doing it in normal conversation," Piper teased and hopped off the edge of the desk, righting her dress.

Leo reached for the box of tissues on his desk. "Wear that, and I won't care what you do to me."

"What is it with men and dresses?"

"You know those knitted knee-high socks you wore to dinner at my parents' house over Thanksgiving break? I'd take you in those, too." He held out the box, and she took a tissue before reaching under the slit of her dress to clean herself. "Just the socks," he clarified.

"Noted." Piper laughed and did a quick swipe over the mess in between her legs. Her underwear was still going to be wet, but it was the best she could do for now. She raised an eyebrow at Leo when he started to rearrange the papers on his desk back to the way they had been before.

"I like my layout," he explained.

"What about the used coffee mug?"

"Casualty of war. I was here too late working on something, and I fell asleep at the desk."

"What were you working on?"

"A side project." Leo moved and replaced a leather-bound journal that she recognized as the one that usually sat in his room untouched. The one he had said he was going to use for something important. The pages were raised with ink and lifting apart from one another, indicating that he had opened and written in it several times.

"Oh? Do tell." Piper was trying to sound casual and not too eager, but it came out that way nonetheless.

"It's a little early. I'll tell you later," Leo said.

Piper's face fell as her hand fiddled with the sunflower hanging from her neck. The unsettled feeling in her gut said Leo would never trust her or feel the same. He would make her feel like she was on cloud nine one moment, desperate for her opinions and her direction in bed, then slam the door closed the next. Maybe she wasn't the person he wanted to tell his ideas to.

"Sure." Piper gave him a curt nod. "I should get going." She whipped toward the door and threw it open, barreling into the hallway as her face went hot and tears threatened to prick her eyes.

"Piper!" Leo stumbled after her and grabbed her hand, pulling her back and flipping her around to meet him. She landed with a thud against his chest. "Why are you running away from me?"

Piper swallowed, her mouth dry and bitter. "Do you still hate me? Or are we friends?"

"Of course I don't hate you." Leo looked pissed. "After everything, how could you think I hate you? That," he pointed aggressively at the door to his office, "that is not what two people who hate each other do, Piper."

She looked back at the door and bit her lip. "I don't know what this is anymore," she whispered.

"I do." He stepped toward her, but then his eyes widened, and he backed away as the sound of footfalls grew nearer. Piper's heart sank. He was still embarrassed to be seen with her. "Elliot." Leo's head bobbed in greeting at the person who had walked into the hallway.

"Hey, just the people I was looking for." Elliot's smile was practically glowing in the dim lighting. No doubt he was still on a high from the ample praise their set design had garnered from the audience earlier. "I locked up." He passed over a large key ring to Leo.

"Thanks." Leo offered a small nod of acknowledgment.

Elliot beamed, and Piper suddenly realized why Leo found her constant cheeriness annoying. "Amazing show tonight."

"You said you were looking for both of us?" Leo raised his eyebrows, and Piper watched a blush sprout across Elliot's cheeks, his eyes sliding over to her. "Oh, uh... just to give you the keys and..." Elliot turned more in Piper's direction, and she blinked up at him, waiting. "Well, this is kind of personal. I was wondering, since we're no longer working together, if you wanted to go out with me sometime?"

Piper's mouth parted, and she immediately got flustered, not from Elliot's question but from the wetness of her underwear that she could feel where Leo had just been. "Like a date?" Her eyes slid to Leo in a panic.

A cold expression took over Leo's face as Elliot yammered on, "Yes if you're up for it." He turned to Leo conversationally. "That's not, like, against the rules or anything, right? I didn't think it was appropriate when we were working together, but now that the set's finished and everything went off without a hitch..."

"It is not against the rules," Leo confirmed, his eyes meeting Piper's. She swallowed, knowing exactly what he was thinking before he said anything further. "I appreciate you waiting for the sake of professionalism. Not a lot of people would do that." He let out a long sigh and messed with the keys in his hand. "I'm gonna go home. It's late." Dread crept up Piper's spine as Leo started to walk to the end of the hallway.

"But we'll talk later, right?" she asked. The question felt shaky coming out of her mouth.

Leo paused but didn't glance backward. "Sure. I'll talk to you tomorrow."

Once the door to the night air had finally shut and Leo was gone, every muscle in Piper's body locked up. She wanted to chase after him or break down, but all she could do was stand there, wishing he would come back.

"Is he okay? He seems off." Elliot peered at the door, looking genuinely concerned. He was so nice. So sweet. The exact kind of person she should want to be with.

"I don't know," Piper admitted.

"I'll shoot him a text. I'm sure he's all right. The show was fantastic."

"Right."

"So…" Elliot's shy smile made the gnawing feeling inside Piper's stomach grow. The feeling that told her to accept whatever was thrown at her so as not to disappoint. "What do you think? Do you want to go out with me?"

Fifty-Six

LEO

A very manly giggle escaped Leo's throat as he wobbled on his unsteady feet. Antonio's forearms slipped under his armpits to steady him, and Leo laughed again. The high of being with Piper in his office had not only worn off but had plummeted into hell. His attitude had transformed from hopeful and excited to all doom and gloom. His laughter sounded like a sarcastic cry for help, but he wasn't about to snap out of it any time soon given the number of empty glasses in front of him. The second he had escaped that fucking hallway, he immediately shot his brothers and Sam a text to see if they wanted to "continue the celebration" before his family headed home in the morning.

"I sink we sood do... *karaoke*," Leo slurred, trying and failing to direct his feet to the stage. "Piper was *so* good at singin' karaoke." The neon-lit signs at the head of the Hot Mic stage were disorienting him further, especially when he realized that the design looked similar to the one Piper had designed for the club scene in *Guys and Dolls*.

"No karaoke for you, hotshot," Alvaro said.

"You understood that? I didn't understand a word," Sam scoffed.

"He speaks fluent drunk," Marcos chimed in.

"I speak fwee languages." Leo tried to hold up three fingers and laughed when it was harder than he thought it would be. "Piper fought it was two, but it's *fwee*!"

"Jesus. Thanks for inviting me, Varo. This is a blast," Carter muttered and dropped his voice even lower. "I'm wasting my fake ID on this." Leo was making an absolute fool of himself in front of Piper's brother, and he couldn't care less.

"Don't blame me! This is clearly your sister's doing," Alvaro accused. "Leo, what the fuck did she do to you?"

"She stwole my howt." Leo swayed. Four sets of eyes turned to Alvaro, who translated it easily.

"Ugh," Carter groaned. "Gross."

"Okay, but this is not new news," Antonio reasoned.

"It's not?" Carter seemed surprised by this.

"I told him this was a bad idea, and he didn't listen to me," Sam said. "She said she didn't want a relationship from the very beginning. Then again, it did kinda seem like she wanted him back, though."

Leo frowned and closed his eyes dreamily. "See's so pwetty and nice. And the sehx was *so* good."

"I don't think you want me to translate that one." Alvaro blanched.

"I am unfortunately catching on now," Carter groaned. "And I swear, if you say anything more about my sister's sex life, I *will* vomit."

"Okay, buddy." Sam cringed and patted the top of Leo's head. "I think it's time we get you home."

"*Noooooo!*" Leo shouted. "I'm having *fun*."

"You're *having* a mental breakdown." Marcos shook his head. "This is worse than that time Antonio got rip-roaring drunk when Saanvi rejected him."

"Oh, fuck off." Antonio shoved Marcos' shoulder. Leo barked

out a delayed laugh, remembering how Antonio had ended up falling on his face and breaking his nose that night.

"One mo' shot!" Leo raised one finger and swayed, happy that he'd gotten the finger up fairly easily that time.

"Absolutely not," Marcos said. "You need to sleep this off."

Leo slumped into Antonio, letting his brother hold up most of his weight. He was too busy with the all-consuming weight of his broken heart bearing down on his shoulders to worry about holding himself up.

"I hate to say it," Alvaro put a hand on his shoulder, "but they're all right. You don't need more. It's not going to help."

"He's cut off anyway," said Sasha, the hot bartender whom Leo had once thought about sleeping with. Leo squinted his eyes at her behind the counter, offhandedly wondering what he had ever seen in her as long as Piper existed. Piper had blue eyes he could fall into and skin as silky as rose petals. Sasha was rough around the edges and dark in all the places she should be bright and happy, like sunshine and sunflowers and everything wonderful. If the bartender was anything like Leo, she would end up with someone as sunny and as warm as Piper, with shampoo that smelled like sugar and lemons.

"Lemon cake!" Leo declared as if anyone could hear his internal thoughts.

"No clue why he's shouting about cake now," Alvaro said when everyone looked to him to decode again.

"Varo, did you know Piper has nithe sampoo?" Leo smiled dreamily then frowned. "Ewiot will wuv her sampoo."

"Who the fuck is Elliot?" Alvaro asked as Antonio and Marcos wrangled to keep Leo upright.

"Elliot?" Sam sat up straighter on his barstool. "What does Elliot have to do with anything?"

"He's going to have Piper's babies," Leo slurred, then pulled his eyebrows together, working out the details. "Or... Piper'll have his babies. I dunno. They'll have cute babies."

"Varo, what did he say?" Antonio huffed.

"He's confused about reproduction," Alvaro informed.

"I would love to stop talking about reproduction in general when it comes to my sister," Carter said dryly.

"It also sounds like he's decided that whoever the hell Elliot is, *he's* who's going to end up with Piper?" Alvaro screwed up his face in confusion.

"That sounds like a conclusion he'd make." Sam sighed. "Elliot's a set designer who worked with Piper on the stage design."

"I have dinner with Piper once a week, and I have no idea who Elliot is," Carter said. "And the last time we were supposed to have dinner, she canceled because she wanted to hang out with *you*." Carter jabbed a finger at Leo's chest, and Leo's wobbly footing became even dicier. Leo wondered absentmindedly if this was how Piper felt just walking around considering he couldn't count the number of times he'd had to catch her from injuring herself. Then again, he couldn't count much of anything except the number of broken hearts in the vicinity: *one*.

"He ashked her out," Leo grumbled.

"So? Does she know how you feel about her?" Marcos asked.

"You gave her the necklace, right?" Alvaro's eyebrows rose. "I spent a lot of fucking time on that thing. You better have—"

"I gave it to her." Leo sniffled. He had never been a drunk crier, but he was starting to think that now might be the time to change that. "And I was gonna tell her when Ewiot—"

"Ah, okay. So Elliot interrupted his love confession," Alvaro translated.

"Then you fight for her." Antonio shrugged after he hauled Leo up to a standing position.

"Get her back," Marcos agreed. "The insane shit I did just so Harper would talk to me was worth it."

"See doesn't wan me," Leo insisted.

"Straight people," Sam muttered under his breath. "You didn't tell her anything, so how would you know that?"

"I weft so I didn't hafta hear the rejecshon." Leo was pretty sure his speech was completely unintelligible at this point, but Alvaro didn't have to translate before Leo's confession was met with groans from the entire group and a smattering of insults slung his way, all in the realm of universally agreeing that he was an idiot.

Even in his drunken state, Leo didn't need anyone to tell him how fucked he was. He already knew.

Fifty-Seven

PIPER

The dried tears on Piper's face coupled with the sticky feeling of her skin made for a terrible way to wake up. She rolled onto her stomach and pushed her head into her pillow. *Coffee*. Coffee would solve everything except for the fact that her heart had practically snapped in two. And her hand was almost permanently latched around the necklace Leo had given her.

One look in the mirror, and Piper was groaning at her appearance. She slipped Leo's hoodie over her pajama top and contemplated just wearing her pajama bottoms to the coffee house but ultimately decided that she needed to put real clothes on. Those real clothes ended up being sweatpants and tennis shoes, but she couldn't fathom putting on her usual dressy attire when Leo had said how much he liked it.

Coffee first. Then she would talk to him. She would confess everything and apologize for crossing the line they had both agreed never to cross.

Piper took a deep breath, prepared for the January air to smack her in the face, and opened the door. She was only vaguely aware of the pain that lanced up her leg when she hit something hard on the porch before she was freefalling.

"¡Ay!" a male voice said.

Then warm hands wrapped around her before her knees hit the floor. "Fuck!" Piper hissed and started to frantically wiggle free from her assailant. She was not getting kidnapped before she told Leo how she felt. "Let go of me, or I'll scream. We have neighbors! They'll hear me."

"Shit." The voice made her halt. "Piper, I'm not attacking you, I'm keeping you from falling over because you're a damn klutz."

"Leo?" she breathed, her vision finally clearing from the rising panic as she looked around. He was sitting on the ground with a blanket wrapped around him. "What the fuck are you doing?"

"I was sleeping. *You* ran into *me*."

"Why were you asleep on my porch? It's freezing outside. Are you insane?" Her mouth gaped open.

"Can you stop yelling?" He groaned and massaged his temples as he rose to his feet. "I'm fighting the worst hangover of my life, and you're screaming."

Piper stood, concern creasing the spot between her eyebrows. She softened her voice. "Why were you asleep on my porch?"

"I was waiting until I was sober enough to talk to you."

"Why didn't you just text me?"

"Carter and Sam took my phone." Leo flashed her a sheepish smile. "Probably for the best considering I was completely out of it."

No part of this was making sense to her. "You were with my brother?"

"Yeah. And then *my* brothers tried to make me sleep at my apartment or one of their hotel rooms, but I needed to talk to you, so I escaped. I was plastered, so I walked." Leo shrugged.

"From your apartment?" Piper blinked and shook her head. "That's three miles, Leo."

He lifted the cloth draped around his shoulders for show. "I brought a blanket."

"I don't understand. Why—"

Leo cut her off and reached his cold hand up to her face. "Don't go out with him, Piper." She shivered under his touch, and he dropped his hand. "Call it off."

"What?" Piper's eyes went wide as she scanned him, taking his cold hands in hers to warm them. "Are you okay?"

"No, I'm not okay." He sighed, and she watched his eyes land on the sunflower necklace around her neck before he took a slow, deliberate breath. "Don't go out with Elliot. I'm begging you. Please don't." Leo pulled one hand away from her to rake through his curls.

"Why don't you want me dating him?" Piper asked carefully. Her heart was racing in her chest. She could see it on his face and in the broken way his eyes pleaded for her to listen. Was it just because he wanted to keep sleeping with her, or was it what she hoped it could be? The fear that it was the former immediately left when he spoke again.

"Estoy enamorado de ti," Leo whispered. She slowly started to translate in her head, but he beat her to it. "I'm in love with you, princesa. Te amo." He gestured from his heart to hers, and Piper's stomach somersaulted. "I've been in love with you for a long time. Before you told me you didn't want love. And I lied. I'm sorry. I didn't want to fall for you, I really didn't. Then I tried to fall out of love with you, but I couldn't. When you smile, and I mean *really* smile, I understand every love song in *Guys and Dolls*. Every book that Sam reads. Why my parents dance and your parents danced, too." Her eyes rimmed with tears as he continued and started to pace on her porch like he was too nervous to stop moving. "Every romance movie I watched as a kid could never adequately explain the way I feel about you. When I'm with you, I have this overwhelming urge to create something—a movie, a play, anything—that will explain it. It's not just romance movies, it's that plot twist that makes a viewer gasp or the way everyone reacted when the fight scene happened on stage last night. I feel harder and deeper when I'm with you. Sometimes it fucking hurts, like in the orchestra pit. Sometimes it feels like joy, the way last night felt after the performance, when I couldn't stop touching you. You're... you're my plot twist, Piper."

When the tears finally built up enough to roll hot down Piper's face, Leo stopped dead in his tracks, his face falling as he stepped forward and caught one rolling tear with his thumb.

"I'm sorry." His pained voice broke her. More tears fell from Piper's eyes, coating her cheeks and the palm of his hand. She shook her head repeatedly, trying to tell him not to be sorry as her words caught in her throat. "I know this isn't what you wanted, but I can't separate sex and emotions. Not with you. I never could with you. I tried, Piper, I did, but I've been falling for you since you tipped that glass of ice over my head. Maybe even before then. I lived to argue with you. I craved the way you told me exactly what you thought of me and how right you were about my flaws. I'm always desperate to know what you're thinking. And then when I kissed you in the library, I couldn't handle that I didn't have more of you. I couldn't handle you smiling for everyone else but me, so I took what I could have. And now that's not enough of you, either. I don't just want pieces of you, *princesa*. I want to be the one you can't stop thinking about, too. And yes, there are better guys out there for you than me—like Elliot, maybe—but I want it to be me. I know you think I'm an asshole, but I'm an asshole who can't stop imagining what it would be like to love you forever, and it's torturing me to not have your heart when you've had mine for months. I don't think I can keep holding you at night if I'm not allowed to love you all day." Piper was freely crying now, frantically trying to wipe at her face so she could speak. So she could tell him he wasn't crazy.

"I—" she started, and before she could get the words out, Leo got on his knees.

"Give me a chance. *Please.* Try with me."

Piper's knees hit the floor again before she even knew what

she was doing. She reached forward to wrap her arms around him and clung to him like he was a life raft she needed to hold onto, his touch keeping her afloat. His arms wrapped around her back, and it felt like home. Every fear she had was right there on the surface. The knowledge that if she lost him, she might just be broken forever.

"Leo, I don't have to try," she said, and let go of the embrace to cup his face. He nuzzled into her palm as his deep brown irises met hers in an agonizing plea. "I told Elliot it'd be wrong of me to go out with him because I was in love with someone else."

"You did?" Leo choked out.

Piper nodded, biting back her bottom lip. "It's you." Leo barely let her finish before his lips were on hers. She pulled back a second later with a sad smile. "You make me want to be a better person. You're thoughtful and hardworking and charming and annoying." Leo chuckled as she smiled at him and continued, "And I love every part of you. I love you, too, Leo."

Leo broke out into a grin and swiped at one of her tears. "Mi vida, ¿por qué lloras?" She sniffled and pulled her eyebrows together, getting partway through the translation before Leo caught on to her struggle and repeated it in English. "Why are you crying?"

"I'm so scared," Piper whispered. Leo's smile softened as he tucked a golden strand of hair behind her ear.

"I am, too," he said.

"I can't lose anyone else." She shook her head and looked away, trying to pull back her emotions. Leo's finger met the underside of her chin, and he tugged her head back to look at him. "Losing you would kill me, Leo."

"I'm not going anywhere."

"You don't have control over that." Piper buried her face in his neck as love, joy, and utter sadness lodged in her chest, mixing like buckets of paint to create an entirely new color. "I didn't want to get close to you for that exact reason, but I couldn't stop myself. You wormed your way in. and now it hurts to not have you. I'm losing something if I don't admit I want you, and admitting I want you means I'll eventually lose you. You're an asshole for making me fall for you, Leo." A half laugh, half sob escaped her throat, and he pulled her in closer, the both of them still kneeling outside her door.

"I know." Leo pressed a kiss into her hair. The first layer of his lips felt cold until he pressed further, and she could feel the heat underneath. It was the way her heart had felt for so long. It looked warm and inviting on the surface, but it was cold to the touch. Leo hadn't retracted from the cold at all—he had dug in, found the warmth underneath, and made her admit it was there. "But if being an asshole got me you, then I'm not sorry. I'd do it again. But you don't know that you'll lose me. We don't know anything, Piper. All I know is I'd rather assume that I'll get to have you forever and love you like I could lose you any second."

"I want what my parents had. And I think, with you, I can have it." It was little more than a whisper, choked back with emotion, but Leo nodded with a soft smile.

"You can have it with me."

Piper leaned in to kiss him again, tasting the salt from her tears and letting her mouth find peace in his touch until they were just sitting, clutching onto each other with Leo's blanket wrapped around them as he slowly stroked her hair.

"What do we do when you go to film school?" Piper sniffled.

"I haven't gotten in yet," Leo pointed out.

"They're idiots if they don't accept you." She laced her fingers in his. "You pulled off something big last night."

"We all did."

"You got us there. But I'm still going back to Archwood. That has always been my dream, and my family is there even if my parents aren't. I want the job I wanted as a little girl. I want to make my parents proud. And it's not even just about that anymore. I love the work, and I know I'm capable of doing it."

"Your set spoke for itself. And, even if I do get in, this will work, Piper," Leo said. "We can love each other and still do what we want. We'll do long distance. We'll do whatever we have to. I'll drive ten hours to come see you every weekend if I have to. I'll work overtime at a shitty side gig to afford the gas or find some rich relative that I didn't know existed to bequeath their entire life savings to me. I don't know, but we'll make it work. If anyone can do it, it's us. We don't back down from fights, Piper, and I'm not going to stop loving you just because I'm far away."

"Okay." Piper nodded, her bottom lip wobbling. "I'll fly out to see you. I'll be so organized with the company that I can take some weekends off. I'll hire a personal errand boy to do all my grunt work."

"That's the spirit." Leo chuckled. "But can we make it a personal errand girl or someone who rivals the sheer amount of gay that Sam is?"

Piper giggled and rose to her feet, flattening out Leo's hoodie against his chest. "On a scale of one to ten, how jealous were you when you thought I was going out with Elliot?"

"The scale was broken." Leo hopped to his feet and scanned his eyes over what she was wearing. "Am I ever getting that back?"

"Nope." Piper grinned as he helped her up, and she pushed open the door. "This has been mine from the second you lent it to me. I'm going to need you to wash it with your laundry detergent, though."

"Figures." His lips met hers in a quick kiss before his face contorted. "Now, I would love to take that hoodie off you, but right now, I think I'm gonna throw up. Where's your bathroom?"

LEO

There had to be a rulebook somewhere that said, "If you're going to confess your love to someone, you shouldn't do it when your body wants to do nothing but eject all of your internal organs." Stone-cold regret for the prior night's drunken pity party didn't come as an epiphany to Leo so much as a learned experience. For the third time that morning, he was curled over Piper's toilet as wave after wave of nausea showed him just how dedicated his body was to the cause of making him look like an idiot.

"Fuck," he groaned and lifted a weak arm to flush the toilet before falling back against the side of Piper's bathtub with his eyes closed. "Do you still love me?"

Piper chortled and answered immediately. "No, this round finally got to me." He peeked out from under his eyelids and found only a look of amusement. "Of course I still love you, but I am kinda starting to think you're more into my toilet than me."

"I am *never* drinking again." Leo enunciated each word with vigor. The headache splitting his head in two seemed to agree. "I can see why you don't."

"I don't, because I'm fairly certain I'm an alcoholic." She said it so offhandedly that it made his eyes snap open.

"What?"

"It runs in my family. My grandpa, Walker, and my dad all are... or were. My grandpa's been in and out of rehab for five years. My dad and Walker both decided not to drink early on. Colin will never touch the stuff to find out, but I figured out pretty quickly in high school after a few rounds with Harden that I can't seem to stop once I start." Her tone was softer and more timid now. "It's not something I tell a lot of people, for obvious reasons." The implication was there, that she *was* telling him, and that it meant something.

Guilt sloshed in his stomach. "I didn't know. I wouldn't have been out drinking if I did. I'm sorry."

"Leo, it doesn't bother me when other people drink, I'm just letting you know because we're together now." Piper was up on her feet, wringing out a washcloth in the sink before she crouched down next to him and pressed it to his forehead. Leo sighed at the touch.

"But I'm on your team," he said. "If it's a problem for you, then it's a problem for me, too."

"That's..." Piper trailed off thoughtfully. "Most of the men I've dated in the past were either adamant about me drinking with them—"

"Harden, I assume," Leo cut in, and she nodded. "I better not see him again, or I'll break his fucking face."

"And the *others*," Piper rolled her eyes and continued, "were happy to get smashed, and they assumed I'd just take care of them because that's what I always did."

More guilt ripped up Leo's insides. "You don't have to take care of me, mi vida. I don't want to do that to you."

"I'm doing it because I want to." She dropped the washcloth away and bent forward to kiss his forehead. "You took care of me when I was sick last night before the show. We take care of each other."

"I'd take care of you even if you never took care of me," he said.

"I'm well aware." Piper's face took on a flirty look before she scrunched both her eyes and blinked. It took him a second to realize what she was trying to do before his face split into a wide smile.

"Was that supposed to be a wink?"

"It *was* a wink!" The confidence in her voice made him chuckle.

"I hate to break it to you, but both your eyes closed." She tried again, and Leo grinned wider. "Not even close."

"Dammit. I really thought I was doing it."

"I mean, you look cute when you're trying, so it's doing it for *me*." His mouth quirked up before he grew serious. "This will be the last time you take care of me because I'm hungover, though, princesa. I promise. I could happily go my whole life without feeling this way ever again. Not to mention that drinking is a very expensive pastime that I don't have the money for." His smirk came back. "I can think of so many other ways to pass the time that are free and much more fun." His finger traced a line down her leg suggestively.

Piper scoffed. "Are you seriously flirting with me right now when you just yakked into my toilet?"

"You started it! And I can't help it. I'm pretty much always thinking about sex with you." Leo flashed her a crooked smile, and Piper's cheeks instantly went red. "I love it when your face does that."

"Does what?"

"I always know when you're embarrassed because you blush." He couldn't help but smile as the color fading from her cheeks came back with a vengeance. "Just like that."

"Ugh." Piper dropped the washcloth and covered her face with both hands. Leo reached up and tugged on one of her wrists to pull it free from her face.

"You blush when you come, too." Leo let his thumb run a circle over the skin on her wrist.

"I'll tell you what. We're gonna go get coffee because that's what I was trying to do when you tripped me, then we're going to eat a greasy breakfast to help your hangover, and *then* I'll let you do whatever you want to me." She attempted a wink again and failed again.

"Deal." The abrupt way Leo jumped to his feet made his head swim and his vision dance with darkness before Piper reached out to steady him, bringing him back down to earth.

"Water and ibuprofen first," she ordered.

Fifty-Eight

PIPER

The snick of the door closed catapulted Piper toward Leo in a crash of tongues, teeth, and lips. He had been toying with the hem of her dress in the booth at breakfast, and she'd been ready to jump him the whole car ride back to her house. Her chest rolled into him as he kept pushing her farther into the living room, their limbs tangling as she worked to remove his belt. Leo's talented tongue trailed up the column of her throat as she slipped the sleeves of her dress down her shoulders.

"Wait a minute." Leo broke away, taking a step back.

"Do you not feel okay?" Piper tried not to let her disappointment show.

"Estoy bien. Will you spin for me? I feel like I didn't really get to appreciate the dress last time. We were too busy pissing each other off." He circled one finger in the air. It was too cold, but the sunflower dress she had worn to breakfast was a calculated decision, one she knew had messed with Leo's head. He had kept her plenty warm with heated glances and his hand resting on her thigh all morning.

"And what do you want to appreciate about it?" Piper let her voice drop into a low and sultry murmur, slowly spinning as she looked over her shoulder at him.

"The way it brushes against your thighs. God, I want your thighs wrapped around my head. I want to bite them till I leave a mark." Leo stepped into her with a fire behind his eyes that she wanted to burn forever. He slipped two fingers into the gap between the buttons holding together the front of her dress. "The way the only thing separating your breasts from me are these four little buttons. I love it when you don't wear a bra, Piper." His fingers swirled behind the fabric and found one pebbled and sensitive nipple. "How do you want me this time, mi vida?"

"I don't want you on your knees," she huffed out quickly. When a confused expression crossed his face, she explained. "I want you with me the whole time. I want it slow until we can't take it anymore. I want to feel every part of you against me, filling me. I just want you."

Leo unbuttoned the top of her dress with slow, deliberate fingers before he leaned in for an even slower press of his mouth to hers. She opened to him, and his tongue dragged unhurried over the entrance to her parted lips.

"I can do that." The low gravel of his voice sent a shiver down her spine, and she could feel her nipples harden more against his chest. Leo, never missing a single thing when it came to her body, brought his hand back up to her buttons to unclasp the remaining three. "And I'm going to suck on these." He cupped her breast, and she relaxed into the warmth of his hand.

"Can I..." Her hand dipped down to the hem of his pants, then further, groping over the erection tenting his pants. "I want to suck *you*."

"You don't have to." Leo shook his head.

"I want you in my mouth." Piper held his gaze for a long moment, unwavering in her confidence, before Leo finally broke.

"Fuck," he hissed. "Sí." He gave a frantic nod, like the opportunity might pass if he didn't agree with fervor. "I want those pretty, red lips around me." Piper went to drop to her knees, but

Leo grabbed her arm, shaking his head again. "Get on the bed. And when you suck me off, I want you naked, with your back arched and ass pointed to the sky."

There was only time for a quick nod of agreement from Piper before their mouths and hands found purchase as they stripped each other bare. Until skin was on skin and the only thing left to do was take, body, heart, and soul. Leo backed through the doorway to her bedroom first and sat down on the mattress, pulling Piper along as he shifted their position back to the billion throw pillows she had adorning her bed. They had never spent time in her apartment before, and she watched in real time as Leo hit pause on devouring her to take in the state of her room, organized right down to the highlighters on her desk.

"I should hire you as my interior decorator. You know, someday, when I can afford you." The smile he gave her was devastatingly handsome as he lifted his hand and brushed his fingertips over her cheek. It was such a simple statement, and yet it hit the nail in the coffin for how utterly screwed she was when it came to loving him. Her heart was soaring. Compliments from Leo were like a golden glue fitting together the broken pieces of herself. "Your parents would be so proud of you."

"You can't say things like that to me," Piper said, but broke out into a wide smile that made her cheeks ache.

"Well, that face makes me want to say it again." Leo cupped the nape of her neck and met her smile with a slow press of his lips that turned heated. He tasted like cool mint, and the reminder of that made her jerk back.

"Oh!" She bounced in her seat, her breasts bobbing with the movement. "I have to show you something."

Leo's eyes dropped to her chest and closed the distance that she had created with all her excitement. He gave her a pleading look and tried to kiss her again, but she wiggled free as his low voice asked, "Right this second?"

"Sorry." Piper giggled and rolled off the bed. "One second." Leo let out a disgruntled puff of air and fell back into her down pillows, which made a dramatic slapping sound at the contact. She ignored his theatrics and grabbed a small metal box off her desk, bringing it to the bed. Leo lifted himself onto his elbows, still fully naked and erect, eyeing her down like he was going to eat her alive. "Here."

Curiosity crossed his face when he sat all the way up and gave a good look at what she was holding. "Is this what I think it is?" Leo gingerly took the box from her hand like it was already his most prized possession.

"That depends on what you think it is." Piper smirked.

"Smartass." He shook his head and opened the latch, slowly nodding as he looked down at the contents. "You made me an inspiration box."

"Yeah, it's not a big deal."

"Don't downplay it," Leo warned.

"You're *right*." Piper drew out the word like a child who had just been scolded and fiddled with the sunflower pendant at her neck, the only thing she was still wearing. "It's a big deal. I made you one because I kept finding things that made me think of you."

"I love it," Leo said reverently. Her shoulders slackened, and the tension she had built up in her head released. She reached into the box, first pulling out a sprig of dried mint in a glass tube.

"The way you taste," she explained and handed it to him. Leo shot her a heated look before he pulled out a piece of obsidian glass. "That's for your eyes. They kind of look like black volcanic glass." She shrugged and took out another item, a small square tile covered in splashes of color, lines, and dots. "I would probably use this in a maximalist kitchen, but it reminded me of how your brain works. Like cohesive chaos."

"Perfect." He took the piece from her and stared down at it before carefully setting it back and grabbing another item. "And this?" Leo held up a small mesh bag of coffee beans.

"Your strength. It's a medium roast."

Leo blinked in surprise. "Medium? Not dark?"

"Dark roasts tend to be bitter. You're strong, and you might come off as bitter at first, but you're not."

"Please don't say I'm a secret softie."

"You're a light roast to the right palate." Piper grinned.

"Like..." Leo leaned toward her and dragged his lips across her shoulder. "You?" He murmured against her skin.

"Exactly." Piper expelled a breath, and her eyes fluttered shut. "There's also a—" Her voice broke off in a soft groan as Leo gently sucked at her pulse point and cupped her breast. "—a piece of a heavy red curtain."

"Theatre?" he asked, kissing his way across her collarbone.

"Mm-hmm." She hummed, unable to form words the second his hot mouth wrapped around one of her nipples. "Argemone mexicana," she managed to get out finally.

He released her breast with a wet popping sound. "What?"

"The dried poppy in resin." Piper heaved out a sigh, arching her back in search of his mouth again. Leo obliged and continued his ministrations. "It's a... resilient flower that—*fuck*." Leo pressed on her chest, and Piper fell backward, her hair splaying across the pillows.

"Keep going, princesita. How resilient is the flower?" Leo slipped his fingers over the outside of her entrance, spreading her wetness.

She moaned. "I can't remember." She was losing her ability to think rather quickly. "Something about being able to grow in rough soil?"

"Mmm, anything else?" he asked, kissing down her torso.

"Charcoal color swatches. And a little moonstone." Piper's eyelids were heavy as she looked down between her legs where Leo was hovering.

"Because night is when we typically do this?" Leo guessed and pushed two fingers inside her.

Her back bowed off the bed, and the remainder of her explanation came out in rapid fire so they could get to the point. "No, because you're the light when it's dark."

"That's sweet," he noted and then stuck his tongue out and dipped down to swipe it over her clit.

"Oh, God."

"Funny, I thought I was the one worshiping," Leo said before flicking the tip of his tongue against her again. Despite the extreme pleasure, Piper vaguely remembered what her original goal was and jerked away from him. Leo sat up abruptly and wiped at his mouth, sighing. "If you keep jumping away from me, I'm going to start getting a complex," he repeated her own words from their second kiss in the hot tub back to her.

"You distracted me," Piper scolded and set the inspiration box onto her nightstand before pointing to the spot beside her. "Lay back."

Leo's eyes were dark pools of lust, ink spreading in water, as he moved like a cat up to the head of the bed, laying back but keeping his gaze fixed on her. "Are you gonna..." He trailed off the second she started to plant wet, sucking kisses down his chest. "No te detengas." She jerked her head up to look at him. "I said *don't* stop," he groaned.

"Sorry, all I heard was the word no," Piper defended. "I want your consent."

"There's no one on Earth who's more consenting than me right now. Don't. Stop," he enunciated pointedly. "You have to learn Spanish, or it'll be detrimental to my health." His eyes shut as she started kissing down the V of his hip.

"I bought an app a while back, and I've been practicing, but I think you should redeem your ineffective teaching methods from high school." She bit the inside of his thigh.

"You're so ungrateful." He barked out a laugh, and to punish him, Piper gripped his cock with her hand and swirled her tongue over the head. Leo let out an indecent sound.

"What was that?" She gave him a coy smile.

"Nada," Leo huffed. "Nothing. I was a horrendous teacher. I'll do better." As a reward, she dragged her tongue from root to tip and was happy to hear the strangled sound at the headboard. "Lengua."

"Tongue?" Piper asked. When he nodded, she grinned and wrapped her lips around his head, sucking him into her mouth.

"Chúpamela." His hips bucked off the bed, and she released him.

"I don't know that one." She narrowed her eyes, trying to find the word in the recesses of her brain.

"Suck." He said it as an order.

Piper grinned. "This is a much better way to learn," she said, then did exactly what he had asked. He didn't wait for her to ask questions once she was planted firmly between his legs and pulling him deeper into her mouth. Instead, he would murmur a word or a phrase, then quickly translate it so she didn't have an opportunity to ask at all. The amount she was legitimately learning was not conducive to becoming fluent, and she doubted she could use any of what he was saying in general conversation, but the game and the breathless way he translated things had the hot ache building between her legs.

"Back of your throat, princesa. Choke on it," Leo directed after the Spanish version of the same command fell uncomprehended on her ears. She did as she was told and sucked him deeper as she looked up at him through her lashes. His hands fisted her sheets as her head bobbed. "Quiero..." The translation started to form in her head—*I want*... before he grabbed a handful of her hair to pull her up his torso. "Ven. I want to be inside you." She released him with a wet popping sound and met him up by the headboard.

"I was going to make you finish like that." Piper pouted.

Leo pressed his forehead into hers, breathing hard. "Later. Not right after I told you I love you. I want *you*." His mouth slanted over hers, and she molded her body against his, kissing him back.

They slowed the pace. Leo's tongue slipped through the seam of

Piper's mouth as her hand traveled up his chest and into his hair. The warmth of Leo's palm cupped her breast, and his knee slowly slipped between her legs, increasing the pressure until she was out of breath and panting into his mouth as she rocked against his thigh. Leo sensed what her body needed, and she responded to each plea that left his lips like they were a well-oiled machine. When she fell onto her back, she didn't have to ask him to move above her—he just did. There was no room for words when she found his mouth again, slowly consuming his every breath. Her hips did all the talking when she tipped them toward his cock. Leo only broke away from her lips for a brief moment to position himself at her entrance and to slowly sink into her before Piper smothered their moans with another kiss.

They rocked together, and when it became too hard to kiss through their mutual undoing, they pressed their foreheads together and breathed with each push and pull. Piper's hands pressed into Leo's back, and she could tell how fast he was nearing his release when his body started to lose its careful precision and control.

"Piper," he breathed, rolling his hips forward with a choppy thrust.

"Yes." Piper nodded, breathing with the incline of her orgasm. Her body jerked as it rose and plateaued at the top. Everything felt like bright splashes of watercolors across the canvas of her mind, each new wave of excruciating pleasure adding a new color like the polychrome tile she had picked out for Leo's inspiration box. And when she watched Leo come apart on top of her and felt the warmth of his cock twitching inside her, she was finally satiated.

Their foreheads met again as their breathing slowed to normal. Leo's eyes were closed when Piper finally opened hers, and she bent her head just enough to brush a kiss against his mouth.

"I love you," Piper whispered. Leo's eyes finally opened, and he slowly rolled off her.

"Say it again." The sex-sated smile he gave her had her curling into his chest with one of her own.

"I love you."

"Good, I'm not dreaming," Leo sighed. "I love you, too."

"I think dream me would still say that," she mused. "But there's only one way to tell if you're in a dream."

"And what's tha—ow!" Leo shouted when Piper's fingers pinched the skin on his ass. "You're ballsy, I'll give you that, but..." He flipped on top of her and pinned her wrists above her head while she tried to writhe free. "Your tactics need some help. If I was really trying to abduct you on your porch, you wouldn't have been able to stop me. We should work on that."

"I would have screamed, and someone would have heard me." Piper lifted her chin and glared back. A sly smirk pulled up the corner of Leo's mouth, and she waited for his rebuttal. When he said nothing, she raised her eyebrows and asked. "You're not going to argue with me?"

Leo bent his mouth next to her ear, his hot breath sending a shiver down her spine as his husky voice said, "That's not the threat you think it is, princesa. I really like making you scream."

Fifty-Nine

LEO

Leo's hand was clammy as he opened the back door to the theatre, holding it for Piper before he walked through. For the first time, he truly understood the internal monologue that must have been going on in Piper's head twenty-four seven. He was about to make himself look like the biggest dick of the century, and he couldn't help but wonder if anyone would have any respect for him ever again.

"You're panicking." Piper paused in the hallway and grabbed onto his arm.

"They're going to think I gave you preferential treatment." Leo scrunched his eyes shut.

"You didn't."

"I know that, and you know that, but that's not how it's going to look. I've been yelling at everyone for months about professionalism and focus when it comes to the show, and I'm a hypocrite." Leo ran a hand through his hair and let out a slow breath.

"What did Moreno say when you told him?" Piper asked.

"He said he had a bet going with his wife on how long we

would last before we hooked up and wanted to know the exact time frame." Leo pursed his lips. "And then he said that as long as I'm still working hard at my job, he doesn't care."

"Everyone sees how hard you work. If they think you're being a hypocrite, then they're wrong." Piper slid her hand down his forearm and laced her fingers in his.

"You're right." He nodded. "I think falling for you actually helped with the show. No one needs a director who's never been in love to direct a love story."

"Probably shouldn't have cast me to play the woman in love, either," Piper noted.

"You were the best casting choice I made. Besides Emma... and Sam."

"Hey!" Piper swung and hit his arm, but Leo just shrugged.

"You and Wes are on equal footing," he said. "But maybe loving you does make me want to give you preferential treatment, because logically, I know that Emma and Sam are better actors and have better vocals, but if you were singing next to the both of them, I'd be staring at you." It was staggering how easily he could find Piper in a room. Even when he had hated her, he couldn't seem to peel his eyes away. Piper jumped on her tiptoes, and he brought his lips down to hers. It was just a quick, chaste kiss, but it was enough to set his head straight. "Okay, let's go burn down my image."

When they walked toward the stage, an entirely different scenario than what Leo had expected was unfolding. Sam and Wes were practically suffocating Emma in a group hug, and the entire cast and crew were cheering. Leo stopped short of the stage and tossed a glance at Piper, who wore the same hopeful look he assumed was on his own face. If this celebration wasn't what he thought it was, he was going to storm the university president's office.

"What's going on?" Piper split from Leo and ran over to Emma.

"Waylen Hornbill is officially no longer a professor at Fletcher

University," Emma announced. Relief sagged Leo's shoulders, and it felt like a breath of fresh air after being stuck in a burning building.

Leo approached the group. "How did that happen?"

"They did an internal investigation. I had to go give a statement and was assured they had already started investigating my original report even before we pulled our stunt. But we made it easy for them." Emma's face faltered. "There were six other women there, including one of my professors." Leo had thought the rage was gone, but it surged back once again.

"It's okay." Piper came to his side.

"That's only the number of people who said something." Leo shook his head. "He had tenure. How many—" He choked on his words before he could speculate further.

"This is a win, Leo." Emma's soft voice broke him out of his spell.

"I've had a class with him every year for four years. I knew there was something wrong with him. I knew it." His voice wavered. "I'm sorry."

"This isn't anyone's fault but his." Emma gave him a stern look. "You are not a mind reader. There wasn't a whole lot to be done until someone called him out. I'm happy, Leo. Is it the best possible outcome? No, because he won't end up in prison or anywhere he truly belongs. No, because his wife dutifully came to get all of his shit for him, and he has children. But it is a win."

"How could anyone be married to someone like that?" Leo grimaced.

"He's manipulative," Piper answered.

Emma nodded in agreement. "Whatever he does on campus, I'm sure it's worse for her." She sighed. "But, right now, I think we need to focus on the good. We accomplished something."

"You accomplished something. We were just there," Leo corrected.

Emma smiled. "People being there and supporting me was half the battle. Handling it in isolation would have been worse."

"Being alone is worse." Piper nodded.

"Plus, you two have something to announce, don't you?" Emma gave Leo a cheeky grin. His eyes went wide as he heard Piper say, "Nope! Nothing to announce." For once in their lives, they were on the same page about something. It was entirely inappropriate to be announcing their relationship on the tail end of more important news.

"So you aren't together, then?" Emma's eyebrows rose.

"We are." Leo shifted his feet and shot Piper a look of discomfort.

"But an announcement?" Piper tossed her hand in the air. "I don't think that's necessary, do you?"

Piper met his eyes with a plea he was already planning on complying with. Leo jerked his head back and forth. "Nope. No announcement necessary."

"You two are idiots." Emma rolled her eyes. "Hey, everyone!"

"Emma, no, that's—" Leo tried to interrupt, but Emma had already gotten everyone's attention.

"Oh my God," Piper groaned, burying her face in Leo's arm.

"Leo and Piper would finally like to announce that they're in a relationship now," Emma stated plainly.

"Uh..." Leo looked around nervously. Everyone—except for Elliot, who tactfully avoided his gaze—was staring at him expectantly. He was going to have to sit down with Elliot after this to make sure he knew there were no hard feelings. "I want to assure you that I haven't been giving Piper preferential treatment. I hope you all have seen how hard I work to keep this environment professional. Matter of fact," Leo tilted his head toward Piper, "you were a little quiet on your duet with Sam last night, so you need to project more from your diaphragm."

Piper glared at him. "I don't think they needed you to show them that you're not biased, Leo, but *thanks*."

"Dude," Sam scolded him.

"Am I wrong?" Leo asked.

"Not wrong in the literal sense," Emma said. "But in the way you timed the delivery? Yep."

"Shit." Leo's mouth popped open as he looked down at a fuming Piper. "Sorry," he whispered.

"I will fix my volume," Piper bit off.

"I was just trying to prove I wasn't—"

"No one thinks you're giving her an edge, man," one of the members of the ensemble called out from the back.

"Plus, we all figured you've been hooking up for a while," said a girl who played one of the dancers in the Hot Box scene. If there was one thing that could be counted on from theatre kids, it was gossip.

Leo whirled on Sam and Emma. "We said nothing," Sam declared. "You're good at telling everyone else what to do, but you can't seem to control your own facial expressions very well."

"People were bound to notice that you look like a lovesick puppy every time Piper walks on stage. We didn't tell them shit." Emma folded her arms over her chest. Leo's face heated as he looked over to Piper, whose cheeks were stained red, and he couldn't help but smile. "Yep. There it is." Emma laughed.

"Fine. I guess I'm obvious." Leo shrugged off their teasing and reached out to tip Piper's head up. "I'm sorry, princesa. I don't need to point out your flaws to make myself look better, and that wasn't my intention. Forgive me?"

Piper let out a long sigh and nodded. "Regardless, you were right. I was too quiet. I was just really nervous. I'll do better tonight."

"I got distracted when you sang your first song last night and fumbled the ASL interpretation," Leo said, loud enough for everyone to hear. The little crinkle that said Piper's smile was real formed on her face, and without thinking at all, he bent to kiss her in front of the entire cast and crew.

The wolf whistles and cheers were ridiculous, but Leo grinned against Piper's mouth anyway before letting go and facing his team. "Anyway, that's it. We're together. You can still expect me to be hard on everyone, and I have several notes on last night's performance from myself and Moreno that we need to go over before tonight's show, so let's get to it."

Sixty

Three months later

PIPER

Piper and Sam hovered over Leo's shoulder as they looked down at the laptop perched on his lap. The thing was loading so slowly that a new laptop immediately rose to the top of the list of things Piper wanted to get Leo before he left for film school—assuming he got in, which they were about to find out presently. When Leo finally navigated to his inbox, he clicked on the bolded, unopened email sitting at the top, and they waited. Piper was reluctant to look and chose instead to watch his face.

Just as Sam broke out into cheers, Piper watched Leo's face frown as he stared at his computer. In a panic, she looked at the screen, her eyes landing on the word *Congratulations* before she relaxed.

"You did it!" Piper squealed and ran around the couch to throw herself at Leo. He set his laptop to the side and caught her cleanly as she wrapped herself around him. "I'm so proud of you."

"Congratulations, man!" Sam plopped down beside them on the couch, beaming. "You deserve it."

"I think you're both going to be really disappointed, then." Leo cringed.

Piper blinked and quickly grabbed the laptop to make sure Leo really did get in and she wasn't imagining things. "No, see, it says right here that you just need to enroll in the fall term," she explained, pointing to the form links attached to the bottom of the email.

"I know I got in," Leo said calmly.

"Then why the hell would we be disappointed?" Sam furrowed his brow.

"Because I'm not going."

"What?" Piper laughed and searched Leo's expression for the joke that must be there. When she didn't see it, the color drained from her face, and she got to her feet.

"What the fuck?" Sam balked.

"You can't just not go!" Piper argued. "This has been your dream for years, Leo. You didn't even get in when you tried in high school. The entire point of this was so you'd get in! Why are you doing this?" Her mind was still racing a billion beats per minute when he answered.

"I want to be back in Archwood."

Piper's eyes blazed. "You better not be doing this for me. I can't be the person that makes you give up your dream, Leo. I can't. We agreed. We said we would do long distance. We said we would still love each other no matter how far apart we were."

Sam rose to his feet. "I'm sorry, Leo, but I'm on Piper's side here. This is insane."

Leo got up from the couch and folded his arms over his chest, his face stern. "Are you two done freaking the fuck out now?"

"No!" Piper yelled at the same time Sam did.

"Do I get a say in what I do?" Leo snapped.

"Not if you're fucking up your whole life for me. I mean,

what the hell, Leo?" Piper threw up her hands. "Where did this come from?"

"Sit down," Leo ordered, jabbing a finger at the sofa. Piper huffed and puffed her way over to the couch and threw herself down on the cushions while Sam sat beside her in equally dramatic fashion. "Thank you. Now, you two are going to listen to me. You're going to wait until I'm done talking, and then and *only* then can you give me your opinion."

"Fine," Piper grunted. Her back was straight with irritation as she waited for an explanation that could not possibly be good enough.

"Please explain." Sam sighed.

"I've had this feeling for a long time that I didn't want to go, and when I opened that email, I felt nothing. I should be elated that I got in, and I'm not," Leo said.

"So, what? You just don't want to be a director anymore?" Piper argued. "I saw the way you were with the spring show, Leo. Nothing has changed. You still love it."

"For fuck's sake, Piper." Leo blew out a breath. "I love you, but I asked you to let me speak."

Piper swallowed and bobbed her head. At least with that, she knew she was in the wrong. He had asked her to listen. They had learned a lot about each other in the last few months they had been dating, and how to resolve arguments was a big one. They still butted heads frequently, but there was never any malice behind it like there used to be. They were both just extremely passionate, and learning the right way to fight was a process. "You're right. I'm sorry. I'll listen."

"Okay." Leo started to pace like he was psyching himself up. "When my abuelita died, I felt this need to be near my family. And I know what you're both thinking, that my family and both of you would support me no matter how far away I am, but I don't want that. I still want to be a director, but I don't want to go to film school. I've taken online classes already, and I can take more, but what I really want is to be with the people I love and to jump right into creating. If I go to film school, who knows how long it'll be before I get to really direct or produce something again? I have this harebrained idea, and the more I think about it, the more I don't think it's a pipe dream." Leo wandered over to the leather-bound journal he had been staying up late writing and poring over for months. Piper had wanted to know what it was he was working on, but Leo continually said that it wasn't ready and that he wanted to show her the finished product as a surprise. When he tossed it to Sam first, Piper was slightly jealous until Leo said, "I think the book you made me read is going to change our lives. There are plenty of directors and producers who never went to film school, Moreno included. So, I've decided that's not my path. Instead, I want to make an independent film adaptation of *The Dating Brigade*."

Piper's body felt like it was going to burst into flames of emotion as she wedged herself next to Sam on the couch and leaned over his shoulder to look at the journal that was flipped open on his lap. Pages and pages of a rudimentary script were written out with scene descriptions, setting ideas, and more. Excitement coursed through her body. This felt like a Leo thing to do—something risky, but fulfilling. Something filled with passion.

"Are we allowed to talk now?" Sam raised his hand.

Leo chuckled and nodded. "Yes. Piper first because I can see how badly she wants to. ¿Princesa, qué piensas?"

Instead of answering, Piper launched from the couch and sprinted into his arms, burying her face in his chest. She couldn't hold back the smile stretching across her face. Leo seemed to relax a little in her hold, like he had been genuinely scared she would hate it. "I take it you like the idea?" he asked.

"You're a genius. I think if anyone can do it, it's you," Piper said. Then, realizing what all this meant, she brightened even more. "And this means you'll be in Archwood? With me?"

"With you." Leo nodded.

"That's good, because," she paused to hold back the tears that wanted to spring to her eyes, "I don't know how I was going to survive being away from you." Since they had gotten together, they hadn't spent more than one night apart, and Piper had pictured what it would feel like to not sleep beside Leo one too many times for the relief of this change of plans to not feel like finally coming up for air.

"I'm sorry I didn't say anything sooner." Leo kissed her forehead. "I was just trying to work it all out in my head, and I was nervous that this idea would go nowhere and that it was a bad idea and that—"

Piper cut him off by cupping his jaw before he had time to spiral. "It's a great idea, Leo."

"Look, you two are adorable and everything, but can I finally say something?" Sam said from behind them. Piper giggled and turned around, wrapping one arm around Leo's waist.

"The floor is yours," Leo said.

"First things first, yes to all of this. You making my favorite book into a fucking movie? Absolutely on board with that. Now," Sam stood up, looking extremely hopeful, "just a quick question. When you say this is going to change *our* lives, does that mean..."

"I want you to play Landon." Leo grinned. "I haven't talked to her yet, but I'm hoping Emma will play Cora."

"Fuck yes!" Sam clapped his hands together. "Did you talk to Walker yet?" Piper didn't know why the thought hadn't occurred to her before, but surely the man who wrote the book would not only need to be apprised of the idea, he would also need to sign off on it. "And what about the funding? How are we doing this?"

"To answer your first question, I was hoping the two of you would want to take a little trip with me to Archwood. And to answer the second, I have a pretty good idea on that front as soon as I get Walker to agree to this."

"Moreno?" Piper guessed.

"Moreno and company." Leo nodded, the corner of his mouth tipping up.

The energy in the room bounced off the walls, and between the three of them. Piper's cheeks were starting to ache from how much she was smiling. Leo's smile was understated in comparison to hers and Sam's, but it was no less wonderful. His joy felt like a secret that only a select few got to know, and Piper could practically see all the possibilities written behind his eyes. Even more so when he took the leatherbound journal from Sam's hand and held it up in the air.

"Let's make a movie."

Epilogue

One and a half years later

PIPER

With her hand firmly clasped in Leo's, Piper stepped toward her childhood home and immediately heard screaming from behind the door. She glanced at Leo, who chuckled under his breath as she opened the door and let the flood of noise cloud her senses. The wailing was coming from the living room, as was the loud chatter. Leo guided her toward the noise, and she smiled when she saw the decorations Talia and Amala had put up, all golden with bouquets of bright sunflowers adorning end tables.

"Hey," Scarlett chirped out a greeting as they passed by her and Colin, who was looking a little green in the face until Scarlett pulled his noise-canceling headphones out of her purse and handed them to him.

"Hey." Piper smiled and reached to hug her before beelining to the biggest source of the noise, a three-month-old little girl who was apparently none too thrilled with the festivities.

"Pay, I promise," Walker begged. "Mommy is getting you a binkie. You ate a half hour ago. You're not starving. I just changed you. Is it gas? Please stop screaming." Walker looked the epitome of exhausted as he pointed across the room to where Paisley's twin sister, Lydia, was happily chewing on Piper's grandfather's finger. "Look, your sister is having a good time. Do you need a finger?"

"I think she just needs her cousin." Piper smiled and made grabby hands at Paisley's chunky legs.

"Take her." Walker held out his daughter, and Piper brought her squirming, writhing cousin into the fold of her arm. "I have no idea where Talia ran off to with the pacifier, but I think Pay is going to make Colin have a panic attack if I don't get her to calm down."

"Here." Leo pulled their car keys out of his pocket and dangled them in front of Paisley's screaming head. Like a charm, her red, tear-streaked little face caught the motion, and her eyes went wide with interest.

"Keys," Walker sighed. "I should have thought of that. I'm just... so fucking tired."

"Babies will do that to you." Lucia stepped in beside her son, putting a hand on his shoulder as she spoke to Walker. "Two at the same time is a lot. I could barely handle Alvaro and Leonardo when they were a year apart."

"I'll bet." Piper laughed. "Leo's enough to handle on his own."

"You handle me just fine," Leo said and then made a goofy face down at Piper's arms as he shook the keys for Paisley's benefit. Piper wanted to handle him right there and then because there was just something about a man enthusiastically playing with a baby that was intrinsically hot. Walker groaned, scrunching up his nose like he could tell what she was thinking. It might as well have been what Leo was thinking, too, because he had once told her that he pretty much always thought about sleeping with her, and all he would have to do was think about the celebration sex they'd had two nights ago to conjure up an image.

"When are you two going to give me nietos, hm?" Lucia demanded.

"Mamá," Leo warned with a cursory glance. "We aren't even married yet."

"So, soon, then?" Lucia asked. Piper looked to Leo to answer that one because, as it stood, her ring finger was looking a little bare. Leo shot his mom an extremely irritated look, and she raised both her hands before wandering off to find her husband.

Leo sighed. "I swear she means well, but I wish she would go back to jumping down Marcos and Harper's throats about when they're going to have kids."

"Isn't Harper pregnant?" Walker asked.

"Yep." Leo nodded. "Hence why my mom's moved on to Piper and me. Both my brothers have given her exactly what she wanted. They've created a monster."

Just then, Talia whirred in from the side and plopped a green pacifier into Paisley's mouth. "Sorry, I was having a hard time finding one. I swear we bought a million of them, but the second I need one, they're nowhere to be found. There's probably a stash under the couch. Lydia likes to throw hers."

"She's going to be a quarterback." Walker beamed.

"Pay could probably be a vocalist," Leo said.

"She's got the lungs for it," Talia mused.

"Hopefully she got them from Piper, not you." Walker chortled. The twins were adopted and had no blood relation to any of them, but the adoption jokes were frequent fliers in Piper's family. Last year, Carter had sat down for Thanksgiving and dramatically declared, "I think it's time to address the elephant in the room." Then he paused for a long while before delivering his punchline of "I think I'm adopted," to which Pearl replied by gasping loudly and slapping her hand over her mouth before saying, "If you're adopted, then what am I?" The only response they received was a few eyerolls before everyone continued stuffing their faces with turkey.

"Mi amor, I'm gonna go check in with Emma, Sam, and Elliot, if that's all right with you?" Leo ran a hand down Piper's spine, and she smiled at him with a nod.

"Of course. It's your party. Have fun."

"You, too." Talia nudged Walker's arm. "I'll watch the girls. Go bask in the glory."

"I'm just gonna go find Roscoe," Walker scoffed and bent down first to kiss Paisley's forehead then Talia's cheek before he wandered away.

"Bask in it!" Talia called after him.

"No," Walker singsonged back. The idea of Walker taking praise from anyone was laughable. Even after he'd hit *The New York Times* Best Seller list for his recent book release, he still barely acknowledged his considerable amounts of success. Leo had somehow convinced him to throw this party in the first place, and Piper wasn't sure how, other than through some sort of bribery.

"Stubborn man." Talia shook her head.

"Maybe you get your stubbornness from your dad," Piper cooed to Paisley. Paisley smiled up at her, and Piper figured that was as good of an answer as she was going to get. For the time being, her baby cousins were satiating her baby fever, but she couldn't help but look down at the tiny bundle of joy and, sometimes, fury in her arms and want that for herself. With Leo. At some point in the future.

"I know that look." Talia smiled. "That's a wistful look if I ever saw one."

"Yeah, I'm just..." Piper shrugged, trying to look indifferent. "I'm not in a hurry, but now that the movie is finally done, I can't help thinking about what's next. I know Leo's already got another project lined up, but..."

"You want him to ask you to marry him?" Talia guessed.

Piper nodded. "I mean, our hotel room at the film festival was so romantic, I kinda thought..."

"We barely got to be in our hotel room while we were there. That would have been a terrible place to propose, Piper," Leo's voice said from behind her. Piper's face went beet red. Talia grinned and shot her a wink before snatching Paisley from her grasp and walking away.

"I didn't mean—I mean, obviously, we can get married whenever you're ready, and if that's later, that's totally fine." Her blush was still going strong as she met Leo's eyes in mortification.

"I love it when your face does that," he whispered and reached up to touch her cheek. "I need to make a thank-you toast. Will you come stand with me?"

"Of course." Piper smiled and let him guide her to the open area behind the couches in front of a long table of hors d'oeuvres and champagne flutes. Leo grabbed a flute filled with sparkling cider and handed it to Piper before grabbing his own. Then he picked up the only metal spoon on the table. She had the brief thought that he must have really planned out this speech if he had planted a spoon on the table before he tapped metal against glass and the sound rang out, alerting the living room.

Leo cleared his throat like he was nervous, which was silly considering this was a congratulations party. He had already won. "Thank you all so much for joining us to celebrate our Sundance Film Festival Grand Jury Award." A few hollers from the crowd had Piper beaming. "There are just a few people I'd like to thank before we celebrate. To Walker." Leo turned toward Walker and Talia, cradling both their daughters in their arms and standing beside the Winstons. "You wrote something that had me immediately inspired. That had my best friend annoying me with his constant commentary."

"Woo!" Sam shouted from the back.

"Without you, *The Dating Brigade* wouldn't have existed at all, nor would there have been so many bids for the distribution rights." Walker raised his glass in a salute. "To Sam and Emma." Leo smiled at their friends. "You brought Landon and Cora to life, and I'm forever grateful for your talent. And to Elliot, for all of your engineering and prop work on this project." Elliot smiled from beside Emma, who leaned into his shoulder as he bent to kiss the top of her head.

"To Alejandro Moreno." Piper watched Leo scan the crowd before she found Moreno and his wife on the other side of the room and pointed them out. The hand on Piper's back brushed up and down in thanks. "Quite frankly, thank you for your money." The entire room let out a collective laugh. "On a more serious note, thank you for believing in me enough to help me find the funding for this passion project. Thank you for giving me the scholarship that led me here. Thank you for everything." Moreno lifted his glass in response, and that was when Piper's eyes landed on someone she had not expected to see. Thea was standing beside her husband Yuri and beaming from ear to ear. Piper's best friend would have had to fly from Minnesota to be there. She was still assembling the pieces in her head when Leo cleared his throat.

"And, finally..." Leo found Carter in the crowd and discreetly signed something to him. Confused, Piper narrowed her eyes between her brother and Leo. Carter was picking up on ASL way faster than she was, but he had a damn good motivator. "I want to thank my girlfriend, Piper." Leo turned back to her and set his glass on the table. Piper bit her lip as he reached for her hand and laced his fingers in hers. "Not only for her design skills on the project, but for being the love of my life." Her heart fluttered in her chest. For a while, she had felt a little guilty that she could feel this happy after her parents' death, but she knew that they would want this for her. Cole and Paisley would want her to find her person, to be loved the way that Leo loved her. To love someone the way they had loved each other.

Carter made his way toward them and handed Leo something before quickly moving away. Piper's heart stopped entirely as every stray piece of this evening snapped into place. The sunflowers. Lucia's comment about grandbabies. The conversation with Talia. Thea. The blue velvet ring box now in Leo's palm. Her eyes widened as she whipped her head around the room.

"I think she's getting it now," Leo said to the crowd in the same way that he addressed a theatre. Everyone laughed as Leo took a shaky breath and met Piper's gaze with vulnerable eyes that sliced right to her heart. "While I did want to thank everyone, the

Sundance award was just a front for the real reason we're here, for what I'm hoping will be our engagement party."

Piper immediately felt the sting of tears welling in her eyes as Leo lowered himself down to one knee.

"Piper Lennon Hartrick." He held up the ring box, flipping open the lid to display the gold sunflower ring seated inside with tiny diamonds inlaid in the center, and she frantically wiped at the tears pooling at her eyes. She reached for Leo's hand, needing some form of contact to keep herself steady, and just as always, his fingers felt warm and assured as his thumb rubbed gentle strokes into the back of her hand. "I love you. I'm never going to stop loving you. When I think about the future, you're always there, pissing me off or smiling at me." Piper let out a choked laugh. "It is shocking how wrong I was about you. I used to think you made me weak, but you're not my weakness at all, princesa. You're my greatest strength. You call me on my shit and take it when I call you on yours. You are my person. The one I want to annoy with my movie commentary forever. The one I could listen to tell me the difference between eight shades of the same color green forever."

"They're different colors, Leo." Piper rolled her eyes, remembering their squabble over the paint color in their living room, and sniffed back more tears.

Leo beamed up at her. "I'd love to spend the rest of my life arguing with you over that. I, uh, I asked your dad. He was very quiet and didn't say much. I took that as a good sign." Piper broke out into a giggle, shaking her head. "I did ask Walker just in case, though." The formality of it all was so fervently Leo that it made her grin even wider. "And now you're smiling at me, so I guess I should get on with it because I'd really love to see that forever." He cleared his throat nervously and shifted on the ground, setting his shoulders back. "Piper, mi vida, will you marry me? Please?"

Piper's body reacted before her brain did, though she was sure she had been adamantly nodding her head the whole time. Her knees hit the floor, and she spilled the sparkling cider all over herself in the process. She barely cared as she ditched the flute on the floor and dove forward, wrapping her arms around Leo's neck and kissing him. She was only vaguely aware of the applause and congratulatory noise in the room when she finally dropped her mouth to Leo's ear.

"Seré todo tuya," she whispered. "Since you asked so nicely."

"Can I look yet?" Leo complained, one hand covering his eyes as Piper dragged him through the house to their bedroom.

"Almost there..." Piper said. She was practically skipping with excitement all the way to the doorway. When they did, she adjusted her knee-high knit socks before saying, "Open your eyes."

Without a word, Leo turned to her and looked down to see she was wearing nothing other than knit socks and jewelry, and his gaze turned molten. His reaction had been completely worth the extra effort of undressing behind him and yelling every time he tried to remove his hand from his face. Piper had kept her body just out of reach as she spirited him away to their bedroom so he would be none the wiser. Then, she finally saw it dawn on him that her naked body wasn't the surprise.

"You want to make a movie?" Leo's tongue swiped over his bottom lip as he stepped toward their bed, where Piper had set up two video cameras.

"I want you to direct," Piper said and reached up to touch the sunflower necklace around her neck, a new nervous energy taking over. She had set up the cameras with meticulous care, but the way Leo was inspecting them made her skittish. "What are you doing?"

"It's all about the angles, princesa." Leo's voice was smooth as butter as he turned to look at her. His director's tone. "What's your favorite part of sex, Piper? I'd like to capture that."

Her face heated as she moved to sit on the edge of the bed. She considered the question for a moment before smiling. "The look on your face when you come."

Leo hummed thoughtfully, lowering the camera and moving it along the side of the bed to where there would be a direct line of sight to their faces during the action. "Not what I was expecting, but I'll deliver."

"What's *your* favorite part?"

"You," he said simply before adjusting the other camera to capture a wide shot of the entire bed at an angle. Piper hadn't quite been able to figure out how to position the cameras well enough to not get the other camera in the shot, but Leo had done it easily.

Piper scoffed. "You can't just say me. Total cop-out."

"Why not? I love every single thing you do. The way you move." Leo hit the record button and moved back over to the other camera. "The way you're so... *vocal*." He smirked and hit the other record button. "And the way you feel when you're so wet and needy." His voice had gotten darker, like he was a movie villain who was about to get exactly what he wanted. Piper could feel how slick she was getting from just his words and the way he prowled around their room, perfecting the cameras so he could get this exactly right.

"Now, I want you to get on the bed slowly," said Leo in a more seductive version of the voice he used on set. "Crawl your way up to the pillows. When you lay down, stretch your arms above your head and roll your body, all the way down to your hips."

The heat between her legs was already unbearable as Piper did as he commanded, arching her back as she slowly pressed inch by inch of her body to the bed, first her breasts, then her stomach, and then her hips, until she was lying down fully. "That's beautiful, Piper. Now I want you to roll onto your back. Again, do it *slowly*." She did, feeling suddenly a bit self-conscious of the cameras pointed at her. Leo must have noticed her sudden shyness because he added, "Find your confidence. You own this room, princesa. I'm the only one here, and you're doing so good. Trust me when I tell you that I'm very, very turned on, but I have to be patient. A good scene takes time." Piper closed her eyes briefly and took a deep breath, feeling her chest rising and falling and wondering what it would look like on camera. "Now," Leo's tone lost a bit of control as he said, "Bend your knees a bit and place your feet on the bed." The soft fabric of her socks felt warm against the pads of her feet. "Slowly spread your legs. Let me see exactly how wet you are, but make me work for it. Tease me."

"Okay," Piper huffed out as she slowly dragged her feet across the bed, parting herself. Her hand moved up to cup her breast because she needed to touch something, *anything*, to release the pressure.

"Fuck," Leo hissed from where he stood at the side of the bed. "That's it. Do what feels right to you. If you want to touch yourself, do it." Piper did. Every motion came with full confidence as she put on a show, her hand dragging at a snail's pace down between her legs and circling her clit with the tips of three fingers. The strangled noise Leo made encouraged her to add pressure. "Tilt your hips with it. Move into your hand like you just can't take it anymore. God, yes. That's perfect. Just like that. You look so good. Switch hands for me, mi vida. I want to see your engagement ring in the shot."

"Leo," Piper panted, writhing against her left hand with slow rolls of her hips.

"You want me?"

"Yes," she moaned. "Take your clothes off in the shot." Leo, the collaborative director he was, moved to where the camera could see him before pulling his shirt slowly over his head. He was doing everything the way he had told her to do it, at a pace that would look good to the cameras. When he was relieved of his shirt, she watched him and shoved two fingers into her heat, bucking into her hand.

"Does that feel good?" Leo asked. The sound of his belt

unclasping filled her ears next, and the promise behind it had her panting hard. "I think you need another finger."

"Not good enough," Piper cried out.

"If you want something, you're gonna have to ask for it."

"Come here." She practically yanked him onto the bed.

He chuckled, scolding her, "I said slowly, and I can't be wearing socks in the shot. That's not sexy."

"I'm wearing socks," she pointed out.

"Those aren't socks, those are torture devices," Leo mused, snapping the band at the top of one.

"Lay on your back." Piper pointed. Whatever director's reserve Leo had had seemed to disappear as he scrambled to the head of the bed and laid back, still wearing his socks.

"Are you gonna ride me?" Leo reached for her, and she let him pull her into his lap, his cock grazing the inside of her thigh.

"Since you're so dead set on going slow, I think I'll make it agonizingly so," she decided. With one hand on his chest holding him down, she started by testing him, rubbing herself along his shaft until his fingertips were digging into her thighs, just above her socks.

"Please," Leo begged. She smiled wickedly as she pressed up on her shins and grabbed his cock, dragging the tip over her wetness. "Please," Leo moaned again. She dropped down a bit and let his crown alone enter her. "Fuck. *Please*, Piper. How much more do you want me to beg?"

"You're going to beg for every inch," Piper murmured. She let him have another and watched him squirm as he tried to hold back. Then, she happily listened to his pleas for every drop of her hips until he was seated completely inside of her.

They moved like water, waves chasing and backing from the shore until they were a storm, thrashing against the sides of their small boat and coming dangerously close to capsizing. The emotions never seemed to stop when Piper was with Leo, but that was what she liked best about him. He knew how to push her buttons, knew what made her cry, and knew how to bring her so much joy that her heart ached from it. Leo knew how to make her *feel*, and while that could be terrifying, he used that power to make her feel seen, not manipulated. She used to think that feeling so much was a bad thing, that emotions were damaging and destructive, but now she knew that it only made her stronger.

Several minutes later, after they both had collapsed into a cuddled heap on the bed, Leo let out a small laugh as he stroked her newly maroon-tipped hair. "I can't believe there was ever a time where I didn't want to cast you."

Piper gave him a wry smile. "I think your casting was spot-on for this movie."

"I like to think I'm good at my job." Leo grinned back. "And directing is ninety percent casting."

She shoved his shoulder playfully. "I hate you."

The sparkle behind Leo's eyes turned downright giddy. "I hate you, too. You're the absolute worst. It's probably why I'm marrying you. Now." He popped his head up from the pillow and held out his hand. "We're celebrating."

"Isn't that what we just did?"

"I have chocolate-covered strawberries in the fridge, more sparkling cider that I can prevent you from spilling all over yourself this time, and your female rage music queued up. I want to dance with my fiancée." Leo pressed a kiss to the back of her hand as she eagerly scooted toward him. "Will you dance with me, princesa?"

Piper smiled easily. "I would love to dance with you."

THE END

Acknowledgments

There comes a point, when you set out to write your second novel, where you start to wonder if the first novel was a fluke, and you don't actually know how to write and publish a book anymore. The fact that I have completed this book means that I have an endless amount of people to thank. It sounds cliché to say that I wouldn't be where I am without a team of people behind me, but sometimes the cliché things in life are true.

To my daughter, once again, you sacrificed some of your time with me and even sat in my lap coloring while I wrote part of this book. I never want you to have to force a smile, but if you do, I hope you know that happiness isn't your only valuable emotion. I hope you know that I fought and I still fight my trauma and depression because I love you and I want to show you what it looks like to heal and chase your dreams. It's all for you (although you're not allowed to read it yet and we haven't quite made it past the ABCs yet).

To whoever left groceries on my porch years ago when I thought I'd be eating Top Ramen yet again, you're an angel. To my mother, who continually brought me along for her random acts of kindness as I grew up: I hope you know that even when you never took credit, I was watching and internalizing every ounce of your kindness toward others. For all the men in my life who would bury a body for me if I asked them to—my husband, my dad, my brother, and my brother-in-law—thank you for having my back.

The truest friends, like all the characters in this book, are the ones who stuck around during my mess. Even more so are the friends that found me at my lowest and helped me come back to life. Crystal, Taylor, Mackenzie, and Lexi, you are everything and more, and I'll celebrate how wonderful you all are until I die. To my built-in best friend who is also my sister, Elli, thank you for every late night and heartfelt conversation in your car.

As far as the physical book goes, I have a whole slew of people that helped make this happen. First off, Allie, you are incredible and an absolute delight. Thank you so much for your hard work on all the Spanish in this book and for giggling with me over the vulgarity of some of it. To my other beta/sensitivity readers: Kristen, Kae, Melissa W., Lauren, and Melissa E., thank you for all of your help to make this book better than I could do on my own. And last, but certainly not least given the amount of times she's had to explain to me how to use a comma, thank you to my editor, Maryarita.

Finally, because I've met some incredible authors who have done nothing but build me up during this entire process, thank you to Letizia Lorini, Kelsey Schulz, and Hannah Bonam-Young for taking my late-night author rants and stress messages in stride and giving me advice when I needed it. I love you all. You make the world a better place.

More by the Author

The Ones Series

The Ones We Fight For - Walker & Talia's Story

The Ones We Hate - Piper & Leo's Story

The Ones We Remember - Colin & Scarlett's Story - Coming Fall 2024

Stay Connected:

@katiegowritely on social media

www.katiegolightlybooks.com

Dicktionary

Whether you wish to skip the smut entirely or return to it, that content can be found in these chapters:

Chapter 7
Chapter 16
Chapter 23
Chapter 24
Chapter 25
Chapter 26
Chapter 39
Chapter 45
Chapter 49
Chapter 55
Chapter 58
Epilogue

About the Author

Katie Golightly is an Oregon girl who thrives on chaos. She lives happily with her husband, daughter, and overflowing bookshelf. In addition to getting serotonin from the outdoors and well-organized spreadsheets, she has always been drawn to the art of storytelling. Eventually, the endless emotional, funny, and spicy stories she fabricated in her head had to be written down somewhere.

- instagram.com/katiegowritely
- threads.net/@katiegowritely
- x.com/katiegowritely
- tiktok.com/@katiegowritely

Made in the USA
Coppell, TX
30 March 2024

30699469R00281